FORTUNE'S DAUGHTER

MARELLA SANDS

Word Posse

Dedication
To Mark Sumner, who sponsored me into the Alternate Historians. How different my life would have been if we had not crossed paths!

Acknowledgements
Thank you to my cover model, Rachel Sullivan.
You're an amazing young woman and I'm sure that, no matter where you go, what you do, or how you travel the road of your life, you will be magnificent!
As always, to my husband Todd,
and to the Alternate Historians: Sharon Shinn, Rett Macpherson, Mark Sumner, Thomas Drennan, Deborah Millitello, and Laurell K. Hamilton.
Also, thanks to Paul Dauben for being a last-minute proofreader.

From Word Posse
The Naturalist, Mark Sumner
Sleeping the Churchyard Sleep, Rett Macpherson
Pandora's Mirror, Marella Sands
The Water Girl, Deborah Millitello
Fortune's Daughter, by Marella Sands

Visit us at www.wordposse.com
Like us on Facebook: facebook.com/WordPosse
Follow us on Twitter: @WordPosse

This book has been typeset in Fanwood. Titles and headers are in Alien League. Cover design by Word Posse.

ISBN-10: 0986151106
ISBN-13: 978-0-9861511-0-1

I

Lythera stirred the soapy water wearily. Laundry day was a smelly, steaming affair involving some of her least favorite things, such as wet wood that smoked more than it burned, lye that chapped her hands, and soaked clothes that had to be churned with a heavy paddle. Her shoulders ached, but if she stopped, it would only be to add more fuel to the smoldering fire. That, in turn, would increase the smoke that stung her eyes and filled her nose with soot.

Her overcloak hardly kept off the drizzle that filtered its way through the outbuilding's heavily patched roof, but the rain, at least, she could overlook much of the time, even when it was dripping onto her head and running down her neck. What she couldn't overcome was the bone-deep exhaustion that came from her incessant grind of chores. She might be a lord's daughter, but the family's fortunes had fallen far too low for them to be able to afford servants. Yet her status was too high for her to find work in town; no one would hire Lythera Halevern, with her aristocratic name and haughty father, no matter how hard she worked.

And she did work hard. But, truth be told, she was not overly talented at the raw effort of keeping the household going. She burned the bread, cut herself when chopping the heads off the chickens, and tripped over her own skirts when carrying buckets of water up and down the steep, uneven stairs of the ancient manor. Perhaps if she'd been training since childhood, or if she could switch into a servant's uniform, which was much looser and had fewer underskirts than her own, she would be better at it. But she hadn't, and she couldn't. Her father's pride would not allow his daughters to wear the servants' livery, even where no one else would see.

Her younger sister Pezia rushed into the outbuilding in a whirl of patched skirts and mud-scented rainwater and coils of damp auburn hair. "A coach is here! A coach pulled by blue deer! He says you're to come to the hall in your best dress!"

The paddle slipped from Lythera's hands in shock and the splash sent water over the edge of the kettle into the fire. Steam flashed around her, but Lythera barely noticed. Blue deer? Pezia could only mean the royal stags, which only the nobility could use.

What would a nobleman high enough in rank to be able to have the royal stags at his disposal be doing at Halevern Manor? Her father had hinted that they might have a well-born visitor, but he hadn't said anything about the person being noble. Or that they'd arrive *today*.

It didn't matter. What mattered was that there was no ostler to take the animals to the stable—where there was no food for them in any case—and no butler to show the royal guest inside. The fireplace in the great hall was cold, fuel being too expensive to waste in an area of the house the family rarely visited. And dinner! How could they serve dinner? Here was Pezia in a stained dress, barefoot, in the laundry building while dinner was being neglected in the kitchen. If the lord's hounds hadn't eaten the unattended food yet, it was likely burnt and inedible by anything but the dogs. Or the mice that overran the kitchen.

Panic threatened to overwhelm her. She took a deep breath and smiled for Pezia's sake.

The laundry could wait. She would have to swallow her embarrassment and play hostess for the royal visitor. Her tutor, back in the days when the family's fortunes allowed the lord to hire one for his daughters, had given her a few lessons in court styles of address as well as some history. She could at least be a knowledgeable conversationalist, if not a charming one.

It was unlikely she could take advantage of her best subject: languages.

"Get some water to put out the fire here," she said, feigning a calm she did not feel. "Then back to your kitchen duties. I'll see what we can provide our visitor."

Pezia's relief that Lythera somehow knew what to do was palpable. Color crept back into her pale cheeks.

Lythera left the outbuilding, pulled her overcloak about her tightly, and navigated around the worst of the mud puddles in the courtyard to enter the drafty interior of the hall.

Once away from the mud, she rushed to her room and looked glumly at the other dresses in her wardrobe. Most looked similar to the patched dress she had on. But at least they were not covered in mud and soaked with rain. She removed her soiled dress and her muddy shoes and replaced them with dry, relatively clean, alternatives. The dress she chose was a dark, unbecoming color, but it had been patched fewer times and also featured the Halevern eagle embroidered on the cuffs. The shoes were a touch too small, but looked presentable. Lythera ran a comb through her hair and pinned it back with the one silver hairpin she owned. Once her toilette was as complete as possible, she rushed toward the Great Hall to greet the noble visitor.

The low rumble of voices came from the Great Hall, but no smell of smoke or beer. The lord had not, then, managed to get a fire lit for his guest, or to provide any sort of refreshments after the traveler's journey.

As she walked into the room, she noted anew how heavily the spring chill hung in the air and how weak the light was; the high windows were too dirty to allow much light inside even on sunny days. Rushes littered the floor and made a shushing sound as she walked toward her father's oak seat. Normally, she could ignore such things but today she looked at the hall as a stranger might and found it terribly wanting. She swallowed her embarrassment.

Lythera strode up to her father's seat and nodded to him, uneasy. The single guest stood to the side, cloaked against the rain and the cold air. He faced the empty fireplace as if he could wish a blaze to arise within it by willpower alone. He was tall but Lythera could determine little more than that.

Besides, her father demanded her attention. He stared at her with a calculating gaze she had never seen before. Lately, she had become used to his sunken eyes and long silences, for her mother had died only six months before. Marlun Lord Halevern had been mourning for his wife and had largely retreated from the rest of the family. But today, something was different.

Her father nodded in return. His iron-gray hair and beard were trimmed for the first time in months; his trousers, shirt, and surcoat clean and unwrinkled. Across his chest was emblazoned the stark white eagle on a green field that was the Halevern coat of arms. Its patches were more cleverly hidden than in Lythera's clothes. Even the lord's boots had been shined for the royal visitor.

The stranger strode across the ancient stone floor with an unconscious hauteur Lythera had rarely seen in her father's guests. Blue and red swatches, covered with embroidered golden stags, adorned his tunic and his coat. Black hair soaked up whatever light managed to make it near him. His eyes were a black deep enough to match his hair, and they held no warmth. The elegantly carved chair which was reserved for her father's guests looked old and ragged beside this shining, cold example of royalty, as if unworthy of supporting such a distinguished man.

The man's gaze swept over her, head to toes, and his lips curled back into a sneer. Lythera kept her face pleasant, but seethed inwardly. Though nobility had never visited this impoverished hall in her lifetime, her tutor had impressed upon her that they all had impeccable manners. This man did not appear to care whether his rudeness was observed or not. Perhaps that was true of all the royal family.

"This is my daughter, Lythera Halevern," her father said to the visitor. "Lythera, this is Ilvinard Segrithr, Lord Novardan, cousin to the king. He's come to meet you."

Lythera curtseyed low to Novardan. She was only the eldest daughter of a sei-Lord—the lowest ranked of the styles of lordship—a man who had nothing but a damp hall and an ancient title. This man belonged to the ruling family itself. His title would be ist-Lord, a First Lord, since he was from House Segrithr, which had held onto the throne of the land for the past four centuries.

"Lord, we are honored by your presence," she said, curious as to why any one, especially an ist-Lord, would come to see her. Without a dowry, she was unmarriageable. Or perhaps the lord had heard that she devoted her time to reading and studying the old languages. Would a royal visitor stop by Halevern Hall for a simple translation? Surely there were scholars enough in the capital.

"You are eighteen?" asked Novardan.

"Almost twenty, Lord."

He looked at her critically, and she felt a stab of anger. Hospitality would not permit her to show such feelings to a guest, though the thought was tempting.

She knew what he saw, anyway. The eldest daughter of House Halevern had inherited her mother's auburn hair and dark blue eyes, eyes so blue they were almost violet, but in other ways she looked like her father. Strong chin, hooked nose, wide forehead. Tall and broad-shouldered, though she had developed a woman's curves in the past few years. Her mother had died believing Lythera would never find a husband. She had often said, "A girl with no dowry had better be beautiful so that a man will overlook her poverty. Or she can be a scholar." And so she was a scholar.

Her younger sisters, at any rate, looked to be growing into great beauties. They might find men willing to overlook their poverty, though Lythera was not sure marriage was the best solution to their problems, anyway. Eternal poverty at their father's side might not be an attractive proposition, but marriage to the wrong man would be worse. A wife belonged to her husband, in every sense of the word.

Novardan walked around her slowly, as if inspecting an animal at market. His dark eyes were black as jet in the angled planes of his pale face. "Not attractive in the classic sense, but she's intelligent, is she not?"

"I was tutored in languages, history, literature, and arithmetic," she said haughtily, her hospitality wearing a bit thin around this pretentious man, who spoke about her as if she were not even present, and whose gaze left her feeling naked and ashamed.

Novardan was not pleased with her answer. "A swift tongue isn't always an asset in a woman. I asked your father."

"If you have a question to ask about me, then ask me. I'm not a cow; I can speak for myself."

Novardan grinned slightly and sat down in the visitors' chair. He scratched briefly at his ear before settling back. "There you are wrong, my dear, for your father and I are bargaining for you in much the same way two farmers might haggle over the price of a hog. Or a cow. And if you are as learned as you claim, you know you do not speak for yourself legally. Your nearest male relative does. And he seems anxious to bargain. After all, you have no dowry."

He was so rude she could not even respond. She just stared. Finally, she turned to look at her father. "Father, what does he mean?"

Her father looked embarrassed at his visitor's behavior, but he could hardly speak slightingly of a guest, especially a cousin of the king. For a moment, Lythera saw fear creep into his eyes, and she wondered just what sort of errand this visitor had with her father. "He means," said her father at last, "there is a way for House Halevern to be relieved of the burden of back taxes. Do as you're told, and a goodly portion of my debt will be waived."

She stiffened. A woman had to come with a dowry if she was to wed, but her father indicated that he would be the one receiving money.

"You are not trying to find a husband for me," she said through the chill of terror in her breast. "What else then?"

Novardan shrugged. "Three years ago Queen Brenicia died. I suppose you know that."

"Of course."

"And she died childless."

Lythera was silent. She did not like where this conversation was going.

"What you may not know is that the king's ministers have convinced him he needs to produce an heir of his body. Therefore, maids from around the kingdom have been presented to him during the past year and a half. So far none of them have become pregnant and all have been sent home."

"You...you would send me to the king's bed as a..." Words failed her. She would not be wife, but a thing. Something to be used and discarded with no legal protections. A cow, indeed.

"Consort is the word you're looking for, scholar-girl. Once your father signs the contract, you will belong to the king, just as you would to a husband," said Novardan. "But in this case, there is a time limit. If you are not pregnant in three months, you will be returned home, no worse off than you were."

"Except that I will no longer be a maid; I will be unmarriageable."

"Then all is well. For, since you have no dowry, you have already attained that state," said Novardan. "Consequently, no harm can be done to your prospects. You'll come with me and become the king's consort for three months, and be grateful for it. It's the closest you'll ever get to marriage."

Lythera was speechless. She turned to her father, hoping he might at least bid their visitor hold his tongue or mind his manners, but he looked just as wretched as she felt, and he would not meet her gaze.

"I will not," said Lythera. "This is disgraceful! I will not even consider it."

Fear flashed across her father's face. He turned to his guest. "Lord Novardan, my library is just in the next room. I will speak with my daughter, and you may leave with her when I have finished."

"Very well."

Lord Novardan took his time ambling out of the room, but Lythera kept her eyes on her father. He had never been a soft, gentle person like her mother, but he had never been outrageous or cruel. That he would even consider selling her to the king was nearly unthinkable.

Nearly, but not truly unthinkable. With five daughters to provide for, and a manor house falling down around his ears, her father had few options. Sending Lythera to the king in exchange for enough money to pay his debts must have been a tempting offer.

Her father grabbed her arm, desperation making him stink of sweat. "Listen, girl, it's time for you to do something for your family in return for twenty years of shelter and food. You'll go with this man, and be put in the king's bed. With any luck, you'll bear him a son, and Halevern blood will one day sit on the throne of Evandia. Now, swear to me you will do this."

Every instinct told her to say no, to reject this offer. To run from the hall, even if it meant a life of exile and hunger. But her practical nature could not countenance doing so. Not if it meant her sisters would continue to suffer poverty.

"Swear it," her father said again, "and allow me to provide for your sisters. I have no other way to see to their needs."

Lythera closed her eyes. She loved her sisters; could she not endure this fate for three months, and then return home to a family that could once again afford a fire in the fireplace, and full meals on the table? She could hardly say no, no matter what the cost was to her personally.

"I swear," she said in resignation. She felt color rising in her cheeks in shame. She could do this. She would do this. For her sisters. In stories, someone who sacrificed so much would be heroic and brave, but Lythera felt only small and abandoned.

Her father grunted. "Good." He called out, "Have no fears, Lord Novardan. She will be a good girl."

The other man strode into the room and nodded briefly at her father. "Then we will depart. Come along, girl."

"What?" Lythera backed away. "I said I would go, but let me say goodbye to my sisters. Let me get my belongings."

"I'm not staying in this rat-infested hole one more moment," said the royal visitor, who had clearly decided that any attempt to be mannerly was unnecessary in front of the local lord. "We are leaving."

"Lythera?" It was her youngest sister, little Narelle, barely five, but already promising to blossom into a lovely woman. The child stumbled across the uneven floor, arms out.

Lythera rushed to the girl and wrapped her arms around the small shaking body. "It's all right," she said. "I'll be gone awhile, but it will be all right. Be a good girl."

"Come," barked their visitor. He had reached the doorway to the drive where the coach waited.

Lythera dropped her arms but Narelle would not let go. "No!" the child shrieked. "Don't go!"

"Allow her a good-bye to her sisters," said her father. His voice was low, despairing. Lythera tried very hard not to hate him, but in the face of Narelle's tears, it was hard.

"We are leaving," said Lord Novardan. "Besides, she will be supplied with everything she will need once we are at the palace."

"No!" said Narelle. Her small face was blotched with tears.

"I'll be back soon," Lythera said with forced happiness. "Do not fear for me. Tell the others goodbye for me, and look for me in three months!" Lythera turned from Narelle or she would start crying herself, and followed their visitor out the door. A crushing sense of loneliness took her breath and she staggered through the doorway as if drunk. But at least Narelle did not follow.

The coach itself was beautiful, except that it was nothing more than a beautiful prison to her now. Gold dripped off of its intricate carvings and designs, and polished stones were inlaid in beautiful sweeps of color that reminded Lythera of feathers. Despite how heavy it must be, it gave an air of lightness and flight, as if promising an escape rather than a humiliating doom.

One of the magnificent stags turned his head to stare at Lythera a moment, its eyes so ice-blue, she could not look away before it did. But then it lifted a leg to stomp in a puddle and the spell was broken, and the world was mud and rain and degradation all over again.

Novardan stood outside the coach and held something out to her. A marriage bracelet, gold and marked by the Segrithr coat of arms. Lythera's mother had worn one similar, but it had been cheap pewter and of course had borne the Halevern eagle.

"Give me your wrist," Novardan said. Lythera's spirit balked, but she had no choice. For three months, she belonged to the king. She held out her wrist.

Novardan snapped the heavy thing on her. The tiny click it made as it closed was the most terrible sound Lythera had heard since her mother's death rattle. Now she officially belonged to the king. No man could touch her, or even approach her without risking retribution from the Segrithrs.

Novardan got in the coach and sat down. "I'd like to get back to the court before the week's out."

Lythera stepped up into the coach and settled herself on the seat opposite Novardan. She had no wish to look at him, but even less wish to sit beside him. Looking was the lesser evil. Lythera rubbed at the gold bracelet and wondered how her life could turn to ashes so quickly. Not that her life had been good at Halevern Hall, but she at least had had her sisters, and the small treasures of her childhood stored up in a chest her mother had given her when she was much younger. Now she had nothing—literally—except a patched dress, a cloak, and a pair of muddy shoes.

And the pretty bauble of a golden shackle.

Novardan closed the door and pounded on the roof of the carriage. The coachman clicked at the stags and they were off. Lythera looked out the window at the drab gray stone of Halevern Hall, with its ivy and its dirty windows, its cold fireplaces and charred meals, and already missed it with all her heart.

2

Lythera's first glimpse of the capital came early in the fifth morning, as they had been forced to stop just short of the city the night before. One of the stags had fallen lame and a replacement had been sent for from the royal stables. The replacement had been acquired early enough that they were able to leave in the hazy early light and arrive at the city while the sun was still ascending. Lythera held her breath and gazed out on all the white stone buildings—not blue, as her tutor had told her—covering rolling hills. The morning sunlight brushed across them and made them appear gold and pink, all the colors of dawn. *Rayn Avinon*, city of birds. The white was gorgeous against the blue of the city's lakes and the sky.

And then there was the palace, which could be seen from every vantage point.

There her tutor had been correct, after all. The palace was an astar, a giant crystal that appeared to have been grown, not constructed. The palace was reputed to be the largest astar in the land, and it certainly was incredibly tall and massive. Thousands of people must be able to fit inside! It seemed as solid and eternal in its central location as if it had been here forever and the city itself sprung up around it later. Its crystal towers sported colorful flags representing the most important families of the realm. Lythera knew Halevern would not be among them.

The gate to the city was a massive structure made of a dark stone. Mounted on top was an odd sigil, consisting of a carving of a full moon, a stork-like bird, and a verse. The coach passed by quickly, but Lythera could just make out the text, which was in Old Evandian and scarred by time and weather. *Moon-bird of Fortune protect us.*

Lythera could not recall reading about a moon-bird before. She had expected to see the sigil of the Segrithrs over the gate, if anything. The phrase, structured like a plea, gave her pause, and she began to look out the window of the carriage in earnest at the buildings and people of the capital.

It didn't take long to notice a few odd things. People made a strange finger-flicking gesture upon meeting. Many women wore intricate lace hair ribbons in various styles and colors, but always tied with a large knot at the nape of the neck and with a tassel hanging off the end. Lythera had never seen anything like it in the towns she had so recently passed through.

In contrast to the ribbons and brightly colored gowns of the women, the men of the city looked decidedly plain, much as they had in other places along Lythera's route. But even with their dress, she noticed some differences. Elaborate buttons, jeweled ceremonial daggers, and heavy rings were worn by many men. Even the commoners of the capital wore such affectations, though theirs were bone or wood rather than precious stones and metal.

All too soon, the carriage pulled up into the forecourt of the palace, a place alive with servants rushing to be somewhere else, and small groups of well-dressed young men and women chatting and laughing together. The entire area was bustling with energy. It was the most interesting sight, besides the astar, Lythera had seen since leaving home. And also the most frightening. The shared laughter, especially, only drove home her own misery. These people belonged here, had a place. Had friends and family. And she was alone.

The coach had barely stopped jostling before Novardan, who had proven to be as boorish a companion as could be imagined, pushed Lythera out of the carriage and into the arms of a middle-aged woman. "Here she is," he said. "Get her ready."

Novardan hopped out of the coach and stalked off without a backward glance. All activity in the courtyard stopped; as one, servants and well-born folk alike stared at her, and Lythera's heart quailed. Lythera did her best to ignore the attention, but the collective weight of a hundred stares drilled into her and cored into her soul.

The woman who stood before her did not seem to notice. She was not as tall as Lythera and appeared to be at least twenty years older. If Lythera had to guess, this must be another royal cousin, for she had the same black eyes and hair as Novardan, the same cool look in her eye. But what captured Lythera was her gown! It was the brilliant blue of an autumn sky, and trimmed in pearls. It was not the blue-violet of the astar, but close. Lythera backed away from the other woman, not daring to touch the dress again.

The woman flicked her fingers in the odd gesture Lythera had noticed on the city street earlier, and Lythera caught a glimpse of the woman's own marriage bracelet. She didn't recognize the design. The older woman said, "Good fortune." Lythera felt very small before this dazzling woman with the tremendous crystal palace behind her, giving her presence weight and importance, whether that was what she had intended or not, and could manage nothing more than a nod in return.

"I'm Metricia Trenstarl," said the woman after a few moments. "The man who just left you and who was, I'm sure, a perfectly atrocious traveling companion, is my younger brother. Don't worry about court customs; they're old and boring, but we just do them anyway. You'll pick it up, I'm sure. I don't suppose my brother gave you any warning of what we'll be doing with you today, did he?"

Lythera shook her head no.

"Oh, it'll be all right," said Metricia. "We'll get you settled in before tonight. Of course, you'll have to be interviewed by the ministers," here Metricia curled her face up in a gesture of disdain, "but that's just a formality. Novardan has agreed and your father agreed, so there's nothing else to be said about that, whatever the ministers like to think."

"Is...is this all your brother does, Lady? Bring maids to the king?"

Metricia shrugged. "Anymore it is. Sooner or later one of you will get pregnant, though, and then he'd better get his head back to thinking about his estates. Our youngest brother's been running them in Novardan's absence. Now, what was your name? Listria?"

"It is Lythera, Lady."

"Nice name. Are you hungry? I don't suppose my brother let you have breakfast?" Metricia guided Lythera into a side doorway off the main courtyard. The crystal floor of the corridor had been covered in thick carpets. Lamps set in niches in the walls gave the hallway an eerie, yet compelling, purple glow that seemed warm and inviting. For the first time in five days, Lythera's heart lifted a little.

"Did he?" prompted Metricia.

"Oh, what?" asked Lythera. "I'm sorry, this is just so beautiful. Everything is. Halevern Hall is, well, has seen better days. And, well, this is an astar. I've never been inside one before."

"Largest one in the kingdom," said Metricia. "By law, all astars technically belong to the king. But, enough of boring things like that! We have other matters to discuss. I'd been wondering when you might arrive— your father wrote my brother almost a year ago, did you know that? Proposing this alliance. He must have been stunned beyond belief to finally have my brother show up on his doorstep."

"He wrote a year ago?" Her father had been planning this even then? Lythera hated her father even more.

"Everyone's doing it—writing my brother, I mean. Especially the lesser lordlings who have fallen on hard times. Sei-Lords, mostly, though a few dau-Lords as well. How to improve the family fortunes in just one small step—sacrifice your daughter! It's disgraceful, but that's the way things are at court now."

Lythera ducked her head.

"Oh, but we were talking about breakfast. Did you get any?"

"Yes, Lady, at the inn."

"Do you want anything else?"

"No, thank you, Lady." Lythera did not add that she had hardly been able to keep food down for the past five days, and certainly couldn't eat anything else now, or possibly for the rest of the day.

"Then I'll show you to the room you're to use. There's a passageway that connects it to the king's suite, so he can come and go as he pleases without running into one of the hundreds of people who clamor for his attention every day."

Metricia guided Lythera through more hallways that all looked alike and were full of people in various costumes, all of them walking quickly as if they had somewhere more important to be than here. The dominant colors were the dark red and blue of the royal family but many other houses' colors were represented as well. Lythera recognized the sigils of a few of the more famous houses, but most of the liveries meant nothing to her. Lythera felt dizzy with all the activity.

"We expected you last night, of course, and then we got word about the stag going lame. It's a shame. They don't heal very quickly, and there are so few of them left."

"There are?"

Metricia shrugged delicately. "There used to be two kinds of them. A crimson kind and the blue. The crimson stags died out about twenty years ago, and the blue ones will probably be gone in ten years, maybe less. For some reason, most of the does just stopped dropping calves. The animals seem healthy enough, but, well, if they won't breed, you can't force them."

"No, I guess you can't," said Lythera. But anger surged anew within her. If animals didn't want to be mated, they could choose not to, but she had no choice! She was less free than the royal stags.

Metricia laughed and waved at a woman who passed by too quickly for Lythera to take in her features. "I see you're drawing some attention. You'd think by now everyone would be jaded, what with girls coming and going for over a year. But there hasn't been a new one in four months, after the last one being such a disaster."

"A disaster?"

"Skinny little thing, hardly old enough to have her courses yet. Hadn't filled out at all, but a fantastically gorgeous girl for all that. Anyway, her father would have her here and my brother agreed. So she was sent to the king, but then all she did was scream for her mother, so he finally left her in the room and had me fetch her out. She was just a little wisp of a thing. After that, the king told Novardan that if this abominable practice was to continue—and those were the king's words, *abominable practice*—that the next one should be older, intelligent, and not chosen for her beauty."

That remark stung more than it should have. Lythera had never been under the impression that she was pretty. "Then he did well."

Metricia shrugged. "Looks are overrated. The very first girl sent to the king was stunning, and everything seemed to go well for them for a few days. But eventually everyone realized the girl was thick as a stick. I mean, you couldn't talk to her about anything and hope she'd understand. But that's the kind of girl my brother likes—pretty, young, and not too smart. That's the kind he's been choosing, until now. But he's a fool—does he really think our next king should be birthed by a stupid woman? What if her child was just like her? That's more trouble than we need."

"So how many girls have there been, Lady?"

"Oh, nine, I think, including you. The others were all failures in one way or another so we're all hoping this time things will be different."

Lythera said nothing to that and allowed Metricia to guide her to a wide oak door in a nearly deserted hallway. Metricia lifted the latch and gestured for Lythera to go inside.

Lythera walked into a room cloaked in white and decorated in gold leaf and rose-colored silks. To her left, a merry fire blazed in a marble fireplace. To her right was a tall wardrobe, and beyond that was a wide bed heaped high with fluffy pillows. On the far wall stretched a wide window covered with gauzy materials. Lythera stared at it all, taking it in. From the angular shapes of the walls, she could tell crystal lay underneath, but somehow, palace residents had discovered some way to coat them with gold, marble, and fine cloth. Lythera was relieved; already she loved the astar, but she was glad her room, while grander than her old room, at least didn't look quite so exotic as the rest of the palace.

"This will be your room," Metricia said gaily. "And see that door on the other side of the fireplace? That leads to the king's suite."

Lythera walked toward a heavy wooden chair that was covered in gilt. A large blue cushion invited her to sit on it, but she didn't dare. Not in her old dress, now stained with nearly a week of travel.

"It's yours for a while, so sit in it," said Metricia. "We're just waiting for the body servants to tell us your bath is prepared."

"A bath?" That sounded wonderful. "Will it be warm or cold?"

"Warm of course! Who wants to bathe in cold water? Why, would you prefer that?"

"No, Lady. It's just that, well, we were never able to afford the fuel for such things. Using wood to do nothing more than warm bath water wasn't done, not even for the Lord." She refused to call him "my father." Though she realized he'd had few options, she had been less and less successful in her goal of not hating him the closer they'd gotten to the palace.

"That won't be a problem here," said Metricia. "You may not be a titled lady, but you'll be sharing the king's bed. We'll be sure to use a little fuel to warm your baths."

Lythera smiled. Perhaps, if she could just endure the king, she would like it here. She glanced up at Metricia. "Lady, what's he like?"

"Who, the king?"

"Yes."

"Well, nothing like my brother, for one thing. The king doesn't appreciate stupid people or fools. He's an excellent hunter and swordsman, and he's been riding horses since before he could walk. Everyone in our family is brought up on a horse. So I hope you can stand the smell of horses because the king's liable to smell like one."

That wasn't very helpful. Lythera clenched her fists and tried to gather what courage she could. Why hadn't her mother told her anything at all before she died? Why did she have to go to the king's bed so ignorant?

A soft knock came at the door. "Enter," said Metricia.

The woman who came in did not seem to be much older than Lythera, though it was difficult to tell. She wore a dark green dress that covered her from chin to toes, and even obscured most of her hands. From one hand dangled a leather satchel. Around her head she wore a strange wrapped veil in the same dark green as her dress; it covered her hair and ears, and from the veil dripped strings of black pearls. The veil hid the woman's hair but her silver eyes were striking. Her face was unlined, but she had an air about her that made her seem old.

"Lythera, this is our family nestriana," said Metricia. "I don't think you'll find them outside the capital—in fact, there's fewer than a dozen left. They're women who live lives of contemplation and service to others. They give up their families, and their personal names, to devote their lives to the study of herbs and medicine, but they're not physicians. They're concerned with women's health problems, mostly. Things like fertility and childbirth, and bleeding problems—subjects the men know nothing about and aren't interested in learning—or teaching—in their schools."

Lythera nodded to the other woman, a bit unnerved by her stillness and quietness. "Good day," she said.

The other woman only blinked. Perhaps she nodded slightly, but Lythera wasn't sure.

"They usually don't speak unless they're teaching their students or explaining a treatment to a patient," said Metricia. Servants now entered the room from behind the green-clad woman. "Traditionally, the black pearls represent their vows of silence. Come along, now, it's time for your bath. I've called the nestriana here to help prepare you for tonight."

Lythera stood and followed Metricia, the nestriana, and the servants down the corridor. Each of the servants wore a white uniform with the starkness broken by a sash with the Segrithr coat of arms embroidered into it. At the doorway at the end of the hall, Metricia stopped. She turned to Lythera.

"I must see to your lunch. These women will care for you until I return." She walked away, leaving Lythera with a gaggle of utterly quiet women with intense stares. Lythera wondered if they had decided not to like her, or if they were only curious. Still, she shivered under their combined gaze.

Abandoned, Lythera followed the silent women into the room where they showed her to a huge brass tub. She had never imagined a tub could be so large! At Halevern Hall, there was a disused tub in a storage room only a third this one's size. But Lythera had never been allowed to use more than a bucket.

The servants tsked over the condition of Lythera's dress and undid the buttons and the laces in the sides. They took the gown away from her and she stepped into the warm water. She didn't care for undressing in front of them; since her father had not been able to afford servants, she had never gotten used to undressing in the presence of others. She supposed the nobility did that all the time here, and that she would be expected to follow suit.

The nestriana opened her satchel and spread flower petals into the water. Lythera liked the smell and relaxed a bit.

The bath was a luxury! She might be willing to do anything in the king's bed if it meant such wonderfully warm baths. The women began scrubbing her skin and rubbing scented soap into her hair. Lythera let them do as they wished and simply lounged in the tub. Behind them, the nestriana held out a long white feather and waved it in the air in intricate patterns.

Eventually, she was clean enough for them. When she got out, the women toweled her off and brushed her hair. The nestriana approached her with a jar. Without a word, she poured some ointment into her hand and began spreading it onto Lythera's body.

Lythera wanted to protest—bad enough to be naked in front of the servants, but also to have ointment rubbed into her skin?—but the scent was so pleasant she decided she could endure this after all. As the scent wafted around her, she felt more relaxed than she had in days. After she finished with the ointment, the nestriana made several broad gestures over Lythera's head, then stepped back.

Now that the nestriana was finished with whatever she had done, the servants fitted several layers of underthings on her, and then presented Lythera with a russet dress that looked almost as fine as the one Metricia wore except that this was trimmed in gold lace rather than pearls. The women slipped it over her head and fastened it up the back. The dress was slightly too short for her, but it was so beautiful she did not care in the least about the faux pas of showing her ankles. It was the most gorgeous thing she had ever worn.

The women put roomy satin slippers on her feet, and then led her back to her room. They left, but the nestriana stayed. Lythera stood there with her odd companion in front of the merry little fire, and looked down at herself.

The neckline of the dress plunged much farther than her father would ever have allowed, and the dress, which was cinched at the waist and midback, lifted her breasts so that they appeared far larger than she thought they were. She knew she had developed breasts a while back, but in her shapeless dresses, she had never seen them like this. She wasn't sure she liked the idea of walking around the palace in such revealing attire.

The door opened and Metricia came in followed by servants carrying trays of food. The servants put the food down on a tray underneath the window. One of them pulled the sheer curtains back, revealing a view of the forecourt several stories below. Men and women moved about quickly, obviously on important business, just as they had this morning.

Lythera looked back at the table, where Metricia was spooning a thick meaty stew on to Lythera's plate. "I know you're nervous, dear, but eat something," the king's cousin said. "This lamb stew is one of the royal chef's most famous dishes. And make sure to drink all the tea."

Lythera would have asked what she meant, but it was immediately obvious. The nestriana approached, opened her satchel, and began preparing a mixture of herbs and oils in boiling water.

"I'm no expert, of course," said Metricia, "but everyone knows some of what a new bride—or consort—should be given before going to a man's bed. Oil of juniper berry, for purification. Lemon balm, for easing of worry. Dried hops, to make the woman eager for a man. Fortune's Rue, for fertility."

Metricia gave the air a sniff. "From the smell of it, I suspect she's already dosed you pretty good with the lemon balm. Spread it in an ointment, I would guess. I got that, too, on my wedding day, though I was pretty eager for the night to come in any case. Well and good, though; we don't want any scenes tonight, do we?"

Lythera frowned slightly. Did Metricia think she was a silly girl like the last one? She was several years a woman, and though frightened, she was no coward. And she had sworn.

The nestriana poured the tea into a cup and set it in front of Lythera. Metricia and the nestriana watched her carefully as Lythera sipped the tea. It was bitter and very strong.

"Three cups is tradition," said Metricia. "So drink one now, then eat. Two after lunch."

Lythera gave herself over to their care. Whatever odd customs they had at court, at least they were seeing to her comfort.

The food smelled wonderful, and the bath and the tea suddenly made Lythera feel famished. She ate with abandon until she was more sated than she could remember being in years. Regretfully, she looked at the remains of the lamb stew; it had been delicious. Perhaps it would be served again soon; it was the most flavorful dish she could remember eating.

Lythera glanced once more out the window at the courtyard surrounded by the glorious blue-violet spires of crystal. The hubbub of the courtyard made her feel small and alone. Everyone seemed to know where to be, how to get there, and what they were to do. Everyone except her. She dreaded the coming night but at the same time wished it were all over. She wished she could close her eyes and it would suddenly be tomorrow and everything over and done. The lemon balm ointment had, perhaps, lessened her anxiety enough for her to eat lunch, but it seemed to be wearing off now. The familiar hot and cold flashes running up her spine returned. When would they send her to the king?

"The king is out riding this afternoon," said Metricia, as if she had heard the unspoken thought. "But he'll be back in a few hours. Then they'll stick him in a bath before they shove him into a bed with you. So don't worry, you still have a while to wait."

Lythera ducked her head, trying to hide her fear. "He's out riding? But you said everyone knew we were coming today."

Metricia snorted. "My cousin is perhaps the person least interested in producing an heir for the realm. Don't ask me why. I can understand wanting a better quality bedpartner than my brother brings to court, but really, having maid after maid brought to your bed hardly seems like such a burden. Yet he behaves as if it were so."

Lythera's ears perked up at that. The king wasn't happy with this arrangement either? Would that encourage him to be understanding and kind, or resentful and cruel? The agony of not knowing tore at her and she couldn't ask. He was Metricia's cousin; she was bound to say he was kind, even though she should have no way of knowing what the king was really like in private.

"The ministers will be gathered near four o'clock, which gives us several hours to wait," said Metricia. "According to custom, you're supposed to wait here until sent for today, but tomorrow you can move about. You won't see me then, because I'll be heading back to my own estate tomorrow and I won't be back for a few weeks."

"You're leaving?" The world lurched under Lythera's feet. Already she felt like clinging to this woman, but to have to give her up so soon? It felt like an abandonment, though she knew the woman was only doing what she'd been assigned to do.

Metricia smiled. "Yes, I know, it seems bad to you, but understand that my daughter is being married soon, so I really should be there now with her. The king asked me to be here for you, so here I am, but I really must go. Now, enough about me. Tell me what you like to do. What diversions are there at Halevern Hall?"

Lythera shook her head. "None, Lady. I teach the younger girls what my tutor taught me and that's about it." This high born lady did not need to know that most of her time had been taken up with laundry, and baking, and mending, and cleaning.

"You teach?"

"Yes," said Lythera, wondering if Metricia would take the news better than her brother. "For a while, my mother paid for me to have a tutor. He was a cousin of hers and allowed her to pay him less than his usual fee. My mother said if a girl had no marriage prospects, she might as well have an education."

"Well, then, we can read the afternoon away."

And so they did. Lythera became entranced with a history of the palace that was so full of gossip and backbiting humor that it was hardly the dry historical tome she'd expected when she'd picked it up. The gossip was centuries old, but she didn't care. The book made the inhabitants of the court feel more like real people to her. People that might be found anywhere, even Halevern Hall.

By the time four o'clock arrived, Lythera was feeling much calmer. Surely everything would be all right.

3

She was halfway through the book when Metricia yawned and stretched. "I need to be getting you to the ministers. Remember, girl, don't let them frighten you. They're just bitter old men who'd rather their own sons were sitting on the throne. There isn't one of them who wouldn't like to be wearing the royal red and blue."

"But then why would they want the king to have an heir?"

Metricia laughed. "Because none of them can agree on which son from which minister would be the best choice. So if Vaiher's son is a favorite, then Landrith wants the king to have an heir. If Landrith's son looks like a better candidate, then Vaiher wants the king to have an heir. They're the worst lot of scoundrels you're likely to meet in the realm, and if they weren't so useful and efficient in running everything from the treasury to the army, I'd happily strangle the lot of them."

Lythera smiled. "I suppose I'm ready, then, Lady."

"Good. And while you're with them, I'll make sure my cousin is made presentable for you. We won't want him smelling of horse or saddle oil."

Lythera blushed, wishing all over again that tomorrow was already here.

"Come along," Metricia said as she opened the door. She walked down the corridor to the end where wide steps led downward. "This is the main staircase. If you can find your way back to it, you shouldn't ever get lost. I'm assuming you'll start wandering tomorrow."

Metricia led her down two flights of steps, down another corridor, and finally stood her before large double doors with men in royal livery standing at attention to the side.

"When they announce your name, go inside and walk to the end of the corridor. They'll ask you some questions, and then tell you when you can leave. Don't worry about any sort of protocol; this meeting is as informal as they get around here. Remember—they're just unpleasant old men. They're all ist-Lords, of course, being the king's council of ministers, so you must address them as *istan*, at least at first."

Lythera nodded, grateful for the reminder, but the sudden coldness of terror in her gut kept her from thanking Metricia. She shivered.

"Lythera, daughter of Marlun Lord Halevern," boomed a loud voice.

The men by the doors grasped the door handles and swung them open. In front of Lythera was a long gallery. At the far end was a table at which sat eight men dressed in shirts and coats decorated with family crests. Lythera stepped forward and walked toward the men. As she passed beyond the doors, she heard them close behind her. She was alone.

She walked the length of the room, glancing at the portraits hung precariously on the fluted blue crystal walls, and at the statuary lined up like two rows of spectators on either side of her. Light filtered down from high windows and danced in a riot of colors around the room. The carpet under her feet dampened her footfalls and all was quiet.

When she reached the end of the room, she stopped in front of the table and waited. No one spoke to her, and Lythera's mouth was so dry, she was sure she couldn't speak. What did they want with her?

Lythera stood before the assembled ministers and tried not to be embarrassed by the amount of cleavage she was showing off in this new dress. The men obviously appreciated the effect, for none of them made any effort to disguise the predatory looks that wandered to her breasts and stayed there far too long.

All except the man in the center, and a large man to her left dressed in teal and brown. The man in the center had wispy white hair and his eyes were milk-white as well. He turned to the man on his left, his eyes unfocused. "Vaiher, she's here now?"

"Yes, of course, Landrith. Right in front of you. Surely your ears work even if your eyes don't."

"Well, then, let's get started."

"Looks like you did what was asked of you, Novardan," said a thin, gangly man to the blind man's right. "She's not what you'd call beautiful.

Still, those eyes—striking in a way. Unusual color. But the important thing is, is she intelligent? That's what the king will want to know."

"She is a scholar. So she should be intelligent enough for the king's taste."

Lythera had not noticed Lord Novardan at the very end of the table. He had changed clothes to match the other lords and did not stand out among these men as he had at Halevern Hall.

"Still, you couldn't find a pretty scholar?" asked another lord.

"Not necessary," said the one in the center very sharply, the blind one. He blinked. "She only has to be a maid. Is she?"

"I have her father's sworn oath," said Novardan. "And her father promises to pay the honor-fee if she is found to be other than virgin."

"She must be," said the old man. "Halevern would never swear to pay money he didn't have."

"You are a maid, girl?" asked the lord on the far right.

"Yes, istan."

"You swear?"

Her pride was stung. Lythera brought her shoulders back and spat the words at him. "I have already so sworn, but if you must hear the words, then I swear that I am untouched."

The old man laughed. "Spirit! The last few didn't have any of that."

"We don't need spirit. Does she have the breeding?" asked another lord, this one near Novardan.

"Halevern's pedigree goes back to the days of the Kandliss wars. His fifteenth great-grandfather was given a title for saving the life of the king."

"Which king?"

"Revast Gomeril."

"Hmph. But that's only fifteen generations."

"If memory serves, your pedigree is no better," said the portly man, speaking for the first time. His gray hair was touched with brown, and his green eyes took in his fellow ministers with a studied disinterest. "Do any of you have any *real* objections?"

A sour-faced minister gave Lythera a look she could not decipher, but finally said, "*I* have no objections."

"Everything is set," said Novardan. "There's nothing more to discuss." The others nodded and stared at her.

Lythera's fear came back full force and all of Metricia's patient work was ruined. These men, they were looking at her like Novardan—like she were a cow at market. Or a bitch with a pedigree put to the male as if they could calculate what sort of prince or princess they could get from her if she should become pregnant.

Lythera's shame and terror twisted around her gut so badly she felt she might faint or be sick. She closed her eyes a moment and concentrated on breathing slowly and evenly. She would not dishonor herself by rejecting her lunch in front of these lords, no matter how cruelly they spoke to her.

She felt dirty, in need of a cleaning more thorough than mere hot water could achieve. Her skin crawled as if insects were walking all over her.

"We're finished here," said Novardan. "She's a maid, she has an acceptable pedigree, and everything is signed." He looked at her. "You have three months to get pregnant. I suggest you rut like a cat in heat, dear, or you'll just be one more disgraced girl sent home to a crumbling manor and an angry father."

The other seven laughed. No, six. As Lythera fought against the tears that wanted to flow, she noticed that one of them, a portly lord whose clasped hands rested on his ample belly, merely nodded his head to her in a comparatively friendly manner. But the others, even the blind man, seemed to think Novardan had made a great jest. They laughed and laughed. Lythera decided the interview was over and fled the room.

4

Lythera found her way back to her room and flung herself onto the bed, weeping in desperation and terror. What awful men! How could anyone bear to be in their company?

She wept until she began hiccupping. She curled herself into a ball and wished with all her strength that she was back home. But what use was that? Her father had schemed to get her here, and now she was here. There was no solace to be had at home. Where else could she go?

Vague half-formed plans of simply walking out of the palace flitted into her head, but her practical nature dismissed them. Besides, she had made a vow to her father that she would...she couldn't even think about that now. If the king looked at her the way his ministers did, she would simply die of mortification. She didn't want to be involved in this charade. One more entry into the pedigree charts.

The door opened. "Lythera?" It was Metricia. She crossed the room and touched Lythera on the shoulder. Lythera hoped for a kind word, but Metricia merely said, "I told you not to be afraid of them. You'll need to be stronger than that if you want to survive around here for three months."

Lythera sat up slowly. "They talk about me like I'm some kind of animal. One of the bitches that wanders around their estates."

"Yes, that's exactly what they're like," said Metricia. "Every woman gets treated like that—I suppose since you were so isolated in Halevern Hall, you were never exposed to it."

"You mean, even you, Lady?"

"Oh, yes, I stood before them and they debated my bloodline for a while, and I was born to House Segrithr! I can trace my line back fifty-four generations to Eistler Segrithr, Lord Warrenhall, who commanded the king's cavalry at the Battle of Nestarak. And my intended was from the Trenstarl family—only five generations in his pedigree! Didn't matter. They still had to discuss me like I was a dumb animal with no understanding. But I'd learned to ignore them long before that, so it wasn't such a trial for me."

Lythera wiped her eyes.

"It's time, child. The king has returned and is bathed and will be waiting for you shortly. As soon as he can pull himself away from the half-dozen courtiers who just had to have a minute of his time on this evening of all evenings." Metricia held out a white dress. "This is what you'll wear. Here, let me undo the stays in your dress."

Lythera turned her back on Metricia and the other woman went to work on the dress. Soon it lay in a crumpled heap at her feet. The underthings followed. Lythera stepped out of her slippers, still uneasy at being naked in front of others. But at least this time, it was only one person, and that one the friendliest one she had encountered so far.

Metricia handed her the white dress. Lythera shook it out and was embarrassed to discover it was no proper dress but a very thin shift with buttons up the front. She stared at it.

"Yes, he'll see through it, but that's the idea. We want him to see your assets clearly."

Lythera pulled the shift on and carefully fastened each button, unnerved by the offhand way Metricia mentioned her *assets*. She felt naked even with the shift on. She glanced down at her bare feet and could easily see the dark skin of her nipples, the paler skin of her stomach, and the dark hair between her thighs. She flushed.

"Here," said Metricia. She pulled a small packet of seeds out of a pocket, reached in and sprinkled a few into Lythera's hair. She said under her breath:

> Blessed the sun, the sea, the bright moon shining
> Blessed the hind, the hen, the fair winds rising
> Fortune lie upon you smiling.

Lythera frowned and wondered if she were allowed to shake the seeds out of her hair. "What was that?"

Metricia looked slightly sheepish. "Just an old custom. No one knows what it means anymore, so we just consider it good luck. You'll find there are a lot of little rituals we do around here have no meaning. They're just old ways that have no beginning that anyone remembers—but no one has any reason to quit doing them."

Lythera nodded, grateful for any good wishes. "Thank you."

Metricia tucked the packet of seeds back into a pocket of her gown. She stepped back and surveyed Lythera critically.

"Well, Teiryn can certainly have no complaints about you being too young or underdeveloped," said Metricia drily but with humor. Lythera did not think it was funny.

"Now we go," said Metricia. She led Lythera to the side door and opened it. Behind lay a narrow passage lit only by a small window high on the wall. The passage was unadorned, making the light sparkle with violet-tinged beauty. Metricia led her through it to the other side, then opened the far door.

Lythera took a deep breath and walked into the king's suite, expecting something like her own, but she was surprised. This suite was larger than hers, but less ornate. Very plain, actually. Metricia led her to the far side of the suite and opened another door. On the other side was huge room, nearly as big as the one they'd just left. Decorated in dark reds and deep blues, with gold everywhere. And on the far wall, a large bed. Lythera gulped.

"Go on, climb in," said Metricia. "He'll be here in a few minutes; don't worry."

Metricia left her there and Lythera walked slowly toward the bed. To the right were two huge wardrobes that dwarfed the one in her room, which she had thought of as large. Next to the bed was a small table with a lamp already lit. And then...the bed.

Lythera pulled back the thick wool blanket that covered the bed and the cotton sheet that was underneath that. The sheets were softer and their weave finer than anything she had ever slept in at Halevern Hall. If she weren't so afraid, she would have been glad to lie on such fine linens. She closed her eyes a moment and tried to gather her courage. Then she crawled into the bed, curled up into a ball, and waited.

The light faded from the windows, though it was not yet true dark. The days were getting longer, but it was still close enough to winter for the twilight to slip by quickly. As the shadows lengthened, Lythera stared at the ceiling and tried not to think about what the king would do with her once he arrived.

It seemed she waited an eternity before she heard the outer door open and a man say, "That's enough. See me tomorrow."

The king. Her heart leaped in her throat and she shivered.

But minutes passed and the king did not come. Finally, Lythera climbed out of the bed and crept to the door in the dim light of the oil lamps. She opened the door slowly.

Across the room a man sat at a table, eating dinner. He was black-haired and black-eyed like his cousins. The king's straight hair fell down past his shoulders and was streaked with gray. He had a beard, trimmed very short and also touched with gray. His tanned face was lined, making him look older than his years.

She stepped out of the room. "Sire?" she asked.

The man stopped eating and stared up at her. "Fortune's Blood, girl, did my cousin leave you in there alone and in the dark? All this time? Blast the woman!"

Lythera dropped her gaze and shuffled her feet. She didn't know what to say.

"Well, come on over here, and let me get a look at you. You get a look at me, too, hey?"

Lythera liked the sound of his voice. It was deep and comforting. She walked over to the table but couldn't help clutching her arms over her breasts. She felt exposed and didn't want to look up to see the king stare at her as his ministers had.

"It's all right, girl, you do get to look at me."

Lythera looked up slowly, dreading what she might see. But the king was studying her in a friendly manner, with an expression on his face that looked like pity, or even sorrow. Up close, she could see his black eyes were sharp and intelligent. They stared evenly into her own eyes, without falling toward her body and remaining there as the ministers' eyes had done.

The slight upturned wrinkles on his face made him seem like a person who enjoyed life and laughter, unlike her father's wrinkles, which caused his face to sag. She liked the king's face. It looked slightly careworn, but strong. And most importantly, kind. The king sat back in his chair and gestured for her to take a seat opposite him. Lythera thought she should probably curtsey before sitting down in the king's presence, but a surge of rebellion in her heart stopped her. She had not chosen these circumstances. If the king wished her to bow or curtsey, that was too bad. She would not. Her body was his, but that did not necessarily mean her heart was. Lythera sat down.

"There's enough food for two if you'd like some," he said. He did not seem to notice her omission of protocol. Perhaps he did not expect it from the maids sent to his bedchamber.

"No, thank you, Sire."

"Not hungry?"

She shook her head.

"My cousin shouldn't have abandoned you here. I'm sorry for that. She's thinking too hard about going home."

"So she said. Her daughter's getting married."

"Yes."

She did not voice the bitter thought that followed and swallowed her hurt pride. *And I'm not married, despite this bracelet. I'm not here to face the prospect of a wedding bed, but a life of shame. I'm here to be used.*

"It's not easy coming here from one of the smaller holdings," he said conversationally. "The court is crowded and busy and not particularly set up for guests. I hope you come to like it here, at least enough to stay for a while."

"I'll try, Sire."

He picked up his meal where he'd left off. "You know, you don't have to stay here," he said in between bites. "You could go home."

She closed her eyes and snuffed out the pang of grief that came with the word home. "I have sworn to stay here for three months, Lord."

He looked at her then, a deep, calculating look. Different from the predatory looks given her earlier by his ministers, and not as unwelcome. He seemed to be considering more than simply what she had said out loud. "You're Halevern's daughter."

"Yes, Sire."

"And he has no other way to provide for his family."

She nodded.

The king washed his hands in the bowl of clean water which sat by the table, and then washed his face. He toweled his face dry and rubbed his short beard vigorously. "I don't care what you swore to your father," he said when he had finished. "You don't have to come to my bed."

"Don't...don't you want me to? I belong to you now," she said and couldn't keep all the bitterness out of her voice. She was rewarded by a startled look from the king.

"No offense, Lythera, but you are not my queen. She and I bedded with great joy, with laughter, and with love. And since she is gone, I haven't the heart for such things anymore. Yet my ministers insisted on reviving this atrocious custom, for the sake of the realm. But it is still too much like the prize stallion being put to the broodmare. There is no love in it. And, really, does the kingdom truly need an heir of mine? I don't think my ministers would have problems finding someone else to put on the throne once I'm dead. A cousin, perhaps; there are so many to choose from. Or one of their own. What they really mean is that by making an heir, I avoid the chaos that would follow my death. But it seems to me the heir should be conceived in joy, not in fear. Would that were the case now."

She had nothing to say to that, but she felt calmer. It was easier, somehow, to realize that the king was even more trapped than she. He would let her go if she asked, but they would just send him another maid later. And then another. He couldn't escape. She was surprised at the great swell of pity she felt. She had never considered kings to be anything but free. She looked him in the eyes with as much courage as she could summon. "If I leave, I am forsworn."

He stared at her, his expression intense and unreadable, but something in his face reassured her. Seconds ticked away. Finally, he nodded and stepped toward her, arms wide. He wrapped his arms around her shoulders and she laid her head against his chest. Her heart pounded but fear was giving way to excitement. At the very least, this man wasn't cruel or angry or violent. *From the marriage bed to the birthing bed, life is nothing but pain,* her mother had said often enough. But the king's talk of laughter, joy, and love did not make the coming night seem dreadful at all, but rather something to be savored.

"You are my *verrika*," said the king softly. Lythera puzzled over the word a moment, but she remembered it from one of the old languages.

Verrikon was an archaic term for a courageous person, a hero. She didn't feel brave, but she was warmed by his compassion.

Being held by another person who was taller and broader than she was a new experience. Lythera had carried and comforted her younger sisters, of course, but her mother had not been demonstrative and she had certainly never been embraced by her father or her tutor. The feeling of being cherished and protected was novel, and delightful, as was the warmth rising from his skin. Lythera looked up to meet the king's gaze. He planted a quick kiss on the end of her nose and she was tricked into a laugh. The answering smile on his face washed away the last of her fears. She stood on tiptoe to meet his lips with her own.

At first, the kiss was tentative, almost shy, as if the king were waiting for her permission to continue. Lythera reached up and held his face between her hands, marveling at the softness of his beard, ready for whatever was next. The king did not disappoint her. He became more confident; his tongue found her own, to her surprise and pleasure. His hands roamed her body, at first lightly, then more boldly, caressing her with increasing confidence. Lythera could not believe the shift she had donned with some embarrassment less than an hour before now seemed heavy and cumbersome. She had to be rid of it.

Wriggling out of the shift while the king held her with one arm and struggled with his own clothing with the other was enough to make Lythera laugh again. Finally, they had to part long enough to finish disrobing.

As the king's clothes fell away, and Lythera saw him naked for the first time, the dread she had thought she would feel had been replaced by a new hunger she had never known existed. He held out his hands to her and she willingly went to him, wedded to him by desire and a rising excitement that she could not wait to use the night to explore.

5

Somewhere in the depths of the night, Lythera had a vivid dream where the world lay under a bright blue sun that was fading to purple in the west. Before her stood crimson and blue stags and a forest of crystals. An old woman, bent with extreme age, toddled toward her. Lythera rushed forward to help the woman sit on a low flat bench of radiant opal. "Here, grandmother," she said, "let me help you."

The old woman laughed. "You have no idea how you could help me. The future could be yours to choose. Or not, but one of you will choose."

"One of whom? Choose what?"

The old woman patted Lythera on the hand and Lythera sat down beside her. The bench was icy cold. "This world has grown old. But what will replace it?"

Lythera was about to tell the woman she didn't understand when the woman lifted her eyes to Lythera. Instead of normal eyes, the woman's sockets were filled with blue crystal which shone with an odd light. Lythera screamed.

It was morning. Lythera took a deep breath and unclenched her fists. She had never had such vivid dreams before, but then, she had never before been away from home, or in a man's bed. Her life had turned upside down. A strange dream or two was understandable. Lythera stared at the gilt ceiling until the remnants of the dream faded. The intricate designs swirled around each other like eddies in a rushing stream.

Thoughts of the night crowded out everything else. The king...no, Teiryn, she could hardly think of him as only *the king* after last night...had introduced her to feelings she had not known she was capable of. She blushed even now to consider how forward and wanton her behavior had been, but she had no regrets. She looked forward impatiently toward the night, toward the next three months of life with Teiryn.

But she couldn't just lie in bed all day, no matter how pleasant daydreaming of her lover might be. Still—what would she do with her idle hours?

She was not yet finished with the book she had been reading yesterday, but the thought of reading books all day for three months did not sound appealing. And she was sure that the palace had enough staff that no one would expect—indeed, even allow—her to make herself useful. Not that she liked mopping or cooking or laundry, but those were, at the very least, time-consuming activities.

Teiryn had said she was free to wander around; Metricia had said the same. So she would wander. Perhaps she would meet some interesting people, or even find a friend. She had time and Metricia couldn't be the only person at court who would speak to her.

Someone knocked on the door and said, "Lady?"

"Yes?"

A girl entered with a basket of materials for building up the fire. She curtseyed at Lythera, then busied herself at the fireplace. Another girl entered with a pitcher of water and a towel. Both girls finished their tasks in moments, nodded to Lythera, and departed. Lythera bathed quickly, certain that other servants would begin arriving momentarily. This time, she was determined to get as clean as she could, and dressed, before anyone else came in the room. Lythera put on the russet dress from yesterday and did up the stays as best she could by herself.

As she finished, more servants arrived, one after another, some bringing food, others bringing clothing. The servants brought her piles of underclothing of cotton and silk, dresses, shoes, even jewelry. Lythera reveled in the luxury of it all.

One of the servants bowed to her briefly. "Your pardon, Mistress, but we're to dress you and see to whatever needs you have."

Lythera hesitated, but it was clear she was going to have to get used to servants dressing her. With as much indifference as she could muster, she allowed the servant to remove the russet dress she had just put on. The servants outfitted her with more underclothing, and then showed her a beautiful dark red dress.

With only the briefest of statements, "Please try this on, Mistress," a girl held the dress out for Lythera to slip into. Lythera did so and the girl fastened it up the back. This outfit had a neckline identical to the russet dress and Lythera realized she was likely to continue getting dresses that displayed her breasts like trophies. But this one fit better than the last one; it fell to the floor instead of just to her ankles. Metricia must have noticed the other gown was too short. The dress had enough extra material in the bodice that the stays could be adjusted for nearly anyone who was close to Lythera's size. It was only the hemline that had been a problem for the palace staff, because of her height.

New slippers were placed on her feet, dyed the exact color of the dress, and another girl placed tortoiseshell combs in her hair. Lythera began to feel she would look like a real court lady today.

The girls—though they did not resemble each other, their uniforms were identical as were their modest, downturned expressions, which made them hard to differentiate one from another—nodded to her and left the room. Lythera eagerly went to the table to eat her breakfast; she had not eaten since yesterday's lunch.

The food was excellent—light fluffy muffins, eggs, delicious sausages, and a whipped fruit compote in a sparkling glass bowl. Freshly squeezed fruit juice, toast dripping with butter. She consumed it all.

There was something else on the table, too. A small wooden box with exquisite mother-of-pearl inlay. Lythera's hand shook as she picked it up. She had heard of the custom of leaving a morning gift for a woman on the day after her wedding, but she did not think to ever receive one. She had never thought to be a bride, and now she was only consort. Not wife. Still. The box was there.

She opened the box and gasped. Inside lay a ruby necklace, the cabochon set in gold, hanging on a gold chain. Small diamonds framed the larger red stone, which matched the red of her dress. She lifted the necklace out of the box carefully as if it would disappear. This necklace alone could solve all her father's financial problems. She grinned, knowing it was hers and not his. A woman's morning gift could only be given or sold at her discretion; it was hers for life.

She put on the necklace, which was long enough to dangle just between her breasts. With this neckline, the jewel was still entirely visible and brought even more attention to her chest than the dress would alone. She wondered if it was the custom of court ladies to display their breasts like this; Metricia had not. But then, she was a mother with children old enough to be wed. Surely she would dress more demurely than women Lythera's age in any case. Lythera had no desire to leave such a wonderful gift behind, so she would wear it whether it caused others to stare at her or not. And if men stared, she would learn to take Metricia's advice, and ignore them. If the other court ladies could ignore men's stares, then Lythera could, too.

The door opened and a short round woman in a dark blue dress entered. She, too, wore a sash like the servant girls, but Lythera did not recognize the livery. The woman's gray hair still showed wisps of red; it had been braided and wrapped around her head. Blue eyes rimmed in deep wrinkles were of a much lighter blue than her dress.

The woman bowed slightly and panted as she spoke as if she had just run up the steps. "Mistress, I apologize for the lateness of my arrival. I was just informed that I shall be your chambermaid. My name is Wenvia. I'll be making sure you'll have food and a bath when you wish, and I'll be spending part of today making sure you have everything you need."

The breathless way Wenvia spoke made Lythera smile. She nodded. "Thank you. I suppose the others came with personal effects, but I came with nothing, so anything you can provide will be most welcome."

"I see." Wenvia's gaze went to the dresser by the bed, which contained the clothing the servants had just brought. She sniffed disdainfully, as if insulted that the king would be presented with a lady so poor. "Well, Mistress, that's not a problem you'll have long. That's a start, but there's more to come, I promise you that. Body oils and perfumes, slippers and shoes of every color. More combs for your hair. Trinkets. Meals are usually provided at eight, one, and six. If you wish to change that, you have only to let me know."

"Thank you." Lythera rose from the table. "I think I will take a walk. Do you know where I might go?"

Wenvia frowned. "I'm not sure you're to leave the palace, though the royal park is across the street. Perhaps the king will arrange for an escort if you wish to go there. Otherwise, the forecourt is close, and the gardens are behind the palace. The shortest way is through the stables," here Wenvia pointed out the window toward the central tower; "otherwise, you'll need a guide to get through this maze on your first day."

"Thank you," Lythera said again. She had never had servants of her own before and was a little unsure what she was supposed to say or do. She settled for nodding to Wenvia and leaving the room.

The main staircase to the right was easy enough. She was passed by people hurrying along in the same bustle as yesterday. The palace seemed like an anthill, with everyone scurrying around her. Lythera hugged the wall and did her best not to get in anyone's way. She went down the steps to the bottom floor and found that if she turned left she could walk straight into the forecourt.

Thousands of flowers lined the courtyard, which was otherwise an expanse of gravel punctuated by patches of grass. Overhead, the towering crystals broke the morning light into multiple rainbows of color that fell all around her. Lythera bathed in the beautiful light for a few moments before realizing she was attracting some attention. Quickly, she followed the gravel toward a large entrance beneath the central tower.

A yellow cat ran past her, chased by a long-legged dog. The cat leaped into an open window and the dog pulled up short, looked up at the window, and whined. Lythera was fascinated. Her mother had once tried to keep cats in Halevern Hall, but her father had thrown them all out. Animals were dirty. No animals were allowed inside, not even a kitchen cat. Lythera could not remember even petting a cat or dog. Perhaps in the palace, she would be able to do so, or be allowed to care for an animal.

Now that she was no longer standing agog in the sunlight, most people who passed paid her no attention, though she received several odd looks and one leer from a guardsman who should have been minding his own business. And that might have been simply a response to her dress rather than an acknowledgement of who she was.

Lythera walked into the dark entrance and waited a moment for her eyes to adjust. When they did, she crowed in delight. To her left and right were double rows of large stalls built of intricately carved wood. Equine heads peered out of them, eyes and ears turned in her direction. Lythera knew nothing of horses; back home, she had only seen them occasionally on the street. Still, she was sure these must be the most beautiful horses anywhere.

"Hey, are you supposed to be in here?"

A young man approached her, his raven bangs hanging in his eyes. He didn't wear the royal colors, but she would have known him for Segrithr kin from his coloring alone. He was her height, and very thin. She curtseyed.

"I'm just taking a walk," she said. "I was told I could get to the gardens from here."

The young man bowed slightly, but he didn't take his eyes off of her. Lythera could almost feel him assessing who she must be. A stranger, wearing a fortune around her neck and a Segrithr marriage bracelet on her wrist, the day after Novardan delivered the newest maid for the king. Surely he could guess.

He could. "You're Lythera Halevern, I bet. I'm Evinard Nivain. Good fortune to you." He made the finger-flicking gesture.

Lythera still didn't know how to respond to that, so she said, "I'm pleased to meet you." She wasn't sure what title Evinard deserved, and waited to see if he would insist on one.

"I don't see any reason you can't be here," he said, apparently unconcerned with her casual mode of address. "I, for one, don't want to have to worry about where you'll be allowed and where you won't since you won't be here long in any case."

Lythera felt she should be insulted by his remark, but he made it so artlessly that she couldn't. Evinard had the air of a boy just growing into manhood who still said what he thought. Unlike her father or Novardan, he gave no indication he knew how to hold his thoughts to himself. She was certain he would learn if he spent much time in court.

"Would you like to meet my horse? My mother gave him to me for my birthday."

"Certainly."

Evinard led her down the row of stalls until he stopped in front of a yellowish head with a black forelock. "Isn't he grand? His name is Black Sunlight."

Lythera looked at the horse. The entire animal was a faded yellow but it had black legs and black mane and tail. He was beautiful. "He certainly is grand. What do you call his coloring?" She held out her hand as she had seen Evinard do and the horse lipped at her palm. His breath was warm and his nose softer than velvet.

Evinard gave her a sideways look, the look on his face one of bafflement. Lythera supposed that, in the court, horses were a favorite topic and Evinard had never met anyone who wasn't intimately familiar with them. "Buckskin. You don't know much about horses, do you?"

She shook her head. "There are no horses at Halevern Hall. And I've never had a reason to travel before."

"Well, have your chambermaid get you some riding skirts," said Evinard. "There are a few old timers around here who are safe to put babies on. Won't startle for any noise. We can see you learn to ride."

"But you admitted I won't be here long," she said. "How long does it take to learn?"

Evinard shrugged his shoulders and scratched his horse under the cheek. "I don't know. Everyone in our family gets put on a horse as a babe. We just grow up on them. But I'm sure you could learn. You're obviously not an idiot like the first girl Uncle Ilvinard—Lord Novardan—brought here."

"He's your uncle?"

"Yes. There's six of them in that set. My mother, Morvania, is the eldest, and I'm her youngest child. Then Metricia, then my uncle Malagert. After that, my grandparents appeared to run out of names that began with an 'm' so then you get Ilvinard, Julinand, and then Vandencia. Vandencia's what we call a fortune's child."

"A what?"

"A baby who comes so long after the last one everyone's sure the mother can't bear any more. A surprise baby. Some people say they're bad luck, but Vandencia's nice enough. She's not much older than me. Seventeen, I think. She's not here now but she'll be in court soon. I'll introduce you. She's a horrible tease, but I bet she'll like you. And then my Uncle Julinand's the one minding Ilvinard's lands while Lord Novardan is out gathering Tei..." He stopped suddenly and flushed. "Oh, sorry."

"About what?"

He shuffled his feet and cast his eyes downward. "It's what's everyone's calling them. You. Well, not you in particular, you know, but the girls sent to the king, Teiryn's Tarts. Some call them Fortune's Flowers, but that only sounds better, it's not any more polite. Just more poetic."

"Why are flowers rude?"

The words seemed dragged out of him. "Because the girls come bearing a kind of flower—their maidenheads, you see—and then the king deflowers them. They give him, well, you know. Everything. Honor, reputation. Even the words they get called—tarts and wilted flowers—they're words used for the women who sell themselves on the street corners. I'm afraid to the court you're..."

"A whore," she said, sick at heart. Lythera had never said the distasteful word out loud before; just saying it made her feel dirty.

"I'm afraid so, yes. Though, of course, no one will say so to your face. I don't suppose that makes much of a difference, though."

Lythera stepped back, too angry and too bitter to say anything. She covered her face with her hands, turned away and would have fled, but Evinard said, "Wait. I know it's a wretched thing, but where could you go to get away from it? Everyone in the palace knows. Even if you left the palace, the people in the city would know just from the Segrithr jewel around your neck. Don't pay any attention to them—any of them."

Lythera took a deep breath and dropped her hands. The air in the stable smelled of fresh hay and manure, of leather harnesses and above all, of horses. Somehow, the earthy, ordinary smells comforted her a little. She knew so little about horses, or any animal, but something about them drew her attention away from her personal pain. The horses in the stable all seemed to be looking at her, their large black liquid eyes friendly and welcoming.

Somehow, she felt strangely at home in the stable. Perhaps she'd be allowed to ride while she was here, and the time wouldn't pass by too slowly. No matter how rude people were to her otherwise.

Besides, where could she go? She had no home. No place. Where could a dishonored woman, even one with an education, find a place in the world—today, or in three months? Despair crept over her, though the warm breath of Black Sunshine on her face revived her spirit a bit. She touched the horse on his velvety nose in gratitude, then followed Evinard to the far end of the stable.

"Dendryl?" called Evinard.

A stocky blond man stepped out of a stall. "Yes, Master Evinard?"

"This is Lythera Halevern. She'll be a guest here for a while, but unfortunately, she doesn't know how to ride. Is Blinky well enough to entertain thoughts of teaching a new rider?"

Dendryl shook his head sadly. "No. His health has failed. We'll have to put him down soon. But Morningbelle would do. Blinky would have been too short for the lady, anyway."

"Is there any reason I couldn't take the lady to the ring in the morning for lessons?"

"No, there isn't. No one else is training right now." Dendryl smiled at Lythera and his smile seemed genuine. She smiled back and hoped he wasn't someone who thought of her privately as Teiryn's Tart.

"Well, that's settled," said Evinard. "Thank you, Dendryl, I'll leave you to your work. Come on, Lythera, let's go to those gardens you were trying to find."

Dendryl bowed slightly to Lythera, and she bowed back, unsure of the protocol, but grateful for the gesture. Then she hurried after Evinard.

6

Evinard led her through further corridors until she was thoroughly turned around. But then one last corner, and through a door, and...they were in the gardens, and they were magnificent.

Ahead of her lay a flagstone path made of the same dark blue stone as the city gate. To either side were well-tended roses of all colors. Farther along, towering, spreading trees guarded benches just big enough for two to sit upon. Birds sang in the bushes and hopped across the well-manicured lawn. Some of them were familiar to her but others were not. A dark purple long-tailed songbird of a type she had never seen before flew into a bush nearby and sang the most beautiful trilled song Lythera had ever heard.

But perhaps the most magical thing was the way the giant crystal castle behind her broke the bright daylight it into a million dancing hues of blue and violet. The entire garden glowed.

She could stay here forever.

"Nice, isn't it?" asked Evinard, who had clearly seen the effect too many times to be impressed. "Come on, let's explore."

Let Evinard be jaded; Lythera could not imagine a time the garden would not look like an enchanting retreat untethered to the real world outside the castle. Lythera could not name many of the trees, bushes, or flowers, but she was sure she could find a gardener at some point to tell her what all these wonderful plants were called and where they came from. In the meantime, she was thrilled just to walk along the path and drink in the heavenly scents.

Her companion noticed her lightened mood and smiled. "So, you must have had a garden at Halevern Hall. Did you like to walk there?"

"No, no, we had nothing like this—how could we? There's a walled-in area behind the manor where we used to grow vegetables." She didn't add that it had been the cook who had raised the vegetables. Once the cook had been dismissed, her mother had tried, and Lythera had tried, but neither they nor the younger girls had had any luck gardening. The changing weather patterns had not helped. "It was usually just a patch of mud. The rains get worse every year and all the gardens and lawns around Halevern Hall suffer for it."

Evinard nodded. "The past few years have been bad. Too much rain in some places, too little in others. I don't know the last time I heard my father say the crops were coming in well. Master Jarris is full of predictions of doom and gloom, but most people seem to think it will sort itself out eventually."

"Who's Master Jarris?" Lythera asked.

"He's..." Evinard was interrupted by a young man who, like everyone else in this place, seemed to have somewhere important to be. He swept by in a whirl of green and black clothing that was heavy enough for travel; certainly too heavy for this warm morning.

"Valeron," called Evinard. "Good fortune to you."

The young man stopped and turned to face them. Lythera blinked in surprise. It wasn't just that the young man was attractive, but that he had eyes like hers. Eyes the color of the astar. Eyes that matched the violet glow all around them.

The young man—Valeron, she assumed—seemed equally flummoxed. He stared at Lythera several moments before catching himself. With a little shake of his head, he said. "I'm sorry, Lady. I did not mean to stare."

"That's quite all right," she said.

"I thought you'd be gone by now," said Evinard. "Your mother kept talking about how she wanted to be out of here by mid-morning."

Valeron shrugged. "Mother doesn't always get what she wants. I still have a few chores to take care of, and others in our train have business to attend to this morning as well. But we're leaving soon." He cast another glance Lythera's way.

Evinard apparently realized he'd been lax with his manners. "Oh, excuse me. Lythera, this is Valeron Trenstarl, Metricia's son. Valeron, this is Lythera Halevern."

This time, Valeron made a formal bow. "Lady," he said again. "I'm sorry I don't have more time to make your acquaintance. My mother spoke very highly of you. Still, with Evinard to guide you, you are well accompanied."

"Yes, I believe I am," she said. "Perhaps I will see you again."

"Perhaps," he said. "As my mother may have told you, we go home to prepare for my sister's wedding. I told her there was no reason for me to be there just yet, but she insists." A quirky smile crossed his face for a moment before his formal demeanor returned. "Mothers are difficult to please sometimes, especially when you're the lord of the manor. Now, if you'll excuse me." He bowed again, not quite as deeply as before, and walked off quickly.

"We used to be pretty close," said Evinard as he and Lythera continued their stroll. "But then his father died and he had to spend most of his time at Trenstarl Manor. Since then, he's gotten pretty grim. Their crops are doing poorly and, though Metricia puts a brave face on it, I think their situation could be dire within a couple of years."

Lythera felt a surge of sympathy for the young man; he looked no older than she, but duties and responsibilities to his manor, his family, and the people of the land had clearly taken a toll on him already.

"I've never met anyone with eyes like mine,," said Lythera, wondering if she were being too bold to bring up such a subject. Her mother had told her many times women were not to comment on the appearance of men outside their immediate circle—and most of the time, not even then. But Evinard, as she suspected, was not bothered by the question.

"It's rare," he said. "Shows up sometimes in a few of the bloodlines, though I don't know of anyone else in Metricia's family who looks like that. But with the way the nobility marry their daughters to each other, you have to expect some slightly odd traits will pop up here and there over the generations. At least it's not two noses or something bizarre like that." He grinned, and Lythera smiled back.

"I suppose that would be quite a detriment when looking for a spouse," she said.

Evinard laughed. "I suppose, though a man who is destined to be a nao-Lord, like Valeron, could have fifteen noses and everyone else would want their daughter married to him."

That was cold water on Lythera's light heart. Yes, men could look like anything at all, have any temperament, and still be desirable if they had wealth. But even a woman whose suitor stood to inherit a great deal from his father-in-law might look twice at a woman who was not perfect.

Still, this was Evinard. He meant no harm by what he said. The two of them continued through the gardens in silence.

As soon as she saw the spreading branches of an ancient twisted tree ahead of them, she forgot any pique she might feel toward Evinard. "Oh, it's beautiful," she said. She ran to the tree and touched its outstretched limbs. Branches drooped nearly to the ground so it took some time before she noticed the bench at the base of the tree.

"Let's sit here!" she said.

"As you wish."

The two of them pushed their way through the curtain of branches and sat down. Lythera looked up into the tree. Her eye could not follow all the twists of the trunks and branches. It was as if the tree had grown itself into a giant knot. Graceful thin branches, covered in long knife-shaped leaves, drooped down around her head. The leaves were the darkest green imaginable, almost black, but silver on the underside. Lythera felt she could stay here all day.

"I always thought this tree appeared rather sinister, but you seem to like it," said her companion. "Except for this one, these only grow in the far east in Hellfren lands, so people usually call it the Hellfren Willow. But I've heard the gardeners call it Old Gnarly. No one knows how old it is; they say it was here even before the palace, and no one knows when the palace was built."

Lythera continued to stare at the tree. She decided she could ask Evinard her question about his title now.

"The stabler called you Master Evinard. Is that what I should be doing?"

She turned and saw furious color in his cheeks.

"No, no," he said. "You can call me whatever you like. My father is Lord Nivain, and so that title will go to my oldest brother. Father's subsidiary title, which was willed to him by mother's uncle when he married, is Lord Aydriel, which will go to the next son. That's not me. So, since there are no titles or lands in the offing, I'm a Master to the servants."

"Then if you'll have no lands, what will you do?"

He shrugged. "My oldest brother will have to provide me with some sort of allowance. But as for what I'll do with my life—well, I don't know. If I want any children I might have someday to have more than scraps, I'll have to figure something out on my own. Most lads in my position look around for the highest-ranked unmarried lady they can find—preferably one without brothers—so they can inherit anything her father bestows on her. But that seems a rather cold way to choose a bride."

"All ways seem cold to me these days," said Lythera absently. She thought for a few moments about what Evinard had said, anger tugging at her heart. She wondered why her father had never mentioned he could offer his title as her dowry. Some younger son of the nobility might have preferred to be a sei-Lord than a titleless burden on an older brother. Then she might have had an honorable marriage and a husband, though a husband who would have taken her for the sake of her father's hall, and not for affection. She tried to imagine going to the bed of a husband who had married her merely to get her father's lands, and shuddered. The arrangement with the king was not an honorable estate, but the king was caring and compassionate.

"Oh, no," said Evinard.

"What?" She glanced around but the drooping branches obscured her view. It appeared some people were approaching, though Lythera could not tell much about them from behind the leaf curtain.

"There, see? Those three girls. My cousins. Malagert's daughters. His eldest is a son, but the man's literally a drooling idiot, so it's well-known that someone who weds one of these three will be his heir. Too bad you have to meet them on your first day here."

"Are they so awful?"

"Judge for yourself. Just keep in mind that if anyone is calling you a tart or a wilted flower behind your back, these three are. So if I were you, I'd spare them any excessive politenesses. They don't deserve it." Evinard got up from the bench and went out to greet his cousins.

So warned, Lythera got up after him and followed him out onto the path and back into the swirling violet atmosphere. The eldest of the three looked to be of a similar age to Lythera, and one was a girl just developing into womanhood. The youngest was probably six or seven. They all shared the black hair of the Segrithr family, but only the eldest had inherited the black eyes as well. The other two had eyes of silver. The eldest wore a dress of rose, the neckline of which matched Lythera's own. That made Lythera feel slightly better; apparently this was the fashion for young women, and not something reserved for the king's consorts. The middle sister wore dark rose, and the youngest was in silver. Their dresses were of a more childish cut—shorter skirts, high collars and loose waists.

"Lythera, these are my cousins Reyva, Holliwen, and Jynarra," he said, naming them from eldest to youngest. "Cousins, this is Lythera Halevern."

Lythera curtseyed to the girls, but they merely stared at her in return. "Welcome to the palace," Reyva said at last, though the spite in her voice voided any possible hospitality in the phrase. "May you enjoy your stay."

The other girls giggled at the emphasis Reyva put on "enjoy."

"Well, at least she has some manners," said Evinard. "I bet the king likes her. What man likes you?"

Lythera blushed at the mention of the king but none of the cousins noticed. Reyva flushed and looked as if she might spit at Evinard, but controlled herself. Holliwen put her hands on her hips and came to her sister's defense.

"And what girl likes you, Evinard Nivain? You spend so much time with the horses that you always smell of manure. Your mother will never find a bride for you."

"My mother isn't even trying," said Evinard evenly. "I have asked her not to."

"For shame," said Reyva, though she actually seemed oddly pleased by the news. "It is your duty to marry and sire another generation of your father's family." This time the emphasis was on "father." Lythera didn't understand the reason for Reyva's strange way of accenting words, or why she would choose Evinard for a target, when he seemed so nice.

"House Nivain is amply represented by my father, his brothers, my brothers, and all their sons and grandsons already," said Evinard. "The world won't end if I don't contribute. Nor will the world end when you can't find anyone willing to bed you, my dear."

"Galladon Standren would dispute you on that, little cousin," she said. "My father is working out the match even now."

Evinard bowed slightly. "My apologies."

Reyva seemed mollified. She raked a disdainful glance across Lythera before departing. Her sisters followed in her wake.

A strange sound came from Evinard. Concerned, Lythera turned to him, thinking he might be choking. But her companion was not in danger; his face was contorted in an effort not to laugh out loud. Lythera glanced around but the girls were out of sight. "They're gone."

Laughter exploded from Evinard and he choked out words in between guffaws. "Did you...did you...hear her? A...a match! With Galladon!" He couldn't stop laughing long enough to go on.

"Yes, I heard. Why is it funny?"

Evinard breathed deeply several times and finally managed to get himself under control. "It's funny because everyone knows Galladon despises her. But he wants Malagert's lands—House Standren hasn't an acre to its name anymore. Yet they do have an ancient name and a large manor with some income from the iron mines. A Segrithr daughter with vast land holdings as a dowry would be a fine match. But more than likely it will be Holliwen in his bed, not Reyva. Holliwen's a woman now and she's not so bad when you can get her away from her sister. All Malagert has to do is declare Holliwen's husband—whoever he might be—as his heir and the deal is set."

"But then why does Reyva say the match is for her?"

"Because she won't admit that she's so unpleasant that her father can't find anyone to take her. Not for any dowry. Not even in exchange for his lands. She's a poisonous creature, and she's the only one who doesn't realize it. Perhaps if she were Malagert's only daughter and marrying her was the only possible way to become lord of his estates, someone would wed her just to get his hands on the land. But with two others who could be chosen instead, well, I doubt there will ever be a wedding for dear Reyva."

"And why did she seem pleased that your mother isn't trying to find you a wife?"

He shook his head. "Just spite. She'd like me to be single forever because she thinks I'd be woefully unhappy in that condition. After all, what man wants to sleep alone his whole life?"

Again, his artlessness kept her from taking insult or even being embarrassed. "So you won't marry?"

"Someday. Maybe. But I'd like to find a girl who would marry me because she liked me, not because my mother picked her for her pedigree. Fortunately, after having schemed to get all her other children married off as well as possible, my mother seems to have tired of the game. So she agreed not to meddle with my affairs."

"I hope you find her someday, this girl of no particular pedigree," said Lythera softly.

"Me, too. Anyway, do you want to see more of the gardens? Or, I know. You're a scholar, right? That's what the king told Uncle Ilvinard to bring if at all possible. Would you like to see the records room? Our records-keeper would love to meet you, I'm sure. He won't be calling you nasty names behind your back. He never says a bad thing about anybody, not even when they deserve it."

Lythera smiled. "All right. Thank you for your kindness."

Evinard flushed red, then white, then red again. He looked away and couldn't meet her eyes. His black hair fell down into his face and he had to sweep it aside.

"What?" she asked.

"It's just that, well, I feel ashamed of myself. When Novardan first began bringing girls, I was one who thought it was funny, or worth mocking, and I feel terrible about it now. But then, when the last one came, it finally hit me how cruel it all is. Anybody who didn't think so before should by now because everyone heard her screaming herself hoarse. They say the king didn't even touch her, but well, she was shrieking like he'd done something terrible. That's when I decided I wasn't going to let my mother do that to me and to some girl who just happened to be from the right family. Anyway, I'm sorry. I'm sorry this has happened to you and I'm sorry I used to be such an ass about it all."

Lythera was touched. "You haven't offered me any insult, Evinard. There's nothing to forgive. And if you were thoughtless before, well, at least you learned you made a mistake. You've certainly been most kind to me and I appreciate it very much."

He blushed and nodded. "All right, then. Let's go to the record-keeper and get you introduced." He glanced up at the palace and pursed his lips.

"But I'm going to take you the long way—back to the main staircase, and then to the records room. That way you can find it yourself when you want."

"That's very thoughtful of you."

He shrugged and grinned. "Come along."

Once again he led her through a veritable maze of corridors, all of them teeming with people who behaved as if they had urgent business. But then, Evinard walked so swiftly that Lythera realized they looked like they had urgent business, too.

Upon reaching the main staircase, Evinard glanced at her as if to ask her if she knew where she was. She nodded and he turned back into the forecourt and crossed it to the far side. Then through another door, up a staircase, and a left turn. Soon Evinard was knocking on a large oak door that was slightly ajar.

"Master Jarris?"

"In here, of course."

Evinard turned to Lythera and grinned, then indicated she should precede him into the room. Lythera walked in and gasped. She had never in her life seen a room like this.

From floor to high ceiling, every wall was crammed with books. Some bound, some tied together with string. Stacks of loose papers lay on shelves, held down by blocks of wood. Additional shelves had been built in the center of the room. All of them filled with more books than Lythera had imagined existed in the whole world. The high narrow windows were situated in between the columns of crystal and the light gave the room an eerie radiance that made the room appear surreal, as if the walls were lit from the inside. Yellow shafts of light filtered down through the dusty air around her, but instead of giving everything a warm glow, they turned everything into violet.

From the ceiling hung dried leaves tied with yellow string. The leaves had a scent that tickled Lythera's nose and partly obscured the smell of old parchment and glue.

An old man hobbled around the bookcases. For a cruel instant, Lythera thought he was the blind minister, but only for a moment. Both men had thin, wispy hair and were bent with age. But this man had merry green eyes and walked with the help of a stick. He smiled and beckoned for them to sit at a table.

"Welcome, young Evinard. And friend. What can I do for you?"

"I've brought you a scholar," said Evinard. "Perhaps she could help you with your work while she's here at the palace. And someday, we may need to find her a place on someone's estate. As a record-keeper."

Jarris smiled at Lythera pleasantly. "Is this what you'd like, girl? Spending your life among dusty old tomes and ancient papers? Wouldn't you prefer to be raising a family, thinking of the future, and not fussing over the past?"

His gaze was so friendly it disarmed her. "I have no dowry, so I don't think I shall ever wed. My mother, knowing I would be poor and seeing I was no beauty, made sure I was educated. If you can help me find a position, I would be most grateful." In fact, Lythera felt intense relief. She had no desire to return to Halevern Hall, although she did miss her sisters. If this man could help her find some way to spend her life other than as a dependent in her father's care, she would be forever in his debt.

The old man gave a cursory glance to her bracelet but Lythera was glad to see he refrained from mentioning that she had said she would never wed. Instead, he nodded. "An education is a wise thing to have, no matter one's circumstances or the condition of one's birth. Can you read Old Vedatic?"

"Yes. And of course Evandic, both modern and ancient."

The old man's eyes widened. "That's quite an education. I haven't met such a talented young person for quite some time. Not since Ulindein. Sadly, most schools won't hire female teachers, but with such skills, we could surely find you a position. In the meantime, you can help me here, though I can't offer any pay."

Lythera was startled into a laugh. She had never dreamed of holding a position that came with a salary! "I don't need anything right now, but I would like to explore the option. It sounds exciting. For now, can I help you?" The idea of reading books was appealing, but the idea of three months of nothing but reading was not; here, at least, she could do something she enjoyed and have activities to fill her time.

The old man shrugged and gave her a calculating look. "I've been staring at these ridiculously obscure manuscripts for so long I'm not sure I even see the words anymore. They're incomplete and some of the authors used a complex grammar I haven't seen elsewhere. It's difficult to sort out."

"Where are these texts?" she asked.

Evinard rose. "I think that's my cue to leave, before the two of you get too wrapped up in moldy books. I'll leave her with you for now, Master Jarris. You can find your way back to your room, Lythera?"

"Yes, thank you."

"Then I'll see you tomorrow, around nine, in the stables. We'll get you on Morningbelle. Don't forget to ask your chambermaid for riding skirts."

"I won't. Thank you again."

He bowed to her and left. She turned to Jarris and he was smiling at her as if he had found a treasure he had not known existed.

"Young lady, would you fetch the red-bound book on the shelf to your right? That one is the most complete record of ancient sayings and prophecies that we have in Old Evandic—unfortunately, the dialect is not that of the court, but something more obscure. It would be the best place for you to start working the puzzle out with your fresh young mind."

Lythera brought the book to the table, opened it, and began to read.

7

Lythera had no more than opened the book when a door on the far wall opened and Valeron Trenstarl strode through. He frowned when he saw her. "Lady, are you lost?"

"Ah, Valeron," said Jarris as he re-entered the room by a different door. "Can I do something for you?"

"The object I gave you to look at. I want it back so I can return it to Trenstarl Manor where it belongs. You've had enough time to study it."

"Object?" Lythera asked.

Valeron's frown deepened and he said sharply, "It's no concern of yours, Lady."

"Valeron," chided Jarris gently as he searched through a box on a table nearby.

Valeron's face cleared and a bit of color flushed across his cheeks. "My apologies; I am in a hurry and have forgotten my manners. You know, if you stay here long enough, Jarris will have you digging in the dirt or cleaning up the things he digs out of the ground. He and his students find all kinds of things. Even my father would dig around Trenstarl Manor and find the odd bit of the past. I don't know what any of it means, but Jarris can get quite excited about it."

"We know so little of our past! We should be studying it, learning about it. How can we face the future as a people with so little history, when there is clearly so much to learn, so much at stake," said Jarris as he continued sifting through the contents of the box. "Fortune's Blood, I thought it was in here. It must be in my office. I'll return shortly."

Jarris limped out of the room, leaning heavily on his cane.

"Do you know what this object is?" asked Lythera.

Valeron shook his head. "It's just something my father found. I've found a few things myself, but nothing particularly interesting. Just be wary of Jarris—if he can sense the least grain of interest, he'll sweep you up into his obsessions and refuse to let you escape."

"You seem to have escaped."

"My father died," Valeron said flatly. "And that was the end of any scholarship for me. I would think you would understand that one's life can change in a moment, and never be the same again." His bitterness was hard to listen to; it matched her own too well.

"Yes, I can understand," she said quietly.

"Well, in any case," Valeron continued in a slightly warmer tone, "Jarris is a good man, just obsessed. And I am supposed to be on the road to Trenstarl Manor. I can't wait to get away from this nightmarish place."

"Nightmarish? Do you have bad dreams here? Does everyone?" Perhaps her visions of the old woman and the ancient lion were common in the palace.

Valeron leveled his gaze at her and stared at her intensely, as if truly seeing her for the first time. "No; I thought it was only me."

His odd reaction made Lythera's blood run cold.

"Found it!" said Jarris from the other room. He tottered back into the archive waving a pointed metal object. It appeared to be the head of a lance, in bronze. It reflected the blue glow of the room so brightly Lythera blinked.

"I've copied the inscription that runs down the blade," said Jarris as he handed the lance to Valeron. "If I can translate it, I'll let you know."

Valeron nodded briefly to the old man, cast an awkward glance at Lythera, and departed.

Jarris came back to Lythera and sat down wearily. "That young man wearies me," he said. "Never a great student, but he used to be more affable, more patient. I suppose that's how you know he's a grown man with estates to run. Now, where were we?"

"Tell me about the lance head you gave back to him," said Lythera. "He said his father dug it from the ground."

Jarris chuckled. "My favorite topic, my dear. I'm surprised Evinard didn't warn you to keep your nose in a book."

"He didn't. Why would he?"

"Because nearly everyone is tired of hearing me talk about the past," said Jarris. "It's all well and good if they can use a good translator to help them decipher some old records that might show they're the rightful owners of some land their neighbor claims, but unless it benefits them right now, they're not interested. If I can help you find a position with a family or school, they will be interested in your translation skills, not my pet theories."

"But maybe I'm interested," said Lythera. "I'd like to hear about the past, anyway. I only know what little I've read in my lessons."

"Those are usually not very informative," said Jarris. "At least, that's what I've found. *The Battle of Oldfield was waged in the year 356. King Glirindol died in 593. The sigil of House Standren is the bull.* Boring. Necessary, perhaps, if your life's work is to be spent among dusty documents, but they're only dry facts, not really the lifeblood of history itself."

"And you know about the lifeblood of history?" It was an odd phrase, but it sounded interesting. Lythera leaned forward, her elbows on the table.

"That has been my life's ambition," he said. His green eyes shone with the fire of his interest. Or, obsession, as Valeron had said. "It started when some farmers came to me with an odd metal disk that had an inscription engraved on it. This was, oh, fifty years ago now. Anyway, the disk fascinated me. I paid them for the item and didn't really think about there being more. But once people realized I'd pay for old things, more items were turned over to me. After a few years, I decided to start looking for them myself. I began digging in the ground. It took me some time to learn where the best places were, and how to go about it. You have to be careful, going just an inch or two at a time. You must make careful records, so that later you can tell exactly where the item was found in relation to everything else."

"Why?"

"Because the farther down you go, the older things are," said Jarris. "So you must know the order in which you find things. Unfortunately, I have no way of knowing exactly how old the items are. I can only date them relatively, not absolutely. Are you sure you find this interesting?"

"Oh, yes," said Lythera. "Do you have some of these items around here?"

Jarris grinned crookedly. "Most assuredly. Come along." He got up and went through the door into the next room.

Lythera followed. The next room was full of wardrobes. That seemed odd. But when Jarris opened one, she realized he had stacked wooden boxes inside rather than clothing. The boxes were on racks so Jarris could pull one out at a time without having to dig through piles.

Lythera stepped closer and noticed each box had a label on the front. Jarris reached for a box whose label read, "Palace Garden Site 3."

"Here," said Jarris. He handed Lythera the box. It was heavier than it looked; Jarris hardly appeared strong enough to handle something of this weight. But he seemed used to it. He grabbed a second box and closed the wardrobe. "We live in an era of silence, Lythera—deep silence. Only whispers of our past have come down to us in books and laws." Jarris led the way back to the library and put his box down on the table. Lythera put hers down beside it.

"What do you mean?"

"The past stretches out farther than you know. We have good records for the past few hundred years, documenting the reigns of the Segrithr kings, and before them, the Gomerils. Before them..." he glanced at her and Lythera realized he wanted to ascertain how much she knew.

"The Uldreths. They were the first family to rule Evandia."

"That's what we're all taught," said Jarris. "But were they? Records from the Uldreth kings are sparse, but they do exist. Before that, we have nothing. But there were people in Evandia before that. People have been here for a very long time."

Jarris opened his box. Inside was a collection of crystals. "Before our own era, there was another era of even more silence. So far I have found no evidence of human habitation; perhaps I'm looking in the wrong places, though. Who knows? I haven't been able to dig up the entire country. Even earlier than that came the Era of Crystals. I believe that's when the astars were created." He pushed the box toward Lythera.

The shattered pieces of crystal glittered prettily in the light. They were a range of colors from clear to blue to fiery red. A few were delicately pink and one was night-black. Lythera picked up one of the pink stones and held it up to the light. The color it radiated around the room was exquisite.

"From these layers, everything is crystal. Crystal buttons, knives, plates, combs. It must have been a beautiful and fascinating world indeed. Most of it is the bluish violet we recognize from the astars, but some of it is very different, as you can see."

Questions swirled around in Lythera's head. If Evandia's history were so old, why did no one know anything about it? And if the rest of that world lay shattered under the ground, why did the astars remain? Who were the people who had created all this?

"There are other layers," said Jarris. "Beneath the crystals is the layer that contains things like the lance head I returned to Valeron. Weapons of every shape and material. Knives of stone, swords of bronze, arrow points in glass. I find things like buttons, too, everyday things, but most of what I find are the weapons. The Trenstarl lance is the most magnificent object of its kind ever found; for one thing, it is all in one piece. Most items that old are broken. I call it the Era of Conflict, though I am not sure the weapons were actually used. Perhaps they were ritual items."

"Ritual items?"

Jarris gestured for Lythera to open her box. As she did so, he said, "Some of them are only shaped like weapons—it's hard to see how anyone could actually have used them."

Inside the box was a small gold item shaped like a knife. But it was only the size of Lythera's smallest finger. She picked it up carefully.

"Is it really gold?"

"Oh, yes," said Jarris. "Solid gold. Fortunately, I found that one—I doubt I'd have been able to get my hands on it if anyone else had found it. But gold's too soft to use as a weapon, so what was this really? It couldn't have been a knife."

"It looks like one." Carefully, Lythera turned the object over in her hand. It was cool but warmed quickly to her hand. The gold knife was very detailed; the handle was fashioned to look like it was covered in interwoven leather straps. It was a perfect knife. Except it was gold.

On the edge of the blade, she noticed a reddish stain that chilled her heart. "What's this? Blood?"

Jarris shook his head. "No, no, even if a gold knife were sharp enough to draw blood, blood wouldn't have survived this long, and would have turned dark brown, anyway. And gold doesn't tarnish, so that can't be the explanation, either. I think it must be the remains of some potion or powder used in a ritual. But what sort of ritual? I can't imagine."

Reluctantly, Lythera replaced the knife in the box. "I had no idea."

"No one does, my dear," said Jarris. "And few are inclined to even guess. The past simply doesn't interest many."

"And before the weapons?"

"Deeper than that, artifacts become very sparse," said Jarris. "Well, who can say how long ago they were made? All the items from the oldest layers are made of a reddish metal that looks much like pure copper, but it has no tarnish. The very soil often seems to take on the same color. I confess I don't understand it. But the most exciting thing is that every single one of the objects from this ancient time are inscribed."

"Really? What do they say?"

Jarris laughed. "I have no idea. The script is unfamiliar. I don't have any idea how to go about translating it. I have made sketches of each item and given a copy to each scholar who's interested in tackling the problem, but so far, no one has found anything."

Lythera was quick to reply. "I'd like copies, too, if that's possible."

Jarris hesitated, then shrugged. "Certainly. Why not? Even if you find nothing, you'll be just as accomplished as anyone else who's tried." He sighed and a darkness crossed his face. "I just, well, I have this feeling that I must know what all this is about, and soon."

"Why?"

"Because the layers are so distinct, with no transition. It's as if something happens to turn the world upside down."

Lythera frowned as some snippet from one of her tutor's books came to mind. "The Uldreths were supposed to have become the first kings of Evandia after some sort of terrible upheaval. My tutor guessed it was a series of wars in which the Uldreths moved into Evandia and forged it into one nation. But he said that was only a guess."

"Yes," said Jarris. "I have wondered about that. It is so frustrating, that we know nothing of it. We can see only that the world was remade in some way, and that Evandia was formed from whatever had come before. I believe that time of upheaval will come again, and soon, and we should be ready for it. What use is learning about the past if not to spare our world another such dreadful period of chaos as the last one? It had to be dreadful, or how could we have lost *everything?*"

Lythera smiled and put a hand on the old man's shoulder. "But that could be a long time away. Centuries. You and your students could have lifetimes to decipher the clues."

Jarris shook his head wearily. "I don't think so, Lythera. I don't have definite proof, but there are signs. Omens. Crops failing, weather patterns shifting. The stags dying. Some of the smaller astars have literally fallen apart into dust overnight. Young animals born with two heads, or six legs, or with no legs at all. And then there was last night? Have you heard?"

"No." Lythera blushed, remembering how she had been worried about much more personal issues the previous evening.

"Stars fell from the sky from the constellation of Fortune's Wheel. That happens every year around this time, but last night was spectacular and the sky toward the north glowed with odd colors. It was very unusual."

Lythera sat down as well. "Evinard didn't say anything about it."

Jarris waved a hand absently. "Oh, well, I doubt anyone in the palace noted or cared. The palace has a tendency to reflect light in ways that makes its inhabitants blind to strange lights in other places. Except me. You see, last night was the old New Year. The one celebrated under the Uldreths. It was the Gomerils who moved the New Year to the date it is today. I had always wondered about that, so I got in the habit of staying up on that night, and that's how I've become so acquainted with Fortune's Wheel and her falling stars. Usually, there are only a few, and they come toward dawn. But last night the stars fell all night long."

"That might not mean anything."

"It might not," said Jarris. He sighed. "However, there's no need to burden you with an old man's worries. Come back tomorrow and I'll have the drawings of the oldest artifacts available to you. They're around here, but I'll have to look."

Jarris suddenly seemed so weary that Lythera grabbed his hand in concern. His warm skin was wrinkled and felt paper-thin, and he seemed to have no flesh on him at all. It was as if his life was poured into his obsession with the past, and the fire of it was eating him from the inside.

"I'll see what I can do," said Lythera, wishing there was something she could say to comfort the old man. Though she had known him only a short while, she felt a connection with Jarris she'd only previously felt with her tutor. He was someone she could talk to, about languages and words, about obscure texts, about history. Someone who would understand her own interest in those subjects.

And who could help her indulge them. Now, during her three-month term in the palace, Jarris could help her learn all that her tutor never could. And in learning, perhaps she could help Jarris in return. If some bit of information could be teased out of the ancient artifacts, Lythera would do it.

Jarris squeezed her hand slightly. "My dear, you give me hope for the first time in a long time. A long time." His green eyes met hers and he smiled.

She smiled back. Suddenly, she looked forward to the next three months. She would have Teiryn and she would be able to indulge her love of learning. Life in the palace was looking to be sweet indeed.

8

Teiryn moved through his day slowly, the courtiers around him seeming more like pestering flies than usual. His experience with Lythera had rerouted his mind somehow. She was nothing like the other girls sent to his bed; she was special. He could not stop thinking about her, the feel of her skin, the smell of her hair.

"Sire?"

He looked up and realized he had ceased listening to the judge. "Your pardon, Lord Yawneil. Please continue."

Yawneil kept talking about some problem in the northern reaches of the kingdom. Some brigands. Why this hadn't been handled by the local lord was beyond Teiryn's comprehension. Oh, wait. The local lord was Gomeril. That would explain it.

Ever since the Segrithr family had taken the crown from House Gomeril, the losing family had, well, been throwing a fit. They paid their taxes late. Every year. They sent the required enlistment for troops for the army, but never quite the number that had been requested. The rest were always "en route." Local problems went unheeded and ended up on the king's lap. Their negligence and lack of cooperation with the crown never quite reached the level of true insubordination or rebellion. Gomeril knew how to toe a very fine line—he never stepped over the line from constant nuisance to treason.

Gomeril had no sons to take the throne, anyway, so Teiryn listened less and less to Yawneil. He would do what he always did; send a detachment of the army to deal with the problem. And Gomeril would be properly grateful in public while planning his next trick privately.

Truly, Teiryn did not mind Gomeril's little schemes. They were so transparent. "Oh, my man didn't get the taxes paid until they were six weeks late? For the twelfth year in a row? I'll look into it, Sire!" Teiryn smiled to himself. Gomeril couldn't think him stupid; he must know that Teiryn was aware of everything he did. The old man just didn't care. "Annoy House Segrithr" had become the unofficial motto of House Gomeril.

If anything, Gomeril's little tricks just proved how little true trouble was brewing in Gomeril lands. A brigand here, an assault there. Nothing unusual for such extensive holdings. Now, Novardan was another matter.

Yawneil glanced at Teiryn and said, "I assume you'll issue the same judgment as last time, Sire?" Teiryn nodded, which satisfied the judge.

Teiryn rose. "That's enough for today, Lord Yawneil. I'll take care of the rest tomorrow."

Yawneil looked like he'd bitten into a bitter root, but what could he say? Teiryn was extremely conscientious about getting to cases as quickly as possible, and often sat in judgment even on Harvest and the turning of the year in spring when everyone else went home except for a few courtiers like Yawneil. It was already noon and Teiryn was weary of this. If he didn't get to many cases on this one day, Yawneil could hardly complain that Teiryn was being slothful.

Teiryn rose and left the chamber. Everyone stood until he left the room. When he was newly crowned, that had bothered him, but he scarcely noticed anymore. That was one problem with being king no one had ever mentioned to him—it was easy to get used to the bowing and scraping. To not notice it anymore. Teiryn made an effort not to fall into that habit, but some days, the effort was too much. Like today.

He had barely gotten into the corridor when his cousin Novardan spotted him. Teiryn stopped to greet him; he could hardly do otherwise, despite the other man being a thoroughly unpleasant person to be around, someone he'd prefer to avoid. But kings could not indulge such personal preferences.

Teiryn stopped before Novardan and his cousin immediately bowed deeply. "Good fortune, Sire. I trust all is well with you."

"It is," Teiryn said in as friendly a manner as he could.

"And the lady?"

Teiryn carefully kept his pleasure to himself. It wasn't kingly; besides, he wanted Novardan on his toes. "Well, I believe. Quite a find. Halevern's daughter, I was told?"

"Yes, Sire," said Novardan.

Teiryn began walking toward the forecourt; Novardan followed a half-step behind. "Is there anything I can do for you this morning, Lord Novardan?"

"It would give me great pleasure if I could host the king at my estate for the Harvest this year."

"That's six months away."

"True, but the royal schedule is always so full. I thought I'd ask now and that perhaps, with some time to think on my petition, you would look favorably upon it."

"But, cousin, why should I look unfavorably upon it?" asked Teiryn. He stepped into the bright blue-tinged sunlight of a beautiful spring day. This particular courtyard was full of gardens growing nothing but blue flowers, constantly tended by an army of gardeners. Flowers that matched the blue of the palace were highly prized and a favorite of most residents, but Teiryn preferred the sunny yellow buttercups in the meadows around the city. They had been Brenicia's favorite.

"No reason. Please consider my request." With that, Novardan bowed and moved off.

What was that all about? Teiryn wasn't particularly popular with any of his cousins of his generation except Metricia—the Segrithr scions could hardly be called close—so an invitation to spend the holiday season at Novardan Manor was more than it seemed. And Ilvinard Segrithr should always be watched. Teiryn wished he'd been king rather than his father when his distant cousin had died childless, leaving the title of Lord Novardan to be awarded to one of the remaining Segrithr males. Teiryn had no idea why his father had chosen Ilvinard and had never felt safe with that man locked away in Novardan Manor, far from court.

That was why, when the ministers had decided to dust off the horrendous custom of finding maids for the king, Teiryn had sent his cousin Ilvinard to acquire them. It kept the man busy and away from his estates. The younger brother currently holding the reins there was no threat. Julinand Segrithr had a sharp mind for arithmetic, tithes, and taxes, and no head for trouble. He might have no fondness for the king, but he liked his comforts and his accounts, and his wife was unquestionably loyal to the crown. Far better for him to manage Novardan lands for now.

"Sire!"

Teiryn recognized the voice of his personal secretary, Velrudin. The man could be as pesky as a horsefly, but he did work hard keeping the paperwork of kingship at bay. Or as much as possible.

"Yes?"

Velrudin bowed slightly. He was a bit of an enigma to the court. Extremely short, bald, and with a frightful scar over his left eye from a childhood accident, he hardly seemed the sort to appeal to women. Yet many women vied for his attention. So far Velrudin had not married, but when he did, there would be a string of broken hearts among the female staff.

"Sire, I just wanted to remind you that the Morovolo ambassador is due to arrive within the week, possibly as early as tomorrow. And I have the Suzahlin Islands documents for you to sign. Ambassador Ghanzia has been asking about them."

"Thank you, Velrudin. I'll see to the papers tomorrow morning first thing."

Velrudin bowed again and retreated. Teiryn walked toward the stables. He needed to ride, needed to escape the palace for just a short time. Riding was the one pleasure not only afforded him, but encouraged. Every noble should know how to ride, and the king should know better than anyone. His father had had him on a pony before his first birthday, and he had loved horses ever since.

The stabler bowed to see him, not quite as deeply as his assistant, but with more feeling. That pleased Teiryn, for the stabler and he shared a love and a respect for the denizens of the stable. Kings had few friends, Teiryn had discovered early on, but certain loyal servants were almost as good. Worth their weight in gold, and willing to stretch the bounds of propriety just enough to let you know they didn't just respect you as king, they liked you as a man. That meant a lot in this nest of serpents.

"Shall I saddle Trailblazer for you, Sire?"

"Please."

The stabler bowed again and departed into the darkness of the stable—or at least it seemed dark to one standing in the spring sunshine. No one but the stabler himself was allowed to touch Teiryn's mount, and the man spent his evenings currying and burnishing the fine black coat, oiling and braiding the mane and tail, and polishing the harness. The care the man took with his charges had earned him Teiryn's gratitude on multiple occasions, especially when his steed threw a shoe or picked up a stone or suffered from some odd sickness of horses that occasionally passed through the stables.

Teiryn couldn't help but see Lythera's face in front of him. He was eager to see her again, which surprised him somewhat. He had thought no woman except Brenicia would ever inspire a strong passion in him. Certainly, the previous eight girls brought to him had not been nearly as exciting or precious as Halevern's daughter. Five of them he had sent away without even touching; they were too young or too terrified, and he had had no heart to force them no matter how badly their fathers wanted them there. The others had been willing, even to the point of hounding him, reminding him over and over that their time was limited, and they desired to be the mother of the next king. But they had approached the actual lovemaking as if it were a chore, opening their legs but closing their eyes, waiting for it to be over. As a chore, lovemaking was not something Teiryn had been able to manage on more than an occasional basis.

He had been relieved when none of the women who had so desired a royal baby but who had no love for him had gotten pregnant in the allotted three months. He couldn't bear the thought of his child being born to a woman who despised or disliked him, who schemed to be in his bed as often as possible for the chance of a pregnancy and not because she wished to be there. It was as he had told Lythera—he did not like playing stud to their broodmares. What child should be conceived in such circumstances?

The stabler brought out his horse and Teiryn patted the white blaze on the black's nose. "He looks splendid, Dendryl. Thank you."

"My pleasure, Sire." Dendryl beamed and bowed. His smile was genuine, unlike so many smiles at court. Teiryn smiled back before mounting the horse.

"Oh, Sire!" called the stabler.

Teiryn stopped the horse. "Yes?"

"There's a fair of some kind in the park. There will be lots of people there. It's to run for three days, I believe."

Teiryn nodded. Normally, the royal park across from the palace was reserved for the use of those at court, but fairs and celebrations were held inside on a regular basis. He had not thought to ask before coming to the stables. He was glad Dendryl had informed him.

Trailblazer was ready for a romp, but Teiryn reined him in. "Not just yet, sir!" The horse flicked his ears back at his rider as if he could understand.

Silently, four mounted guardsmen followed him across the forecourt and out of the palace. That was another thing it was easy to get used to—a constant guard in public. But it was necessary. Several kings throughout Evandia's history had been assassinated.

Teiryn kept a tight rein on Trailblazer as he maneuvered the large horse into the park. There were a lot of people, at least near the entrance where the booths, tents, and stages were set up. Farther on, he could see that the central corridor of the park, used only by horsemen, was not occupied.

The people around Teiryn bowed to him and waved. Small children were pushed toward him for him to touch. He plastered a kingly smile on his face and reached down to touch whom he was bidden, nodding to everyone who caught his eye. The people of the capital were not strangers to seeing the king, so he was through the crowd quickly and on to the horse track.

Trailblazer was not content to walk; once on the track he could barely be held back to a canter. Teiryn finally tired of fighting the restive horse and gave him his head. The horse would wear himself out soon enough.

After Trailblazer had had a good run, Teiryn slowed him to a walk. This time, the horse was glad to obey. The horses of the guardsmen were not as energetic as Trailblazer; the guardsmen sat on their horses in the shade of an ancient oak to the side of the track. Their horses were content to stand hipshot and nibble on the grass. Their riders split their attention between Teiryn and the surroundings.

Brenicia had always loved riding in this park. When he was here, sometimes, it was almost as if he had never lost her. He could picture her so clearly, smiling at him in the bright sunshine, cheeks high with color, laughter floating on the air.

You like this young woman, said the voice of his dear wife in his head. Since her death, Teiryn had engaged in the habit of talking to her in the privacy of his thoughts as if she were still alive. He could do so because he and Brenicia had always understood one another. A glance or a gesture had been enough for them to communicate whatever was needed. As youngsters, they had been constant playmates and companions, though their friendship had blossomed into love as they grew older. Teiryn had been grateful that Brenicia Hellfren's family was old and well-connected. No one doubted she would make a suitable queen for the realm. He had been seventeen and she sixteen when they were wed.

Their wedding night had been more than he could have dreamed. They had been thrilled to express their love for each other with their bodies. And they had spent the next twelve years teaching each other the intricacies and forms of love.

Until that day three years ago when she had clutched at her chest and collapsed in front of him. Her life cut short by...well, that was the crux of the matter. No one knew. Poison? Disease? The physicians couldn't say. The nestriana had only shrugged and wept. Brenicia was just...gone. So quickly. Leaving him alone. Leaving him to face the ministers and their plots, their petty cruelties, their frightened maids and their leering glances.

Why did you leave me?

He always asked, but she never answered. Well, there was no answer. And ever since Brenicia's death, though he had tried to disguise it, he had trudged through his life, eternally exhausted by the effort of keeping up appearances and doing his best to manage his ministers and their plots. But his own inner weariness had no place on this grand day. His thoughts could not be kept from Lythera for long.

Do you like her? he asked his late wife.

Yes. Her answer was swift and clear. But then, it wasn't hard for him to guess what his queen would have said. Lythera was intelligent and educated as well as honest and brave—just the sort of person Brenicia would have befriended and adored.

Will she get pregnant? No answer to that, but then, he was only talking to himself, after all. Brenicia had suffered five miscarriages in their years together, and no physician had been able to help her. The children would be conceived, and carried a few months, and then die in the womb without even the chance to draw first breath.

Perhaps he was fated to be the last of his line, and there would be a civil war when he died. But he hoped not. The land was his, and the people were his, and he could not bear the thought of them destroyed by war.

He had thought about naming one of his cousins heir, but he doubted anyone would actually obey his wishes once he were dead. There was no point in appointing one of his ambitious relatives who would then have a fine motive for wanting him out of the way. Or would hate Teiryn for making him a target.

Teiryn was tired of thinking. His head hurt with it. Besides, he had walked the stallion enough for him to cool down. He turned Trailblazer back toward the palace.

At the fair, he was stopped by a baker holding out a muffin. The man bowed low. "It would be an honor, Sire, a true honor, if you would accept this." Teiryn had long ago learned to accept small gifts from the people; it pleased them and they did not have to know that his staff wouldn't let him eat their food without having a food taster try it first.

Teiryn smiled and took the muffin. "Thank you."

After that, Teiryn was approached by several other people but one woman in the back caught his eye. She was an old woman, bent with age, but her fingers still moved quickly with her tatting. She was selling lengths of lace ribbon dyed many bright colors. One of the ribbons had been dyed the deep red of Segrithr rubies; it had the traditional tassel on one end. It would look perfect in Lythera's hair.

See? said the voice of his dead wife. *You are already buying her love gifts.*

Teiryn considered getting off the horse, but the press of people around him made that unwise; people who were cautious of a horse's hooves might move closer once the king was on their level. And the guardsmen would feel the need to push people away. Better to stay above the crowd, even if it felt strange to be talking to people from Trailblazer's back.

A man selling silk handbags noticed Teiryn's stare. "Sire," he said, coming to stand in front of Trailblazer and bowing. "If you're interested in hair ribbons, then I can help you. This is my grandmother, and she makes everything herself, as you can see."

"Thank you, yes, I'm interested. The red ribbon."

The man beamed. "A fine color, and dyed to match the royal livery. As if we could know you would come by our stall today! Tati," the man said to his grandmother, using the expression of deference to an elder, "the red ribbon, please."

The old woman looked up, saw Teiryn, and bowed in her chair. Her toothless face drew up in a wide grin; it was clear she was pleased. She handed the ribbon to her grandson.

Teiryn always carried a few coins on him for just this reason. He reached for them, but the man shook his head. "I could not take money, Sire. Please, accept this gift with my compliments."

Teiryn took the ribbon. "Thank you, goodman. What is your name and where is your home?"

"Relf, Sire. We live in the city of Ensdrun, but we have relatives here and come to the capital often for the fairs. Good business here." He bowed. "Good fortune, Sire."

Teiryn nodded to the man once more and then continued back to the palace. Ensdrun was only a day's travel to the east. Coming to fairs in the capital would be an easy journey on good roads, even for Relf's grandmother, especially when they knew they would have family to stay with rather than trying to find a place in an inn.

Teiryn continued back to the palace and left Trailblazer in Dendryl's devoted hands. He folded the ribbon several times and put it in the small coin pouch at his belt. He would give it to Lythera tonight.

But first he had an afternoon meeting with the ministers who wanted him to look over some boundary disputes. Teiryn glanced at the muffin and decided to eat it whether his staff liked it or not. He could order food during the meeting, but he disliked upsetting the kitchen staff's routine; by now they would be deep in preparations for dinner.

He ate the muffin and endured the meeting. Idrant and Landrith were squabbling over some worthless section of land, which tempted Teiryn to judge the matter immediately. But Landrith was an oily fellow—what did he want with that patch of land that most likely truly belonged to his neighbor? Teiryn wanted to know before he made a decision; he had learned long ago that just because Landrith was blind did not mean his mind wasn't sharp. And rapacious. Teiryn left the meeting in a foul mood.

He was besieged on the way to his quarters by the usual crowd of petitioners. He listened to a few, sent a few more to see Lord Yawneil or Vaiher or Ryllmaren. At last he got through them and entered the sanctuary of his room.

To find Lythera sitting at his table, eating dinner alone, resplendent in a dark red dress. She looked up when he came in and smiled. "Good evening, Sire."

He managed to walk over to the table and sit down opposite her without embarrassing himself by stammering or tripping, like he had done as a young man around Brenicia.

She didn't seem to notice. "I hope you're hungry," she said. "I asked for a lot of food to be brought. I hope that is all right?"

The look she gave him was slightly teasing, but there was a note of pleading in it, too. She wanted to please him, and she wasn't sure this was the way.

He sawed a piece of bread from the loaf on the table. "Yes, it certainly is. I'm quite hungry."

She looked relieved and continued her dinner. He ate his bread slowly, taking the opportunity to look at her more closely, in the light of late afternoon.

He knew Novardan and the rest would have labeled her plain, but he didn't think so. She didn't have the sort of beauty that was fashionable at court nowadays, which had more to do with small noses, heart-shaped faces, blond hair, and milk-white skin, than the character of the woman. Lythera had a beauty of a quieter, deeper sort. There was strength in her face, determination in her glance, pride in her carriage. She had faced shameful circumstances in being brought here, and had not allowed them to overcome her.

She smiled. "Are you going to eat more than bread?"

"Perhaps." He lowered his gaze to the jewel around her neck. "You liked your morning gift?"

Blushing, she touched the jewel. "It's magnificent. And unexpected. Thank you very much."

"Unexpected?"

"A morning gift is for a wife," she said softly. He saw her frown slightly and he felt ashamed of himself, ashamed of this dreadful custom his ministers felt was so necessary for the preservation of the realm.

"A morning gift is for my lady, whether she is wife or consort," he said. Actually, it had been last-minute inspiration. None of the other women had been given a gift. As soon as she had left him in the morning, he had ordered that a fine jewel be given to her, one in the dark red color that only rubies from the Segrithr mine displayed. The steward had brought him three to choose from, and this one had been the most spectacular; it was meant for her, he was sure of it. "And I have another gift for you." He reached into the pouch and pulled out the ribbon.

She beamed. "It's beautiful! I shall wear it tomorrow."

"I thought we might place it in your hair tonight," he said and was rewarded with a blush. "But before that, we must finish dinner, and I should bathe or I'll come to bed smelling like a horse."

She smiled shyly. "I don't mind."

"I'm glad you won't mind smelling of horse tonight."

He looked down at his empty plate. If he kept staring at her, he'd have to have her. Just the thought of touching her was enough to drive him crazy.

"You are not eating," she noted.

"No, I guess I'm not."

She stood up and came around the table and held out her hand. "Then, perhaps we should eat later."

He laughed, a deep belly laugh such as he had not had in years. "I agree," he gasped.

She led him to the bedroom where she suddenly looked down with despair at her dress. "I can't get out of this myself."

"I'll help. My...my wife's dresses were much more elaborate and I could usually get her out of those without shouting for the servants."

She turned from him and he undid the stays of the dress. He helped her pull it up over her head. Today she wore more layers underneath and he helped her out of those as well. By the time she wore nothing but her morning gift, they were both lying on the bed giggling at nothing at all.

"Now you," she said.

"No, first your present. Give me the ribbon."

She handed him the ribbon and turned her back on him. "I didn't think you would know how to weave ribbons into hair," she said.

"Then don't be offended if I tell you that I spent much of my childhood in the stables plaiting ribbons into manes and tails. You know I do not consider you my broodmare." He lifted her hair and kissed her on the nape of the neck. Then he concentrated on the ribbon and was silent for a minute. But this was a task made easy by years of practice and it went quickly. Her hair was thick and silky and brown, and was alive with hints of red; he loved the color and the feel of it in his hands.

"And did you do this favor for the queen?"

His hands froze in their work. How was it that mention of his queen could still affect him so? It had been three years. But he still felt her loss keenly.

"I'm sorry," she said.

"No, don't be," he said. "Yes, I helped my wife sometimes, too, but she had four or five hairdressers who puttered over her hair daily. She didn't really need me to help."

"But I'm sure she enjoyed your attentions more than the attentions of the hairdressers."

He finished weaving the ribbon into her hair and secured it with a knot. He reached around her and hugged her. "Yes, I suppose she did. Do you mind when I mention her?"

"Why should I?" She turned in his embrace and stroked his beard tenderly. Her touch sent a thrill through him. Her eyes looked into his with compassion and sympathy. "Rather, I am thankful you loved her so deeply. It tells me what kind of man you are."

"What kind is that?"

She grinned, then said, "One who should be getting his clothes off. After all, I'm sitting here naked!"

She undid the buttons on his shirt and helped him pull it off. She sat back then and ran her hands over his body, staring at him hungrily, eyes bright with desire. He was pleased she was so eager.

"I did not truly see you last night. You are beautiful," she said.

"I'm glad you think so, though that compliment sounds strange coming from a woman. Handsome, perhaps?"

She shook her head. "No, beautiful."

"Just don't say that too loudly in front of the court, all right?" He pulled off his boots and socks, then stood and undid the laces on his trousers and dropped them to the floor. He sat down beside her and buried his face in her hair. The ribbon scratched his nose. "My beautiful Verrika."

"I am right here," she said calmly. "I am not going anywhere. And we have time. Come."

He kissed and touched her in a hundred different places, learning all the curves and lines of her body. He showed her where to touch him, how to please him with her hands and mouth, and she proved eager to learn. Her touch fired his passion again and soon enough they were loving in a tangle of hair and bedsheets and bodies.

8

Wenvia brought the riding skirts the next morning, though she seemed unsure that Lythera should engage in such an activity. "You'll likely shake any newly-made babe right out!" she had exclaimed. But that sounded like nonsense to Lythera, so she had just accepted the skirts and ignored the chambermaid.

She had slept late and uneasily, for she had had more dreams of the old cackling woman with crystal eyes, and only had a few minutes to dress and eat breakfast. Wenvia had awakened her with a respectful shake and said, somewhat disapprovingly, "The sun's been up for hours, Mistress."

Lythera just smiled. The remains of the dream melted away in the sunlight and what remained of the night was all wonderful.

The king had been as good as his word. After they had made love, they remembered they were hungry, and they had repaired to the main suite to finish the food Lythera had had brought. The king had requested a bottle of wine and it had arrived with some speed even though the hour was late. Lythera assumed that was a prerogative of kingship—anything you needed, at any time of day or night, was at hand with merely an order.

The food and the wine made them both giddy and somewhat silly so that their next encounter in the bed was often interrupted by giggling or outrageous remarks that sounded inane when she thought about them now. But last night the two of them had simply been delighted with each other. When they had finally dozed, sated and exhausted, she had snuggled up to him and tucked her head under his chin. His arm had been around her waist. She had never felt more safe and loved.

Dawn had found her still in the king's bed though by then they had moved apart. Still, the king's hand was on her shoulder, as if, even in sleep, he wanted to be sure she was present. Neither had the energy for more than a few kisses, and Lythera had departed sleepily for her own bed to doze for a while longer before Wenvia came.

Wenvia braided her hair quickly, but did not want to use the red ribbon on this day. "Your riding skirts are blue. I have a fine silk ribbon of the same color that I should use instead." But Lythera insisted, and in the end Wenvia wrapped her braid in the red ribbon, though she never lost her disapproving expression.

Lythera hurried to the stables, still smiling, finding it easy this morning to ignore the occasional stare or indecent glance. She had a friend waiting for her.

Evinard stood in the entrance to the stables and grinned as she approached. He took one look at the circles under her eyes and winked.

Yesterday she would have blushed, but today, she felt much more confident, and Evinard was her friend now, after all. She lifted her chin and looked down her nose at him. "Good morning," she said with as much haughtiness as she could manage. "Or what is it I'm supposed to say?"

"Around here, people usually use *good fortune*," said Evinard and Lythera nodded.

"Then good fortune, Evinard."

"And to you." He laughed, but not in a teasing way. He seemed genuinely happy for her. "And a good morning to you, as well. Come along; Morningbelle's already waiting for you." He bowed and gestured for Lythera to precede him. She bowed in return and followed his direction down the row of stalls on the right hand side of the stables. At the end was a door to a large indoor room with a sand floor. The ceiling was lost in the darkness above. To her right, a tall red horse with four brilliant socks and a white nose stood saddled. She flicked her ears at the two young people before heaving a big sigh.

Evinard untied the horse from a hitching post and brought her to Lythera. "Belle, this is Lythera. You be good to her or it's no oats for you!"

The horse stared down at her morosely and chomped on her bit.

"She looks sad," said Lythera.

"Belle always looks that way. Don't mind her. You could put Malagert's drooling son on her; she's completely reliable. If you want to see her look slightly happy, come back later with a carrot or an apple and see how eagerly she takes it from you. Come on, I'll help you on."

Evinard dropped the reins and stood by the side of the horse with his hands cupped. Lythera stared up at the flat saddle. It did not appear to have anything to hold onto. This did not look like it would be easy.

"Just step in my hands; I'll get you up."

Lythera did as he requested and he tossed her lightly onto Morningbelle's back. Her skirts easily fell on either side of the horse. Lythera glanced around, amazed at how tall she felt.

"Hang on a minute while I get the stirrups adjusted," said Evinard. He began lengthening the stirrup straps until she felt the metal bang into her ankle. "There. Point your toes up and put your foot in the stirrup."

Before long, Lythera sat on Morningbelle with both feet in the stirrups and felt as if she were on top of the world. Then Evinard picked up the reins and walked the horse forward. The sudden lurch forward startled her and she grasped desperately at the red mane.

"It's all right," said Evinard over his shoulder. "She's not going to let you fall."

Lythera tried to relax and listen to the shuffling of the horse's hooves in the sand, the twitter of birds in the high open rafters of the room. Soon she felt confident enough to loosen her grip on Morningbelle's mane.

The lesson lasted nearly an hour and consisted of getting Lythera used to the feel of the horse moving under her at a walk. At one point, Evinard stopped the horse and gave Lythera the reins, though he attached a lead rope to the horse's halter and continued to control the pace. Lythera attempted to get used to the feel of the leather reins in her hands. By the time the lesson was over, she felt as though she'd been engaged in heavy work, and all she'd done was sit on a horse! It looked so much easier from the ground.

Evinard helped her dismount. Lythera was glad to feel the sand of the ring under her feet but was surprised by the sudden pain running up and down the inside of her legs. She winced.

"Yeah, you'll be saddle sore for a while," said Evinard. "But tell your chambermaid to give you some liniment. That'll help some. And if you come back every morning, by next week you won't be sore at all."

Lythera thanked him warmly and he ducked his head and smiled. "It is my honor," he said.

She walked away, but Morningbelle tried to follow. Evinard held his ground. Lythera stopped and turned back to the horse, feeling a pang of loneliness at the thought of leaving her behind. Strange. She shook her head. "It's all right," she said. "I'll be back tomorrow."

The horse snorted at her. Lythera walked out of the training ring and Morningbelle remained placidly with Evinard this time. Lythera returned to her room. Wenvia was adding more wood to the fire as she entered.

"Lady," said Wenvia with a small bow. "A bath has already been prepared for you." No doubt Wenvia did not want the lady she served to bring the smell of horse into the room.

Lythera was more than ready for a long soak. She let Wenvia and two silent girls bathe her, then towel her off and rub liniment into her legs, all while she thought about something besides being naked in front of them. But it was clear she would just have to get used to it, and indeed, today she was more comfortable than she had been yesterday.

After the liniment, Wenvia insisted on spreading a floral-scented lotion into her skin and spraying perfume on her neck. Lythera tried not to sneeze at the strong flowery scent. She no longer smelled like horse, but neither did she smell like herself; she smelled like a rose garden. She wasn't sure she liked that, but Wenvia obviously approved.

Wenvia presented her with a silver dress that was trimmed in delicate lace with a lily design. Lythera let the women dress her but still did not allow Wenvia to get her way on the ribbon. She would wear the red one, or none. Tomorrow she could wear something else, perhaps, but not today. The ribbon was precious to her; a morning gift might be tradition, but anything else must come from a generous heart since it was in no way required. Besides she had told the king she would wear it and she would consider that a vow.

Lythera wished she could think of something to give the king, but she had nothing of her own, and no money. Besides, what could a king lack?

By the time they returned to her room, lunch was just being set out. To her surprise, a man sat at her table. He was dressed in green with a red cap. Lythera had heard that professional musicians sometimes dressed like that, but she'd never met one before.

He bowed in his seat. "Your chambermaid asked me to come and serenade you while you eat."

Lythera tried to hide her discomfiture. No one had ever looked after her like this! "Thank you for coming." She turned to Wenvia. "Thank you for your consideration." The chambermaid blushed and spooned food onto Lythera's plate.

She sat down, wondering why the musician did not have his own plate. Lythera felt famished, but she had been brought up never to eat in front of a guest. So she looked at her food and wondered what to do.

"Please, eat," he said. "I eat in between everyone else's meals; that way I'm ready to sing for my supper at the regular times."

Lythera picked up a bun, then put it down. She just couldn't. "Please, it would make me feel better if you would eat something. Even a little bit."

He smiled and bowed slightly in his chair. "For you, Mistress." He picked up a piece of bread and smeared butter on it, then took a large bite. Lythera smiled at him gratefully and began eating her own lunch.

"I can sing if you like, but I thought I should find out what songs you like to hear first. What did you hear at home? Perhaps I can sing you a favorite of yours."

"I have no favorites. My mother would sing to me at night sometimes, when I was very little, but I don't know the names of the songs. I always thought she had just made them up, little lullabies, you know. What do you like to sing at lunchtime?"

He smiled, but the smile did not reach his eyes and Lythera felt a grain of unease. What had Evinard said about some people using more poetic terms for Teiryn's Tarts? Wouldn't a musician know all the more poetic terms?

"I know many songs," he said.

"And have you sung many of them to other Fortune's Flowers?" she asked as sweetly as she could. Wenvia gasped.

He flinched, so she knew he was one of them. One of those who would make fun of others' misfortunes.

"You have been listening to gossip," he said. His charming demeanor slipped further.

"You are hardly in a position to approve or disapprove of anything I do," said Lythera in sudden anger. Her fingers trembled with it and her face felt flush. "So have you come here merely to find out more material for this gossip of yours? Because I will not help you mock me behind my back."

He leaned back in the chair, the smiling musician gone. What remained was a cold-eyed, calculating man. "That's my job, little wilted flower. You might say I *am* gossip. If there's anything that should be known around court, I'm the one the news comes to. Eventually. I mock high and low alike, from the king to the boy who empties the chamberpots, so you're hardly special there. And I also sing sweet lullabies to babies as the occasion demands; I can be accommodating of most circumstances. Even these."

"Leave now," said Lythera. "And do not return to this room again while I am staying at the palace."

He left. Wenvia cleaned up the remains of the piece of bread the musician had nibbled on. She started babbling, "So sorry, Lady, I thought only about your entertainment. I didn't think he would be so rude."

"*So* rude?" asked Lythera. "Then you must have realized he wasn't necessarily the best choice."

Wenvia looked near tears. "Lady, few of the musicians of the guild are in the palace at present, and he *is* very talented. I know many lords ask for him specifically when they give parties. But I didn't think beyond that. I'm so sorry, Lady. Please forgive me."

"Still, there must be others."

Wenvia wrung her hands. "Yes, but few outside the ministers and lords think this custom of bringing girls into the palace is worthy behavior for a king. The songs they sing about it can be quite cutting. I can only assume the king hasn't heard them or he would be angry about it. It's hard on everyone on the staff, sorry as I am to say it."

Lythera thought for a moment over that. "Difficult to be the chambermaid to one of Teiryn's Tarts? Does that mean you have been put in a bad position?"

Wenvia pursed her lips. "Serving you is the same as serving the king. How could that be bad?" Her voice was strained and belied her words.

"Easily enough, I suppose, since apparently the cruelty of this court extends beyond the nobles to the servants as well. Who assigned you to me? And why were you late that first morning?"

Wenvia apparently felt this was safer territory and spoke quickly. "The woman who was to serve you was pregnant—it was thought that perhaps being served by a pregnant woman would somehow, well, encourage you, I guess. But she was brought to bear two months early."

"And the babe?" Lythera was concerned; early babies did not live long.

"The little one died just this morning. And a boy, too. She's heartbroken."

"If you see her, I would appreciate it if you would extend to her my condolences," said Lythera. "I'm sure she is terribly distraught by this tragedy."

Wenvia nodded. "I'll tell her, Lady."

"And so who assigned you to me, then?"

"The Lady Trenstarl. She'd heard about the early birth and called upon me to see to your needs. If I may say, she said she had a good feeling about you, and that if any maid would be the one to bear a child for the king, it would be you. She gave me explicit directions on how I should care for you, and I'll do my best. And I know the signs to watch for, so don't worry; if a babe takes root, I'll make sure it's as snug as can be."

Lythera smiled. "Thank you."

Wenvia seemed encouraged. "Don't you worry about the gossip. The musician speaks evil of everyone, and good, too, depending on his mood or what's requested of him. But even if he trumpeted your praises, it wouldn't change much."

Lythera mulled over that for a minute. She was sure it was true; she doubted that those who were determined to dislike her would change their minds over a song. She sighed. Why did people have to judge her without meeting her, or knowing anything about her?

"I'm sorry," she said at last. "Is there nothing to be done? Even if my reputation is ruined, why should you suffer for it? That's unfairness piled on unfairness."

"There's little that's fair at court, Lady," said Wenvia. "By the time your three months are out, you'll know it's true and be glad to leave. If there's anything that's fair, it's..." Wenvia caught herself, and stopped speaking.

Lythera was intrigued. This sounded like it might be gossip. Perhaps gossip Lythera could use to her own advantage. "Won't you tell me?" she asked.

Wenvia wrung her hands again. "I shouldn't. It's not my place."

"Oh, never mind that," said Lythera with frustration. "Can you not tell me anything that might be fair?"

Wenvia didn't stop wringing her hands, but she did start speaking. "Well, it's cruel and you know it to be, that you and the others are ruined for life. No man will have one of the king's consorts for his own, even if the king didn't touch her. That's the unfair part. The fair part is something you may not know: your father will suffer just as much."

Now that did sound interesting. Lythera was intrigued. "How? Tell me how!"

"The nobility keep a watch on their daughters, as you well know. It's of vital importance to them that their sons have virgin brides. So it's a father's utmost duty to protect his daughters from shame."

"So fathers who have failed in this duty share in the shame?"

Wenvia nodded. "Your father may have eased his debts, but he'll have no friends in court. Nor the other eight fathers, either. That's why only the daughters of penniless lords have been made consorts. They're desperate enough to do anything to better themselves. But years from now, when they have other daughters to arrange marriages for, there will be no suitors."

Lythera's heart quailed. "I knew I was ruined, but my sisters must share this with me? If only it were just my father!"

Wenvia shrugged. "Who's to say? If your father dies, or fosters your sisters elsewhere, there is still hope for them. But for yourself, there are only these three months, and then you'll be turned out. It will take longer for your father to feel the pinch, but it will come."

Lythera sat dumbly for several minutes, trying to absorb the information. That her sisters might be affected by her circumstances had never occurred to her. But that her father might be affected—oh, she only hoped that it were so. Let him suffer a little of what she had suffered, and would suffer as a ruined woman with no place in the world, no money, and no prospects.

At last, Wenvia bowed and said, "I'll just clean this up now. Oh, and a messenger brought something by for you while you were riding. I didn't want to leave the package out; it's in the top drawer of your dresser."

"Thank you." Lythera went to the dresser and opened the drawer. Inside was a thin leather satchel. Her heart skipped a beat. Master Jarris had been as good as his word. He had sent her the sketches of the oldest artifacts for her to peruse.

Lythera went back to the table, which Wenvia had cleaned, opened the satchel, and pulled out the parchments. There were five, each covered in several diagrams and many notes. But the most fascinating drawing of all was one of a star-shaped object covered in runes. Lythera couldn't tear her eyes from it.

The object was circular with eight points radiating from its edges. The runes spiraled around the center, and each of the eight rays had one rune upon it. Lythera ran her fingers lightly over the drawing as if she could tease some meaning out of the sketch by willpower and touch alone.

When she could finally look away, she noticed that Jarris had listed some letter equivalents in a column to the side. He had apparently deduced that each rune stood for a letter. But his notes indicated that this assumption had not helped him breach the object's secrets.

It was somewhere to start, anyway. Lythera scanned the other images quickly. Most were circular, though a few were square. Only the one had the rays. Lythera wondered if the object were meant to represent the sun, and if so, what the number eight meant. Eight days? Eight hours? Eight years? Eight solstices?

Well, without more information, she could guess forever. Lythera looked over the drawings until she felt her eyes growing tired and decided to take a walk. She replaced the drawings in the satchel, replaced the satchel in the drawer, and left.

Her feet seemed to take her to Master Jarris' library door without asking her the destination. She smiled. She liked Jarris and the library felt more like home than home ever had. She pushed the door open.

Jarris was shuffling through piles of loose parchments when she arrived. He glanced up and the smile on his face was broad and genuine. "Lythera, how glad I am to see you. I was just going to send for a guardsman, but you're young and strong. Do you see that thick book over on the third shelf down?"

Lythera looked in the direction he pointed and nodded. "The one with a cracked brown cover, underneath the black one?"

"Yes, that's the one. Would you please get it for me? I wanted to take another look at it after our session yesterday since you helped me so much with Old Evandic. This is the oldest text we have, and I have been perplexed for years over some of its more ambiguous passages. You're tall enough to reach the shelf, I believe."

Lythera retrieved the large thick book. It smelled of mildew like the books back at Halevern Hall, and Lythera could see the damage on the cover was not limited to the crack of age. Yet this book was in better shape than the ones she had at home. She brought the tome to Jarris. "This one should be copied out onto new parchment," she said. "It won't last much longer."

He shook his head sadly as she placed the book in front of him. "Impossible, I'm afraid. No one's interested in this book, and except for a few scholars such as ourselves, my dear, who could even read it? Parts of it are beyond me, and most likely beyond you, too. It is simply too old and too obscure. The subject matter is interesting, but not relevant to modern life."

Lythera sat down beside Jarris with the odd feeling he wasn't telling all he knew. If this book wasn't relevant to modern life, why was he so interested in it when there were so many other books that needed to be translated? But she had other things on her mind today.

"Master Jarris?"

"Yes?"

"Thank you for the drawings. They're fascinating."

"You're welcome, Lythera. Perhaps your young mind will discover something mine is too tired to sort out these days."

"Maybe. Would it be possible for me to see any of the items? Touch them?"

"Why?"

Lythera hesitated. She wasn't sure why herself. Finally, she shrugged. "I don't know. I just have this feeling. I'd like to touch the items. It sounds silly, doesn't it?"

"No, not at all," said Jarris. "I can have some here shortly. Someone else is looking at a few of them, and he's due to return them to me at any time." He shook his head. "But as for these items, I'm afraid they will always be mysteries. But perhaps mysteries should not all be solved."

"Why do you say that? I thought you wanted to know enough to avoid any future upheavals in history."

He smiled. "Well, yes, definitely *some* things we should know. But there will always be a few mysteries, and that's all right. Where would the beauty in life come from if we understood all there was to know?"

Lythera thought about that. "I think beauty would still be beauty. It might even be more beautiful for the knowing."

Jarris raised his hands in concession. "You may be right. Is there anything else?"

She glanced up at the herbs hanging from the ceiling and decided to interrupt him again. "Could you tell me why all the dried leaves are hanging up in here?"

"It's Fortune's Rue," he said without looking up or missing a pen stroke. "Soaked in hedgethorn juice for three days, then left to dry in the sun. It keeps the insects away."

"I thought Fortune's Rue was for fertility," she said, remembering what Metricia had said the other day.

"Prepared another way, yes," said Master Jarris. "But this is the way to use it to keep books safe from the silverfish and roaches. Here, while I'm looking at this book, see if you can finish this list for me."

"A list?"

Jarris nodded but seemed perplexed. "Yes, yes, they can be found everywhere in the oldest of texts, but they don't make much sense. This one seems to equate items with certain symbolic meanings." He scanned the sheet before him. "*A lark is good news of bright events which shall greet you soon. A storm is the conflict centered within you. A sword is the power that resides in us all. A knife can be for your healing or for your wounding.* Things like that. I believe the ancient seers used to memorize these lists and then use them to determine messages in the world around them."

Lythera was intrigued. Could messages really be found around her all the time? "If that were true," she asked, "who sends the messages? They'd have to be arranged by someone."

Jarris shook his head. "I don't know. There are hints of an unnamed entity of great power, perhaps something like what the Selandi believe lives in the sea and provides them good fishing. If our ancestors believed in anything like that, I don't know of it. But just because someone believes or doesn't believe doesn't necessarily mean anything."

"What do you mean?"

"If I said I didn't believe in the ocean, would that make the ocean disappear? No. So what if there really is some entity that looks over us— what if it is watching us all the time? What would such a thing want?"

Lythera shook her head. His questions made her head spin and reminded her too much of her dreams. The cackling woman, the odd world under a blue sun, the crystals, the animals of unusual colors. A fantastic world she didn't understand, and which frightened her.

Jarris passed the list and the paper he was writing the translation onto to Lythera. She gratefully turned her thoughts away from her dreams, took them from him, and began where he had left off.

A feather is a message from the one who rules the moon-bird. Rain on your fields purifies the land. The stork is the contentment found within all life.

It did not take long for Lythera to finish. The previous copyist had had a steady hand and the spellings weren't tricky. The comment about a feather caught her eye, though. She had found a feather on her windowsill a week before Novardan arrived at her father's house. Had it been a message? If so, she didn't like the way it mentioned the ruler of the moon-bird.

Quickly, she scanned the list for the other items in her collection at home. A rock indicated strength, though the milky coloring indicated strength that was hidden. A shell was a protective covering, shed when the situation no longer required it. Even the comb she had from her mother indicated that Lythera had been in hiding and would soon emerge.

The list gave her pause. If everything she had kept in her room back home had had a different meaning, she would have dismissed it out of hand. But everything she had kept near to her indicated hidden strength, hidden purpose, kept safe for a special time when it would be revealed. The thought sent a shiver up her spine.

Lythera scanned the rest of the list to take her mind away from that disturbing discovery. *A cricket is long life for those who understand its song. The star with a tail indicates great change and transformation is undeniable and cannot be avoided.*

A craving to know more came over her but she wanted time to study, time to think. She needed to take notes of the things around her and see if she could find the messages that the feather had foretold. That is, if she weren't crazy. Lythera shook her head. Only peasants danced naked under the moon to make crops grow or burned mouse fur to chase away sickness. This list was no different, a legacy of a bygone age when people believed in such things.

Lythera put the list aside and sat quietly, not wanting to disturb Jarris, but unwilling to return to her room. She didn't mind spending time here in silence as long as Master Jarris didn't think she was interfering. She loved the feel of the smooth walnut table, marked by ink stains and candle wax. And she loved the quality of the light coming in the windows as it adopted the blue cast from the crystal walls.

"Here," Jarris said at last. "This is taking me longer than I thought. Take a look at the book you carried over and see what you think. I'd be interested in your opinion."

Lythera opened the book to the cover page, but was disappointed that even the title had a word she did not know. "What is this, Master Jarris?" she asked, pointing to the word. "It is Something of the Realm. Or The Realm's Something. What is this word—*veyardante'ina?*"

"That is what the book is about. Long ago, people believed they could make things happen with songs, or potions, or herbs. Not like a physician or even a nestriana, but with the help of spirits of some sort. Nowadays there's nothing like that. The best translation is magic, though perhaps that's not entirely accurate."

Lythera frowned. Magic?

Jarris reached across the table and flipped the book open to a page marked with a ribbon. "Look, here's a passage I've fumbled over for years. What do you see in it?"

Lythera squinted at the cockeyed handwriting. She could strangle the scribe who wrote it; she was laboring under not only a language barrier, but under the difficulty of reading his sloppy, crazily slanted hand.

"*Ghreinvar nastorvun yalva, pled*...no, *plakestreai korendun veunt ieroval ansvorda klisteai*...something. I'm not sure about that next word. It seems to be a foretelling of the future. At the end of the age, a warrior will take the throne. I'm not sure *ansvorda* is a warrior, but it's definitely a title and it looks like *ensvorden*, which I was taught meant a foot soldier."

"That's what I thought," said Jarris. "But what is this end of the age? What sort of warrior is an *ansvorda?* The word for a mounted soldier is completely different. I can't find the term anywhere else and the context doesn't help."

Lythera glanced farther down. "There's something about a circle and a struggle of some kind. And a...a moon-bird. And then it says *elenvi vaurrikas bandrynoi*. A Bandryn hero?"

"That was the motto of House Bandryn—*ever courageous,*" Master Jarris was saying. "Or *ever heroic,* or even *ever faithful* depending on how you wanted to translate it. But there are no more Bandryn to wield swords, and no more magic in the realm in any case—if there ever was any to begin with. Or maybe there is. I don't know. It's just an interesting passage. I'd appreciate it if you could look through this book for the next few days, and take notes. That would help me a great deal. There's so much I have never understood." For a moment, a deep care settled on his face, and Lythera shifted in her chair uneasily, full of foreboding. But then Master Jarris smiled. "Oh, never mind me, dear. When you're my age, time is always precious."

"I'd be happy to help in any way I can, Master Jarris," she said, relieved he seemed to have put aside whatever dark mood had touched him briefly. She looked forward to having something concrete to do; trying to translate this passage was just what she needed to occupy her mind.

"Write in the margins if you like," he said. "I have. And no one else will come calling for this book to see what you've done. So you can't harm it more than time and decay already have."

He patted her on the arm and went back his sheaf of parchment. Lythera turned the book back to the first page.

9

Lythera clutched a blanket around her and sat in front of the fire in her room that evening. A spring chill had swept through the capital that afternoon while she had been in the records room and it had made the hot tea Wenvia had brought after dinner most welcome. After eating, Lythera had sent Wenvia away and had looked in on Teiryn, but he wasn't back in his room, and his fire was no more than coals.

So she had returned to her own room, and she dozed. This time the odd woman did not visit her. Instead, her dreams took place in a brilliant verdant pasture. Before her stood an odd mockery of a creature; head of a lion, body of a goat, feet of an eagle, and tail of a serpent. The creature's mane was white with age and its head drooped in sorrow. Lythera could feel the anguish in it. Slowly, it raised its brown liquid gaze to her own. *Will you be the one to release me?*

She turned and suddenly she was at a beautiful mountain lake. The water was so flat, it was a perfect mirror for the sky. An old man sat on the shoreline, tossing stones into the water. The stones disappeared without disturbing the surface at all. Everything was completely still, except the old man. And Lythera.

"Hello?" she asked.

The old man shook his head. "It's not you. I don't want you. You can't be the one."

"I can't be what? What is it you don't want me to be?"

"At Harvest, you'll find out."

Someone touched her and she startled. It was Teiryn, who knelt beside her.

"Sorry, love," he said. "Perhaps I should have just gone back to my room."

She yawned and shook her head. "Don't you dare." She grabbed his outstretched hand as he sat down on the carpet next to her. He retrieved his hand and put that arm around her shoulders, then reached over with his other hand and she clasped it.

They sat in silence for several minutes. Lythera was happy to spend this time with him being quiet. Just having him near caused her heart to race and her stomach to flutter, and at the moment, the contentment she felt was so complete that she almost felt she could drown in it. The strange dream puzzled her, but she had no desire to keep hold of it. She let the tattered remains of it fade.

After a time, he sighed. "It's been a long day. Everyone has problems that they want me to fix. I know that's what being a king means but some days I'd like to tell them to solve their own problems."

She let go of his hand and reached an arm around his waist. "Then I promise not to ask you to fix any problems tonight."

He looked down on her suddenly in deadly earnest. "Is there something I should know? Has someone treated you cruelly? You'd tell me if they had, wouldn't you?"

She was alarmed as his seriousness. "I was only making a jest," she said. "I was only saying that I would not make the same demands on you as everyone else. No one has treated me badly."

He hugged her tightly. "Be sure to tell me if that changes."

She frowned. "Why would it change?"

"The customs of this court are old, and sometimes heartless. I've tried to change that when I could, but old ways die hard sometimes. It may take more than one king to stamp them out."

She cast her mind back to see if she could understand what he meant. Some people had stared at her. She knew what people called her behind her back. But outright cruelty? So far the spitefulness of the court was of a more insidious kind, rumor and gossip.

Teiryn seemed despondent over something, but she wasn't sure she had the right to ask. She was only his consort. But he had treated her like a wife, with respect and honor. Perhaps she could behave like one, at least here in the privacy of her room.

"Will you tell me what sits on your mind?"

He hesitated, then shrugged. "I suppose there's no reason you shouldn't know. Novardan is asking me to come to his estate for the Harvest. He asked me yesterday, and again today. He's getting rather insistent. That bothers me. Novardan must have a reason he wants me at his estate. He has hinted he has another consort lined up for me already and she'll be there."

Lythera stiffened. She had only been here two days and already Novardan had planned her replacement?

"I think his hints are supposed to attract me, but I find them repellent."

"So don't go."

"It would wise for me to do so simply because most of House Segrithr and our kin will be there. When my father was king, his younger brother—who was then Lord Novardan—had a great family gathering every fifth year, but that hasn't happened since his death. He died childless, and his will named Ilvinard his heir. So the gathering will be at the same place I went as a child and since it hasn't happened for some time, it would be good if I would go. Besides, Metricia thinks it would be a good idea, and if I have one cousin who likes me, it's she. She has been here to try to introduce each consort into court life as gently as possible, and that hasn't been easy considering her duties at home, so I owe her a great deal. Plus, she can usually blunt the edges off her brother at social gatherings."

She ran her fingers through his hair. "It seems to me that being king means performing a number of duties you'd rather not do."

"Sometimes. However, I am glad to say that as reluctant as I was to have yet another maid brought to me, I have been happy to perform my duty with you." He kissed her on top of the head.

"And I with you," she said.

A knock came at the door. "Lady?" It was Wenvia.

"Yes?"

The door opened and the chambermaid entered, several other serving girls behind her carrying trays of food. "I was told the king had not yet had his supper, so I've had some brought up."

If Wenvia or the girls with her were nonplussed at the sight of Lythera and Teiryn sitting before the fire with his arm around her shoulders, they did not reveal it.

"I'd forgotten about dinner," said Teiryn. "Thank you."

Wenvia nodded, took a last look at the food on the table, and herded the serving girls out of the room. "We won't disturb you again, Sire. Lady. Just cover the food with the cloths we've placed on the table and we'll take away the remainder in the morning."

"Thank you, Wenvia," said Lythera.

Wenvia closed the door.

"Efficient," said Teiryn. "I'll see her rewarded."

"That would be kind of you. I would like to see her rewarded," said Lythera. "But now, you need to eat, especially if you're to keep up with Lord Novardan and all your other ministers."

Teiryn groaned. "True enough. It can be so trying; they never stop plotting. Never. I get exhausted just thinking about them; I don't know why they're not exhausted, too."

"Some people seem fueled by pettiness and cruelty," she said, thinking of her father. "But again, that's a discussion for another time."

Teiryn got up and went to the table. "I didn't think I was hungry before, but now that I can smell it, I'm famished." He looked at the array of trays and dishes before him with a faint frown. "There's only one plate— what about you?"

"I already ate," she said as she sat down opposite him. "Please, Teiryn, *eat.*"

"How can I refuse, when you use my name so prettily?"

She grinned, buttered a roll, and put it on his plate. "As you requested. And kings always get what they request, don't they?"

"Not always," he said, and the light atmosphere grew darker.

Lythera kept a smile on her face but cursed herself for being so reckless. She should have known better than to say that.

"And how have you been spending your time?" he asked. "I hope you are getting out and seeing the palace, at least."

"The gardens are likely to become my favorite place in all the world," said Lythera, eager for a chance to change the subject and help Teiryn think of more pleasant things than his ministers and their squabbles, and the decisions he had to make. "Not only because of the birds and flowers, but because of the way the sunlight reflects off the palace and turns everything blue and violet. It's so lovely."

"That it is," said Teiryn in between bites of roast. "I haven't spent much time there myself. Brenicia did sometimes, but she didn't really like how the gardens—well, everything in the capital—takes on the hue of the astar. She loved yellow best, and there is little of that here. I grew up with everything tinted blue and violet and never thought much about living in a giant crystal palace. Buildings made with stone, like Segrithr Fasthold, were where I spent holidays. But the astar was home."

"It seems a strange place to be a child," said Lythera as she tried to imagine it. What would running through the garden as a very young girl have been like? Would she have found it as enchanting as she did now, or would it have seemed like an ordinary place until she left it and realized how singular it truly was?

"Most people don't raise their children here. They choose to keep them on their estates with their tutors and nurses. But when your father is king, well, you end up being here most of the time. Sometimes, when Brenicia was pregnant, I would think very hard about sending her and our child away for part of the year, to live with her parents in Hellfren Manor. Besides being a more normal place to grow up, a child could have playmates there. The astar is a lonely place when everyone besides your parents has their children living elsewhere." Teiryn's gaze dropped to his plate, where he stared blankly at the remains of his roast and buttered bread.

Worse and worse. She wanted to help Teiryn think of lighter, happier things, but his thoughts continued to slide into dark places full of loneliness and loss. Lythera cast around for some thing to say that might not relate back to an unhappy childhood or the loss of Brenicia. She spotted the drawings from Master Jarris on the small table against the far wall.

"I received a package from Master Jarris today," she said, as light-heartedly as possible. "He's a very interesting man."

Teiryn blinked a few times, then nodded. "Yes, he is." He went back to eating his bread, but she had his attention again.

"He said he had some drawing he had made of ancient inscriptions that he hasn't been able to decipher. He sent them to me, but they are as mysterious to me as they are to him.'

Teiryn put down the remainder of his roll. "I've heard him speak of those runes. I'm not sure why he puts such time into understanding them.

They're from an ancient time we know nothing about; why not let the past alone? The present is difficult enough to understand."

"But what about our history? Shouldn't we understand what's happened before, and try to learn from it?" Her voice rose and she couldn't help but gesture pointedly and keep Teiryn's gaze trapped with her own. How could Evandia survive without its own history? "It's terrible, how much we've lost, not to mention how much no one cares that we have lost it!"

Teiryn laughed. "So passionate! I'm glad you found Jarris, then, so you can indulge your interest in the past. It just seems like knowing everything about the past would be like a terrible weight on us all the time. When my counselors want my decisions on their issues, they tell me what kings of the past have done, and what tradition demands, and what the law says. The past becomes a box I don't know how to evade. I'm cornered; much of the time, I feel like a rat about to be stepped on. And it's always the past, filtered through people like Landrith, that are wearing the boot."

That wasn't a happy topic, either, but at least Teiryn seemed to be able to approach it with some humor.

"We don't have to be enslaved to it," she said lightly. "But we could use it like a tool. Your ministers hone it as a weapon to use against you. But what if we found wonderful works of art, forgotten solutions to problems, beautiful poetry, or the secrets of how to build the astars? Perhaps there are even older laws you could use against Landrith, if Jarris could only find them, and translate them, for you!"

"Now that idea has merit. I'll talk to him about it immediately. But don't spend all your time in dusty archives, *verrika*. That is a place for old men and dead things. You are meant for a more sunlit world of love and family."

The comment struck her in the heart. She couldn't lose the one place where she might find purpose in her life if, after her three months here were up, she had not gotten pregnant! "But you wouldn't forbid me from spending time with Master Jarris?"

Teiryn looked startled. "No, of course not. I just meant, well, there is more to life than looking through dusty and worm-riddled parchment. That's a task for men like Jarris. Of course you can visit him, and look at his curiosities, but is that really where a young woman should be spending most of her time?"

She almost blurted out "Who are you to tell me where to spend my time?" but the weight of the marriage bracelet reminded her to keep her silence on the matter.

"You should really spend time around other women, not just old men," he continued. "If Metricia were still here, I'd say she could introduce you to some of my cousins, invite you to spend your days with them. I think several of them go to one of the private gardens whenever the weather is good, to work on their embroidery and gossip. Perhaps your efficient maid could give you directions to them."

The thought of showing up to a tight-knit group of noble women uninvited, unannounced, and without introduction froze Lythera's heart. She supposed women like Reyva would be there, women who had already decided to dislike her, no matter what kind of person she was. But she smiled; she was sure Teiryn meant well. "Perhaps. I've never had women friends before, so I know very little on how to go about it."

"No friends?" Teiryn seemed genuinely shocked.

"I don't know how you could be surprised, knowing the poverty of my family," she said with more bitterness than she really wanted to display in front of her lover. "It wasn't as if my sisters and I were allowed to mingle with the local children. Without family nearby, we had no one except each other. A palace isn't the only lonely place to be a child."

He was silent a moment. "Of course, it isn't. So how did you spend your days there?"

She doubted he wanted to hear about the incessant demands of the household, how she hated to struggle with the damaged and smoky flues in the fireplaces, how she scalded herself when doing laundry, how desperately she'd wanted a bath every time she had to treat the latrines with lime. "I had a tutor for a few years. He taught me whatever he knew about history and languages. Master Jarris liked that; he is interested in finding me a position, he said. When my time here is up, I will have to find something to do with my life. And if I can, I should earn some money to send some coins to my sisters. Perhaps they will be able to use them to find positions of their own, or even amass enough of a dowry to find husbands. I wouldn't want any of them to be trapped at Halevern Hall, to spend their lives shivering in front of cold fireplaces with only a bitter father for company."

"No, I suppose not," said Teiryn softly. "You know, I will make sure you are well cared for. You will never have to worry about having enough to live comfortably. No matter what happens, you will have what you need."

Until the next maid is sent to you, she thought. If, in three months, she were not pregnant, she would be sent away, and Novardan would put another young woman in Teiryn's bed. What if he came to care for her, too? Would he even remember Lythera then?

But then, why be so bleak? She might become pregnant, and then her worries would be over. She would not need to hope that Teiryn would bother to remember a childless woman he had once loved for a few weeks, and she would not need Jarris to find some lord willing to hire a woman archivist. She could have Teiryn, and her child—a prince, or a princess! Her life could become very good, indeed.

"You are my *verrika*," he said. "I will always take care of you." He stood and held out his hand formally. "Come, lady."

To her surprise, her resentment was strong enough to make her hesitate, though it also shamed her. She was grateful to Teiryn for so much—how could she let such a little thing make her so disturbed? Teiryn had promised to provide for her; she did not have to worry about anything at all, for the rest of her life. Wasn't that everything she could ever have asked for?

And yet, a small voice at the back of her mind whispered, *It is not enough.* When Jarris spoke of finding her a position, she felt as if her life opened up before her. When Teiryn spoke of caring for her, she was relieved and happy—she *was*—but she could feel the walls of her life, walls she had always resented, being reinforced instead of being torn down.

Slowly, she stood and took Teiryn's hand. While she belonged to him, she could do nothing else. The marriage bracelet and her father's signature on the contract dictated that.

He sensed her mood, and was as solicitous as he had been their first time together. Lythera tried to respond with the same carefree abandon she had shown before, but tonight, no matter how many times Teiryn hugged her and spoke lovely phrases in her ears, she could not quite let her anger go. Eventually, he sat up and looked at her with a strange and wounded puzzlement, "Lady, am I suddenly so foul that you do not welcome me into your bed?"

Fear lanced through her—he couldn't think she would refuse him, could he? If she did, she would have no chance to stay in the palace, no chance for a life beside him, no chance to bear a child and raise him or her as her mother and her mother's mothers before her had raised theirs.

With an effort, she smiled at him and drew him back down onto the bed. With lips and hands and body, she encouraged him in any way she could think how.

When he left her afterward, she lay awake in bed and stared at nothing at all, until exhaustion finally sent her tumbling into fretful dreams.

10

Valeron Lord Trenstarl's stomach was aflutter with nervousness. Today was his wedding day. He stared out his window at the fertile fields of the river valley where the crops grew green for mile upon mile in the strong light of a bright day. This was one of the smallest, but richest, land holdings in the kingdom, as far as mud was concerned. You could grow anything here, or at least you used to be able to. For the past generation, the soil of the Trenstarl fiefdom was failing, and no one knew why, though the problem hadn't become a financial disaster for the family just yet. Master Jarris had some crazy theory about the failure of the soil being one with the mines being exhausted, and the weather changing. That was nonsense, of course. If anything, the changes in the land meant it was also time for a change in the capital. At least, that was what Valeron's mother kept harping on.

As a child, Valeron had learned early to stay quiet when his mother launched into her vision of a future with her son on the throne. He just wanted to play with the other children and catch frogs in the ponds behind the manor. While at the palace, he and Evinard had even snuck into the stall of the king's own steed and fed Trailblazer carrots they'd swiped from the garden. Dendryl had never discovered them.

And then his father had died and there was no more running around with Evinard, or with anyone else.

His mother had worn her widow weeds for a short time, but while it seemed to everyone else she was the proper, grief-stricken noble lady, behind closed doors, she had turned on Valeron with a vengeance. No longer did he merely have to sit through her lectures on how he was destined to take the throne, he was to be actively involved in the plot to overthrow Teiryn and make himself king.

Every report on a failed harvest, or drought, or epidemic, had been fuel to her fire. "See?" she would say as she pointed at him. "Teiryn's line has failed. It's *you* who will rule Evandia and restore our family to its rightful place. You are destined to be the next great ruler of the land."

At first resentful, he had slowly, grudgingly, realized she must be right. How could she be wrong, after all? His birth was the culmination of five generations of planning. The signs all appeared to point to him. Even Jarris, with his nose buried in those dusty old books, had kept coming up with ancient texts that seemed to presage the birth of someone like Valeron. Not that Jarris, or anyone else at the palace, seemed to realize that the prophecies they discussed in such an academic fashion, were actually about to be realized.

For a few years, he had lived in terror that Teiryn would find out. That Master Jarris would finally see the truth. That someone, anyone, would realize that Valeron constituted a threat to the crown. But no one had.

Since then, he'd gotten more cocky, but still, no one seemed to consider him a threat. That had been both thrilling—that he could sit among them and be so unsuspected!—and annoying. After all, wasn't his greatness obvious?

He had thought, if anyone could have spotted his new role, his new purpose, it would have been Evinard. But even Evinard had continued to treat him as he always had. Evinard still thought he was Valeron's friend. His equal. He had no idea he was chatting with his future overlord.

Valeron held the mysterious lance his father had found years ago. It was just one of the many items that had come to light on Trenstarl lands. Some of the items Valeron had let Jarris inspect, including this one. But he never left anything for long with the old fool; the items belonged to him. Especially this lance. In his hands, it felt familiar, as if it whispered secrets to him as long as he was in contact with it. It was proof, if any were needed, that his destiny was greater than sitting as a nao-lord over a failing land. He was the hero the land required to be reborn. Evandia needed him.

And he would do it for House Bandryn, not House Trenstarl. His true name and parentage were known only to a few, but those few were absolutely loyal.

The old legend that stated that the Bandryn were due the crown was unclear on just why it had never been claimed by them. Some said it would have destroyed the land if they'd done so. Others said it merely would have meant bad luck, though for the family or the land as a whole, no one knew. And if no one knew, then Valeron could not see any reason to assume the old tale was simple superstition, and that there was no real reason he could not be king, and rule in the name of Bandryn. He bore their blood, even bore the violet eyes and auburn hair that marked those of Bandryn lineage. No one else remembered what that meant, not even Jarris, or they simply didn't care.

He had been startled for an instant when he'd seen Teiryn's new toy, and *she* had also had the Bandryn coloring. Probably some Bandryn had dallied with a Halevern some generations back; by-blows were not so uncommon among the nobility. But still, it had been a shock to see someone who looked so much like him.

He didn't wish to think any more on her, though. Today was his day. Or, perhaps more accurately, his mother's day. She had schemed and plotted and even killed in order to get him to this day: a day for him to claim his proper name, to take a royal bride, and make that first irrevocable step toward the throne.

In the distance, on the main road from the south, he saw a single carriage. Good. His bride was approaching. As nervous as this made him, he was even more excited. At long last, to be taking this plot to the next level! To have achieved this after five generations. Today was indeed a momentous day.

Only a few people knew of the wedding today; that was why this wedding would be so informal and held the day after his sister's. Not, perhaps, an ideal situation for a bride, but the woman chosen for him was eager for a chance to be queen, even if it meant a secret marriage. News could not be allowed to leak out before all was ready. Not even the bride's father knew the true reason why his eldest daughter traveled to Trenstarl lands; as far as he knew, she was merely visiting her newlywed cousins.

His mother came into the room, her dress the shining purple of House Bandryn. No one had worn it for generations until now at this wedding. His mother wore it, he wore it, and his bride would be gowned in it from neck to toe. His surcoat also sported the golden lion of House Bandryn, signifying his right to claim the lordship. Today, House Bandryn would be reborn.

"Come along," his mother said, kissing his cheek briefly. "They're almost here, and my brother's waiting in the great hall. You need to inscribe your name in the pedigree book."

Valeron watched his mother stride out of the room smartly. She had been hinting lately at what she wanted once he was king. Idrant's lands, perhaps, or Hellfren's. She wanted a wide demesne in which to rule. Technically, she'd still have to rule it in his name, since she couldn't have the title herself. But with him busy running the country, she seemed secure he'd let her have a free hand. Valeron could see her excitement growing the closer it came to Harvest and he knew his mother spent her days dreaming of all the riches—all the power—she would have when he ascended the throne.

He walked down the airy passages of Trenstarl Hall, buoyed by the idea of a noble woman in his bed instead of the chambermaids and scullery girls he'd had to choose from up to now. His mother didn't care for his behavior, but she did not gainsay him. She merely kept track of the female staff and if one started to show a pregnancy, it was dealt with. Just as all of Queen Brenicia's pregnancies had been dealt with.

The whole situation also proved how weak a man Teiryn Segrithr really was. No real man would have failed to notice how tired he was all the time, how incapable of making decisions. No real king would have allowed himself to be so bullied. If it were Valeron in Teiryn's place, he would have realized something was wrong long ago, and set a trap for those acting against him. But Teiryn was too kind-hearted, and not nearly suspicious enough of his ministers and friends. He thought he was tired because of grief over his wife, and that he was being fair and just rather than timid and biddable. Which had worked so well in Valeron's favor, he had realized long ago that his mother and her nestriana would need to die for him to ever be secure on the throne.

His mother had schemed her whole life to see him crowned, but she and her nestriana would not hesitate to dose *him* if he did not give them what they wanted. Exactly what hold his mother had on the healer, who was supposedly sworn to heal and never harm, Valeron did not know. Nor did he care.

He and his mother emerged from the corridor onto a gallery that went around the entire great hall of Trenstarl Hall. The marble railings of the gallery were festooned with purple ribbons and purple flowers. Swaths of matching material hung from between the newel posts of the rail, shrouding the entire room in a haze of violet.

Valeron went down the stairs ahead of his mother and walked down the great hall toward a small side chamber where the family marriages were recorded. The book was a precious one, for inside was a carefully guarded secret. The secret that would make Valeron king.

His mother's brother, Lord Novardan, stood over the book with a quill. "It's about time you got here," he said. He held the quill out to Valeron and opened the book to the proper page. There lay recorded Valeron's pedigree. In most ways, it would have matched the books of other family members, with one important difference.

Valeron ran his fingers over the name list before putting his own name at the bottom. The top of the page interested him most, and he had never tired of looking at it. It recorded the name of Valeron, the last Lord Bandryn, and his wife, Princivia, who had given him only daughters. By the time the last Lord Bandryn was old, the Bandryn line had lost much of its former influence. Newer lines that did not bear ancient names or have the majesty of House Bandryn had the ear of the king. With only daughters to his name, Lord Bandryn had known he would have to do something desperate.

Bandryn had gone looking for a lover. Someone of noble blood, not to marry, but to bear a bastard son in secret. Valeron wasn't sure why the secrecy was necessary at the time; the old lord surely could have been more open. Perhaps it had something to do with an odd family legend about a great Bandryn heir arising out of obscurity, hidden to all until the time was right.

In any case, the old lord had found Islara Segrithr, youngest sister of the king. Young and innocent, and far too easily lured to his rooms, where he had forced her to accept his attentions. He kept her until it was obvious she was pregnant, then had arranged a quiet marriage with Aylward Lord Trenstarl, who was not very intelligent and more than willing to have the king's sister in any condition. Islara herself was too shamed by her circumstances to tell anyone, and had died a few years later, supposedly by her own hand.

The son of Lord Bandryn and Islara Segrithr had been given the name of Vandian Trenstarl. But the old Lord Bandryn knew the child was his whatever his official name. He sent his trusted steward to serve in Trenstarl Hall and keep watch over the child. To tell him his birthright when he came of age, and to urge him to keep the line going. Until, someday, the time would be right for House Bandryn to re-emerge as a power in the land. Along the way, the steward had told select others of the existence of the child, and eventually a small cadre of those loyal to House Bandryn had developed. Even his mother Metricia and her brother had been willing to be swayed from their loyalties to the crown. Metricia had married Borganden Trenstarl knowing his true name and vowing to give him the son that would one day rule the land.

Valeron wrote his name into the book, but not as Valeron Trenstarl as it appeared on the birth record earlier in the book. In bold letters, he signed Valeron Bandryn.

Novardan brought out a small leather purse. "This is yours now," he said. "It belongs to Lord Bandryn. It is your legacy."

Valeron took the purse with excitement. He knew what this must be. He opened the purse and dumped its contents out into his hand. A heavy gold ring sat in his palm, gleaming in the morning light.

"The signet ring of Lord Bandryn," said his mother. "Wear it with pride, my son."

The ring had a thick band, but the size wasn't terribly big. Valeron slipped it onto the last finger of his right hand, his heart swelling with pride. With this, he was Lord Bandryn. No one could doubt it.

A rustle of silks came from behind him. "The bride," said Novardan. He held out his hand.

Valeron turned to look at the woman who would be his queen. They had met before, being cousins, but rarely since he had inherited his father's title and his time was consumed by running the Trenstarl estate.

His bride-to-be was his uncle's daughter and so custom forbid this union. But there were too few women who knew the secret, who could be trusted. This woman had been asked years ago to be the one, and she had agreed. And as a scion of House Segrithr, she would be acceptable to the people after Bandryn sat on the throne. It would ease the transition.

The woman bore the stamp of her Segrithr heritage, the raven hair and black eyes. Valeron himself was proud of his Bandryn coloring, so unlike his father's. He felt his auburn hair and dark blue, almost violet, eyes were proof that he was the one everyone had been waiting for. He had the name, and he had the appearance. He was Lord Bandryn. It was a sign that he was right, that he was the one Evandia required to regain her former glory.

"Lady," he said and held out his hand. She held her head high and took his hand gracefully. Her gown's bodice was covered in thousands of pearls his mother had patiently sewn onto the dress. The effect was magnificent.

"Valeron Bandryn," said Novardan. "Do you agree before witnesses to take Reyva Segrithr as your wife? Do you swear to honor her and be faithful to her? Will you accept her dowry..."

Novardan stopped. The dowry was a sticking point, since Malagert was bestowing his lands on the husband of his second daughter, Holliwen.

"The woman herself is the dowry," said Valeron.

Reyva's eyes shone with joy. Valeron was pleased. He would need this woman's cooperation if all were to go as planned. He could afford to be gracious.

"Do you so swear?" asked Novardan.

"I do swear to accept this woman as wife, to honor her and be faithful to her."

"And you, Reyva Segrithr, do you renounce your claim to that name and take the name of Bandryn for your own? Do you agree to wed Valeron Bandryn, to be faithful to him, to surrender yourself to him, and to bear him children of his body?"

"I swear."

Novardan handed Reyva the quill. "Then write your name beside that of your husband."

Reyva's hand shook slightly but she inscribed Reyva Segrithr in bold letters. Then, as according to custom, she scratched a single line through her birth name and wrote Bandryn next to it. Valeron smiled in approval. It was important to go back through the pedigree to note which families the women had been taken from, but their husband's name took precedence. His bride handed the quill back to Novardan.

"Then you are now husband and wife until death."

That was normally the bride's family's cue to greet their new son, but no one in Reyva's immediate family was present. Metricia filled the awkward pause; she stepped forward and kissed Reyva on the cheek. "Welcome to the family, darling." After her came her other children, Valeron's younger brothers and sisters, and his sister's new husband.

Reyva beamed. "Thank you."

The entourage went to the dinner prepared for them. The cooks had not been able to prepare the traditional wedding items lest word get out too quickly. So the small sugary delicacies Reyva might have looked forward to were missing; however, instead, the cooks had prepared several enticing puddings and cakes to follow the roast pig and baked lamb. Valeron glanced at Reyva but she didn't seem disappointed in the fare. If his mother were right, Reyva was as eager for a crown as his mother was to be the mother of a king. Today might not be the wedding a royal woman would dream of, but Reyva could look forward to a coronation that would have everything her wedding lacked, and more besides.

His attention was pulled away by the mention of the king's whore, Lythera.

"The way he behaves around her, you'd think he's in love with her," said Metricia. "The fool."

"One woman's much the same as another," said Novardan. "This one was a wretch. You should have seen the horrendous dress she wore when I picked her up at Halevern Hall. It was more patches than dress. Dark brown, almost black. Loose, like a child's dress, and she almost twenty! And with that brown hair, just tied behind her head with string! She looked more like a scullery maid than a member of the gentry. And her father! Greedy to get her sold away from him as quickly as possible. A despicable man."

"I'll need to get back to court as soon as possible," muttered Metricia. "In case she gets pregnant."

"She is very plain," said Reyva. She screwed up her face in a moue of disgust that did not make her appear particularly attractive, either.

"I'm just glad I never met any of them," said his youngest sister Joula. Her new husband was the most recent addition to their group, chosen for Joula because his loyalties were easy to sway. In fact, Joula had been the reward for his change in loyalties from House Segrithr to House Bandryn. He was Ulstar Yawneil, grandson of the king's lead judge. His dirty blond hair and matching eyes gave him a washed-out look and he was as plump as a goose ready for eating. Valeron was just glad he did not have to bed anyone with so much excess weight; he didn't know how Joula could stand it, and didn't care. She had been given to Ulstar and she seemed happy enough with the arrangement. Now he just hoped his own bride would be happy with her arrangement. A happy bride would make the upcoming months pass more smoothly. He had too much to do to prepare for the Harvest to be distracted by an emotional woman.

"Well, the consort's not important," said Novardan. "I'm sick of this duty, but I'll need to find at least one more before Harvest so nothing seems suspicious. I have just the perfect girl in mind, too. A scion of the Hellfren family."

"Must we discuss this now?" asked his mother. "Bad enough I have to smile and simper and be their friend. I don't need to hear about the next one before the current one is sent off!"

"My lady mother is correct," said Valeron before Novardan could scold his sister. What Novardan never seemed to understand was that, underneath that beautiful exterior, Metricia Trenstarl was made of pure steel, honed to a fine point and aimed directly at the throne. Her single-mindedness was both a gift and, at times, a burden, when she could not shake the quest to put her son on the throne long enough to take some enjoyment out of life. At times like that, Valeron had learned to placate her in such a way that she did not suspect his interests differed from hers. Once she was calm again, he could generally get her to do anything he wanted, or would merely leave her to concentrate on his own interests. Novardan had never figured out how to handle his sister as her son had, and Valeron had always been amused by that.

"So, Mother, you choose the topic. This is your day more than it is mine. Even more than it is my bride's, though it pains me to say that in the face of such a lovely example of royal womanhood." Reyva beamed with pleasure. Valeron put his hand on her thigh, wondering if his eagerness for her was matched by any eagerness of her own.

Not that it truly mattered, he supposed. She was his now, even without a wedding bracelet. Her name was in the pedigree book. She did not have to be eager or willing.

Still, he would prefer that she was. If this woman were to rule at his side, and support him, and help him outmaneuver ministers, and bear his children, and raise them as he wanted them raised, he could not afford to have her hating him. With the serving girls, that was never an issue. Hate him or fear him, they merely had to do what they were told.

This woman, technically, also had to. But he needed her for so much more; life would be easier if he could figure out how to win her heart along with her body.

The afternoon passed with more food, and more drink, until nearly everyone in the room was leaning back in their chairs half-asleep. Valeron held his hand out to Reyva and was gratified by the strong grip she gave him in return.

"It's time to retire to our chamber, my lady and my wife," he said.

She trembled slightly, but her eyes shone with excitement. "Yes," she said. "It is time."

Still, they could not leave without one more toast from the other guests, and a hug from his mother, and one last surprise from the cook, who had prepared a sweet and sticky concoction that tasted divine. But at long last, he managed to lead Reyva to his rooms, where his mother had already prepared the bed with purple sheets and throws covered in more pearls.

"I know it's not quite the right time," he said, "but I want to give you this." He went to the wardrobe, opened a drawer, and brought out a small cedar-scented box.

Reyva stopped pulling hairpins out of her elaborate upswept hairstyle, and took the box. "What's this?"

"Well, your morning gift," he said. "I know it's not morning, but I just couldn't wait for you to have it."

Reyva opened the box and gasped. Inside lay a lazy serpentine curl of gold dripping with amethysts. Not the most expensive jewel, but the only one that matched the Bandryn heraldic color. His new lady, his new *queen*, would be a wonder in purple and gold.

It was clear she thought so, too. She picked it out of the box, and after admiring it for a moment, slipped the long and heavy chain over her head.

The central stone was the size of a robin's egg and was surrounded by brilliant diamonds that reflected the candlelight onto the walls, where each glittering star danced with every movement his bride made

"It's beautiful," she said while she continued to stare at it. Valeron began shrugging off his clothes and, when he most of them removed, he started undoing the stays on his bride's dress. Together, they managed to remove Reyva's clothing and then what remained of his own. Reyva touched the egg-shaped amethyst and started to remove the necklace, but Valeron placed his hand on hers to stop her.

"No," he said. "You are my lady, one day to be my queen, and this is yours forever, along with my heart."

He was rewarded with adoration in her eyes, her arms wrapped around his shoulders, and her lips on his own, eager and hungry. He responded in kind and together, they sank down on to the bed and made themselves truly husband and wife.

I I

The library had become Lythera's usual afternoon haunt. She never got over the otherworldiness of the place, with the glowing blue walls, the high thin windows that let in beautiful shafts of light, and the strange tangy smell of Fortune's Rue that clung to everything and overpowered even the mustiness of the old tomes. In some strange way, she felt at home here. She couldn't explain it, and didn't really care. It was a feeling she'd been missing her whole life, and now she had it in abundance—here in the library, and anywhere with Teiryn.

Her heart warmed to think of him, her resentment a distant memory. She was almost embarrassed to think how much she had dreaded coming to the palace, and how much she had feared going to bed with a stranger. But Teiryn was a wonderful lover and was becoming a treasured friend, even if sometimes he could not see what was important to her. Just being near him brought Lythera more contentment than seemed possible, and she was sure she could find a way to explain her feelings to him eventually. She was happier than she could ever have imagined just a few weeks ago.

Books lay piled haphazardly on the ink-stained, wax-laden tables of the library as usual, but Lythera did not hear what she expected—the low tones of Jarris mumbling to himself over a text.

"Master Jarris?"

Her own voice echoed oddly back at her from the fluted walls. Lythera went to the room where Jarris kept his wardrobes full of artifacts, but the room contained nothing but furniture.

"Bloody fortune!" shouted someone behind her. Lythera whirled. At first, she was confused because she saw no one, but then she noticed a whiff of smoke coming out from under a door opposite her.

Lythera went to the door and pushed it open slightly. Before her was a room she had not yet been in; through the smoke, she could see it was entirely blue as the records room was, but in the middle was a large crystal table. On the table lay a pile of parchments, herbs, and a small assortment of metal items.

A man stepped through the smoke and stared at her. He had snow-white hair and ice-blue eyes. His face was unlined, so Lythera felt he must be fairly young despite the hair.

"And you are?" he asked.

"Lythera. I heard you say something and then I saw the smoke. I came here to see if you were all right."

"I'm fine. Cursed thing blew up in my face, though. Hasn't happened before, but I should have been expecting it." The man's attention went back to the items on the table and he sorted through the herbs as if looking for something in particular.

"Can I help?"

He looked up again. "With what?"

Lythera shrugged. "Whatever you're doing...what *are* you doing?"

"Ask a lot of questions, don't you?"

Lythera decided to ignore that and walked forward to the table. From a closer vantage point, she saw the pile of objects contained the gold knife of which Jarris was so proud, several broken crystals, and one of the inscribed metal objects from the oldest layers. Without thinking, she reached for it.

The man slapped her hand away. "Careful. That's not yours."

Lythera drew herself up straight and stared him eye to eye. "I dare say it's not yours, either."

The man stared back for a few moments, glanced down and noticed her marriage bracelet. He blanched, no doubt recognizing the Segrithr crest. "No, it's not, Lady. I beg your pardon. You have a point. But you should wait for it to cool down, anyway. I was using it as the focus of the spell, and so the flash initially came from the object before setting my herbs on fire."

"A spell? Like peasants dancing under the moon to make their crops grow?" Lythera couldn't entirely contain her amusement.

"Well, something like that, Lady," said the man. "The thing is, these spells used to not work. When Jarris started trying them in his youth, nothing would happen. Over the years, the results have become more unpredictable. Something usually happens now, though the violence of this particular reaction was unexpected."

Lythera glanced back down at the object with intense curiosity. "How odd. What do you think that means?"

"I'm not sure, but Jarris says it's because we're approaching the end of an age. He's sure there'll be another upheaval soon. Wars, famine, a new ruling family. Who knows?"

Lythera's heart tightened at the off-handed way the man mentioned a new ruling family. That would mean Teiryn would be dead. She couldn't fathom a world where Teiryn was not king.

"No," she said softly. "That can't happen."

"Might not," said the man. "No one really knows what happens when the tides of history turn. All we can say from the record Jarris has uncovered is that whatever it is, it will happen quickly. But that doesn't mean it will all be bad, Lady. I'm sure you won't have to worry."

Lythera sat down. "But such extensive changes...how could they be good?"

The man shrugged. "For one thing, if we can educate people that something is coming, perhaps they could be prepared. Or perhaps, if we study enough, we can figure out what will happen ahead of time. If we really knew, then it would be easier to let people know what to expect. We could deal with it."

"Could we really predict what will happen? From what little Master Jarris said, there seems to be no pattern. An age with odd metal artifacts, an age of weapons, an age of crystals...then nothing as if Evandia were deserted, and then the Evandia we know now. What could be next? I can't even imagine."

"Nor can I, Lady."

Lythera shook her head. "I don't have a title. My name is just Lythera. And you?"

The man nodded. "My pardon again, La...Lythera. I'm Avaidan. A student of Jarris' for many years now. I've learned enough that he's trusted me with this summer's dig."

"A dig?"

"A place where we dig through the layers of the past inch by inch and record what we find. I'll be taking a team to an area just outside the eastern city gate. A lot of artifacts have turned up there under the plow. It looks promising."

"So you just keep collecting items? What good will that do?"

Avaidan shrugged. "I'm not sure. But every summer we learn a little bit more. Two years ago, we found a site where we discovered the crystal foundations of a house. The crystal was a much lighter blue than the astars, almost green."

"How do you know it was a house?"

"In this case, it was fairly easy to tell. One room held personal items like combs, mirrors, buttons. Another held kitchen utensils. The kitchen area also turned up a few small animal bones. I don't think the lady of the house was too good about sweeping up—or else her last meal was interrupted suddenly and she never returned to the kitchen."

"But what could do something like that?"

"War? Natural disaster? On the coasts, they occasionally have giant waves that wipe out entire villages. And towns near rivers sometimes are flooded. But you'd think a flood would have washed away the artifacts and left us an empty house—or a house full of things like fish bones! So I don't know. My guess is war."

"War," repeated Lythera softly. "That would be terrible."

"Indeed," said a new voice. Lythera turned around. A large man with a smith's shoulders stood in the doorway. He had short curly brown hair and a tightly-curled beard. Lythera had never known a man with such a beard; it gave the man a pastoral look even though his clothes were expertly tailored and he stood with an unconscious grace.

"Lythera, this is Master Mandlarin. He's on loan to us from a school in Thavinar. That's in the far southern reaches of Evandia, near the sea, in case you haven't heard of it. They breed good linguists there, if Mandlarin's any indication."

"We are excellent breeders of many things," said Mandlarin. "Good fortune, Lythera."

"Good fortune, Master Mandlarin," she said.

Mandlarin strode forward. "What have you been doing, Avaidan?" His demeanor was somewhat friendly, but Lythera sensed a reserve. This man was still unused to dealing with those of lesser station on a regular basis. Though he was no lord, the Master title meant Mandlarin came from some good family. Jarris and Evinard did, too, but they'd never let that hold them back. But this man was different.

Avaidan seemed used to the tone of the other man's voice. "I tried using the fire-starting spell with the sundial, and instead of sputtering as usual, it exploded in my face. I'm lucky I'm not hurt."

"Sundial?" asked Lythera. Mandlarin gave her a look that, from her father, would have meant for her to hold her tongue. But Lythera had no intention of obeying. She had too much to learn, and Mandlarin couldn't do anything to her anyway, not with the Segrithr wedding bracelet around her wrist. For the first time, she felt some gratitude toward the custom.

Avaidan touched the metal object briefly, then picked it up. "It's cool now. We call it a sundial just because it looks like a sun with rays coming from it. And there's a dial in the center. It appears that the various pieces of this once moved in different directions, but it's too old. It's fused together."

Avaidan held out the sundial to Lythera. She took it and a strange vibration shot up her arm. She dropped the sundial and backed away from the table so quickly she knocked the chair over. "What was that?"

"What?" asked Avaidan. "It's not hot."

"It was moving, or vibrating, or something," said Lythera.

"Nonsense," said Mandlarin with a gruff laugh. "Why don't you leave us to our work, girl?"

Lythera ignored him. She couldn't take her eyes from the sundial. That was not what it was, really. It was a calendar. Its maker had called it a *nauvynnor*. How did she know that?

Carefully, Lythera approached the item again and grabbed it. In her hands, it vibrated, then emitted a humming sound so loud she knew the men heard it when Avaidan's eyes widened.

"What's that?" he asked.

"She's broken it," said Mandlarin.

"No," said Avaidan. "She's only holding it, and more than one of us has accidentally dropped it before." He stood up and came around the table's corner.

Lythera ignored the men. She studied the item carefully and saw how the different thin layers of metal were marked in days, months, and years. She didn't understand the runes, but she could see the intent. She used her thumb to move the day disc forward.

"Wait, don't do that," said Mandlarin. "That's an ancient artifact, and you're destroying it!" He grabbed for the nauvynnor but Avaidan put himself in between Lythera and Mandlarin.

"Be still. We've never gotten this far with it on our own. For whatever reason, she can work it. Let's see what we can learn."

Lythera spun the dials on the object in the ways they seemed to want to go. Months ticked by, then years. Another dial was, she thought, probably centuries. It had twelve runes on it. Twelve hundred years and then some. Marking time. But marking it for what?

As the dials marked out time, every so often, a hole in a disk would reveal a rune on a disk underneath. Lythera thought those must be holidays or other special events.

The starting and ending points on the disks were marked with small arrows. Lythera spun the centuries disk to the twelfth position, then continued counting the years and months upward. The humming grew louder.

"I think we're approaching today," she said. "Twelve hundred and ninety-seven years since the upheaval." She kept spinning and the humming grew louder.

"What's going on here?" Jarris entered the room, leaning heavily on his stick. "Avaidan?"

"Lythera can work the sundial, and it's making noise," said Avaidan.

Lythera clicked the final disk into place into what she thought— hoped—matched today's date. Suddenly, all was quiet for a brief moment. Only Mandlarin broke the silence by saying, "She's ruined it, Jarris."

"Shush."

What happened next stunned them all. A sonorous voice of no special quality spoke out of nowhere. It echoed throughout the crystal room.

The time for change has arrived.

The cycle is nearly complete.
Only a Bandryn hero can save your land.
Thus speaks Fortuna.

Lythera stood, stunned, as the voice faded away.

"Fortuna?" asked Avaidan. "Not fortune?"

"It's a name," said Jarris. He alone of the men seemed to have noticed Lythera's paralysis. He approached her and took the nauvynnor from her. "It's all right, my dear. We're all surprised."

"Surprised, yes, but think of what she did!" Avaidan's features were suffused with wonder. "We should show her everything, see if she can work any of the other objects."

Lythera rediscovered her will and backed away slowly. Though the voice had not said so, the object in her hands had seemed to glint at her as if it knew something, tickled the back of her mind with its vibrations, as if to tell her she was important, someone who would be needed when the change came. But the voice held neither approbation nor approval. It just was. All over again, something was deciding Lythera's fate for her, and it wasn't even human, wasn't even from her own time.

Lythera fled the library, and did not stop running until she reached the Hellfren Willow. She flung herself down upon the bench underneath its sheltering branches and wept in terror.

12

For the next five weeks, Lythera avoided the library on days she could hear voices inside. Instead, she tried to find hours when no one else was about and continued looking through old texts. Nothing she found gave her any indication of what changes were in store—or where she, or Jarris or Avaidan, could find a Bandryn hero, the one the nauvynnor said would be needed.

Lythera kept up her lessons with Evinard and had developed a good seat, but was still uneasy on Morningbelle's back. She doubted she would ever be a good horsewoman, but she did enjoy learning to care for the horse. The cats and dogs of the stables were a continual wonder for her, and she learned all she could about them. She even managed to get Evinard to show her the special stable where the royal stags were kept and was thrilled when one old male allowed her to stroke his nose.

The strange dreams continued, and developed, until Lythera felt comfortable in the colorful world with the pitiable lion-creature. It would lay its head in her lap and purr. But the dreams weren't peaceful; she could see very well that the creature was dying. Its fur was patchy and its body covered in sores. Lythera was saddened by its condition but didn't know what was wrong. The creature never spoke to her again.

Occasionally, she saw the old man at the still lake. Sometimes, he threw pebbles, and other times, he did not. But he refused to speak to her again, no matter how often she inquired where she was, or who he was, or what she was to do. Once, she knelt and placed her hand on his shoulder in entreaty, but that broke the dream and she woke up, sweating and nauseated, in her bed. She had not returned to sleep that night.

Then one morning, after a particularly annoying dream in which the old man literally turned his back on her, Lythera rejected her breakfast. She did not understand why Wenvia seemed so excited by her illness. She felt exhausted and irritable and just wanted Wenvia to go away so she could go back to bed.

But Wenvia would not be put off. She was so thrilled she kept patting Lythera on the shoulder. Lythera finally snapped at her. "Get away from me!"

"Oh, I must find the king! I must tell him!" babbled Wenvia.

"Tell him what?" Lythera tried to lie down, but Wenvia grabbed her arm and dragged her to the large chair by the fireplace.

"No, don't lie down; you'll just feel worse. Tell him you're pregnant of course. Don't you know the signs?"

Lythera fell into the chair, stunned. Pregnant? It shouldn't be a surprise; she was here for that reason, after all. But she had been so wrapped up in her new-found emotions for Teiryn, her studies, and her odd dreams, that thoughts of a pregnancy had largely fled her mind.

Now she would have time to figure everything out. If she had a baby, she'd have to be permanently installed at court. She would never be a wife or a queen, but she would have everything else: the king's love, and his child, and all the days of her life to read and study and learn. The secrets of the runes could not evade her forever.

"I was suspicious when all these weeks went by without your courses," said Wenvia. "So I've been watching you carefully."

"I...I never had regular courses," said Lythera. "That wouldn't mean anything."

"Don't lie down," said Wenvia again. "Oh, this is terribly exciting! I'll be back."

The chambermaid left in a flurry of skirts. Lythera relaxed in the chair and put her hands on her belly. Pregnant! Her thoughts whirled as quickly as the fluttering in her rebellious stomach. She could not recall her mother being sick when carrying a child, and she had known no other pregnant women, so she had not expected this development. But if Wenvia said it was a sign, it must surely be.

Lythera tried to concentrate, but her thoughts were too scattered and joyful. She was happy with the news, but had a hundred questions about how her pregnancy would develop, and about the birth. It was not considered proper for an unwed woman to aid in a birth, so the midwife had come from the town to help her mother. Perhaps Wenvia would be willing to explain what she could expect. Or the nestriana. Metricia had said they could speak if they were giving information to a patient.

A few minutes later, she was still sitting peacefully in the chair when the door to her room flew open and she heard Teiryn say, "Later, later," to someone. The door closed.

Lythera's chair was turned away from the door. She waited for him to come to her, and he was there in moments. His eyes shone with a joy she never seen in them before; that combined with her own happiness brought tears to her eyes.

"Your chambermaid gave me the most welcome news," he said through his own tears. The morning light reflected off his black hair, almost turning it navy. Lythera could not resist and ran her fingers through it.

"Is it true?" he asked. "How long have you known?"

She shrugged helplessly and laughed. "I don't know. She just told me herself, but I didn't know before that. I wasn't even thinking about a pregnancy."

He looked sheepish. "Neither was I. I mean, I hoped. But even with Brenicia, it was two years after our wedding before she first conceived. I never suspected three months would be enough time and with the other maids, it was far too long a time at that. But with you..."

He leaned forward and kissed her. She returned the kiss eagerly. He kissed her nose, her cheeks, her ear. "Now I do not need to lose you, my sweet *verrika*," he murmured into her neck. "Not ever."

"You will not lose me," she said. "I'm yours forever. I swear it."

Teiryn sighed. "I wish I could marry you."

She stroked his cheek, angered at the thoughtless law which forbade him to take a second bride, but thrilled that he would have her for a wife if he could. "It doesn't matter. As long as you love me."

"I do love you. I have since that first night. Tell me you love me."

"I love you, Teiryn. I will always love you."

He kissed her, then sat back on his heels. His smile stretched across his entire face; joy radiated from him. "I could stay here with you all day professing my love and kissing your tempting lips, sweetheart. But perhaps we should do something a bit more public today. So far I haven't been seen with you at court functions or dinners because it simply isn't done. I never despised the custom before because I didn't love the others. Since you came, I have ached to have you near me at all times, but the court protocol is strict. But now that you will be the mother of my child, who cares if anyone disapproves?"

"All right."

He frowned. "That is, if you're feeling well enough. Should I send for Wenvia? Or a physician?"

She laughed. "I don't think the situation is as desperate as all that. And I feel much better than I did. I take it this sickness is a passing thing?"

"Well, Brenicia was sick a few times with each pregnancy. But she didn't carry them long, so...I would prefer that you had all the help it is possible to give. I don't want the little one hurt in any way."

"Nor do I."

"I know," he said. "You haven't been out of the palace since you came, have you? Why don't we go to the royal park? You said your lessons with Evinard have gone well, right? Perhaps that will make you feel better."

Her stomach rolled at the thought of climbing on a horse today. "I don't know. I've never ridden beyond the training ring. Do you think that's a good idea?"

"Well, Segrithr women ride horses until the last weeks of their pregnancies, and I've never known one to take ill from it. I suppose it's possible, though, so if there's any chance, we shouldn't risk it."

"But Evinard will be waiting for me," she said. "I'm already late. I should send word to him that I'm not coming."

"The news of a royal pregnancy will have spread to every corner of the palace by now. Still, you're right; it would be polite to inform him directly. Just a moment." Teiryn stroked her cheek lightly, then rose and went to the door. He said something in a low voice to someone on the other side, then came back.

"If we don't go riding, what shall we do? A stroll in the gardens?"

"Absolutely!" Suddenly, she had an overwhelming desire to return to the Hellfren Willow and sit under its curtain of branches. It had become her favorite place in the entire palace complex and she went there often on afternoons after she had stared for too long at ancient puzzles. She had become such a fixture that the songbirds never bothered to leave its branches when she came, and sang the entire time she was there.

Wenvia returned and shooed Teiryn out of the room "just while my Mistress is dressing." Lythera thought it was silly; after all, Teiryn was adept at undressing her, why shouldn't he stay now? But Wenvia apparently had court protocol on her side and Teiryn left meekly. He did wink at Lythera once before he went through the door.

Wenvia helped Lythera on with her layers of underwear, then opened the wardrobe and stared inside. "Let me see, now, the king was wearing the royal red, wasn't he? I think you should match today, don't you, Mistress?"

"Certainly."

Wenvia pulled out the same dark red dress Lythera had worn on her first full day at the palace, the one that matched her morning gift. She put it on eagerly and couldn't wait for Wenvia to fasten the stays in the back. For the first time, the king himself would be seen with her in public. They had only met so far in his room or her room and no one had seen them together except the occasional servant who brought them food or wine.

And Wenvia, who had caught the king in Lythera's bed one morning when they had both slept too late. The chambermaid had given a little screech that woke both Teiryn and Lythera. When Lythera glanced up, she realized who was standing over her bed...and who was lying naked beside her. Teiryn appeared amused by the situation, but Wenvia went white and Lythera worried for a moment the woman might faint. But the chambermaid had gathered herself and said, "I'll return shortly, Mistress. Sire," and had fled the room as quickly as she could.

Lythera had wondered what sort of court gossip had come of that encounter. That there was court gossip she was sure, not just because of Radi's admission, but because of the way stares had changed around her by the week. At first, they had been haughty and spiteful, like Reyva Segrithr's. That had changed to curiosity over time. The curiosity had been intense and not at all friendly. Now, she hoped that curiosity might become something more sociable since she was carrying the king's child.

Wenvia braided her hair and wrapped it in the red ribbon. Nowadays she never argued with Lythera over which ribbon she would wear; she knew Lythera would only wear the red one. Fortunately, the maker had been skilled and the ribbon hadn't frayed even after being in her hair every day, and occasionally at night, too.

She rejoined Teiryn and they walked to the violet-tinted gardens. Lythera was gratified that in the presence of the king, no one dared stare at her, or push past her as if they had not seen her coming. Instead, the king's presence demanded respect. People bowed as he passed. Lythera was worried that he would be mobbed by people demanding his attention, but they reached the gardens unmolested. Perhaps her presence had also helped him by keeping her detractors away from him.

Lythera immediately pulled Teiryn toward her willow. The garden was bright with blooms on nearly every tree and bush, as if reflecting her own inner joy in a more colorful, expressive fashion. For the past two weeks, Lythera had watched as bushes brought forth flowers, glad that she had come to the palace in the spring when she could witness the glorious bursts of beauty. Even the Hellfren Willow had put out thousands of tiny delicate white flowers. Lythera wanted to share their beauty with Teiryn, but on the way they saw someone she knew. He stood at a sad, wilted bush Lythera had noticed before; she had always wondered by the gardeners had not removed it long ago.

"Master Jarris," she called out. "Have you heard the good news?"

Jarris blinked and looked up. He smiled at her and hardly seemed to register the presence of the king. "What news is that, dear?"

"I'm pregnant," she said.

Jarris' smile got wider. "Congratulations, my dear. I am happy to see you so full of joy. I admit I was somewhat reluctant to discuss your situation, as dishonorable as it is." He glanced at the king. "No offense, Sire, but such a woman deserves better than a consort's lot."

"On that we agree, though now her lot is much improved," said Teiryn. "And I'm glad to discover that Lythera has some champions at court."

"She is an able translator, from what I've seen, and she had the most unusual way with ancient artifacts," said Master Jarris. "I'm only sorry she has not come to the library more often. There's so much we could explore and possibly little time in which to do it."

"Ah, yes," said Teiryn with a laugh with a bit of that puzzlement returning to his face, as if he couldn't understand what could possibly interest Lythera in the library, or why Jarris should want her there. "I remember you saying something years ago about the age coming to an end. I didn't realize you still believed that."

Jarris shook his head. "I don't think it is a matter of belief, Sire. The end of the age is at hand. But what will happen, and who will help us through it, remains hidden." He stared meaningfully at Lythera and she recalled he had heard the voice from nowhere. The one that said a Bandryn hero was called for. But he said nothing; he merely smiled and bowed. "Good day to you both. And congratulations again." He limped away.

Teiryn took Lythera's hand and they walked through the garden slowly. Lythera pulled Teiryn toward the willow and parted the curtain of branches so they could get to the bench. She sat down and tried to put Jarris' words from her mind. "This is my favorite place," she said.

He looked around. "It's very quiet and private. I can see why you'd like it. I didn't even know there was a bench here."

She snuggled against him, soaking in his love. "Do you have a favorite place in the garden?"

He was lost in thought for a moment. "I suppose the fountain with the fish. I like to watch them sliding around in the water, with no worries, no duties. They just swim."

She laughed. "I can see where that would be an attraction to a king."

Teiryn put one arm around her shoulders and with the other reached over to run his fingers over her morning gift. She turned her head toward him and they kissed. She thought the kiss would be over quickly; they were, after all, out in public, even if they were sheltered by willow branches. But Teiryn showed no indication that he was aware of their surroundings. His lips lingered on hers, and his tongue followed. His hand dropped from the morning gift to her breasts. She lost herself in his embrace, overcome by her love for him. Let the court see. Let them gossip. Teiryn loved her, and she carried his child.

Branches rustled. "Oh, sorry," said Evinard.

Teiryn's lips left hers and she glanced over toward her friend. He was as red as the royal livery.

"I, uh, heard the news," he said. "And thought I'd be able to find you here. Congratulations, Lythera. Sire."

Teiryn laughed. "Everyone will want to find us to offer their congratulations today, I'm sure. Thank you, Evinard."

"And I thank you, too," said Lythera. "I hope Morningbelle wasn't too disappointed at missing our lesson this morning." She felt flustered, but grateful that if someone were to discover her kissing the king in public, with his hand on her breasts, it was Evinard and not someone like Radi. Or Reyva Segrithr.

"I gave her a carrot and she got over it," said Evinard. "But you should apologize to her later, I think, and explain to her you won't be having any more lessons for a while."

"All right." The thought of apologizing to a horse seemed strange, but she had noticed from the beginning how much Evinard talked to his Black Sunshine, and how the horse responded to him when he did so. She had taken some pains, after that, to talk to Morningbelle as if the horse could understand her. She didn't think the horse really understood, but Morningbelle was definitely more attentive when Lythera spoke to her often.

"But you'll get to stay at the palace now, so you can start your lessons again after you have the baby. And you can visit Belle in the meantime so she won't miss you too much."

Teiryn threw his head back and laughed. Evinard frowned and looked at her, but Lythera shook her head. She wasn't sure what the king found so funny, either.

"Oh, Evinard," said the king when he could breathe again. "I'm so glad to hear that someone in this court is looking forward to my lady being here for a long time."

Evinard grinned. "Sire, I hope Lythera stays here for the rest of her life, and is always as happy as she is now. Fortune willing, may you both be as happy as you are today. For now, though, I believe I shall retreat. Good day, Sire. Lythera." He let in the midst of fluttering branches.

"I'm glad you have one friend," said Teiryn. "But you need more. Even if I can't marry you, we need to end your isolation. Metricia will be arriving soon, with her sister Vandencia. Vandencia's a sweet thing, more like Evinard than anyone else in my family. She had a healthy baby girl last year so you should find her advice helpful. Those two would be a good start."

She was glad he had not brought up the idea of visiting the rest of his female relations uninvited, wherever it was they spent their days. At least she knew Metricia, and if Vandencia were anything like Evinard, having her around would be most welcome.

"I'm sure they will be." She leaned her head on his shoulder and closed her eyes in contentment.

12

Teiryn sat in the biannual tax meeting with the full complement of his ministers. They met in the same room where Lythera had been questioned on her first day at court. Teiryn endured the meeting in the chair in the center with two ministers on his left, two on his right and four across from him. Two empty seats had been left at the far right end.

The original ten families that had united to form Evandia had each placed one family member on this council of ministers. During the succeeding centuries, two families, Houses Bandryn and Uldreth, had become extinct, leaving eight houses and a chair for the king. Because House Segrithr currently held the crown, they were represented by both the king and Lord Novardan. But familial loyalties were rarely a factor in council discussions. Lord Hellfren, his beloved Brenicia's uncle, was usually his most ardent supporter, with Vaiher and Ryllmaren close behind. Nathros, Idrant, and Landrith, as well as his cousin Novardan, were as likely to support him as oppose him, and Gomeril usually took an opposing viewpoint. Usually, but not always. Gomeril was an enigma to Teiryn; never unfriendly, yet often exasperating, as if he knew more about Teiryn's life than Teiryn himself did.

Teiryn turned his attention back to the tax rolls they were studying. Several sei-Lords had not paid, claiming they had nothing. It was probably true; enough of them were writing to Novardan to try to get their daughters in Teiryn's bed just for the money that Teiryn knew some lords were in desperate straits. As of yet, he had not devised a plan to help the impoverished without incurring the wrath of his ministers, who seemed to think that any lord who couldn't manage his financial affairs deserved to be destitute. His ministers, ist-Lords all, were not good judges of the matter, he thought. Their incomes were assured through large land holdings. Hellfren also owned large tracts of forest; Nathros owned most of Evandia's gold mines.

Lords like Lythera's father, however, had no such income. Most of them had titles given for some heroic service in the past, and their incomes were generated by the taxes from small towns or tiny estates that were not generally on the best land. One bad crop, or a plague, and their revenue disappeared for at least a year, if not longer.

Those in the middle, lower-ranked ist-Lords like Standren or Yawneil or nao-Lords like Trenstarl, often owned fine lands or had part-interests in mines or shipping companies, but they did not hold the huge tracts that the great lords did. Yawneil wouldn't go under with one bad harvest, or one lost ship. It would take a string of bad luck to ruin him, but it could happen.

In between the nao- and the sei-Lords were the dau-Lords, who were often in straits as bad as those of men like Lythera's father. And within each classification were men of varying ranks and status granted over the years by royal writ or economic reality or tradition. It was enough to make one's head spin. Teiryn was just glad that when relative ranking was truly important, as in taxation or state dinners, there were others to make sure everyone was treated properly and no feathers were ruffled.

It had been Yawneil who had originally explained some of the realities of paying taxes to the young Teiryn when he was still learning to be king. He could hardly believe, now, that he had survived those first few years, having been crowned at sixteen shortly after his father's death. Within six months of his wedding. How little he had known of the people he was to rule, or how to rule them! Learning to be a good husband, and then a good king at the same time, had overwhelmed him. Brenicia had been his strongest support and his constant companion.

His mind wandered to Lythera, three months along with her pregnancy now. She no longer got sick in the mornings, and had become a fixture in the dining hall, eating beside him as if she were his queen. The ministers hadn't agreed to support him in that decision unless he ordered the removal of the queen's heavily carved chair and a simple chair put in its place. He'd agreed—one fight at a time. At least she was beside him at dinner, where everyone could see how he honored and adored her.

A guardsman entered the room, and bowed to the assembled lords. "Sire, I have a message from Lady Trenstarl. She says you should come to the consort's chamber immediately."

"Did she say why?"

"No."

"Did you hear anything else?"

The guardsman looked uneasy. "Sire, there was talk of blood, but I'm not familiar with such things concerning women."

Blood. That had always been the first sign with Brenicia. The sign that the babe had died and was being expelled from her body. An icy chill fell onto Teiryn and a terrible weight settled on his shoulders, like nothing he had felt since the day his queen had died. He couldn't move.

After a few moments, it was Gomeril—Gomeril!—who slapped his flabby hand on the table. "Well? Go to her, man! She's losing the baby. She needs you."

Teiryn's paralysis lifted and he surged out of his chair. Without a word to anyone, he rushed from the room. From behind him he heard Gomeril's voice say, "Terrible shame." But he had no time for his ministers. He could only think of Lythera, bleeding out their child. Losing the one thing that would tie her to him forever.

In moments he was at her door, and flung it open. Lythera lay on her side in her bed, with Wenvia, Metricia, Vandencia, and the nestriana hovering around her. Vandencia bathed Lythera's face with a cloth. Wenvia wadded up some towels spotted with blood.

Metricia looked up at him with sorrow in her eyes. "I'm sorry, Teiryn," she said.

"Out," he barked.

Wenvia and the nestriana hastened to obey. Metricia patted Lythera on the shoulder and left. Vandencia departed only after surrendering her cloth to Teiryn. He took his cousin's place by Lythera's side and continued bathing her face. She was weeping uncontrollably. Teiryn wanted to weep, too, but not now. Not until he knew she was all right. He couldn't lose her, too.

He had never found the right words to say to Brenicia, so he said nothing. After a time, Lythera stopped crying, but lay still and pale on the bed, eyes closed, barely breathing. He put the cloth aside and took her hands in his. She had to know this wasn't her fault; if it were anyone's fault, it was his. All of his children had died in the womb. His problem was not that his women were barren. No, they conceived. The trouble must lie with him.

Eventually, she opened her eyes. "Teiryn?"

"Right here, love."

"I'm sorry."

His heart broke for her, but he couldn't let her see that now. She needed him to be strong. He leaned over and kissed her brow. "There is nothing to forgive, love. I know you wanted the baby as much as I."

"I love you." Her voice was so weak her barely heard her.

"I love you too, my *verrika*, my brave lady. Rest now. I'll stay here with you."

She closed her eyes again and slept. He got up and put more wood on her fire, and ordered a light supper to be brought to her room. And some soup. He didn't know if she'd be able to eat it, but he'd try to get her to do so. She would need to regain her strength.

Vandencia came with the food and the soup. A servant followed her with a bottle of wine and some tea. After delivering the food, Vandencia hugged him and kissed his cheek. She had inherited the looks of her mother, Keliani Ryllmaren: amber eyes, dark blond hair, and a stocky frame. Her hair was unruly and she kept it fiercely bound back, yet little strands were always escaping.

Vandencia's eyes were red; she must have been weeping. She had changed into a pale green gown of mourning.

He hugged her back. "Thank you for being with her."

She sniffed but seemed unable to find her voice. With a woeful little smile, she nodded and left the room.

Teiryn went to the table. His stomach rebelled at the thought of food, but he had to eat something. Lythera needed him. He couldn't afford to wallow in grief as long as she was weak from the miscarriage. He sat down and ate the meat pie Vandencia had brought, but he didn't taste it. His eyes could not leave the bed and the small form lying under the covers so motionless.

She did not wake all night, and he let her sleep. So it wasn't until morning when Wenvia brought some breakfast that he managed to get some food into her. The nestriana also returned with some sickly-sweet smelling potion she mixed into Lythera's tea. Lythera was pale and didn't speak. He wasn't sure he got her to eat more than three bites, but she did finish the tea, so that was something. Teiryn kissed her and assured her over and over that he loved her. But she didn't seem to hear him.

Toward noon he finally went to his own room to doze. When he awoke, his heart still heavy and sore, he stumbled out of his bedroom, hoping to get a bite to eat and some water to splash on his face. What he got instead was his cousin Lord Novardan, who sat at his table. Behind Novardan stood Velrudin, looking sorrowful in his pale green tunic. He looked at Teiryn apologetically; no doubt Novardan had barged in, overriding Velrudin's efforts to keep him out. Teiryn nodded slightly to his secretary. It wasn't Velrudin's place to keep Ilvinard Segrithr in line.

Novardan looked up at his approach. "I took the liberty of ordering you some food," he said. His manner was completely genial and full of regret. The regret was belied by the royal blue and red the man wore. If he were really sorrowful, he would have changed into mourning colors. Teiryn wished the man would go away.

"Thanks." He sat and gulped down some soup, then followed that with a thick slice of dark bread slathered with butter. His appetite hadn't returned, but he would force himself to eat. If Brenicia were any indication, then Lythera would not be interested in eating, either, and he would have to beg and wheedle to get her to eat and grow stronger. He would spend as much time with her as he could.

"I regret that you and your lady have suffered this tragedy," said Novardan. Some of his sincerity slipped.

"Thank you," said Teiryn with an equal amount of insincerity. "I need to get back to my lady. Is there some reason you're in my room?"

Novardan tapped his fingers on the table as if pondering the right words to say. Knowing him, he'd had his words chosen long since. Teiryn wanted the man to just spit out whatever it was and be gone.

"Ah, not to seem rude, Sire, but arrangements are already being made for the lady's return to her home. My sister says the lady should rest for at least three weeks, but then she shall return to Lord Halevern."

Teiryn's jaw dropped. The nerve of the man! Separate him from Lythera now, when she needed him? "Why?" The word exploded from him in shock.

Novardan tried looking sorrowful but didn't manage it. "It has been over three months."

"But she got pregnant!"

"That is regretfully no longer the case."

Teiryn could do nothing more than stare at the man. Had he no heart at all? Not one compassionate bone in his body?

"It's the law, Sire."

Teiryn struggled to find his voice. "Get out. Get out right now."

Novardan rose, bowed, and left. Teiryn sat in his chair, shaking with rage. They couldn't do this to him, Novardan and the other ministers. Now that he'd found love again, he couldn't let it go.

"My apologies, Sire," said Velrudin softly.

"I understand," said Teiryn, fighting for control. "Is my cousin the only one avoiding mourning, or will I find the court has decided to dismiss this incident."

Velrudin bit his lip before replying. "All the ministers are in mourning, except for Lord Novardan. The staff as well. Among the nobles, some do, some do not. Lord Novardan has not made an issue of his refusal to recognize your tragedy, and though some have followed his lead, the majority have decided to show some decorum, however they feel about the lady in question. If there's one thing that they all want, it's a prince, so in that regard, their mourning is genuine." Velrudin gestured toward a side table, where a tray sat, covered in the black and gold crest of the country of Morovol. "As usual, the Morovolo ambassador was among the first to express his condolences. House Gomeril, however, was also prompt in its display of support." He handed Teiryn a note in Gomeril's flowing hand. Teiryn put it down to read later, wondering what Gomeril was up to this time. He'd never showed more than polite regret with any of Brenicia's miscarriages. Why do more now?

Teiryn sighed and decided to ignore Gomeril for now. "One thing I can count on, at least. Manners from Ambassador Lororo, if not from my cousin."

"Indeed, Sire."

Teiryn gestured for Velrudin to sit. His thoughts were in a fog, and he didn't want to leave his secretary standing while he sorted them out.

He glanced again at the tray, and felt a surge of gratitude. Evandia and Morovol had been allies for centuries, though they remained, for the most part, strangers to each other due to a nearly-impassable mountain range that lay between them. Teiryn liked the current ambassador, Lororo, and had enjoyed a congenial relationship with his predecessor, but he could not say he understood either of them.

One thing he did understand was their deep sense of personal responsibility toward the people around them. At the death of each of his parents, at each miscarriage of his queen's, and after Brenicia's death, it was the Morovolo who had offered the deepest and most heartfelt sympathies. Though the Morovolo could sometimes seem inscrutable to Teiryn, he had never doubted the sincerity of their good wishes in times of grief.

He knew what was on the tray: three cakes of heavy bread dripping with honey to honor the dead, four pieces of fruit to honor the ancestors, and a wreath of flowers to bring the promise of grief eventually assuaged.

Teiryn's thoughts turned back to Lythera. It was true, the law said that consorts could remain in the palace for only three months. Before, he hadn't wanted any of them to stay even that long. But he wouldn't give up Lythera so easily.

"Velrudin, do you know the exact wording of the law about kings and consorts?" he asked. He was pretty sure he knew the wording, but Velrudin would definitely know.

"In the case that the queen should predecease the king, the king may not remarry," said Velrudin. "Any consort the king retains in the palace may remain three months unless she becomes pregnant. If she bears a live child, she may remain indefinitely. Otherwise, she shall be returned to her father's house."

Teiryn mulled that over in his head for a few minutes. Velrudin stared at him with a small smile on his face; perhaps he was thinking along the same lines.

"The law doesn't say what happens to the consort after she returns to her father's house," said Teiryn.

"No, sir, it does not. I would also like to point out that it only pertains to consorts retained in the palace. I believe the Water Street property belonging to your family has no residents at the present time."

Velrudin was ahead of him, as usual. Teiryn nodded. "See that the property is prepared for a guest," he said. "I'm not giving her up."

"I would not advise such a course of action, in any case," said Velrudin with a wicked, though slightly sad, smile. "I have not seen you so happy in years. I'll make all the arrangements."

Teiryn was more relieved that he could say to have an ally in this. He choked up, glad that, for all his ministers' machinations, there were still people he could count on. He nodded again and stood. He would have Lythera as his consort whether anyone else liked it or not. At this point, he didn't even care about the legitimacy of any children she would have by him. He just had to have her. Against the coldness of court life, she was warmth and comfort. He hoped he could be the same for her.

His ministers might not like his plans, but they didn't have to know right away. Eventually, they'd all know about the arrangement, of course—something like that couldn't be kept a secret. But from what Velrudin had said earlier, he suspected most of his ministers would keep their feelings to themselves. Kings had kept women in the city before, although as far as Teiryn knew, it hadn't happened for some time.

If anyone objected, it would be Novardan and Idrant. Novardan was fairly well respected by some, but Idrant wasn't. They wouldn't be enough to sway the ministers to push Teiryn to get rid of Lythera.

Teiryn had never been an expert at the political game the way his father and grandfather had been, but he had learned a few tricks over the years. He would obey the letter of the law, and then do as he pleased. He would have Lythera, and no other, for his consort, for the rest of his life.

But first, he had to face her sorrow again. Teiryn dismissed Velrudin and returned to the heavy pall of despair that hung over Lythera's room like a shroud.

13

Lythera was still numb by the time the coach let her off at Halevern Hall. The loss of her baby had cast her into a pit of despair she thought she would not escape, yet Teiryn's patient and constant attention had soothed her spirit. She suspected the nestriana's teas and ointments had something to do with that, as well. She had drunk everything she had been directed to, and sometimes it had seemed to ease the tightness in her chest and the despair in her heart.

The court and Novardan had cruelties to deliver upon her, though—to cast her off, send her home. To be thrown out, to lose Teiryn, as well as their baby! But Teiryn had surprised her with his plan to return her to the capital. That shred of hope was all she had to sustain her during the five-day trip back to Halevern Hall.

Her hand went to the wrist which, until recently, had borne her marriage bracelet. Now it was gone, and she missed the heavy weight of it. That surprised her, for she'd hated wearing it. But it had tied her to Teiryn, and now it, too, was gone. Like her baby.

She thought she would die of the grief of her baby's loss and being separated from Teiryn, but five days in the coach had proved that grief could not kill. In time, it turned into a stone. Occasionally, she was swept with a fit of weeping, but more often than not, she was quiet. She didn't think she had finished crying, but she was too tired now. And she had to face her father.

The footmen unloaded her trunk, then climbed back up on the carriage and left her standing there, alone with her trunk at her father's door. The door was the same slab of oak, black with age, that she'd seen a thousand times before, yet it seemed different. Or rather, it was she who had changed. The entire dilapidated state of the drive, the lawns, and the building seemed just as sad, but so much more lonely, than they ever had when she'd lived here.

The dress she wore to face her father was a simple woolen gown suited for traveling, gray and unexceptional. When she'd left the palace, she'd been given several of these, each one a dark, dull color. Perfect for what she intended to do, for she would not stay at Halevern Hall but one night. Just long enough to see her sisters, and to obey the letter of the law. Teiryn had already left instructions with the coachmen that they were to retrieve her the morning after they brought her home.

All of her fine dresses—except the dark red one, which she insisted on keeping—were still back at the palace. She didn't mind; she would have nowhere to wear such finery anymore. But she couldn't give up the red one, not even for the duration of this journey. Novardan had protested but Teiryn would have let her take anything she desired.

She also had the red ribbon and of course her morning gift. The woolen dresses had high collars so she could wear her morning gift under them without it being seen. She didn't want to attract attention to it; better if no one knew about it. She had once wanted to show it off to her father; now she wanted to keep it secret, something close to her heart that was hers alone.

Besides that, there was a pouch buried in her trunk, a pouch Teiryn had pressed into her hand the day before she left. "Novardan doesn't know about it," he'd said quietly. "But I can't let you go without something. Something to help you until we meet again. I will not have you destitute, even for a day." Inside was enough coinage for her to buy her food and lodging for several weeks, even though the crown was already paying for her way home and back to the palace. Still, she appreciated the gesture. Even if something went wrong, or if she became stranded, she would have the means to return to Teiryn—no matter what.

She took a deep breath. It was silly to stand out here like a stranger. Like it or not, she was home. Only for a short while, and for the last time, but she was still home. She pulled at the door handle and the door swung open as slowly and with as much groaning as it ever had.

If the outside looked the same, the inside was nearly unrecognizable. The great hall was no longer dark. A fire blazed in the fireplace and new linens in the Halevern green were laid on the long tables. The windows had been cleaned, and the broken ones replaced. Fresh white plaster covered the walls. Her father had not been idle since his financial situation had been restored.

Her father was deep in discussion with his steward as she approached. Neither looked up until she was almost upon them. Her father's hair was the iron gray she remembered, but his face was no longer so lean, and his belly was larger. Apparently he had been eating very well since she left. Lord Halevern spied her and frowned. He waved the steward away.

"My trunk is outside," Lythera said to the retreating steward. "Bring it to my room."

"So you couldn't do it, could you," her father said. "There will be no Halevern on the throne."

"If that is true, then it's because of you," she said evenly. She had never spoken to her father like this before, but now she felt she had the right. She was no longer a child, but a woman who had suffered loss. Her heart was so far gone in grief she couldn't even cry anymore. Or fear her father. "You were the one who sold me away from here. You are the cause of my shame."

Anger and shame colored his face, and he said nothing. Nor would he meet her eyes.

"Oh, we've been waiting for you!" someone said brightly.

Lythera turned to see a short woman whose head was covered by a riot of yellow curls. Her face was delicate, heart-shaped, and pale, and her eyes a bright blue that matched her dress. She was fine-boned, her waist tiny. Her hands made tiny, flickering movements, almost as if she were dancing. She reminded Lythera of a bird.

The woman approached Lythera and hugged her warmly. Lythera looked back at her and thought the woman seemed terribly young. Probably not more than fifteen or sixteen, at the most, more girl than woman.

"Lythera, this is my wife, Nestira Daynar—now Nestira Halevern, of course." Lord Halevern moved to Nestira's side and took her hand. She smiled up at him, not in adoration, but at least in gratitude. What could this girl have to be grateful for from a wretched man like Lord Halevern?

"Come," said Nestira with enthusiasm. She dropped her husband's hand and grabbed at Lythera's. "Tell me all about what's going on at court. I didn't really see that much when I was there."

"One moment." Lythera turned to her father. "I have only come to see my sisters. I will be gone in the morning."

"And go where? You have no place in the world," he snarled.

She shrugged. "I kept my vow to you and owe you nothing more. You, at least, owe me the courtesy due a guest, for I am no longer your daughter and will never again use your name. Where I go from here and what I do are no concern of yours."

Lord Halevern turned away and walked out of the room. Nestira tugged on Lythera's sleeve. "Come," she said quietly.

Lythera followed Nestira to her old room. It was as empty as it was when she'd left it. "Where are my sisters?"

"In town. They have a nurse who is taking them to be measured for Harvest gowns. They'll be back soon." Nestira sat down on the bed and smiled up at Lythera. Lythera sank down onto the bed as well. She wanted to ask Nestira so many things, but there was no polite way to begin. The silence between them stretched out.

Finally, Nestira grinned and blushed a little. On her fair skin, the blush was immediately apparent and Lythera could watch it spread across her face. "It must be a surprise, coming here and finding out your father has a new wife. We've been married for two months now."

Lythera found her voice. "And are you happy with him?"

Nestira sighed. She hesitated, as if weighing her words, but Lythera did not sense any despondency in her. "Yes, more than I thought. He's not a very patient man, but he's not cruel, either. He yells less than my father does. And I get to be Lady Halevern. It's not much right now, and well, you know what it was like before. But we have plans to fix it up. It'll be so grand! With your father's debts gone and with my dowry, we can begin to restore the house and the family."

"There is nothing to restore," said Lythera. "A man who sells his daughter is a worthless wretch."

Nestira's gaze fell to her hands, which were clasped together in her lap. "But he's not the only one, is he? My father was another. You were the ninth sent to the king. I was the second."

"You?" asked Lythera. "But then how could my father…" she stopped. She couldn't ask Nestira how her father could take a ruined girl for a wife. She could ask him, accuse him of an indiscretion, but not Nestira. With no other prospects, what girl would turn down the chance to marry a lord? Even an old, bitter one whose manor house was crumbling around him? Who wouldn't want to go from ruined girl to a titled Lady, even if that title did not come with enough food or fuel for the fire in the dead of winter?

The younger girl bit her lip. "Well, the king took one look at me and said I was too young. That was over a year and a half ago and I've filled out a lot since then. Lady Trenstarl—I assume you met her—said it wasn't my fault but I was sent off home the next morning. My father then tried to find other suitors for me, but it turned out no one was interested in one of the king's consorts. Except, as it turned out, the father of another consort. My father scraped together a dowry from the funds he had received from the crown and sent me here. It's really worked out for the best, you see."

Lythera was surprised at how relieved she was that Teiryn had not touched this girl. He must have bedded some of the others, but she didn't want to meet them. Didn't want her mind to call up visions of the woman and Teiryn in bed together. This one he had turned away.

"It's nice to meet you and I hope you have a happy life at Halevern Hall," said Lythera sincerely. "But I'll be leaving in the morning, so I haven't a lot of time to visit with my sisters and see how they are doing."

"The three of them will be thrilled you're home. They talk about you all the time."

Lythera's heart sank. "Three? What happened?" She couldn't keep the edge of panic out of her voice. Could one of her sister have died and her father not informed her? How could he keep such news from her?

"No, no, nothing happened. Nothing bad, anyway." Nestira's smiling face eased Lythera's fears. "Another lord who'd sent his daughter to the king was looking for a bride for his son. And he'd been finding it difficult to acquire a girl because, well, you know. The ones who are wealthy enough not to have to sell their daughters aren't going to be eager to deal with a man who will. So your father used part of my dowry to send with her as her dowry. Now your sister Pezia is wed to Struven Janneren. I know it should have been Adrina, she's older. But Pezia and Struven seemed drawn to each other, so she was the one to marry him. And now, when his father dies, he'll be sei-Lord Janneren, and she'll be Lady Janneren. Isn't that wonderful?"

Lythera sat stunned. "My sister, married? But she was only fifteen."

"Sixteen now," said Nestira. "Same age as me. Settling in well, according to the letter she sent back. So all is happy with her and with me. And Adrina has had a nao-Lord's youngest son come asking after her, so who knows how long before she finds a better situation, too? It may be that, by spring, only the two youngest will be left here, and their futures may look much brighter by the time they're of age."

"I'm glad," said Lythera, though her heart was so shocked she felt little at all. Later, she thought. Later, it will hit me that my little sister is a married woman. A wife. Wenvia had been wrong, after all. The wealthier gentry might be willing to make men like Lords Halevern, Daynar, and Janneren suffer for their shameful acts, but the lords had found a way around that. They would simply trade their children amongst themselves. By the time the next generation was old enough to be wed, the old dishonor would be forgotten. Her father would not need to suffer for anything. He had been rewarded instead, with new wealth and a new bride. In fact, his situation was so vastly improved, it was difficult to remember just how hard life had been before.

"I'm sorry, but I need to rest. It's been a long trip," she said quickly. She needed some time alone, to think, to reconcile that her father had a new wife, and her sister a husband.

"Of course. Stay as long as you like," said Nestira. "You're welcome here anytime, of course. This is your home."

Lythera looked at this young woman who was now lady of Halevern Hall. Her father did not deserve such a young, pretty thing who was so open, so friendly, and so eager to please. Yet she could not feel sorry for Nestira; if Nestira did not consider herself ill-served, then Lythera would not.

"No, it's not," she said. "But it is yours now. May you find happiness here."

Nestira smiled and left her. Lythera sat alone in her empty room while the light faded toward evening. Eventually, she got out the small bag she'd brought just for the purpose of gathering the few belongings she wanted to have with her in her new life: the feather she'd found shortly before

Novardan's arrival; a few pretty rocks; her mother's favorite hairpin. The pile was extremely small. It seemed she should have more accumulated from nearly twenty years of residence in this hall.

It didn't matter. The few things that had sentimental value were now packed with the rest of her belongings, the ones she had from Teiryn. And she would be returning to him as soon as she could. Though she looked forward to seeing her sisters, her heart's home was far from here, and her thoughts were already back there with him.

14

Lythera's sisters had been thrilled to see her and had cried to hear she was leaving again. She promised to send them presents for Harvest, and that cheered them up enough that they could wave goodbye to her the next morning with dry eyes. The most surprising thing to Lythera was how well the girls had taken to Nestira, and she to them. Lythera had watched the younger woman holding up the littlest one so she could see Lythera's carriage a short while longer. Open-heartedness appeared to be one of Nestira's defining qualities, and Lythera felt better about leaving her sisters than she thought she would. Yesterday, she had thought she would be abandoning them to her father once more, but now they had a nurse whom they adored and a step-mother who, though young, younger even than Adrina, had accepted them eagerly and doted on them. She need not worry about them.

She had little to do during the five days it took to return to the capital except dream of being reunited with Teiryn. Every mile that went by brought her closer to him, and her heart lifted a little.

Master Jarris had promised to search for a teaching position for her at one of the schools in the capital. If he could find her something, then for the first time in her life, she would be free. Free of her father, even free of Teiryn. At least, she wouldn't belong to either of them, not legally. She wouldn't belong to any man; the thought was new and exhilarating. But also frightening—belonging to a man meant safety. Protection. She would not have that. But it would be worth it, to live her own life—with a lover, certainly, but without husband or father. A life she could not have imagined a few short months ago now stretched out before her as an enticing and exciting possibility.

It hadn't occurred to her, during her life at Halevern Hall, that the world held anything for her but what her father decided. And then he had decided upon a shameful course of action. Still, she should be thankful; if he hadn't, she would still be in her father's house, unloved, with no future beyond laundry and cleaning and cooking.

But she didn't consider what her father had done a favor. He hadn't cared what Teiryn would be like, or how his daughter would fare as a royal consort. Whether Teiryn were kind or cruel, it would have been one and the same to her father. It was Teiryn to whom she owed the most. From the beginning, he had treated her with honor, as a person with feelings, and not a thing. Not like her father or Novardan. And now he was giving her a chance at a new life.

When Teiryn had first approached her about his plan to bring her back to the capital, she was too trapped in her grief to truly understand what he meant. As the days wore on, and the edge of her despair dimmed, she had thought about his words, and realized how perfect the plan was. She could return to the capital, and have Teiryn.

And with Master Jarris' help, she could have even more.

The very air of the land seemed to smell better, be fresher, every time she thought about her future. She wondered what sort of position Master Jarris would be able to find for her. She had never taught before, and wasn't sure how to go about it. The thought was intimidating, but at least teaching would mean presenting lessons about the languages she loved to students who were there to learn.

Finally, late on the fifth day, she passed once more under the city gates with its odd inscription; *moon-bird of fortune protect us*. The coach traveled past the palace into an area of large houses spaced out on wide boulevards. They might not be palaces, but they were still at least as large as Halevern Hall. Eventually, the coach turned onto a smaller street and pulled up in front of a large house of white stone and she was stunned with its beauty despite her time in the crystalline palace.

A doorman, wearing the royal livery, stood at attention in front of the house, and walked quickly to the coach as soon as it stopped. He opened the door and Lythera climbed out.

"Mistress," he said with a small bow. "I will get your bags in a moment. The housemaid awaits you inside."

"Thank you," said Lythera. She walked up the steps, prepared to open the door, but the doorman sprang in front of her to get it first. Lythera blushed slightly. No one at Halevern Hall opened doors for her, and at the palace she had only seen doormen in front of the state rooms. "Thank you," she said again as she stepped inside.

The interior of the house was as overwhelming as the exterior. The huge entryway was as big as the great room of Halevern Hall. Marble in white, black, and red ran in giddy spirals on the floor. Lythera had no idea how much time it had taken the workmen to create the design, but the resulting floor was a stunning achievement.

"Mistress?"

Lythera glanced up. She had been so entranced with the floor, she had not heard the housemaid's approach. The woman wore the Segrithr colors and the same sash that the palace servants had worn. She was elderly and slightly plump, and her watery blue eyes were carefully neutral, neither hostile nor welcoming.

"Yes?"

The housemaid curtseyed slightly. "I've been instructed to give you a tour of the house."

That was also neutral enough. Lythera began following the housemaid through the house, but the wonders of the stonework, the beautiful tapestries, the delicately carved wood furniture, began to run together in her mind. It was all beautiful, but there was so much of it! Lythera's eyes could barely register one piece before being distracted by others. The house was similar to the palace, except Lythera had expected a palace to be so ornate. But a house? Especially one that no one even lived in?

The many rooms of the house flowed into one another; Lythera was sure she could not find her way back out again by the time she and the housemaid returned to the front room. She was glad to see the spiral floor again if only because it was a little more familiar than everything else.

"I'm sorry," said Lythera. "I didn't get your name. I'm Lythera."

The housemaid nodded slightly. "I'm Inveora, Mistress. Now I'll show you to your room."

"Oh, no," said Lythera quickly. "Please, I'm sure you have duties to perform. Just tell me how to get there." Inveora's calm but dispassionate demeanor was becoming unwelcome and Lythera longed for the chance to get away. Besides, something was bothering her now that she'd seen the house and she wanted time to sort out what it was. Certainly it couldn't be the house itself—who could object to such a beautiful thing?

Inveora looked as though she were about to protest—it was the first expression Lythera could recall seeing on her face—but she schooled her face into blankness once more. "Up the steps, Mistress, end of the hall, a walnut door with brass handle. Next to the door is a small table with a vase of purple flowers on it."

"Thank you." Lythera fled up the stairs and found her door easily enough. Later, perhaps, she would look into all the other rooms, though she was sure they were all grand and full of ornate furniture.

Her room looked just as she imagined. A huge four-poster bed was on the far wall, with a marble-topped table to each side. On the wall by the door was a huge armoire. A chest of drawers was on the wall to her left, and above it hung an exquisite tapestry showing peasants performing a circle dance. The gray marble floor had been partially covered by thick woolen rugs. Everywhere she looked, there was another small table, a candlestick, a tapestry. The room was full of Segrithr belongings.

Lythera's trunk looked awkwardly out of place in the center of the floor. Lythera went to it to unpack, but something stopped her. Absently, her hand went to the wrist where, until recently, she had worn her marriage bracelet. She stood up and looked around at all the opulence, none of it hers.

She walked around the room, touching things, examining the furniture. Why did this house unsettle her so? Why did she feel like leaving her belongings in the trunk? The armoire was empty—she checked—and so everything was ready for her to move in.

Except she didn't want to. Which was ridiculous. She wanted to see Teiryn again, she was desperate to see him. Thoughts of him had sustained her in all the days they had been apart. She had missed the feel of his arms around her, his lips on hers. The warmth of his breath on her neck in the darkness of the night as he slept. Just thinking about him, about being apart from him, pained her. But she'd see him soon. She was sure he'd send word as soon as he knew the coach had brought her to the house.

Yet something in her rebelled. This house was hers to use, but it wasn't hers. Like another sort of marriage bracelet, it bound her to Teiryn by laws of property. Perhaps she was no longer legally his, but the house was, and she was in it.

That was it. The freedom she had cherished on the road was diminished by the house. By living in it. But if she didn't stay here, where would she go? And how would she tell Teiryn?

Lythera sat on the wide windowsill and looked outside at the street and the people passing each other, some quickly, others more slowly. All over again, Lythera saw the finger-flick greeting, the carved buttons, the hair ribbons such as her own. In this, the largest city of Evandia, there had to be a place for her. In Rayn Avinon, surely a woman could find her own way. Her own place. A place that didn't belong to Teiryn.

She thought of the pouch Teiryn had given her. She hadn't had to use any of the money. Why couldn't she find somewhere else to stay, a room to let, just like any other visitor to the city? This house was far too large for one person, anyway.

Guilt gnawed at her. She owed Teiryn so much. He had treated her kindly, fought for her with his ministers when they didn't want her to eat beside him in the dining hall, stayed with her after her miscarriage. He had given her money in case she needed it, and provided this house for her to use. Bought her the hair ribbon, given her a morning gift. What right had she to turn his gifts away?

Besides, what had she done for him besides lose his baby? She didn't care what Teiryn said about that being his fault, she knew she must have done something wrong. Especially since she'd had the care of Wenvia and Metricia and the nestriana. All over again, her grief welled up and threatened to overwhelm her. She took a deep breath and closed her eyes. This was foolish. The baby had died and that was that. She hadn't done anything that she knew of to cause that, and neither had Teiryn. It had just happened. If she could do everything over, she wouldn't do anything differently. So there was no use in berating herself for her loss.

Lythera got up and opened her trunk again. She needed to unpack, to find a way to feel comfortable in this house. Though her unsettled feeling did not leave, she ignored it.

The light had hardly begun to dim outside before Inveora was at her door announcing dinner. Lythera, already bored and glad of the distraction, followed the expressionless woman down the steps and through several well-appointed rooms until they arrived at a huge dining area. A single plate had been set on a long cherry table that could seat at least thirty. A servant stood behind her chair, prepared to pull it out for her.

Lythera balked. It might be an honor to be allowed to live in such luxury, but she could hardly force herself to eat in this lovely room all by herself, staring at dark red walls and magnificent oil paintings, gold candlesticks and carved cherry chairs. Listening to the sound of her own chewing and nothing else! She couldn't enjoy a meal under such conditions.

"No, thank you," she said firmly. Inveora opened her mouth, but Lythera cut her off. "I'm honored by your attentive service, but I simply can't eat in this room by myself. It's much too grand for one person. Surely there's a smaller breakfast nook, or a table in the kitchen, where I can eat."

The man behind her chair frowned. Inveora's face reflected confusion. Since it had never reflected anything else in the short time Lythera had known her, Lythera was relieved to see the woman could be startled into showing something on her face.

"It's probably untoward," she continued, "but please, couldn't I eat somewhere a bit more informal? It's not that I'm ungrateful, it's just I can hardly imagine eating in this room. It's so beautiful and, well, not a room to put one in a good appetite if one is alone."

Slowly, Inveora nodded. "There's a table in a side room off the kitchen. Usually only the servants eat there, or we use it to stack dishes when we're finished washing them. It's not fancy."

"I'd love it, I'm sure," said Lythera. "Please, show me the way."

The other servant had lost his frown and just looked doubtful. Lythera walked past him as Inveora strolled out of the room. Like it or not, the new resident of the house would not fit into the same mold any previous residents had.

The smaller room was delightful. Painted a sunny yellow with dried herbs hanging in a window which overlooked a backyard flower garden. Birds hopped along the ground outside, pecking at objects in the grass. A wall surrounded the entire yard so that it appeared to be a small patch of peaceful seclusion even though it was in the midst of the bustling capital.

Even here, the sunlight was tinted blue; the radiance of the astar in the center of the city caressed even the birds in the back yards of the nobles.

"It's beautiful," said Lythera, meaning both the room and the view. She sat down at the simple oak table. The servants placed her meal in front of her along with an opened bottle of wine, and retreated.

Lythera ate well from all the dishes put before her. She lingered over her wine, drinking most of the bottle from a small crystal glass etched with the Segrithr sigil, and ate until she felt she could burst. Instead of getting up and returning to her room, though, she stared out the window at the garden. Most of the flowers appeared to be the same varieties of roses that grew in the palace gardens. Creeping vines climbed trellises around a walkway that was interrupted by charming wooden benches. Lythera would have liked to explore the garden, but she didn't know how to get out there. She'd ask Inveora. For now, it was enough to watch the birds, and follow the flights of the bees as they visited the red blossoms on the vines.

"Mistress," said Inveora.

Lythera turned to her. The housemaid held out an envelope to her. "This arrived for you."

"Thank you."

Inveora turned to go.

"Wait," said Lythera. "Could you tell me how to reach the garden? It's so lovely I'd like to walk in it."

Inveora pointed behind Lythera. "Through the kitchen is the best way. There's a door to the garden in the salon, but it's kept locked unless there's a party being held in the house. If you want to use it, the house warden would be happy to open it for you, and then wait to lock it again when you return. The door in the kitchen is unlocked dawn to dusk."

"Thank you. There's no need to bother the house warden."

Inveora nodded and left. Lythera took the envelope and walked through the kitchen and past several startled-looking cooks. The door was propped open to allow the fresh cool air of the summer evening into the stifling kitchen. Lythera stepped over the threshold and strode into the yard.

The shadows were long but it was still quite light as she strolled through the garden nearest the door. The small garden was aromatic and obviously used to grow herbs for the cooks. Beyond that, the flowers began. Lythera walked to a bench and sat down to open her envelope.

On the front of the envelope was one word, "Lythera," in a flowing script. Inside was a card written in a different, tighter hand. It read. "I've counted the days until I could see you again. We will be together, my Verrika. Tonight."

Lythera's heart skipped a beat. She blushed and returned the card to the envelope. Teiryn was coming. She shivered with anticipation, and gratitude. His schedule was always busy, yet he never failed to find time to spend with her. He found ways to show his love to her every time they were together. It was time now for her to find ways to show him her love.

Lythera didn't stay in the garden long; her yearning for Teiryn was too strong. She went to her room and sat in the window in the gathering twilight, waiting, imagining the things they would say to each other, the kisses, the caresses.

Near dark, a coach pulled up in front of the house and disbursed one cloaked passenger. A few royal guards rode behind the carriage. The coach pulled away and the passenger entered the house, though the guards remained. In only a few moments, the door to her room opened, and he was there.

She drank in the sight of him, not having had such pleasure in ten days. His lined face, his night-black hair with flecks of gray. His dark eyes. She couldn't stop staring.

He seemed just as entranced with her; it was several moments before he came into the room and threw his arms around her. The moment he touched her, she felt a shock of relief, of love. The grief she had carried for weeks slipped away in the comfort of his arms.

Thoughts of what she would say, or what he would say, vanished from Lythera's mind in an instant. Now was the time for feeling the warmth of his lips touching hers, the scratchiness of his beard against her cheek. His hands fumbled with the ties on her dress, and she giggled as she helped him undress her.

Eagerly, she helped him shrug off his cloak and shirt. The room seemed to have become very warm and small, just large enough to contain the two of them. Everything she wanted and needed was within the circle of his arms. He embraced her and she forgot the world contained anything, or anyone, else.

15

When she woke up at the first faint glimmers of dawn the next morning, Lythera discovered one of Teiryn's feet draped over her legs and an elbow poking her in the ribs. She smiled and turned slightly in the soft bed. Just enough to take some of the pressure away from her rib, but not enough to get away from Teiryn's touch. The gentle sound of his breathing soothed her back to sleep.

The morning had brightened considerably when she woke again and realized Teiryn was out of bed and dressed. He was just fastening his cloak. She smiled at him and climbed out of the bed.

He smiled back and leaned down to kiss her. "You look ravishing, my dear," he said with a slight chuckle. "If you're not careful, you'll entice me to stay the entire day here with you."

Lythera hugged him. "Why would I wish for anything else? Ten days without you was enough. I don't want to be without you for so long ever again."

He sighed and stepped back slightly. "There are still duties today I can't get away from. And a reception this evening that the Morovolo ambassador is giving. It's their version of the Harvest fest, though it precedes ours by a couple of weeks. If he were at home, the ambassador would be in a capital that was celebrating in the streets—fairs and games, booths, friendly competitions, poetry readings, music. And food and drink of every sort. In the evenings, the revelry goes indoors, and everyone wears their best and travels from one party to another and dances all night long."

"And so the ambassador does this here?"

"No," he said and smiled. "But he does throw a party. I suppose he misses all the celebrating when he's not at home. I know I'd miss Harvest and the New Year celebrations if I were an ambassador somewhere else."

Lythera thought about that as she grabbed one of her traveling gowns and threw it over her head. Though she was no longer shy about being naked in front of Teiryn, it did seem strange to be naked while he was fully clothed and preparing to leave.

"Oh, yes, there's something I was going to tell you last night," said Teiryn, "but, uh, I was distracted." He came up behind her and wrapped his arms around her waist. She leaned against him slightly and looked out the window at the bright summer morning. He shifted uncomfortably and said nothing more, as if he had bad news he did not wish to speak out loud.

"Yes?" she said, wondering what he had to be so hesitant about.

"Master Jarris came to me and told me he has found a position for you at the Aynwren School, teaching languages to students who are having difficulties keeping up with the rest of their classes."

Lythera's heart soared. "Oh, that's wonderful news! I thought perhaps something was wrong."

"No," Teiryn said after a pause. "No, nothing's wrong. I'm not clear why you should want to work at a school. You can have everything you desire here."

"This is a lovely house, but there's no one else here. I wouldn't have anything to *do* with my days. This way, I can talk with other scholars, who certainly know more than my old tutor, and I can learn all the things he didn't even know. I can help others learn, too. It's perfect!"

Teiryn was silent. Lythera turned in his arms so she could look up into his ebony eyes. "What's wrong?"

He started to say something, stopped, and frowned. Finally, he said, "I guess I never thought about what Brenicia did all day. I know she enjoyed riding, and growing flowers, and embroidery. I assume she gathered with other women and participated in court gossip, like Metricia and the others still do today."

"You assume?" Lythera was puzzled. "Didn't you ever talk to her about her days? About who she saw, and what they shared?"

"Of course," he said quickly, but the frown only deepened.

"Then when I see you again, I can tell you about the school, and about what Master Jarris would have me doing there."

Teiryn kissed the top of her head. "I really must go."

"I know." She kissed him one more time and then let him go. He walked through the door without a backward glance. Lythera watched him enter the coach below—it had been nearby and approached the house at the doorman's signal. The coach rumbled off down the street.

Someone knocked on her door. "Mistress?" It was Inveora.

"Yes?"

"Your bath is ready and breakfast is waiting."

Lythera smiled, surprised at how hungry the mention of breakfast made her. She followed Inveora to the bathing room, bathed and dressed quickly, and ate at the same table where she had dinner the night before. Then she sat in the garden and waited for Master Jarris. She was eager to go to the school and learn about her duties, but a knot of fear kept her from truly enjoying the morning and the songs of the birds that sat in the trees and hopped among the bushes. She'd never tutored anyone before, much less several people. How would she do it? Would there be anyone to help her? She hoped Master Jarris would have the answers.

It wasn't until nearly noon that Master Jarris finally arrived. Inveora showed him into the garden from the kitchen door and he smiled and waved as he spotted Lythera on a bench nearby.

Lythera stood and smiled back. She walked up to him and hugged him briefly. "It's good to see you again," she said.

"And you," he said. "Did the king tell you I was coming?"

"Yes. He said you found a position for me."

Jarris nodded. "Let's sit and I'll explain some of the particulars. Besides, we have something to discuss. I know you were avoiding me before you lost the babe, but it's time we talked about that sundial."

Lythera's heart lurched. She didn't want to talk about the object. The nauvynnor. She didn't like the way odd dreams and old words just came to her. It was unnerving. She wanted to have her own life now, something of her own, and it seemed that the past would take that from her. Would assign her a fate she had no choice in and wanted no part of.

Lythera walked to a bench under a large oak tree and sat down. Jarris followed. "But first, the school. I had a bit more trouble than I thought I would in arguing with the schoolmaster that you should be considered for the opening. I say this to let you know right away that there are some who oppose your appointment. But you are so talented that I knew you could be invaluable on the faculty, so I told him that if he wouldn't accept you, I'd quit myself."

"Master Jarris, you shouldn't say such things," said Lythera. Shock warred with confusion in her heart. She loved the old man dearly, even if his strange hobby and the artifacts it brought troubled her, and she knew he liked her, but she'd had no idea he would go to such lengths. "Surely there would be another position somewhere if this one weren't available."

"Yes, yes," he said irritably. "But this is perfect. You'll begin by tutoring some students who are having problems with their Old Evandic. You may wish to offer private lessons in any of the other languages you know; they are all part of the school curriculum, and few students gain much proficiency in any of them these days, in my opinion. And I believe the old languages will become more important to us in time. We must make sure the young are educated correctly. It is the least we can do to prepare them for what is coming."

Lythera avoided the subject of change. She didn't want to discuss the nauvynnor or the odd voice in the library. "And when will I start?"

Jarris rubbed the side of his face with a withered hand. "Oh, let's see, this afternoon is when the four students in the Old Evandic class meet. They meet three times a week at four in the afternoon, and another instructor has been filling in until now, but he's no expert in languages, so the students haven't learned much under him. Oh, yes," he said with a frown, "the schoolmaster—his name's Sanborl Geryton—insisted that your first month will be unsalaried. I couldn't argue him out of it, I'm afraid, but I agreed finally, since it seemed the only way to get him to accept you."

Lythera's gratitude toward Jarris melted away slightly. An uneasy knot settled in her stomach. "But, Master Jarris, don't the other instructors get paid for their first month's work?"

"Certainly!"

"But not me?"

"Well, no, he wouldn't agree to that."

"Then perhaps I should turn down the position and look elsewhere," said Lythera. "It's true I haven't worked in a school before, but there's no reason I should work without pay if no one else does."

"I made the decision, and it's final," said Jarris. "Besides, there's no need for you to worry about anything. Your living expenses are being taken care of by the king, so what's the first month's salary to you? Women don't usually worry about such, especially you, my dear. Teiryn will provide anything you need."

Lythera's happiness with the day faded. She had thought of Master Jarris as a friend, and she knew he was; she was sure he meant well. But she was surprised to have him dismiss her concerns so lightly. All over again, men were making decisions about her life without asking her, without considering her desires or her goals for her life. She was trapped again, just when she had started to take the reins of her life for herself.

"It's just, you should have asked," she said. "It's to be my job, I should make the decisions concerning it."

Jarris shook his head. "Unnecessary, my dear. I've taken everything into consideration and made the best decision for you. Also, I'm hoping you will come tonight to the meeting of my own private study group. We work on texts the students never get to see. Artifacts, too. I know you were upset by the sundial. But that's just why we need to know more about it! What is it, and why did it respond to you—and in modern Evandic! These questions are too important to lightly set aside simply because you are uneasy. Also, there's another woman in the group. Surely that will please you. Please say you'll come."

Lythera hesitated, but her conscience goaded her to accept. Master Jarris was so worried that Evandia was in danger, that a new upheaval would destroy many peoples' lives, perhaps kill thousands, and she was being obstinate because she didn't like what it might mean to her. What kind of person did that make her? Not one she could respect. "All right."

Jarris smiled and patted her on the arm. He got up and leaned heavily on his stick. "The doorman can hire a cab for you to bring you to the school. If you arrive by three, I can introduce you to the headmaster before your class starts."

"I'll be there," said Lythera. She watched him go, torn between excitement and irritation. Up until just over four months ago, she had never questioned that her father had every right to decide her life for her, even to sell her. With the marriage bracelet on her wrist, she had not questioned Teiryn's right, and, indeed, any other male Segrithr's right, to watch her and set limits on where she could go and what she could do. She didn't have to like it, but she had accepted it.

She had thought, while daydreaming in the coach on the way back to the capital, that now that she had no father, and no marriage bracelet, and some coins in her possession, she could start a new life, her own life, one not bounded by the decisions of men. Or at least not as bounded as it had been. Yet Teiryn provided her the house. Jarris found her an appointment, and even agreed to the terms of her employment. Even getting a cab would require the doorman's help. Everywhere she turned, from large arenas in her life to the small, there was a man deciding what she would do. When she would do it. Where she would live. How she would live.

Lythera went back to her room. Perhaps the woman in Jarris' study group would be a source for her, someone to talk to about these new thoughts and new dreams, about how she could stretch herself and find a true place in the world.

Lythera went back to her perch on the windowsill and watched the morning slip away in the bright colors worn by the pedestrians and the ever-present blue sparkling aura that covered the city of Rayn Avinon.

16

The coach dropped her off a few minutes early in front of the Aynwren School. Unlike the white and gray marbles that covered the buildings in the central area, the stones of this building were a softer, rosier color, interspersed with a darker stone similar to that which had been used in the city gate. The school's gate was wrought of iron and tied open. The sign on the gate read AYNWREN SCHOOL, PRIVATE CLASSES AVAILBLE. SCHOOLMASTER SANBORL GERYTON.

Lythera stepped inside the paved schoolyard. Small weeds with bright yellow flowers peeked out from cracks in the stones.

"Are you lost?" someone asked. Lythera was reminded of her first day in the palace, when Evinard asked her if she should be in the stable. She smiled and turned to see a short, portly gentleman staring up at her. He was frowning.

"No," she said. "I'm here to see Master Jarris. He said I should meet him here at three. Are you Master Geryton?"

The man snorted. His short gray beard matched his eyes, though what hair was left on his head was still dark. He wore a strange long burgundy robe with gold roping down the front in two parallel lines. "No, I'm Instructor Reyston. Well, I suppose there's no harm in you waiting out here, girl."

Lythera continued to smile in a friendly fashion, wondering if Reyston would amble off, but he seemed to prefer to stay in the courtyard to keep an eye on her. His eyes kept falling toward her wrist. Finally, Lythera decided she should break the silence.

"My name's Lythera," she said. For a brief moment, she felt like adding her father's name, since it would mark her as a higher social class than Reyston, who could not even put the title Master before his name. But that was ridiculous. She had put that name behind her. She didn't need titles now, anyway. "Master Jarris has found me a position here."

Reyston jerked his head to his right. "Servants enter through the back door."

"I'll keep that in mind if I need to find a servant," said Lythera, momentarily angry, but determined not to let such comments get to her. She was sure she would hear more as the days went by. "But I'm to be an instructor in languages, so I'll use the front door like anyone else."

Reyston choked back a laugh. "An instructor? Jarris is joking with you, girl. Doesn't seem like him, he's such a sincere old stick. But, really, you don't seriously believe you'll be working here?"

"Why not?" Jarris asked from the top of the steps that led into the building. He also wore a burgundy robe, but his sported six gold ropes down the front.

Reyston glanced at him once and nodded. "Master Jarris. You can't be serious. A female instructor? The parents will be most upset."

"The parents won't care—much—as long as their boys are getting the education they're paying for. Come along, Lythera, Sanborl's waiting to meet you."

Lythera nodded to Reyston, who stared back at her with a pensive expression. Lythera climbed up the steps and entered the building. She noted the crumbling carvings around the doorframe had originally been of roses intertwined with lilies. According to the lists she had translated back in the palace library, that meant success and luck. Lythera took comfort from the symbolism.

Unlike the house where she was staying, the school building was dark on the inside, with tiny windows and few lamps to light the way. Layers of soot blackened the ceiling that no one had bothered to clean, and the stone floors had been walked on so long they had ruts worn into their hard surfaces. The parents might be paying for an education for their boys, but none of the funds seemed to be going toward the upkeep of the building. It reminded Lythera of Halevern Hall: dusty, dank, and dark.

Perhaps the school did not have enough students to afford its own upkeep, which seemed odd to Lythera, since the palace record-keeper taught here. Surely everyone would prefer to have their sons taught by such a man. Or, perhaps Jarris was right about the state of education in Evandia, and that the parents simply were not sending sons to schools that often anymore. Sadness swept over Lythera at the thought.

"Sanborl's office is just this way," said Jarris. He led her up some narrow, twisting stairs to the second floor, which was slightly brighter than the first, but no cleaner. The door directly across the hall from the steps was labeled SCHOOLMASTER in paint that was faded nearly to invisibility in the dim light.

Jarris swung the door open and went straight in. Lythera followed. The office on the other side of the door was cramped and dusty. Small tables groaned under stacks of papers. In the center of the room was a desk, also hidden under piles of papers, and behind that sat a large man with flame-red hair and piercing green eyes. He had on the same style of burgundy robe as Jarris and Reyston, but along with the six golden ropes he also wore a gold chain around his neck with a heavy sigil pendant at the end. It rested on his chest.

"Good afternoon, Lythera," said the schoolmaster. "Welcome to our school. I hope you'll find teaching here a fulfilling experience." His voice was sweet, like soft silk against the skin.

Lythera smiled, a little awed by Sanborl's presence. He behaved like a man who liked what power he had, and was comfortable with it. "Good afternoon, Master Sanborl. I am looking forward to it. I understand my first class is in an hour."

Sanborl spread out his hands. "It's not so much a class as an extra study session. The four boys in it haven't learned much so far and if they don't get their grades up, they'll be dismissed at the end of the autumn term." The schoolmaster seemed not to care if the students picked up their grades or not, which Lythera thought was odd. Didn't the tuitions of the students pay for the instructors' salaries?

"You'd be glad to see them go?" she asked.

Sanborl shrugged. "These four are not our best students, and they're always in trouble. They cost more to control and teach than their parents pay to send them here. I'd be tempted to dismiss them in any case, but one of them is the son of nao-Lord Ulfton, so the situation is more delicate. A few boyish pranks may have to be overlooked, but poor grades certainly can't, and the lord will have no room to argue with us over that."

Lythera didn't know what to say. It sounded as if Master Sanborl wanted the boys to fail. If so, then he must not expect her to be able to teach them anything. Perhaps that's why he didn't want to pay her the first month of her salary—he thought he could fail the boys and dismiss her, too, before he would owe her anything. Well, if that were his plan, then she would show him that she was not that easy to dismiss.

"I'll do my best," she said.

He smiled, but his eyes belied the sincerity he appeared to wish to project. A seed of anger took root in Lythera's mind. Sanborl might not take her seriously, but he would have to eventually. She was going to succeed. "That's all we can ask. Now I'll ask Jarris to show you to the room you'll be using."

Jarris led Lythera down the hall, around a corner, and up one more flight of rickety stairs. The third floor corridor was completely unlit. "The study rooms are up here," said Jarris. "Woefully cold in the winter, I'm afraid. But there's a window to let the heat out in the summer."

Jarris opened the fourth door down the corridor on the left and motioned for Lythera to go inside. She did so. The room was small, with only a round table surrounded by six rather rickety looking chairs in the center. A small trunk sat in the corner. "I already put some supplies in the trunk," said Jarris. "Fresh ink jars, parchment, and a few texts for you to use. Also, a book for you to use to keep track of assignments and grades."

"Thank you, Master Jarris."

"Look over the texts until the students arrive. They can tell you where they are in their studies. Don't expect much," Jarris cautioned.

"All right."

Jarris closed the door, leaving Lythera alone in the room. She went to the trunk and opened it. Everything was neatly stored in it just as Jarris had promised. Lythera got out the quills, ink jars, and parchment. Most of the parchment had already been used on one side—she supposed it was too expensive to use fresh parchment for classroom work.

Lythera looked through one of the books and selected a text for the boys to translate. She copied it neatly onto four pieces of parchment.

A knock came at the door.

"Yes?" called Lythera.

The door opened and a lanky man walked in. His golden hair matched the pair of golden ropes on his burgundy instructor's gown. "Good fortune."

"And to you."

The man came into the room and sat down in the chair opposite Lythera. "I don't mean to stay long, I just heard there was a new instructor and decided to come by to welcome you to the school."

Lythera smiled. "Thank you. You're the first, unless you count the headmaster's welcome when I was introduced to him in his office."

The man looked rueful. "I suppose that's to be expected. We've never had a female instructor before. I'm Kavinel, from Stowvald. I've been here two years now, teaching languages and history."

"I'm glad to meet you," said Lythera. "From Instructor Reyston's example, I thought all the instructors might be unhappy to see me here."

Kavinel nodded slowly. "Some, certainly. But, in the end, what can they do? Sanborl can't do much with his uncle, what with Jarris being the palace record-keeper."

"His uncle? He didn't say anything about that."

"Oh, yes, Jarris' younger sister married a younger son of a younger son of the Geryton family. I think it was actually Sanborl's great-great grandfather who was the last lord in his direct line. The Gerytons have a small holding in the west but I'm sure they have no idea who Sanborl is— the connection is too remote. I think the hereditary title is sei-Lord and the main crop there is apples and, um, they raise fish in huge man-made ponds."

Lythera smiled at the speech. "You sound like an instructor," she said. Her tutor had been the same, dropping facts and figures as they occurred to him, whether it was germane to the conversation or not.

Kavinel flushed slightly. He was as pale as Nestira and the blush was just as obvious. His muddy brown eyes showed a glint of humor. "Can't help it," he muttered.

"I suppose not. I'm sure I'll sound the same in time."

"Perhaps. Well, Lythera, I should go. I don't want to keep you from preparing for class. But if you like, perhaps we could get something to eat after your class. Jarris said something at our group's last meeting about you joining us, and you'll want to have something to fortify yourself before one of our study sessions. They can get quite intense."

"I, well," Lythera began. She was flustered and unsure of the protocol. It wouldn't be seemly for her to accompany a man to dinner as Lord Halevern's daughter or Teiryn's consort. But she had no father anymore, and she no longer wore Teiryn's bracelet. What would a woman with no rank be free to do without commitment?

"I doubt Jarris will be there; the man hardly ever eats," said Kavinel. "But Avaidan might. No doubt Oluraun will be there. You can't keep him away from food with a team of horses."

Lythera relaxed. It seemed the study group often met beforehand for dinner. At least she had met Avaidan before. "All right," she said. Then she realized where the money Teiryn had given her was: back at the house. She had never had to pay for a meal before. "Oh, I'm sorry, but I can't. I didn't bring any coins with me today."

Kavinel stood. "No worries. I'll make sure whomever's there provides a coin or two for your meal. Consider it a welcome gift to our study group."

Lythera blushed, grateful for his kindness. "Thank you. I'm looking forward to meeting the group tonight."

Kavinel left. Lythera sat at the table and waited for her students. They were not long in arriving and came all at once in a flurry of elbows and knees and awkward adolescent energy. The boys stood just inside the doorway and gaped at her.

Lythera stood and kept her nervousness to herself, "I'm Lythera, and I'm your new instructor. Come, have a seat, and tell me your names."

A boy with dark red hair and wide shoulders pushed his way to the front. "I'm Gelsinar Ulfdon. My father's Yairven Lord Ulfdon."

Lythera bit back a childish retort that her father was a lord, too. She merely nodded and the boy sat down. The others all sat as well.

"Brellin," said a skinny lad with a face full of freckles.

"Eald." He was as skinny as Brellin, but his coloring was much darker.

"Janlon." The last was the shortest of the four. Unlike the other three, who were busy staring directly at Lythera, Janlon's gaze never left his lap.

Lythera handed out the copies of the text she had made. "Here. I'd like to see where your skill levels are. Please translate this."

The boys each took a copy and stared at it. "I don't know most of these words," said Eald.

"Then guess," said Lythera. "I'm not going to help you with this. I want to see how well you can do on your own."

The boys obediently began their work. Lythera kept her gaze fixed on then, wondering how much trouble they were going to be in the weeks ahead. Right now, they were unsure of her. But she was not convinced their obedience was likely to endure.

The class hour had nearly passed before Lythera collected the papers. She looked over them. None of the boys had done very well, though Gelsinar had at least managed to translate the first sentence almost entirely correctly. It was evident the boys had no idea how to decline a noun or an adjective, and two of them had mixed their past and present tenses.

"I see," she said as she put down the papers. "How much schooling have you had in Old Evandic?"

The boys shrugged. Eald volunteered, "Our last teacher didn't know much, and was half-blind. He couldn't tell what we were doing in the back of the room most of the time. Some days, he never even knew it if we skipped class. And the study instructor didn't know much Old Evandic anyway, so he couldn't teach much."

Janlon hissed Eald to silence and slapped him on the arm.

"I see," said Lythera. "So, I need to know something. Do any of you want to learn Old Evandic? And if not, why are you even in school?"

Gelsinar leaned back in his chair. "I'm here because my father sends me. He says I should do something with my life besides go to the races."

"Well, shouldn't you?"

"Why? My oldest brother will have to give me an allowance."

"You wish to live on your brother's allowance?" asked Lythera. "What if you want a wife, or children, or a house? Will your allowance cover those expenses as well as your basic needs?"

Gelsinar frowned. The other boys looked at each other as if the thought had not occurred to them before.

"When you leave this school, where will you go?" asked Lythera. "Home, to sit for the rest of your life as nothing but a drain on your family? On the road, as an itinerant musician or tinker? In a roadside inn, as a hostler? Have you given any thought to how you want to live, and what it will take to get what you want?"

The boys all were suddenly busy looking at their hands. Lythera let the silence stretch out for several long moments.

"If you want to learn, then I'll teach you," she said with a confidence she did not feel. She had never tutored before—what made her think she could do it now? And with students with no desire to learn! "But if you don't want to, then don't come back. For those who do come back, well, next time we'll start with basic vocabulary and strong verbs." She glanced at their papers again briefly. Considering how little they claimed to have been present or paying attention in their classes, she decided they had learned quite a bit. "I see that most of that will be review. But we can move on to more difficult issues quickly if you're up to the challenge."

Janlon snickered. Brellin rolled his eyes. Eald nodded. "I'm up for any challenge," he said. He brushed dark hair out of his eyes. "No woman is going to know more about Old Evandic than me and I'm not getting kicked out of this school to make Old Firehair happy." He fixed the other three in his gaze one at a time. Then as one, the four turned to her.

Gelsinar stood up with unconscious grace and a touch of hauteur. "Until next time, then, Instructor. We'll see who learns enough Old Evandic to satisfy the schoolmaster." He walked out of the room. The other three followed him without a word.

Lythera took a deep breath after they were gone. She was not surprised to find she was shaking.

17

Teiryn walked into the main palace ballroom nearly two hours after the festivities had started. The paperwork that he had let sit during Lythera's illness continued to require his attention—it seemed he had two days of work to do for every day she had been ill, and he had not been able to leave it before now. But he had managed to get away at last. Now he looked forward to an evening simply mingling with others, eating and drinking, and maybe even dancing. His heart felt a pang that Lythera was not here with him tonight, but at least she was nearby. By the New Year celebration at the beginning of spring, he hoped her presence in the city would be well-accepted enough that she could attend the festivities with him.

He walked across the ballroom floor, smiling at those who smiled at him, kissing a few women on the cheek and complimenting them on their couture. The familiarity of the mindless side of court life was a kind of balm over the heartache he'd suffered over the past month. First his child's death, then Lythera's illness, then her absence. But now his life had returned to a state in which he could be content, even happy. He did not have to try to find a smile out of the depths of sadness as he had some years. This year his good spirits were genuine.

In fact, this year his spirits were higher than they'd been in ages. Which was strange, because he'd spent so much time at Lythera's side, night and day, and his schedule had been so crazy, he'd just assumed he'd be exhausted. He'd barely gotten to ride, couldn't concentrate on anything, and had grabbed whatever food he could out of the kitchen. But instead of exhausted, he'd begun to feel invigorated, even energized. He supposed that came from having a purpose again; someone to love and protect.

Whatever the reason, for the first time in years, he felt light on his feet and ready to face his ministers, whatever Novardan was planning for Harvest, and the mountains of paperwork that needed his signature. For the first time in years, he felt truly alive again.

Alive, and reunited with Lythera. And now, he had a pleasant evening to look forward to, as the Morovolo intention of setting guests at ease was paramount in everything they did, including parties. Teiryn could look forward to an evening of good conversation, pleasant music, and exquisite food and drink.

The room had been decorated in the royal black and gold of Morovolo, even to the yellow flowers that graced every table. Palace servants, who passed among the guests with trays of Morovolo delicacies and drink, wore black and gold sashes for the occasion. The candles and lamps that had been lit to illuminate the party gave everything a cheerful golden glow.

"Good evening, Teiryn," said a familiar voice. Teiryn's good mood faltered slightly. He turned to Lord Gomeril. The portly man was dressed in his house's colors of teal and bronze, not too different in the candlelight from the dark green Teiryn had affected for the night. As always, Gomeril's clothes were impeccably tailored to be as flattering as possible to his large frame. A large topaz brooch was pinned to the ist-Lord's shirt.

"Good evening, Lord Gomeril," said Teiryn. He had never quite felt relaxed enough with this lord to use his first name. He thought Gomeril liked that, actually. "Enjoying the ambassador's party?"

"Of course." Gomeril spread his arms wide and nearly swiped off a lady's hat in the process. "The Morovolo always provide the best for their guests. I look forward to the Selandi red wine every year—it's so hard to find. I'm not sure how the ambassador does it."

"I'm sure the Selanadi ambassador has something to do with that," said Teiryn. "I haven't yet had an opportunity to sample it myself this evening, but I'll make a point to do so on your recommendation."

Gomeril smiled and bowed slightly. "Thank you. May I also offer my congratulations on your recent victory over certain, oh, shall we say, court peccadilloes."

Teiryn went cold. "Whatever could you mean?" He didn't think Lythera was a secret, could hardly keep her a secret, but he hadn't really considered that having her in the city would be so interesting that court gossip could have spread across the palace and the city so quickly. She had only arrived yesterday! He'd known that eventually people would begin to drop hints to him about it, but he hadn't considered anyone would be bold enough to say something so openly so soon. He cursed himself for not considering the matter long enough to have thought up a few pleasant non-answers for the inquisitive.

Gomeril smiled again, the smile of a fox who has the mouse sighted and in range of a leap. "Your happiness concerns me greatly, Teiryn, whether you realize it or not. I'll say baldly that I liked the young lady and was sad to see her go. A spirit like that should not be wasted in the provinces, in some decayed House's darkened hall. Perhaps by next year, you'll be bringing her to the ambassador's party."

Teiryn pasted a smile on his face, wondering what Gomeril wanted with Lythera. He had noted, during her tenure in the palace, that Gomeril had never stood in Teiryn's way when he wanted something for her. And now he plainly admitted he thought she belonged in the city. But Gomeril was a man to watch. What did he really want? He had to have a reason. Ulindein Gomeril might be a man who loved his food and wine too much, but when it came to court politics, he was a master such as Teiryn could never hope to be.

"I'm glad my lady's presence pleases you," he said. "Now, if you'll excuse me, I would like to find the host and thank him for his efforts."

Gomeril bowed and retreated. Teiryn, disturbed and a little confused by the other man's attitude, turned and immediately gasped. Across the room stood a woman who could have been his queen. Brenicia, with her wavy golden hair and brilliant blue eyes, her willowy form and delicate pink-tinted cheeks. The wide mouth and oval face. Teiryn was frozen to the spot. How was this possible? His queen was dead. This woman could not be her.

Yet he could not drag his eyes away from her. The woman approached him, every move, every glance, exactly like Brenicia. The lamplight turned her bright hair to flame. He trembled and could not advance, could not retreat. Even the pale pink of her gown and the opals around her neck were Brenicia's favorites; she had always worn pink and opals to court functions.

The woman glided up to him, her perfume preceding her slightly. The scent of rose wafted from her pale skin. Brenicia's favorite scent. Teiryn's knees almost buckled and he grasped the back of a chair for support. He did not believe in the ghosts that roamed the dark tales his older cousins had told him when he was small. But here was Brenicia, as beautiful and delicate as she had been in life.

The woman smiled and bowed her head but said nothing. Teiryn's tongue was frozen in his mouth as his feet were affixed to the floor beneath him. Brenicia. It was not possible.

"Teiryn, I see you've met my latest find," announced a familiar voice that grated on Teiryn's ears. Novardan. The other man approached from the direction of the drink table, wine glass in hand. He laughed at Teiryn's expression and clapped him on the shoulder. "Thought this would please you. This is Eithnira Nevelein, a third cousin, I believe, of your late queen. It seems some of the Hellfren traits do breed true."

The girl curtseyed. Teiryn bowed automatically, but still couldn't collect his thoughts. He knew he was staring, and that the people around him were beginning to notice.

"Ah, welcome to the court," he finally managed to say with a shaky voice.

Eithnira blushed. "Thank ye, Sire. I have never been anywhere so lovely as this afore."

Whatever spell her appearance had on him, her voice broke it. Instead of Brenicia's soft tones, Eithnira had a raspy voice and spoke in a thick coastal accent. Teiryn blinked, the image of his dead queen banished from his mind immediately. He let go of the chair and his heart started beating again.

"The palace is lovely," he said. "Living here, I often forget. But when I've been away and return, I realize it all over again."

"Well, I'll just let the two of you get acquainted," said Novardan.

Teiryn realized where this was heading, though of course the presence of Novardan and the resemblance to Brenicia should have warned him that his cousin had a new plan to coax more women into Teiryn's bed. If Gomeril knew Lythera was in the city, then no doubt Novardan knew as well, and this was one of his ways of making Teiryn aware that at least some of his counselors were determined he would give her up.

He couldn't let Novardan leave him alone with this woman. Her voice wasn't that of his queen, but in every other way, she might well have been a copy. He didn't want her near him, didn't want her reminding him of what he had lost. "I'm sorry, cousin, but I haven't yet had a chance to talk with our guest of honor. Please, continue to introduce the lady to others and make sure she enjoys herself. She has obviously come a long way. Enjoy the evening, Eithnira. Now, you will excuse me." He bowed to Eithnira and turned away to seek Ambassador Lororo before Novardan could say anything. Tearing his eyes away from the image of his queen was one of the hardest things he had ever done.

Fortunately, the ambassador was not far away. Teiryn welcomed the chance to talk to someone who suddenly seemed more familiar than anyone in the room. Gomeril and Novardan had shaken him. Teiryn wanted to escape their maneuverings and carefully crafted plans. Talking to Ambassador Lororo would be a welcome relief, especially since the Morovolo valued good conversation which put the people around them at ease. Sometimes, Teiryn wished he could find more of that among his own people.

The ambassador stood near a divan on which a young woman was sitting. The animated motions of his hands seemed to indicate he was telling her quite a tale. Teiryn hesitated, then approached. Lororo noticed him and stopped his story immediately.

"Good evening, Sire," he said. "Welcome to the celebration."

"Please, don't let me interrupt."

The young woman rose gracefully. She looked familiar but Teiryn could not place her. Probably a younger daughter of some noble who was not at court often. "I've taken up enough of the ambassador's time as it is," she said with a smile. "And I see my father approaching with the latest young man he wishes me to dance with. Excuse me." She was gone in the swish of sky-blue skirts.

Teiryn and Lororo bowed to the lady as she turned and left. "A fine lady," said the ambassador. "I hope the young man is a good dancer."

It seemed an odd comment—Teiryn would have been more concerned about the young man's rank or prospects. But he often felt he didn't quite catch the significance of what Lororo said.

Teiryn considered the ambassador. The man was about his own age and had come on hunting parties with Teiryn on several occasions in the past year. He was always friendly, never cross, and seemed to have an endless supply of patience. Just the sort of man to make an ambassador, though his predecessor had been exactly the same way, which made Teiryn wonder if all Morovolo men behaved in similar fashion.

One thing was certain: they were endlessly occupied with their appearance. Tonight, Lororo's waist-length hair was divided into multiple braids—at least a dozen, maybe more -- which swayed gently down his shoulders and back. Gloves covered hands which Tieryn knew were perfectly manicured. Everything about the ambassador was expertly coiffed, buffed, starched, and perfumed. The Morovolo obsession with personal appearance had always amused Teiryn, as every Morovolo man he had ever met—though admittedly the number was very small—spent at least as much time on his toilette as any noble Evandian lady.

Lororo's costume was of deep burgundy, forest green, and gold, accentuated by gold earrings and a diamond brooch. Ribbons bedecked his sleeves and trousers. When he went hunting with Teiryn, even his horse's tack was decorated with ribbons. He always smelled like exotic flowers and even here in Evandia where men did not wear cosmetics, he maintained a light coating of rouge on his cheeks and color on his eyelids. A very fine pale powder was dusted across his face.

It was a common joke among Evandian men that Morovolo men wished they were women. Teiryn had never wondered just why the men chose to look so feminine—so ridiculous—to Evandian eyes, especially since there was no doubting their courage. Morovolo army units were famous for their bravery in battle and the fearless way they faced death. In small Evandian towns, pub patrons who had never seen a Morovolo could be found singing the Ballad of Foaloro, which told the account of Morovolo general and hero Foaloro and his two hundred men at the Battle of Sava Plain. They had held off a force many times the size of their own, sacrificing their lives so that the main army had time to advance into position, to be ready for attack. Without Foaloro, Morovol would have been overrun by desert tribesmen hundreds of years ago.

"That's a rather serious face on such a beautiful night," said Lororo in his deep voice. His accent made the Evandian language somehow more elegant and lyrical. Teiryn liked to listen to the ambassador. "Might I inquire as to the content of your thoughts?"

Teiryn smiled. "Foaloro, actually."

Lororo laughed and handed Teiryn a glass of wine. The sound of his laughter was bright and shining and matched his personality perfectly. "Really? Are you planning any final battles?"

"No," said Teiryn. He took a sip of the wine and found that it was excellent. "I was thinking." Suddenly, he realized that interrogating the other man on his odd style of dress was unacceptable, especially since he would be questioning the host of the ball. Evandian manners might not be the same as the Morovolo, but even Teiryn knew inquiring further would be rude. Morovolo were nothing if not properly mannered and he could not afford to insult the ambassador. "Never mind."

Lororo cast him a sideways glance. "But, please, speak. You were thinking of one of my country's greatest heroes. What is wrong with that?"

Teiryn cleared his throat. Perhaps Lororo would forgive him the indiscretion, but he wanted to word this carefully. "I, uh, well, forgive me if this is rude, and ill-suited for discussion at your ball, but I was wondering why, since the men of your country are such great warriors, you dress the way you do."

Far from being offended, the other man actually laughed again. "But this is an excellent question!" he exclaimed. "After a year of riding and hunting together, you have yet to ask me anything about myself or my country. I have been waiting for such."

Teiryn was bemused. "Really?"

"You Evandians know little of Morovol," said the ambassador with a slight air of reproof. "I am not sure why. Perhaps your kings have simply never been that curious about us."

"Our countries have been allies for generations..." began Teiryn.

"I think mostly because we stare at each other in incomprehension," said Lororo. "And also because it would be extremely difficult to move an effective invasion force over the mountains; the passes are simply inadequate for such a maneuver. And as we are a landlocked country, we have no navy to attack you by sea. Perhaps it would be better to say we are acquaintances rather than allies."

"All right," said Teiryn. "But that doesn't answer my question."

"How correct," said the other man. "Morovolo men dress the way they do because it is what Morovolo women want."

"What women want?"

"Indeed. I know your custom is to trade your women between families to cement alliances, but that is not the way of it in my country. In my country, a man must attract a woman. The way he dresses, the style of his poetry, his skill at riding or with weapons, his attention to philosophy—all these are things which will be judged by a potential bride."

"But her father..."

"No, you do not understand," said Lororo. "A father does not find a match for his daughter. The daughter—with the aid of her mother, grandmother, aunts, and sisters—must take care of that. I know that your name, Segrithr, you have inherited from your father, and he from his, back to Evandia's beginnings. But my name, Oanolowa, is from my mother. It identifies her lineage. All the women of her line are Oanolowa. The sons take on the name of their mother, and their children will have the name of his wife."

Teiryn frowned, his initial reaction one of outright disbelief. "But how do you inherit your titles, then, if you have your mother's name?"

Lororo's smile did not falter. Perhaps Teiryn was wrong about the rudeness of his request. It seemed the ambassador was more than willing to speak about his country and its customs. "Property is not inherited in the same manner. A man's wealth passes to all his children, though royal titles go from father to son—this keeps one lineage from holding the throne. As you might imagine, the contest among the women to see who will marry a prince can be quite entertaining."

Tieryn was lost in a sea of incredulity. "I don't understand. If I had daughters, I would have to secure husbands for them, or they would have nothing."

"I know," said Lororo with a sad shake of his head. "But wouldn't daughters also be worthy of your property? Your pardon, Sire, but to Morovolo eyes it seems incalculably cruel to disinherit your women in this way."

Teiryn was too confused to be insulted. He gazed around the room a moment, not truly seeing anything, trying to grasp the concept of women being able to inherit wealth. Or of choosing their own husbands! Though Brenicia had wanted to marry him, the matter had been entirely in her father's hands. If he'd been a younger son rather than the crown prince,

Lord Hellfren would never have consented to the match, no matter how much Brenicia had desired it.

"So your women choose their husbands," said Teiryn, moving back to the earlier topic. "I'm not sure I see why this involves the men dressing up in ribbons and earrings, and the cosmetics, and the rest."

Lororo shrugged modestly. "Every man wants to look his best. A woman wants a man who is beautiful, who is learned, and who is intelligent. Who can dance well, as my young friend should be discovering about her would-be suitor just about now. A Morovolo woman wants to know her prospective husband will either inherit wealth or knows how to make it. Proper grooming is expensive." Here Lororo flashed his diamond brooch and the gems sparkled in the candlelight. "A woman will take a man's manner, poise, and charm into consideration as well. It is important, if you wish to find a wife, to be exceedingly polite, to know how to settle arguments rather than start them, and to be knowledgeable about theater, music, and literature, as well as the things I mentioned earlier. Knowing how to play a musical instrument is considered an advantage."

Teiryn took a deep breath, as if the weight of what Lororo had to say had settled on his shoulders. In Evandia, only the lower classes learned to play musical instruments. Musicians were respected and often commanded high prices, but they were still hired servants. "So you know how to play an instrument?"

"Three," said the ambassador with obvious pride. "The recorder, the lap harp, and the guitar. I compose, as well. I prefer the harp, especially as a composer, as I feel it has the most ethereal sound, but my wife prefers the guitar."

"You're married?"

"Of course. A man who has wealth, can write poetry, speaks several languages, and plays three instruments is not one to stay unwed unless he has some serious flaw in his character. I am happy to say that my wife and her, well, her *aolo*, were delighted with her choice."

"Aolo?"

"A term you do not have. All the women in one lineage are an aolo."

"And were you also delighted in her choice?" Now Teiryn was becoming intrigued. The ambassador hadn't chosen his own wife? Nor had his father been involved at all! Nor his wife's father! It was nearly impossible to understand.

"Oh, yes! My wife is an accomplished musician, as well as being well-read. She also speaks several languages, and writes excellent poetry. Better than my own, I must admit, for she observes some of the most ancient and strictest forms which are almost impossible to utilize in a competent manner. The king's mother is a member of that aolo, though a distant female relation, so my marriage put me closer to the throne than I would otherwise have been. My mother's aolo was noble, and of ancient lineage, but their demesne was far from the capital. My father was wealthy, but his wealth was of his own creation, for he was a financier. Between them I had enough status and wealth to get to court, but I would never have been ambassador to Evandia if I had not married my wife."

"But she does not come with you to Evandia?"

Lororo chuckled. "It is difficult to get a woman to leave her aolo. We men are more free to move about since we have no such attachments."

Teiryn couldn't think of anything else to ask; he was afraid any question he'd come up with would result in another incomprehensible answer.

The ambassador smiled. "Our countries are very different in some ways, it is true. But I think we have more in common than most imagine. I miss my wife, but I do not regret my time in Evandia. It is a lovely country and breeds honorable people."

On anyone else's lips, Teiryn would have suspected insincere flattery. But Lororo, though never discourteous, did not lie. Or at least Teiryn had never known him to lie. From Lororo's description of his own country, Teiryn felt he had a slightly better idea of why the ambassador was always so pleasant, so supportive. It made him wonder what the women were like.

"Perhaps your wife will visit us one day so we can have the honor of meeting her," said Teiryn. "I would like that very much."

Lororo's smile broadened, and his eyes lit up briefly. If Teiryn were any judge, he would say this was a man who adored his wife. "I will extend the invitation to her, Sire. Thank you."

One of Lororo's personal attendants approached and began whispering to the ambassador quickly. No doubt Lororo's ball, as with any party, was faced with the occasional wrinkle which needed to be ironed out. A lack of wine, running out of certain ingredients for the delicacies. Teiryn excused himself and wandered toward the dance floor.

His mood lightened as the evening progressed. He saw no more of Gomeril, Novardan, or Eithnira Nevelein, and after an hour or so without sight of any of them, he relaxed enough to dance with Yawneil's wife, and then with several other court ladies. By the time Teiryn pleaded exhaustion and left the ball near midnight, he was in a good mood. The food had been excellent, as well as the wine, and the dancing. He had not enjoyed a party so much in a very long time.

Teiryn yawned and opened the door to his quarters. He stopped short. A woman sat at the table, precisely where Lythera used to. Eithnira.

She smiled and struggled to sit upright. She looked exhausted; no doubt Novardan had rushed to get her to the palace today so that he might ambush Teiryn with her at the ambassador's reception. Her traveling schedule had probably been hectic, and now she had been left in his room, alone and exhausted, with the expectation that she would share Teiryn's bed.

He was in no mood for this, and was tempted to find his cousin to tell him precisely what he thought of this right now. But the smile faded from Eithnira's face and he knew he had to deal with her first. She had seen his hesitation.

Teiryn entered the room and sat down opposite Eithnira. He tried to smile at her, but it was hard, when all he wanted to do was go to Lythera. This woman did not tempt him, despite her resemblance to Brenicia. She wasn't his queen. His queen was dead.

What should he say to her? This had always been awkward in the past, especially when the girls had been so young, he knew he wouldn't touch them. But this was different. Novardan knew what he was doing—he wanted to put this woman in between Teiryn and Lythera. Wanted to see Lythera gone, this time forever. Teiryn wasn't going to permit that, but how did he deal with this woman now, in this moment? None of this was her fault.

"I'm sorry," he said. "You're probably tired, as am I. Perhaps you should return to your room and get some sleep." That sounded like a cowardly way out, but he couldn't order her away. Couldn't be rude or angry, not at her, not when it was Novardan who deserved his ire.

She looked confused, and a little hurt. He hated to see that. "I'm sorry, Sire, but don't I please you? Yer cousin said you would be happy to see me."

"My cousin presumes much," he said. "I'm sorry, lady, but you can't stay here with me tonight. My heart is already given to another, and I have never been one who could betray my love."

A tear rolled down her cheek and a cold shadow crossed her face. For the first time, he wondered if she were as innocent as he had supposed. Perhaps she had been coached on what to do, how to manipulate him. Not all women were as straightforward and honest as Lythera or Brenicia.

"I have to stay," she insisted. "Lord Novardan told my father his debts would not be relieved until after our three months together. He said...he said the last girl was gone and that I would be just the one to make up for that. He said..." She heaved her chest upward in a deep sigh, but the display didn't entice, only disgusted him. Now he was sure she was as insincere as Novardan.

"I don't care what my cousin told you," said Teiryn as gently as he could. "I'll talk to him about the money he owes your father, which should have been paid when you were brought here. The funds should be released as soon as I can arrange it."

She did brighten up a bit at that news. Maybe she wasn't so much a schemer, as just someone who came across as insincere, even when she wasn't. Or he was being suspicious enough to see ulterior motives even when there were none. It didn't matter. He could be kind to her and still send her away.

"Lady, it would please me if you would go back to your own room," he said.

For a moment, he thought she might collapse into hysterics as a blush rose on her face, and his heart quailed at the thought of being trapped in his quarters with yet another hysterical girl. But he had misjudged her. It wasn't hysterics he saw on her face. It was rage. It rolled up her cheeks and inflamed her eyes until they practically glowed in the firelight. She slapped both hands on the table. "I will nae be sent away like some disobedient child!"

Teiryn sat still, stunned.

Eithnira pushed her chair back and stood. She pointed a finger at him. "I came here in good faith, with promises that my father's debts would be relieved. It's not the choice I would ha' made for myself, but I accepted it. Ye can't turn me away!"

An answering rage rose in his own cheeks. "I most certainly can," he said in a low voice. "Sharing a bed takes two people, and I never agreed to this bargain. I won't have you in my bed."

For a moment she seemed speechless, and she blanched white, then blushed bright red once more. "This is insane! Why not? I can't go home until I've lain with you. Why should I be ruined, with no chance of dowry or marriage, and not even ha' the barest chance of providing an heir for you? You've taken everything from me and you'll give me naught, not even one small hope!"

Teiryn stood. "I've taken nothing, lady. Go home. Once the funds are released to your father, he can find you a husband."

That only infuriated her more and she launched herself at him. Teiryn was so surprised that she managed to slap him twice in quick succession before he grabbed her wrists. "I hate you," she screamed. "Ye never had to live like me, with a noble name and no money to support it! My mother and I have to pick herbs and mushrooms in the forest and grow a garden if we're to have anything to eat in summer, and in winter, there's barely bread to go around the table. My father is a dau-Lord who has had to bend his pride and take work around the village like a commoner. He fixes saddles and repairs harnesses for the same wage any day laborer would receive. And now all that could be over and done—my family could eat well again. My father could be a lord again. But ye have to lie with me first!"

Teiryn thrust her away from him. "No, I will not. Your father will have his money. So there's no need to get so angry."

She clenched her fists, then ripped open her gown and dropped it to the floor. Her form was trim and youthful, with curves just like his Brenicia. She was the image of his queen, and he couldn't help but stare, remembering the many nights he and his queen had explored each other's bodies by the firelight.

"Love me," she said. "Only once. It's my only chance."

He blinked and shook his head. No matter how much she tried, she only had to speak to break the spell. He was glad it was so easy. He had loved Brenicia with all his heart, and this woman was like having her back again—but in form only. "No."

Her anger seemed spent and she sank to the floor. "This is the only way. Besides, what woman would not want to be in the king's bed?" She gave him a look that he supposed was to appear seductive, but it merely looked scheming. "The king must be a mighty lover, yes?"

This was ridiculous. Why had he even agreed to this plan a year and a half ago? Kings could get laws changed; there was no reason he couldn't have cobbled together a coalition of lords to allow him to marry a second time. There had to be enough promises to make, enough favors to hand around, to make it possible for his ministers to see their way clear to blessing a second marriage. For some reason, he had not even tried; perhaps Brenicia's loss had been too near and too devastating. But that time was over. He would never participate in this sorry charade again.

"Lady," he said. "I am truly sorry. I will make you this promise, if you leave now and return home to your father once I have straightened out the situation with the money."

A look of annoyance crossed her face. Apparently, neither Novardan nor she had considered she might be sent away like this. She almost said something, then shook her head. Quickly, she grabbed her gown and wrapped it back around her as if her modesty, which had so recently deserted her, had returned full-force, and she stalked out of the room. Teiryn sank down in the chair again, his heart in turmoil. For the first time in years, tears threatened.

Brenicia. He had thought he had gotten through most of his grief over her loss, that Lythera had helped him wash the last of that sadness away. But seeing her living image before him this evening had rattled him deeply.

He got up and paced before the fireplace, restless in his soul, not knowing why. He only knew one thing. He needed Lythera.

It was just after midnight, but he didn't care. He needed to see her. To escape the palace, his cousin, and all the scheming. To be with the one person who cared about him above all else.

Teiryn wrapped a cloak around him and went down to the courtyard. People were still leaving the ambassador's ball, so he had no problem finding a coachman who was awake and prepared to take him somewhere. The ride to the property on Water Street seemed interminable. As soon as they arrived, Teiryn leapt out of the coach, only peripherally aware that he had not shaken his permanent retinue of guards, and went to the door. The night watchman who kept vigil over the house after the regular doorman left for the evening, was startled, but opened the door without question. Teiryn rushed up to Lythera's room, contemplating all he could tell her, swearing to vow to love her forever, if only he could feel her arms around him.

He opened the door to her room, but facing him was a shock he was not prepared for. The bedcovers were turned down for the night, but Lythera was not there. She was gone.

18

The inn where the study group met was dark and crowded, with straw on the floor and soot from the huge main fireplace staining everything. The smell of old beer permeated the air. Kavinel had guided Lythera to a back table where three other men already sat, bowls and mugs in front of them.

The three men largely ignored her, which gave Lythera a chance to observe them quietly during dinner. Oluraun was a hefty man with short brown curls and a thin beard that was redder than his hair. His features were coarse and stout; his hands made Teiyrn's hands look tiny in comparison. He spent the meal slurping his fish stew.

Frawvin proved to be nearly Oluraun's opposite. Skinny, with bones seeming to protrude from his wrists and shoulders, as if his skin were stretched over a frame much too large for it. His hair was straight and of a nondescript color halfway between blond and brown. He chatted nervously with Kavinel for most of the meal about things of no consequence; the weather, the greeting he had exchanged with the guard at the city gate the other day, a dog he had seen on the street. Kavinel had little to do but insert an occasional "hmmm."

The other man she already knew. Mandlarin, the bearded man she had met in the library. He sat on the other side of Kavinel from Lythera, so she didn't see much of him during the meal. He was as quiet as Oluraun, but that might have been due to Frawvin's never-ending monologues rather than a lack of anything to say.

The men made no comment when Kavinel took up a collection to pay for Lythera's meal. Lythera was glad they did not protest, but their dismissive manner worried her. She had thought they would at least speak to her at dinner. Could they continue their silence even through the study meeting?

Kavinel gave her a friendly grin as they exited the inn, though, so she felt heartened by that. Even if the others ignored her, she would have Jarris and Kavinel to talk to. And perhaps the woman Jarris had mentioned.

Frawvin kept up a monologue on they walked through the warmth of a summer evening on their way back to the school. His speech was a long, disjointed, and pointless story about how a coach had splashed mud onto his new trousers the other day when he'd been visiting relatives on the outskirts of the city. Lythera couldn't help but smile at the ridiculous lengths to which the story was stretched. It was as if the man couldn't stand to not hear the sound of his own voice. The others put up with him in silence, with only one "come now, Frawvin, get on with it," from Mandlarin as they approached the front gate of Aynwren School.

The gate was locked, but Mandlarin produced a key and they were soon inside. Lythera followed the others into a different building than the one she'd taught in earlier; this building was taller, having four stories instead of three, and built of dark granite. The interior was just as threadbare as in the other building, with only wall lamps lighting the way, and chunks of mortar missing from between the stones.

Lythera wondered how long the building would remain standing in this shape, but she kept her worries about the building's stability to herself and followed the others to the top floor.

The uppermost floor of the building was one large room with the beams of the peaked roof exposed above. Fortune's Rue hung from the rafters much as it did from the ceiling in the palace records room. The smell permeated everything, but it was familiar, and Lythera welcomed it.

Master Jarris sat at a large round table in the center of the expanse, three other people already with him. One was Avaidan, the white-haired young man whose magical spell had nearly burned him. One of the others was a large-framed woman with mud-brown hair and green eyes. She looked familiar, but Lythera could not place her. The woman wore a green dress in the same style and fabric as Lythera had worn in the palace; no doubt she was one of the noble ladies who occasionally dined near the king's table. But if so, what was she doing here? Lythera had never heard of another nobleman's daughter who was well-educated enough to hold her own with scholars such as Master Jarris.

The last person was dark and non-descript, with wide-set hooded eyes and a scowl on his face. He looked up and nodded, scowl intact, as if it were permanently affixed.

Master Jarris looked up at the group's approach. "Ah, there you are," he said. "I was beginning to think you'd decided to drink the evening away."

"Frawvin, as usual, kept us," said Kavinel. He took a chair, and gestured for Lythera to sit next to him. Mandlarin took the chair on her other side. Oluraun and Frawvin commandeered chairs beyond Mandlarin.

"Well, Lythera, you've already met everyone except Aiza here and my other student, Threndayl. Aiza is the daughter of my former brilliant pupil, Ulindein, who can no longer study ancient texts as that conflicts with his current duties. Threndayl is a youngster from the northern provinces who was sent here a few years ago as one of our charity cases. He's made quite an impact in his classes."

"Let's get started," said Mandlarin. "I'm anxious to see if I can work out that numerical progression."

"Last time, we were trying to decipher a particularly difficult text from Master Daidanar Fallows from the time of the second Uldreth king," said Avaidan in explanation. "It has a string of numbers in it that are obviously a code for something, but no one's been able to even guess what they might mean. It is a real treasure—one of the few texts we have from Uldreth times."

"That's a task for Mandlarin tonight," said Jarris. "I'd like Lythera to begin work on the Book of Fortune."

The others looked doubtful, except Jarris and Avaidan. Kavinel looked intrigued. Lythera nodded. "I'll do my best. What problems are you encountering?"

Jarris passed a thin booklet to Oluraun, who gave it to Avaidan. Avaidan laid it in front of Lythera and opened it to one of the last pages. "This is a book that Jarris was able to acquire only recently, so we have not had much chance to study it. Here's the passage we were looking at last time," he said. "We all have notes on it already. Take a look for a few minutes and see what you think while we rehash our pet theories with each other."

Lythera looked at the page, and was glad to see the scribe had had a decent hand, at any rate. The text was legible. It just didn't seem to make sense. The title said *Fortuna's Soul.*

At the end of the Rulikarien Cycle, in the appointed hour, the world shall be changed in a great striving. Yet the striving shall not always have a victor; both may lose and the cost will be high. Nothing is certain. The lion can be restored, but only if the moon-bird returns to grace the skies above the healed land.

There was the mention of a moon-bird again, but Lythera still had no idea what that might mean and doubted she would be any help to the others. If Jarris and the rest of this study group had not made any headway with such odd language, she doubted she could provide any further insight.

"Their origins are kept secret from everyone else," said Avaidan. "But I still think the root is the same. Nysteron, meaning to rule or to guide. Nowadays we'd normally gloss it as to heal, but that's not the meaning in these older texts."

"The nestriana are an ancient order," said Jarris. "You may be right, but I feel there is more to the word than simply something about rulership. Healing must be a part of it, otherwise why would the nestriana be a healing order?"

"It must be something to do with power," said Aiza. Her voice was low and calming, and Lythera liked listening to it. The woman's accent was as strangely familiar as her face. Aiza was from somewhere west of the capital where vowels were elongated and some consonants softened. "Look at the number of personal names that have the same root. Nasrilla, Nestira, Annistara, Enistraila, Nystillayn. Everywhere in Evandia, some form of the name is commonly given to the eldest girl. And we're talking about some sort of war between fantastical creatures or entities, who are surely symbolic of two families vying for the throne."

"Daughters do not inherit power," said Frawvin. "On one occasion, when my father..."

"Now is not the time for more personal stories, Frawvin," said Avaidan. Lythera was grateful for the interruption; she had had enough of Frawvin's endless prattling for one night. She supposed everyone else had, too. "I agree that, in our world today, daughters inherit nothing from the father. But in the beginnings of Evandia, the eldest daughter had a special place in society. It was considered fortunate to marry the eldest."

"And unfortunate to marry the youngest," said Aiza drily. "Power is probably the wrong word to use. Influence might be better. Or something more subtle."

Jarris tapped his quill pen against his cheek. "So, we have a word that must encompass rulership, guidance, healing, and power of some sort that's less obvious. Luck, maybe. Or something more. Anything else? Lythera, do you have anything to add?"

"Only a question," she said and raised her head. All eyes except Mandlarin's were turned to her. "I saw the city gate when I arrived and the strange stork-like bird on it. And the phrase *moon-bird of Fortune protect us*. Yet here the word is Fortuna, like it's a proper name, not an idea. What does a bird have to do with anything, and what—or who—is Fortuna?"

The others were silent. "Yes, I had wondered about that," said Jarris at last to Mandlarin, whose dark eyes had finally risen off the text he was reading.

Lythera was confused. "What?"

"It's one of Jarris' ideas, but Mandlarin dismissed it," said Oluraun. "I think, though, that many of us are in agreement that Fortuna is an entity of some sort, vastly powerful, that has something to do with the turning of the seasons, and the beginning of a new era. Perhaps even the one who made the astars and the royal stags."

"I still think it's a misspelling, or an archaic spelling at the least," said Frawvin. "And why are we letting this girl speculate on it, anyway? She has no familiarity with these texts."

"Perhaps not," said Threndayl, scowl still in place. "But not having read it several times before, nor having heard us argue until deep in the night over every nuance in the passage, she can approach the text with a freshness we can't. Perhaps it's a misspelling or just an archaic form. It's worthwhile to consider that it is not. We can argue about it, anyway. That's what we always do with every new idea—as if I should have to tell you."

Lythera tried to be as still and unnoticeable as possible. She had only said one thing and already she had caused contention in the group. She didn't feel she had done or said anything wrong, but she couldn't understand Frawvin's hostility. He had seemed affable enough at dinner. And if the group were accustomed to arguing about every new idea, he should know better than Lythera the sort of discussion that would take place. She would have thought he would welcome a new twist to their old, unresolved arguments.

"Don't mind him," said Threndayl. Lythera looked at him, surprised to find his scowl had been replaced by a small smile. "Frawvin likes to throw fits. You should have seen him when Aiza first joined us."

He glanced at Aiza, who returned his gaze briefly with a slight blush. The others ignored their small exchange, but it intrigued Lythera. She assumed, from what Aiza had said earlier, that she was the youngest daughter, and from her dress, she was noble-born. And not of some bankrupt sei-Lord, either, but of much higher birth and station. A friendship between someone like her and a charity case like Threndayl should be impossible. Lythera was surprised even further that Aiza's father allowed her to join these sessions, knowing his unmarried daughter would be alone until late at night with unattached men of lower station. Lythera's father would never have agreed to such a thing. It had been difficult enough for him to agree for a tutor to come to the house, and even then, the man was his wife's cousin. Noble, if not well-off. Like Marlun Halevern himself.

"All right, what if Lythera's right?" asked Oluraun. "We know the Morovolo honor their ancestors, petition them for luck or health, and think they watch over their descendants. And the Selandi offer sacrifices to the sea beings. We've just never had anything like that here in Evandia."

"But what if we did at one time?" asked Avaidan. He sat forward in his chair, his hands on the table before him, obviously excited. "What if Fortuna was the one to whom people used to make propitiation? That would explain our New Year's and Harvest customs. They're sacrifices to Fortuna."

Mandlarin sneered and went back to his text. "I don't smash old pottery and distribute food to the poor and burn incense to honor some...some being."

"He didn't say you did," said Jarris calmly. "He said it might be what people used to do. Customs haven't changed, but the world has. If Fortuna were the entity that people used to appeal to for assistance or for good crops, or for rain, then it makes sense that some of those ancient ways remain, even if we don't remember their original meaning. But we have forgotten our past. We no longer know about Fortuna, or the moon-bird, or why a Bandryn hero is required at the end of the age."

"A Bandryn hero?" Lythera asked. "But there are no more Bandryns."

"No more males of the direct line," said Aiza, "but plenty of people are descended from Bandryn daughters. Perhaps this entity, Fortuna, does not care if the hero is born of a male or female scion of the family."

"Then the hero could be anywhere," said Avaidan. "Surely, over the past thousand years, plenty of Bandryn daughters have married in to other families and their children have borne a different name. So we can hardly go looking for this Bandryn hero if it could be anyone."

"Anyone noble," said Threndayl.

"Not necessarily," said Aiza. "A Bandryn daughter or even granddaughter could be matched with a younger son who inherited nothing, or whose family went bankrupt. A couple generations after that, no one would remember that a child's great-great-great grandfather was Lord Bandryn, especially if that child is starving at the gate, or a pickpocket in the slums of some city or abandoned to a foundling home. Bandryn blood could be anywhere at this point. I agree, there's no way to figure out who the Bandryn hero might be."

"Maybe there is," said Jarris. "The Bandryn line was said to have bred true when, as the texts say poetically, *the eyes of azoreth are revealed.*"

"Eyes of what?" asked Lythera.

"An archaic word; I'm surprised you haven't come across it before. It means, eyes the blue-violet color of the astars," said Jarris. "Like yours."

The others stared at her, and Lythera felt even more naked than she had ever felt with Teiryn. She squirmed in her chair. "I'm not the only one with...with..."

"No, you are not," said Jarris quickly. "We aren't saying you're the hero we're talking about. After all, it could be Valeron Trenstarl or Mileli Nivain. I can think of four people that I know personally with this eye color, though only two also have the auburn hair of the Bandryn family. Mileli's hair is blond, and Nihael's is almost white, like Avaidan. I'm sure there are others who bear the mark of the eyes of *azoreth*—many years ago, I met a merchant from the far east of Evandia who had the same eyes. He was old then, but who knows how many of his children might have inherited the trait? So, again, we have a rather large pool of possibilities, and no good way to narrow down the choices."

"Then we waste our time with that line of inquiry," said Olaraun. "What about Fortuna and the nystraia, the moon-bird?"

"It's not so much that the nystraia *is* the moon-bird, but that the nystraia *becomes* the moon-bird, in the text I studied," said Aiza. "That text reads as though a woman is going to turn into a bird. I took it to be symbolic."

"I have always assumed so," said Jarris confidently. "We know that no one can change their shape, and even the magicians in the town squares around Evandia are only playing tricks on the eyes. I don't think the text is speaking about a trick, but rather a deeper meaning that ties up ideas of healing and flight and rulership."

"The text says the woman will take flight and definitely uses the archaic term for bird flight," said Avaidan. "We might say *awing*. That could mean many things which I'm sure we'll enjoy discussing again some other time. It also says she'll assume the throne. Both seem to be exaggerations at best. What I'd like to get to tonight is something we haven't covered yet—what is the end of the cycle?"

There was silence a moment, and Jarris shrugged. "Most of you have been involved in our summer digs at one time or another. You're familiar with the sudden changes from a world of one kind to the world of another. But when this happens and why is still a mystery. Though perhaps not much longer if Mandlarin manages to solve the puzzle he is currently working on. It involves sequences of numbers."

"What are the numbers?" asked Threndayl.

"Does it matter? They don't mean anything yet," said Mandlarin. "Do you think you can do better?" He caught Threndayl's gaze and held it. Threndayl looked away after only a moment.

"No, I just asked what the numbers were. I don't have a head for numbers like you do."

"Mandlarin is quite clever with numbers and came to us most highly recommended," said Jarris to Lythera. "Yet even he is stumped by this string of digits without context."

"Which hardly needs to be explained to her," said Mandlarin. "After all, what are her recommendations?"

"She has mine, and that's enough," said Jarris before Lythera could say anything. "Really, do you think I'd invite anyone to our group who wasn't qualified?"

That settled Mandlarin, and Lythera saw a thoughtful glance cross Frawvin's face as well. Aiza smiled slightly and nodded to Lythera.

"We might add, Lythera, that the last number in the sequence matches this year. The year 1297," said Aiza.

"Coincidence," said the man. "I already thought of that, but the other numbers do not fit with years."

Aiza looked like she might say more, but Threndayl glanced at her and she didn't. Lythera was intrigued. What could Aiza think she knew that Threndayl didn't want her to say? Or was he just tired of hearing from Mandlarin tonight?

"No doubt we won't settle anything tonight," said Jarris.

"We never do," said Avaidan with a small laugh. "But this is certainly an interesting twist. Think about an entity powerful enough to do things like change the weather, or raise one family to the throne and displace another. What if this entity fell asleep, or was trapped, or for whatever reason, left. Would people even remember it had ever existed? What about terms like *fortune's child* and plants like *fortune's rue*. You don't see terms like...like *charity's child* or *prosperity's rue*. What if, at one time, they were Fortuna's children and Fortuna's rue?"

Oluraun snorted out a laugh. He sounded like a cat sneezing. "Really, Avaidan, you can get quite taken with an idea when you want to be."

"I'm just saying we should consider it."

"And we will," said Master Jarris. "While Mandlarin gets on with his consideration of the numerical sequences, I'd like to hear if anyone has any fresh ideas on the moon-bird."

"Lythera doesn't know our old ideas," said Aiza.

Jarris shrugged and looked at Lythera. "We really don't have much, just some doggerel that the peasants still sing, about moon-birds and purple flowers. You might never have heard them."

"I grew up hearing them," said Threndayl. "Why wouldn't she have? They're not just sung in the north. Haven't you sung about the moon-bird at Whidsayl and Trilsayl?" His scowl was back. Lythera barely recognized the terms he used, but recalled one lesson from her tutor concerning festivals held by the peasants during midsummer and midwinter. As they had nothing to do with the gentry, he had not expanded on the topic further.

Despite having apparently befriended Aiza, who was far above him in station, Threndayl seemed suspicious about Lythera's station, and seemed to be daring her to state her birth rank unequivocally, as if she were hiding something just to spite him personally. Lythera didn't know what to say.

"Well?" asked Threndayl. He caught Lythera's gaze in his own and did not look away.

The challenge in his eyes angered Lythera. "My father is sei-Lord Halevern," she said. "But I have disavowed using his name ever again as my own. My father had five daughters and he rarely let us leave Halevern Hall. Even my tutor had to come to me. But if I am not mistaken, I am not the only one born to a noble house at this table, so why are you angry with me?"

Threndayl just stared at her. Aiza poked him in the ribs. "You're right. No one's said so, but I'm Aiza Gomeril. My father is Lord Gomeril, whom I know you've met in the palace."

Gomeril. Now Lythera knew why Aiza looked so familiar. The Gomeril mud-brown hair and green eyes. The large frame, though Lord Gomeril carried a great deal of weight on his and Aiza merely looked a bit broader in the face and shoulders than was fashionable. Lythera couldn't remember actually meeting Aiza, but she was sure that at least one or two Gomeril daughters had been in the palace at one time or another during her tenure.

That meant that Lord Gomeril was Jarris' former prize pupil. The thought seemed strange to Lythera; the man had never struck her as any sort of scholar.

"Enough," said Jarris softly. "We have other business. Threndayl, you know I don't consider rank important when conducting scholarship. All scholars are peers, no matter the class they were born into. There's no place for surnames here."

Lythera was glad when the topic turned back to the moon-bird, but the truth was, no one at the table had any idea what a moon-bird might symbolize.

The night wore on, and Lythera got caught up in listening to everyone's opinions. No one hesitated to argue for their own position, and the serious discussions, broken by friendly banter, was exciting. This could be her life now—among scholars! Among those who could discuss languages and philosophy and history. Lythera nearly pinched herself to make sure she was actually awake and present.

Toward the end of the evening, Jarris said something which brought back her uneasiness. He produced the nauvynnor and held it up. "I believe you've all heard the story of Lythera making this sundial work, and about the amazing result of her effort. I propose that for the next meeting Avaidan, Lythera, and I will work with the oldest artifacts while the rest of you continue with the texts. In fact, I have the sundial with me here. Lythera, I want you to take it. Perhaps it will do other things which you can discover."

Avaidan nodded and said, "Good idea."

Lythera bit her lip, unsure she wanted to cooperate. But, why not? A perverse sort of pride filled her chest. She could make the odd thing perform tricks like no one else could. "All right."

Jarris put the nauvynnor inside a small leather pouch and passed it to her. She could feel the sharp edges of the nauvynnor vibrating as she held it, but she was relieved when that was the only odd thing it did when she held it.

The meeting finally broke up. Lythera wondered about getting back to the house; she hadn't thought far enough ahead about arranging for a coach. Being free of a man's subjugation did make one responsible for things she was unused to. In the future, she needed to remember to arrange her transportation and carry money. This was her new life, and no man, not even Teiryn, could take it from her.

But she still had to adjust to it.

On the way out of the building, she glanced at the dark street in front of the school.

"It's too late to hire a coach," said Threndayl from behind her. "Why don't you come with us?"

She turned. Aiza and Threndayl stood nearby, hand in hand. The sight discomfited Lythera; she was embarrassed by the public display. Though since the other scholars were rapidly disbanding into the night and no one else was about, she supposed it wasn't quite so public after all. She just wasn't used to seeing such things. Especially between an ist-Lord's daughter and a peasant.

"Where is that?" she asked.

"Threndayl rents a room at a boarding house nearby," said Aiza. "I have a room there, too, but I only stay there on study group nights. There's a second bed in my room you can use. It's only a block away."

Lythera wasn't sure about the offer. The two of them seemed very cozy together; she wasn't sure how welcome her presence would truly be.

"I really should get back to the house. Teiryn might be waiting for me. And I didn't leave a note saying where I'd be—I had no idea this meeting would go so late!"

Aiza smiled. "I can have a message sent. For tonight, though, you should come with us."

Threndayl nodded. "Now is no time for a woman to be alone on the street. Come on." He turned, apparently expecting Lythera to follow. Lythera tried to keep her worry and frustration to herself and followed Threndayl and Aiza to the boarding house.

19

The boarding house was indeed only a block away. Aiza produced a key that let them inside and the three of them wearily climbed the steps to the third floor. Threndayl said "good night" quietly and slipped into the first door on the right. Aiza went to the last door on the left.

"Here we are," she said as she let Lythera into the room. Aiza lit a lamp quickly and sat down on one of the cots in the room. Lythera sat down gingerly on the other. Neither cot looked terribly sturdy, certainly nothing she would expect an ist-Lord's daughter to sleep on.

"Well, what do you think of our little troop of scholars?" asked Aiza. "I could hardly wait to meet you—I think it's the first time there have been two women in Jarris' group."

Lythera yawned and shook her head to clear it of the sleep that threatened to overwhelm her. "I think my mind is spinning too much for me to know," she said. "I've never sat in on a session like that before. My tutor never invited discussions on the nuances of words. And he would certainly have never permitted an argument!"

"I think it's very exciting," said Aiza. "When I showed an aptitude for languages, my father pushed me to get enough learning to be good enough for Jarris to consider. He used to belong to the group, you see, back when my grandfather was Lord. I think he still misses it."

"I can hardly imagine your father in Jarris' study sessions," said Lythera carefully. "Though he was always polite to me, even when the other ministers were not, he didn't seem, oh, I don't know, scholarly. I wouldn't have guessed he had been in the group."

"No one would," said Aiza. "My father is a great man, you know. He always schemed to get one of his children into Jarris' inner circle, and since he had no sons, and I had the talent, it had to be me."

"Why had to?"

Aiza smiled. "Because my father and I know what those numbers mean. The ones Mandlarin is working on. He's thinking too hard, missing the obvious. I'd love to tell Mandlarin what they mean in front of everyone but my father doesn't want the knowledge widely known yet. Only a few whom my father has specifically chosen have been made aware of the significance of the Rulikarien Progression. I and my sisters know. Threndayl knows, too."

Aiza stopped speaking and the silence stretched out. Lythera wanted to ask what the numbers meant, but it didn't seem Aiza was going to volunteer the information just now, and besides, Lythera's head was too full of words and their meanings and numbers and artifacts to fit anything else in there tonight. It also seemed odd that Lord Gomeril should tap someone like Threndayl to know whatever secrets he had uncovered. Whatever was going on, it was more than Lythera could deal with after her first day of class and her first study session. She decided to change the subject.

"I assume your father knows about you and Threndayl?" she asked.

"What about me and Threndayl?" Aiza said with a sly smile.

Lythera blushed. "You seem very close. But he's hardly the son of an ist-Lord."

"No, he isn't," said Aiza. "You know how it is, Lythera—there are only so many men you can marry when you're noble. And ist-Lords do not give their daughters to just any noble. If I marry as everyone else would assume I would, then there are Segrithr boys my age that are unwed. Metricia's eldest, Valeron. Idrant's two grandsons. A Hellfren boy two years younger than me. Several Landrith scions. None of them appeal to me. Threndayl's had to work for his living. There are days he's gone without food. Times when his family had no shelter. He had to work odd jobs even as a child to be able to afford to go to the little village school. He had to fight to get sent here as the northern province's charity case. He's had to struggle for everything. I respect him a great deal. And, yes, my father knows. But he trusts me. I've sworn to lie with no man before marriage. And I won't. Even if it's Threndayl."

Lythera lay down on the cot, her limbs feeling like dead weight. Aiza blew out the lamp. "We can talk more in the morning."

Lythera wanted to frame a reply, but it seemed she only just closed her eyes and sunlight was streaming into the room from a high window. She opened bleary eyes and blinked slowly. Aiza was moving peering into an oversized armoire that seemed to fill half the room.

"Good morning," said Lythera. "How late did I sleep?"

Aiza glanced at her and grinned. "Good morning. Don't worry, it's not as late as it seems—this window faces east so it's always bright in here at breakfast time. We can get a bite to eat at a small pastry shop down the street. They know me there and I already sent word I'll want a table."

"One of the advantages of rank," said Lythera with as much good humor as she could summon in her weariness.

"Absolutely," said Aiza. "I look forward to having some time to get to know you. I heard all about you coming to the palace, of course, but I was busy at Gomeril Hall and couldn't come to the capital. When my father sent word that you were there, my sisters and I were simply giddy with excitement. For my father's reasons, of course, but also just for the gossip. The queen was a sweet woman and I miss her, and I feel sorry for Teiryn, but the drama of having young, penniless noble women brought to him like brood mares has been the entertainment of the social season for almost three years now."

Lythera ignored the comment, surprised it still stung after all this time.

"Sorry," said Aiza airily. "But it's true. Maybe it's not so true in the home of a sei-Lord like your father, but all the nao- and ist-Lord families have been more animated at the balls than I've seen them. Gossip is the favorite activity of the upper nobility. Threndayl says it's a popular pastime in the villages, too, but of course, nothing nearly so interesting happens there. Nothing like you and your predecessors. The whole thing is so romantic and tragic at the same time. A king without a child. Desperate women. Love. Or lack thereof—I know Teiryn didn't deflower them all."

All over again, Lythera heard Reyva Segrithr's voice. Wilted flower. She shuddered. How could Aiza be so friendly and so thoughtlessly cruel at the same time? The rest of the court considered her no better than a whore. Everyone said so, and even Aiza, companionable as she seemed to want to be, couldn't help but let it slip. The brightness of the morning seemed to dim.

Lythera tried to change the subject again. "But your father," she said. "Why does he care about old manuscripts? He has lands to rule and daughters to find husbands for." Husbands who weren't village boys, even highly educated ones. Aiza's life was like a tragic romance in itself: ist-Lord's daughter and peasant boy, bound by love, separated by custom and law. Aiza was entangled in a drama which was just as prone to be the focus of cruel gossip as Lythera's life.

"He cares because he loves Gomeril lands, and he loves his daughters. Because change is coming, and my father wants to be prepared. My father has no sons, you know, and he's forbidden by law to give the title to one of us, so he'll have to pass Gomeril lands on to a distant cousin or a son-in-law. If things change, perhaps he would have another choice."

"But what does that have to do with me?" Despite the fact her mind was muddled with exhaustion, Lythera was sure this conversation made no sense. Not even if she'd slept a dozen hours. Her eyes felt gritty and her hair was matted. She longed for a hot bath as she'd had in the palace.

"Sorry, I'm telling it out of order," said Aiza. "And it's before breakfast besides. Let's get some crepes and compote into our bellies before we discuss weighty matters like inheritance."

"I'm not inheriting anything," said Lythera, aware she sounded petulant but too tired to care at the moment. "So I still don't see why Gomeril cares about me. If I were a man, I could see he might be wondering about my qualities as a possible son-in-law. But I'm no one of any importance, especially now that I've disavowed my father's name."

"You are very important," said Aiza. "Though it will take a lot of explaining. Here's a brush—at least get the worst tangles out of your hair before we leave."

Lythera took the brush and managed to get her hair into a reasonable condition within a few minutes. She returned it to the armoire to find Aiza gazing down at her own form.

"What?" asked Lythera.

"Oh, nothing, it's just that I hate wearing the same thing two days in a row, and I'd forgotten to have my maid bring some things over this week." Aiza looked up, a little sheepishly, her muddy green eyes slightly embarrassed. "I'm frightfully shallow when it comes to clothes and jewels," she said. "It annoys Threndayl no end."

Someone knocked on the door.

"And speaking of our northern friend," said Aiza, "it would appear he has arrived." She went to the door and opened it. Threndayl stood in the hallway but did not enter the room.

"We're just coming," said Aiza. She turned to Lythera. "Come along, I'm starved."

Lythera followed the pair down the stairs and to the right. The morning was already warm with no hint that autumn was steadily approaching. In less than a month it would be time for Harvest, a time of plenty when people offered food to the poor and held grand banquets for relatives and friends. The autumn was the height of the season, especially as the evenings grew cool enough to keep everyone comfortable in formal clothing while dancing until the wee hours.

Not that Lythera had ever been to a Harvest ball. But her mother had told her of a few she had attended as a young woman, before she had been married to Lord Halevern. At Halevern Hall, no one threw lavish parties, and certainly, no one danced.

Lythera looked around the room as Aiza straightened her bedsheets slightly and closed the armoire. It was small, but neat and bright and welcoming. It had been a good idea for Aiza to rent it. Perhaps Lythera should think of doing the same so that she would have somewhere to stay on nights that the study group met.

She couldn't live in the Segrithr house on Water Street forever; it was simply too imposing and grand for one person, and it was far from the school. Her gratitude to Teiryn for providing for her overfilled her heart, but she wanted to learn to live on her own. Yesterday, she had done badly—no money to buy dinner, no pre-planning to make sure the coach knew when to pick her up. She had to be more alert now, more attuned to getting what she needed. Thinking ahead to know when she'd need money, and how much. What she'd need to live her life. Dresses, toiletries, food. The sheer amount of details she would need to keep in her head from now on seemed staggering, but if other people could do it, so could she. She just wasn't used to caring for herself, that was all. She'd learn.

Of course, since she'd never gotten back to the house, she still had no money. She would have to go there after breakfast and remedy that situation. For now, though, she didn't want to be more in debt to others than she needed to be. When they arrived at the pastry shop, she whispered to Aiza, "I'll be happy to repay you later, but I have no money with me now."

To her relief, Aiza only nodded and ordered her own breakfast. Perhaps even an ist-Lord's daughter could understand the need to be responsible for oneself. But then, Aiza Gomeril did not seem like the normal ist-Lord's daughter. She probably knew many things that her peers did not.

Lythera scanned the pastries available for breakfast—all tempting and sure to be delicious—and selected something filled with the first of the autumn apples. She loved apples, especially when they had been cooked down into a pastry or pie.

The three of them sat at a table on the street outside that the owner of the shop had clearly set aside for them. Threndayl left them briefly to enter the tea shop next door. Lythera watched him go, but Aiza said only, "They know my preferences there. Hope you like the southern red-root Cassledown tea, heavily sweetened and flush with cream."

"I'm sure it will be lovely," said Lythera, though she had never heard of that tea variety. The painted sign above the shop promised fifty-five varieties, and Lythera had had no idea there were nearly so many. At home, Lord Halevern always simply requested "tea." Her mother had taught Lythera the distinction between green tea and black, and had sometimes tried to find her favorite, which she referred to as Sunsweet. But the vendors around Halevern Hall did not know the variety, or at least the name. And so only one kind of tea had ever been served at Lord Halevern's table.

Threndayl returned after only being away moments, a waitress in tow. The waitress bowed slightly to Aiza, "Lady, please let me know if you need anything else." She deposited the teapot and three cups on the table, bowed again, and left. Aiza poured for herself, sampled the brew, and nodded. This appeared to be Threndayl's signal, and he then poured for himself and Lythera.

"Their usual quality," said Aiza. "Not as good as home, but then, my father has close ties to some of the tea importers. He always gets the best, unlike some other ist-Lords who don't know one tea from another. But for a small shop, this place is able to acquire some fine products."

Lythera took the time over her breakfast to observe Threndayl and Aiza, who chatted between themselves quite happily and didn't seem to mind that Lythera was not joining them. Aiza kept her eyes on her companion, but Threndayl's gaze traveled from Aiza to passers-by as if he were worried he were being watched. Or even simply judged harshly by strangers. And yet he couldn't keep his eyes from Aiza for long. Sooner or later, his blue eyes and her green ones met and held their gaze for several moments before letting go.

They didn't touch, or talk of anything more important than the blackberry tarts which, last week, had put this week's apple cobbler to shame. But between them there was an undercurrent of tension and raw emotion that Lythera could sense.

She wanted to ask them about the numbers and about how Lord Gomeril had managed to crack a code that Mandlarin had not, but she couldn't bear to interrupt her two companions. She could ask later. If Lord Gomeril thought she was important for some reason besides her relationship to Teiryn, Aiza was sure to tell her. In the meantime, Lythera wondered what would happen to Threndayl when Lord Gomeril finally found a husband for Aiza. He couldn't possibly believe a poor boy out of the north was suitable for his daughter. Even Lythera's father, a sei-Lord of low rank, would never mate a daughter with a peasant.

On the other hand, Aiza hinted that her father was unorthodox in many ways besides his intense scholarship. Would he be willing to endure the scandal of a daughter wed so far beneath her station? The ostracism that was sure to follow from his peers, even his subordinates? Every dau-Lord and sei-Lord who heard the news would instantly feel superior to Gomeril, even though the Gomerils were one of the ten founding families of the realm. Would Gomeril even be allowed to remain on the ministerial council, no matter how much his bloodline gave him the right to be there?

Lythera didn't want to think about it. She was sure heartbreak was the only future for Threndayl and Aiza, and was sorry for it. It reminded her of her mother's maxim that a woman's life was bounded by pain. And that made her wonder—had her mother had a secret love before her marriage to the unloving and foul-tempered Marlun Halevern? Had her mother been forced to give up the man she loved to marry at her family's whim?

Lythera would never know. The thought saddened her.

She finished her breakfast and her tea—which was excellent—and quietly waited while her companions chatted about the weather they hoped Harvest would bring. Sunny days and cool evenings. Clear skies and bright moonlight. The perfect Harvest.

Aiza laughed at something Threndayl had said that Lythera had not bothered to listen to. "Come, Lythera, we can't leave you out of the conversation all morning."

Lythera smiled. "I don't mind. I have a lot to think about."

"Like what?" asked Threndayl, more bluntly than Lythera expected. The nobility were almost never that direct.

"Well," Lythera tried to figure out what to say, or how to say it. And what she was willing to say to Threndayl. "I would like to find a place to live, for one thing."

Aiza frowned. "I thought you were on Water Street in one of the Segrithr properties."

Threndayl's face drew up in a small moue of disgust; it was plain to see what he thought of women who were given their living by others.

"I am, but I don't want to stay there," said Lythera. "It's hard to explain—I'm not sure I understand myself. Teiryn, I'm sure, would let me stay there indefinitely. But it's far from the school, and, well, it's not mine. I'm just a visitor there. I'd like to live somewhere that's mine, or at least that I pay for."

"Pride," said Threndayl unexpectedly. "I didn't think any of you fine ladies had such a thing."

"What?"

"Pride," he repeated. There was a note of respect in his voice it had not held before. "You want to accomplish things on your own. I swear that until I met Aiza, I thought all noble women were unable to do anything without someone telling them to. Someone to tell them whom to marry, what to wear, whom to talk to, what to say, how much education to have, where to live—it never seems to end. I noticed it with our local sei-Lord's wife, and once I came to the capital, it was everywhere. It's bad enough with the women in the village, but it seems many times worse for the nobility. Then I met Aiza and realized that, even though her father wanted her to be a scholar, she wanted it, too. She wasn't learning just to please him. She wanted it for herself. Now you want something for yourself."

Lythera thought for a moment. "I suppose so. I have a little money, and I'll earn some at the school. I could pay for a room, buy my own food. I've never done anything like that before, but I want to. I'm not even sure how to go about it—I left yesterday with no money and so everything has been provided for me by others ever since. I want that to change. I want to learn to live on my own and make my own choices."

Threndayl nodded sagely. His out-of-control black hair suddenly made his wide eyes seem wise rather than startled. "I'm glad to hear it," he said.

"Well, there's no problem there," said Aiza. "Split the rent on the room I have—I'm only there a few days a month, anyway. Threndayl will be down the hall if you need an escort somewhere, and it's so close to the school. Couldn't be better."

Threndayl nodded even more vigorously. "Yes, yes, an excellent idea. I don't know your salary, Lythera, but most young men aren't able to afford a place by themselves right away. So if you split the cost with Aiza, you'll be doing no worse and no better than most youths who are on their own for the first time. And it is in a very convenient location."

Lythera thought about it. "That sounds perfect. But I don't think I should leave the Water Street house entirely; that seems ungrateful, and Teiryn's been so good to me. I'll split my time at first, like Aiza. Stay in the room on the nights I need to be at the school, and at the Water Street house the rest of the time."

Her companions nodded, which made Lythera feel as if she'd made a great step. But would Teiryn agree? A nagging worry that could not be banished dampened Lythera's enjoyment of the morning. Surely, Teiryn would see that she needed some space of her own, at least part of the time. Surely, he would agree to her plan.

20

The doorman gave Lythera an odd look as she walked up to the house some time later, but opened the door wordlessly. Lythera nodded to him and entered the house, amazed all over again at the lavish furnishings and amazing marble floor. As pretty as it was, though, she would not mind leaving it sometimes. The formality and the display of wealth and power were not appealing to her, a woman who had grown up in poverty at Halevern Hall. Perhaps, if she had purchased these things herself, or if they were hers by some right of inheritance, she would feel more comfortable among them. But these were Segrithr things.

Lythera climbed the stairs wearily and went to her room to lie down for a few minutes. The soft bed wrapped itself around the contours of her body and she was asleep within moments.

It did not seem long before someone was shaking her awake. Lythera opened her eyes, glad to feel more rested, and looked up to see Inveora. The woman's usual expressionless face today appeared to register her disapproval over Lythera's absence and unexplained reappearance.

"It's past noon," said Inveora without preamble. "A bath is waiting for you, as is your lunch. And there are two messages awaiting your pleasure."

"Thank you," said Lythera. She got up and stretched, then followed Inveora to the bathing room. After bathing, Lythera opted to put on one of the drab travel gowns she had been given when she left the palace. The gowns weren't fine enough to attract attention on the street, and looked like they might be worn by any woman of a mercantile family. Lythera missed her beautiful dresses she had worn in the palace, but these were much more practical.

Inveora made a brief gesture toward another dress which Lythera did not recall seeing before—a sky blue dress with matching lace on the bodice. Lythera fingered it briefly. "It's beautiful," she said. "But far too fine to wear today." Inveora did not insist.

Inveora left to set out lunch and Lythera took the opportunity to put her small pouch of coins around her neck. It was unadorned, so she hoped it, too, would pass without much notice. She had not discovered how other woman carried money with them; she would have to watch more carefully, or ask someone.

Lythera felt immensely better now that she had money on her person. She would no longer have to rely on the kindness of others. She went down to lunch with a light heart.

Inveora had set Lythera's plate on the small table near the kitchen, and Lythera was glad of the chance to look out at the garden while she ate. Inveora waited until Lythera had finished eating before she brought two small envelopes of fine bright white vellum on a silver platter. She set the platter on the table in front of Lythera and retreated with one last disparaging glance.

Lythera ignored her and opened the first envelope. The message on the card inside was intriguing. *Lythera. Please grace my home with your presence this afternoon for tea. My daughter and I will await you. Ulindein Gomeril.*

Lord Gomeril wished to speak with her. Lythera was interested to know why Gomeril had any interest in her or why he thought she was important. No one in House Halevern was anyone special.

The other note was in a familiar hand. *Lythera. I was beside myself when I could not find you at home last night. No alarms have gone out so I will assume you are safe with Master Jarris. Be home tonight.*

It was unsigned, but of course it was from Teiryn. Lythera was somewhat taken aback by the imperiousness of the last line, but then, Teiryn had no idea where she'd been. He'd obviously been worried. Lythera had no idea he would have come to see her after Ambassador Lororo's ball. She smiled to herself, pleased that his interest in her, his love, was unchanged from her time in the palace.

The note from Lord Gomeril did not include a particular time; Lythera waited until Inveora returned to replenish her wineglass to find out.

"He'll expect you between three and four," said Inveora. "I do hope you'll consider changing before going to Lord Gomeril's house. The blue dress just arrived from the palace and I'm sure it will look stunning on you."

Lythera didn't really wish to, but she realized she needed to look appropriate when calling on an ist-Lord. "I'm sure it'll be perfect," she said. "Have the coach outside at three. Right now, I'm going to the garden for a while."

Inveora nodded. Lythera got up, ignored her newly refilled wine glass, and went out to sit on a bench. Her thoughts were awhirl. Part of her was worried about her class tomorrow—now that she knew the skill level of her four miscreants, she would need to plot out a course for them to get their skills to the level they should be. She'd never done that before. Perhaps Avaidan or Jarris would have some advice for her on that. In the meantime, she would give them word lists and set them to more translating.

Part of her missed Teiryn more than she thought possible, considering she had seen him as recently as yesterday morning, and would see him again tonight. Her heart yearned to see his kind face, to run her fingers through his smooth black hair. To feel his lips on hers and hear him say her name. She wanted to tell him all about the study group, and her new friendship with Aiza, and of her plan to live on her own. Her soul bubbled up with the excitement of all her life could hold unbounded by father or husband—she could have Teiryn, and still have a life apart from the palace, away from the nobility. She had everything.

She knew she was grinning insanely at nothing, and didn't care. She sat in the garden and let her thoughts drift through her experiences with Teiryn in the palace, and found herself eager for the night to come. The scent of the roses filled the air; surely there was no more beautiful place in the land than this garden.

Toward three o'clock, Inveora came to fetch her. Lythera obediently went to her room, to find the blue dress already laid out for her. This one was simpler than her palace gowns and she managed to get it on and arrange the stays on her own. However, the plunging neckline did not give her a place to put her money pouch. She wasn't going to leave it behind again, though she could see that was what Inveora would prefer.

"I'm taking it with me," she said firmly. "So what's the solution? Do I tuck it under my bodice?"

Inveora hesitated, then shrugged. "I'll fetch something you can use." She left the room and returned in less than a minute with a silk purse held at the top by a drawstring. The purse was in Segrithr red. Lythera transferred her money to the purse and looped the drawstring around her wrist after Inveora demonstrated. Lythera recalled seeing women of the palace using the little drawstring purses, but as far as she could tell, these had always contained perfumes and handkerchiefs. Doubtless ladies of the palace never carried money.

Satisfied, Lythera went down to the coach and got inside. The drive to the Gomeril residence was not long; the ist-Lord's house was only five houses away from the Segrithr house, in the opposite direction from which Lythera had come this morning. Lythera was embarrassed to have used a coach for such a short distance; if she ever visited the Gomeril house again in the future, she would walk.

The house sported a banner with two brilliantly blue-green storks, necks intertwined, on a bronze field. The house, too, reflected the Gomeril colors. The trim had been painted a brown that was close to the bronze on the sigil, while the door and shutters were bright teal.

Otherwise, the house looked very similar to every other grand residence on the street. Except for color, Lythera could hardly distinguish one house from another. The body of the house was white; the columns and portico constructed exactly the same as the house where she was staying. And a doorman stood in exactly the same spot, though he wore Gomeril livery.

The doorman bowed and held open the door for her. Lythera thanked him and walked inside. The foyer of the grand house looked, in some ways, like she was expecting. Ancient, worn pieces of furniture, coupled with fine, shiny new items like brass candlesticks and colorful glass vases. However, where the foyer differed from the Segrithr house was in a sense of hominess. Rugs, most of them in shades of green, blue, and gold, covered the floor several layers deep. Tapestries depicting parties and dances rather than hunting scenes hung on paneled wood walls. Lythera immediately loved the house.

Lythera expected a servant to find her and usher her further inside, but it was Lord Gomeril himself who entered the foyer moments later. Before Lythera could react, he hurried to her and wrapped his arms around her briefly in a quick hug. She stepped back, bemused and a bit confused by his behavior.

She bowed her head slightly and said, "Istan, thank you for your invitation."

He waved off her statement. "Now, now, none of that. I'm so glad you've come." Then, to her great surprise, he bowed to her. Lythera's heart skipped a beat and she took a step backward. For all of Aiza's reassurances that her father was a great scholar, and a great man, he suddenly seemed lunatic.

Gomeril noticed and smiled offhandedly. "Come on inside, my child. Aiza will be with us shortly, but some of her friends decided to go for a ride in the park, and she couldn't help but join them. It's good for young ladies to get out in the open air and not be cooped up all the time with books and dusty old furniture—or with dusty old fathers, either."

Gomeril gestured for Lythera to follow him and set off down a hallway. Lythera obeyed, interested to know why Gomeril felt the need to be so polite to her. Why didn't he think she was a wilted flower, the same as the others? Or at least an embarrassment.

Lythera followed Gomeril through the huge rooms. Each had a polished stone floor and large, finely woven area rugs of intricate designs. The furniture was heavily carved and covered in throws and pillows. It was grand and yet somehow friendly at the same time. Cozy. Perhaps because the furniture was arranged to form small seating areas where three or four could easily chat away from anyone else who might be around. The arrangements made the expansive rooms seem more intimate and welcoming.

Lythera could imagine living in a place like this, wandering through its rooms, being surrounded by its beautiful rugs and furniture and tapestries. The palace and the Segrithr house, though beautiful, were colder and impersonal. In this place, Lythera could feel the stamp of all the owners who had lived here, as if by making this a home, they had each left a piece of their spirits behind.

At the back of the house was a glassed-in room which was full of trees and bushes in pots. Small flowering plants in ceramic containers hung from hooks in the ceiling. The room was shaded by several huge oak trees so that the sun did not hit the glass directly. It was a lush, gorgeous place, second only to the palace gardens in Lythera's estimation. She tried to take in everything at once and bumped into Gomeril when he stopped.

"Oh, Lord, I'm sorry," she said in embarrassment. "I was looking at...at this. It's beautiful."

"Quite right; it is beautiful," he said, dismissing her apology with a wave of his hand. "Come, sit. This is my favorite room. I come here whenever I can to get away from the palace and even from the house."

Lythera sat down in a wrought iron chair covered with a white cushion. "The house?"

"Can't you feel it?" he asked as he lowered his bulk into a much larger chair on the opposite side of a small table from her. "The centuries of Gomerils who have lived here have each left their mark. Their favorite pieces of furniture, or portraits, or sculpture. The whole house is alive with the whisperings of a hundred-and-one ancestors. I find it a difficult place to stay in at night sometimes, as if the voices I can almost hear were scolding me."

Lythera looked back toward the house. "I felt it. But it felt comfortable to me. Friendly. Halevern Hall is bare of anything that makes it a home. That's changing now a little bit. But I think it will take many years to turn that place into a building that welcomes people again."

The steward appeared with a tray of food. "Wine is being fetched from the cellar, Lord," he said. "I will have it to your table in moments. And the tea is almost ready."

Gomeril nodded. "Thank you, Daelar."

Lythera's estimation of Gomeril went up. Neither her father nor Novardan had ever bothered to thank anyone in their service. Not even Metricia had done so. Teiryn did sometimes, especially when the service rendered had been unusual or at a late hour, but many times, he did not.

Gomeril didn't speak and seemed content to wait until their food and drink had been delivered. Lythera occupied herself by gazing at all the glorious blooms in the room. Their combined scent was marvelous.

Within minutes, a bottle of wine, three glasses, tea, a tray of sweets and a large tray of pastries, had been delivered to the table.

"Please see we're not disturbed except by Aiza when she returns," said Gomeril.

"Of course, Lord." The steward left and closed the door that joined the conservatory to the main house.

Gomeril poured the wine and took a flaky pastry from the tray. "Please, help yourself."

Lythera took a smaller pastry that had colorful sugary sprinkles on it and put it on her plate. Gomeril poured wine for her. "Or tea?" he asked.

"Either is just fine, Lord," she said, embarrassed by his solicitousness.

"Now that we have something to fortify ourselves with, I suppose you'd like to know why I asked you here. My daughter told me that she revealed to you that we know the secret to those numbers Jarris and his cronies are carrying on about lately."

"Yes, she did."

"And do you want to know what they mean?"

Lythera hesitated. "I'm not sure, Lord. I mean, I'd love to learn. But Aiza implied that this has something to do with me, and I can't see how that could be."

"That is the simplest thing to answer," said Gomeril. "You are a Bandryn, through your mother's line. The Bandryns founded the kingdom, but did not accept the crown, offering it instead to the Uldreth family. That much everyone knows."

The man *was* a lunatic. There were no more Bandryns, and her mother had not borne that surname.

"What is not so well known is that the Bandryns were forbidden to take the crown. From what I have been able to glean, they were charged with making sure a hero would be ready at the end of the age, not to worry about administering a kingdom."

"That sounds preposterous," said Lythera, before realizing disagreeing with an ist-Lord in his own house was unbelievably rude.

Gomeril did not seem offended, but then, he had been part of Master Jarris's study group and had therefore been party to many late-night discussions and arguments over the most arcane things. "Perhaps so. But the texts also appear to suggest that in return for not claiming the crown last time, the Bandryns would be due it at the next change of history. Remember that we are speaking of people who did not necessarily think like us. Today, someone who was offered a crown and who refused would be considered a fool. But back then, well, if the Bandryn family truly believed—believed utterly—that their line had a separate destiny if they refused a crown, perhaps it would not have been considered so odd."

Lythera didn't know what to say to that. She knew people in different lands had different customs and beliefs, but it was hard to imagine what Gomeril was suggesting—that the Bandryns believed they had had a special destiny. She searched for the Old Vedatic word. Holy.

"Yes," said Gomeril, and Lythera realized she must have said the word aloud. "A holy charge. Something sacred. It's not something taken seriously today. But the Bandryn may have been quite devout. And perhaps they had more intimate contact with the divine than we do. Jarris let slip the story about the voice that spoke to you in the library. Do you see why I take Jarris' theories seriously? We must be prepared for the change and you are instrumental in that change. We must be ready."

"And you think the change is to be soon?"

"This year, in fact. The Bandryns spent the centuries waiting, serving first the Uldreths, then the Gomerils, then the Segrithrs. Until a century ago, when the male line died out. But here you are."

"My name was Halevern."

"Bah," said Gomeril. "That's the problem with people today—everything is so black and white. Everyone says, all the male Bandryns are dead, therefore there are no Bandryns. Everyone says, women have never inherited property, therefore women will never inherit property. That's what is truly ridiculous, Lythera. Being too comfortable with old ideas and traditions to see when they need changing."

Lythera bit her lip to keep from laughing. "So you will insist I'm a Bandryn and I'll take the throne this year? That's insane. I'd never harm Teiryn, and no one would support that sort of madness, anyway."

"You're right, of course," said the portly lord. "But I have a feeling things aren't quite what they seem. The last Gomeril king, after all, lived fifteen years in Gomeril Hall after his abdication. The texts don't say Teiryn dies, only that a Bandryn assumes the throne. There are a hundred-and-one ways that might work itself out, some of them more satisfactory than others."

Lythera stiffened. "And what would be satisfactory to you, Lord?"

"To see all of us alive and happy when the year 1298 arrives," he said.

Lythera shuddered. Gomeril spoke as if such a thing were not guaranteed. Of course, accidents could happen, people fell ill, but she knew that wasn't what he meant. He was speaking of war, or insurrection. Something terrible that would cost many lives. She struggled for something to say that would drag the conversation elsewhere. She couldn't think about Teiryn deposed, even if he lived in exile on some Segrithr estate.

"So, what are these numbers that fascinate Mandlarin?" she asked. "The Rulikarien Progression—what does it mean?"

"It's the way of knowing which year is *the* year. There are two sequences in the Progression. The first is 23, 13, 11. Well, not so obviously. There are formulas and one must work the mathematics of them correctly. If you do, then you get those three numbers. All magic numbers—numbers which cannot be divided by any number other than themselves and one. Uldreth had twenty-three kings. Gomeril thirteen. Segrithr has had eleven. Teiryn is therefore the last. The sum of the sequence is 47, the number of kings of Evandia. The cycle is complete."

Lythera's heart pounded against her ribs but she forced herself to listen without comment. Still, if she had anything to do with it, nothing would happen to Teiryn no matter what some prophecy said.

"That's why the Gomerils never tried to get the crown back. The last Uldreth king had given the numbers to the first Gomeril king, and the last Gomeril king knew when he was crowned that another family would take the crown from him. But for some reason he did not give the numbers to the Segrithrs—bitterness, perhaps?—and so they have never known that they would have only eleven kings on the throne. Or if they found out, they put no stock in it and dismissed the prophecy generations ago. I have never seen any evidence that Teiryn or his father had any idea that the Rulikarien Progression even exists."

"Is that why you oppose Teiryn so much? Because you are bitter about your family being denied the throne by some magic numbers?"

He laughed and took a sip of wine. "Hardly. We have made it a habit to plague House Segrithr, but only with minor things. Call it a hobby. We've never been involved in anything treasonous. Rather, I like Teiryn a great deal. He's an honest, sincere, forward-thinking man, and you don't always get that in a king. His main failing is he's too easily led. Neither of his parents were like that; perhaps, between the two of them, they managed to stamp out some inner strength he was born with. Who knows? He seemed headstrong enough as a child, but the man?" Gomeril shrugged. "I hope you will be stronger on that front."

She didn't know what to say to that, it was so ridiculous. Even if a Bandryn hero were to arise, it wouldn't be *her*. The conversation simply got stranger the longer it got. "So that's the first sequence? There's another?"

"Oh, yes. Again, more equations must be solved first, but the answers to the equations tell us that a total of 47 kings is the answer to the first one progression. The 47th magic number is 2 1 1. The 2 1 1st magic number is 1 2 9 7. This year is the 1 2 9 7th year since the first Uldreth king was crowned. This is the year when both cycles coincide. The entire cycle is complete. By the end of the year, someone else will be sitting on Teiryn's throne. That someone will be you."

Lythera gasped at his brashness. The sheer treason he spouted so casually. "No," she whispered.

"It was easy to spot you," Gomeril continued calmly. "You look so much like the Bandryns—dark hair with a touch of red, violet eyes, strong bone structure, height. A fine-looking family. When you came into the hall that first day, I said to myself, *she's the one*. But it has not been so easy to confirm the signs that are supposed to presage your arrival."

"Signs?"

"Yes. I kept you under watch, you know. I knew this was the year that Teiryn's throne would go to another. But who? And then there you were. And a Bandryn by descent, though on the female side. Which it had to be, since the male line is extinct."

"Women can't inherit the throne," said Lythera weakly. She was sorry now she had ever come here. Gomeril was indeed mad.

"That has been the law until now. I do hope you will change that—and a few other things—when you have the opportunity. As you may know, I have no sons and my daughters are as yet unmarried. I would be happy to leave my title and my lands to my eldest—she is richly deserving. As it stands, though, I would have to leave my lands to the crown, or to a distant male cousin. Or find a man I thought worthy and wed him to my eldest daughter, no matter what she thought about it. I find the idea distasteful."

Lythera closed her eyes. Gomeril spoke as if it were a foregone conclusion that she would rule Evandia before the year was out.

"I know it's a lot to take in. I've had my whole life to consider it. It'll be a shock to Teiryn, too, I imagine. Having a consort and then becoming consort—well, I assume you still want him or you wouldn't have returned to the capital. Most men would refuse, but I doubt he could refuse you anything. After all, he's smitten enough with you to remain by your side to morning."

Lythera blushed, realizing that Wenvia must have told Gomeril about that incident. She had wondered about the court gossip. She had no idea it was Gomeril and not Radi or another chambermaid that was the one listening to Wenvia's tales.

"I have to go," she said.

"I'm sure Aiza will be here shortly," said Lord Gomeril. "Won't you wait for her?"

"No, I have to go," said Lythera. "I have to think."

Gomeril looked disappointed. "Very well, child. But do think hard. There are troubled times ahead, and Teiryn is likely to need all those who are loyal to him to stand by him. And you will need friends, too. The Gomeril family will support you, whatever you do. I pledge my honor upon it." He fingered his topaz ring, and Lythera was reminded that, to some people, the topaz meant loyalty. But loyalty to whom? And for what reason?

Lythera got up and fled the room.

22

Valeron sat in the coach, anxious to arrive at Novardan Manor. If all went well, his retinue would reach it by sundown. From the messages he had received from his mother and Novardan, the king would be approximately three days behind him. Novardan had remained in the capital until the departure date for the king was assured. No one wanted Teiryn to arrive at Novardan Manor before all was prepared.

It would be tricky—Julinand and his wife, Elliya, were the de-facto lords of the estate, even if Novardan held the title—and they were not in on the plot. Even the whisper of treachery could not reach their ears, or the king would know. Julinand himself was not particularly fond of Teiryn, but didn't dislike him either. It was Julinand's way to be equally cool to everyone in the family; he was more concerned with the details of running the estate than in parties or other forms of socialization. Elliya, on the other hand, was outspoken on her preferences. She liked Teiryn, and her father, nao-Lord Fallows, was fanatically loyal to the throne. If there were any trouble at Novardan Manor in the upcoming days, it would come from her, not her husband.

Valeron was sure he could succeed, though. It wasn't just that his mother had groomed him for this; it was an inner peace, a sort of confidence he'd never had before in anything. He could feel the rightness of his plan in the very core of his being. He was Lord Bandryn, he had his Segrithr bride, and it was time to take the title, and the throne and become the greatest ruler Evandia had ever seen.

It had been vital for the male line to be saved a hundred years ago when the last Lord Bandryn's wife had given him only daughters. The lengths to which the lord had gone to obtain a son just proved how critical it was for a Bandryn—Valeron—to be here. It was as if history and destiny had come together just to create him. His mother had drilled that into him almost every day since the day of his birth.

Everything was prepared. He had recruited a secret guard, mostly from the port cities, of men who cared for nothing but money. They would be loyal to him as long as he paid, and he had paid them plenty. Trenstarl lands were still just fertile enough; he could divert funds for a small, well-trained force without bankrupting himself. Most of those men were in his train even now, with a few more having been sent ahead with his mother as "servants" which she would offer to Julinand and Elliya as household staff. Their own staff might not appreciate the extra hands around the estate, hands unfamiliar with their schedules and routines, but it was essential for him to have men able to get close to the food preparation when the time came.

His mother, Reyva, and the nestriana had prepared a large quantity of poison and needed to be able to distribute it on the night of the Harvest feast. It wasn't a killing poison, but it would drug everyone enough that they would be unable to protest his ascension to the throne until it was too late. Teiryn would be dead, and Valeron would be in control of Novardan Manor, and then the nation. All he needed was a few minutes for everyone to be stupefied, aware of what was going on, but unable to resist.

A few wouldn't get the poison, and he was sure a few wouldn't eat enough to be affected. He wasn't worried, though his mother was. He had laughed at her—as long as most people were drugged, his men could handle those few who might try to stop him. And no one would be armed at a family Harvest dinner. The drug was only insurance; even without it, he would prevail.

He sighed and glanced out the window. They were approaching a town, some desolate mud hole on the borders of sei-Lord Falchan's lands. The people of the village didn't even glance up as his carriage rode through; no doubt they didn't recognize the livery or they'd have known him for a nao-Lord. When he was king, that would change. Everyone would know who he was. People should be proud to be Evandians. They had a glorious history; they would have an even more glorious future. Valeron fingered the lance head he kept with him at all times now, and imagined how beautiful and magnificent the new age would be under his guidance.

The village quickly faded behind them, and the road began winding through a dark pine forest where the only the sound was the rustling of the wind through the branches. The forest floor was carpeted thickly with fallen needles and cones and there was a hush over everything. Even the clank of the horse's tack seemed subdued in this place. Valeron had always preferred the plain to the forest—on a plain one could look out over one's domain easily. In a forest, one could see hardly beyond one's nose. A forest made one feel small, insignificant. On a plain your eye could expand its view outward into the distance. And you knew that wherever you looked, and whatever you saw, you were the lord of it.

Along the road, he noticed small heaps of food. Bits of bread, an apple or a bunch of grapes. It was very odd. But the oddest thing were the stones along the trail. They seemed to have been deliberately carved into vague bird-like shapes.

And then there was a lion. Valeron stared at the carving, intrigued. The Bandryn crest had a lion, and the odd dreams that plagued him in the palace often featured a lion. Sometimes the lion was old and wretched, and grotesque, being made up of the parts of different animals and only the head remaining distinctly leonine. Other times, the lion was perfect and huge, and roared loudly enough to wake Valeron from sleep. The dreams had been one more sign to him that he was fated to be the Bandryn to rule at the end of the age. The Bandryn lion lived in his dreams.

Only at the palace, though. His mother had wondered if this had to do with the palace being an astar. She thought it could focus, or even create, dreams. That sounded like nonsense, but Valeron could not deny that the Bandryn lion had only appeared to him there.

Valeron stared off into the trees. Something moved. He blinked and looked again, not believing his eyes. It was a lion. That was impossible; there were no lions in Evandia anymore! Yet there it was.

Didn't the coachman see it? The lion stood in full view just yards from the road yet none of the men in Valeron's train seemed to have noticed it. Everyone was quiet; even the coach horses hadn't missed a step.

Then he understood. The lion was just there for him. It was *his* lion, the Bandryn lion. He didn't know how it was here, or what it meant, but surely it was an omen of good fortune. That he was doing the right thing. He was the one to secure Evandia's future in the new age.

With an impulsiveness that he rarely displayed, he rapped on the front wall of the coach. "Halt!"

The coach stopped. Valeron jumped out. The coachmen and his guard stared at him curiously. He shrugged. "My legs are stiff. I'm going for a walk. We'll leave in half an hour."

Without waiting to see if anyone cared to respond to that, he turned and began walking toward the lion. The lion ambled off between the pines and up a steep slope. At times, it seemed to fade away, but if Valeron concentrated hard enough, the lion would soon become more apparent to him. Though he was in good shape, he was out of breath by the time he made it to the ridge of the hill. The trail crested the ridge and started down into a small valley. The lion faded from view and no matter how hard Valeron tried, he could no longer determine where it was. It had vanished like mist.

Perhaps it had led him as far as it needed to. Valeron peered through the trees, and saw the ripple of a lake and the smoke from a single fire. Who would live in this desolate spot? Someone the lion wished him to meet? He couldn't imagine who that might be.

Valeron broke out of the cover of the trees and found himself on the shores of a tiny lake—hardly more than a pond, really—a few yards from a hut with a fire pit just outside the door. He glanced around, but now couldn't see how he had arrived; the trail was obscured by low hanging branches that dipped into the lake.

Valeron walked toward the hut and around the fire pit, which was producing nothing but smoke at the moment. Perhaps whoever had built it had used green wood. He glanced inside. The hut held a thin blanket and piles of small figures whittled out of pine. Lions, mostly, and a few stork-like birds.

Valeron felt for the knife at his belt. If someone lived this far from anyone else, they must be an outcast. Perhaps a violent criminal, or a thief.

"There you are," said a thin voice. Valeron turned around and immediately dispensed with any thoughts of a knife. The owner of the voice was only about half Valeron's height, probably a quarter of his weight, and at least four times his age. The old man was stick-thin and his white hair stood out from his head crazily. Pine needles and clumps of dirt were caught in it. Skin hung loosely around his neck and bare arms. The rest of him was covered in a filthy brown homespun robe that fell to the ground.

"If you were expecting someone, I am sure I am not he," said Valeron. "I am nao-Lord Trenstarl. Who are you?"

"I'm, um," the old man ran his gnarled fingers over his face and tugged at his hair. "Oh, I'd remembered just this morning. Mu . . . ma . . . no, maybe mo . . . Meldan? Yes, I think that's it. Name's not important here, you know. Fish don't care, trees don't care. Don't see anyone. I'm the last one, you know."

"How do you live?" Valeron was intrigued despite himself. A hermit in the woods—that was something out of children's tales, not someone one met along the road.

"Oh, people leave things at the edge of the forest," he said. "Bread, meat, fruit. Sometimes a pie. I like pie." The old man lowered himself onto a log and glanced at his smoking fire pit. "Fortune's Blood, it's all smoke. The birds don't like that. They won't sing for me this afternoon. They're Fortuna's favorite, you know, especially the moon-bird."

Valeron sat down near the man, wondering if this man would ever say anything that made sense. "Why do you live here?"

"The birds don't sing for me anywhere else. Besides, I'm waiting, you know. For Fortuna's return. Someone has to do the waiting. We're an old order. The, oh, I forget. The nastroi? That sounds right. Used to be more of us, but I'm the last. Been alone here most of my life. Waiting for the changing of the tide. Or is that the turning of the tide?"

"What are you waiting for?"

"She's coming back soon; I can feel it. The deer tell me about it. Can't you feel it? Well, you must if you got here. Only special people find their way to this lake. No one not touched by her can make it up the trail. Yep, touched, that's what they used to call me, you know."

Valeron laughed. Why was he even listening to this? "You don't make much sense, old man, but you are amusing. A lion showed me the way."

The old man just nodded and grinned toothlessly. "I never imagined! The lion! Well, then you must be the Bandryn who comes at the end of the age. Or one of them, anyway."

"What? What do you mean?" Valeron's heart skipped a beat. This man knew him for a Bandryn!

"There's always a striving, you know. At the end of every age, Fortuna gives us choices. Bandryns fight it out, whoever wins will determine how the next age goes, whether we gain something or lose it. All the magic went last time, that's what I was told. Or, oh, something like that. It's up to the Bandryns, but they're chosen by Fortuna."

"Who?"

"Fortuna." The old man threw an arm out in a gesture that encompassed the lake and the forest. "She's in everything, aware, watching. I wonder if she ever gets tired. I get tired a lot lately myself. Sometimes too tired to see if people have left me food or not."

Valeron's thoughts were in turmoil. This man didn't make any sense, and yet a lion no one else could see had led Valeron here, a place where he was identified by this strange man as a scion of the Bandryns of old. Valeron bit his lip and stared at the old man. Should he take the man with him? Would this man's word be worth anything to Jarris and the others once Valeron had seized the throne?

Could he use this old man to secure his rule against any who might oppose him?

The old man didn't seem to notice Valeron's discomfiture. "Sometimes Fortuna's turning brings us great deeds and magic, and sometimes war, and sometimes fabulous wonders. Or that's what I was told by one of the old men who was here before me. How time passes! I can't even remember how long ago that was. Years and years, I don't know how many. The fish keep the time, you know. They know the seasons better than anyone else. Except maybe the trees." The man frowned. "Or was it something else? I can't remember anymore."

"Perhaps you should come with me," Valeron said. "It's time for Harvest, so you know there will be good food. And you can tell everyone about how the Bandryn will rule over everyone."

"Come? With you?" the old man finally stopped jabbering about fish and trees and stared blankly at Valeron.

"Yes. The tides are turning, as you said, and I'm the Bandryn who rises at the end of the age. You could witness my ascent, tell everyone that it was foreordained."

"Come? With you?" the old man said again, a little more loudly. He laughed. "No, I must stay here. My life springs from this place now, you know. I can't leave. Well, I can get to the road briefly, to fetch food. But I must be back to the lake."

"You're mad," said Valeron, "but you might be useful. You can tell everyone else who I am." He grabbed the old man by the arm and pulled him toward the trees. "Let's go."

"I can't be gone long," said the old man, who allowed himself to be hauled through the tree line and up the slope. "And I need to rebuild my fire."

"You'll be warm enough in the coach. And we'll get you better clothing, too."

"The road is more to your right," said the old man helpfully. "It's not far. But once I've gotten you there, I'll need to go back to the lake."

The road was much closer than Valeron would have thought, considering how long he'd followed the lion. But there was his coach. Men sat under trees or stood by the horses, chatting.

"Get this man a cloak," said Valeron as he approached, the old man's arm still firmly in his grasp.

One of the guards immediately pulled off his own cloak and threw it around the old man's shoulders. The old man stared at it quizzically, then looked at Valeron. "You're back to your people now, young man. It's time for me to return to my lake."

A snort came from one of the local men he'd hired. "Lake? There's no lake around here."

Valeron rounded on the man. "Of course there is. I was just there. This old man lives in a hut on its shore. It's just over there." He waved his free hand in the general direction from which he'd come.

The man said bowed his head and said, "Pardon, Lord," but his expression was troubled. Others among Valeron's train cast doubtful looks at each other.

Let them. He'd been to the lake; he knew very well it existed. He pushed the old man toward the coach. "Time to go."

For the first time, the old man resisted. "I can't leave. In fact, I should get back now. I can't be gone long."

The note of fear in the old man's voice almost made Valeron let go, but he quelled the sympathy he felt and tried again. "Good food awaits you," he said as winningly as he could. "And I will give you servants to provide anything you need. You just need to come with me; there are others who need to speak with you about the turning tide and Fortuna."

The old man shook his head. "I can't go any farther, don't you understand? If I don't return now, I will die." He looked directly into Valeron's eyes. "The trees are not happy with you, but the birds, they tell me what you need to know: you have a choice. Let me go, or do not, but remember that you had this choice, and that from this moment forward, you must live with the choice you make."

The old man's gaze shook Valeron; for a moment, it was as if something ancient and primal looked out of those watery pale blue eyes, something that watched him, and measured him, and wondered if he were worthy of...of something.

The man blinked and the effect was gone. Valeron shoved the old man into the coach. "You'll be fine," he said. "Better than you've been in years, with good food and wine to fill your belly, and no fish or trees to whisper in your ear. Won't that be nice?" It would certainly be nice to stop hearing about talking trees, anyway.

Valeron hopped into the coach and one of his men closed the door. The coach rocked briefly as the coachman climbed aboard, then jerked as the horses pulled it forward. Valeron smiled at the old man, wondering if he could be won over with good food. Surely he was too old to want a woman, but who knew? There would surely be a servant girl who could be persuaded to join the old man in bed for a few coins.

The old man stared at Valeron and said nothing. The weight of the unblinking stare made Valeron uneasy and he realized he was nervously twisting his Bandryn signet ring around and around his finger.

"Stop staring at me."

That had no effect on the old man. Valeron looked out the window, determined to ignore the other man for as long as possible. By the time they got to Novardan Manor, the old man would welcome a hot fire, some good food, fresh clothes, a bath, and a bedmate. How could he not? Valeron would be as good to the old man as he would be with Evandia once he ruled it. He would provide everything that was needed, and those who received his largesse would be grateful.

At last, he couldn't stand it and glanced back. The old man had slumped against the wall of the coach, mouth hanging open, skin slack. For a moment, Valeron told himself the old man was merely sleeping, but the gray pallor of the skin and the way the man leaned against the coach like a dead weight made the situation far too clear. The old man had died.

"Stop the coach!" yelled Valeron.

The coachman yelled "whoa!" to the team and the coach jerked to a halt.

"Lord?" asked the men who ran up to the coach. One opened the door. "Are you all right? Why did you shout?"

"The old man died," said Valeron. "Get his body out of here!"

The men glanced at each other. Valeron pointed toward the old man. "There! Get him out of here. I refuse to sit in the coach with a body."

"Lord, no one is there," said the man slowly, as if Valeron were an idiot.

Valeron turned back to the old man, but the other seat contained only the Trenstarl lance. Not even the cloak that had been thrown around the shoulders of the old man remained.

"What about the cloak?" asked Valeron. "One of you gave the old man your cloak."

The men glanced among themselves, and Valeron heard whispers, though he could not tell what the men said to each other. Every one of the men that Valeron could see from the coach wore a cloak.

"Never mind," he snapped. "Continue." He reached out to grab the door and slammed it shut.

A few moments later, the coach jolted into motion again. Valeron stared at the seat where the old man had sat. He didn't know what had happened, but he did know one thing. The man had been a messenger of some kind, and he had declared Valeron the Bandryn who would come at the end of the age.

If he'd had any doubts, he could put them to rest. Forces were moving him into place. It was only a matter of time before Teiryn was dead and he was king.

The long miles that lay between him and Novardan Manor passed quickly as Valeron dreamed of his glorious reign.

23

Lythera was calmer by the time she returned to her room at the Segrithr house. Scholars often tended toward odd thoughts and though Gomeril's thoughts had taken surprising turns, his pledge to her that he would stand by her and Teiryn relieved her of any anxiety that he would be behind any trouble. Whatever his true plans were, she could not credit him with outright treason, and Aiza was already someone she wanted to know better. She'd had so few opportunities to meet women her own age, she had been unable to recognize how lonely she'd been for female friends until now. At last she had the chance to build a friendship such as she'd read about in books, but never been able to experience.

It was only an hour or so past dark when Teiryn's coach stopped outside the house and a cloaked figure emerged. Lythera's heart doubled its work, and a tingle of anticipation ran down her entire body, from spine to toes. He was here. And she had so much to tell him.

The moment he entered the room, she flung herself into his arms. He hugged her hard for a moment, but then stiffened. She looked up into his deep black eyes. "What is it?"

"You weren't here last night," he said in an accusatory tone.

She laughed. "Well, I wasn't with another man. I will have no other man than you. How many times do I have to tell you that I am yours forever?"

His expression lightened, but only slightly. "It's not safe to be alone after dark on the streets."

"I wasn't alone. I was with Master Jarris' study group, and when that ended, it was so late, Aiza invited me to the room she rents..."

"Aiza...Gomeril?"

"Yes," said Lythera happily. "I'm sorry I didn't meet her earlier; we have so much in common! And she keeps a room near the school so I could stay there on days when our meetings go too late in the night for me to get back here. She's already said I could share the rent with her."

Teiryn gave her a quizzical look, "You have a place here."

Her heart faltered slightly. "I'm grateful to you for everything you've given me, and the house is beautiful. But the meetings are so interesting, and I am learning so much, and they go so late into the evening."

"I could have a coach waiting for you at the school whenever necessary," said Teiryn slowly. Lythera sensed he was annoyed but at least he hadn't immediately rejected her idea.

"Come," she said, gesturing for him to sit with her on the divan by the window that overlooked the street. There were so many things they had to talk about; her room with Aiza could wait. "Tell me about your day. And the party. What is the ambassador like?"

Teiryn relaxed visibly as he sat down, placed an arm around her shoulders, and told her about the party. Lythera closed her eyes and tried to imagine the splendid décor he described, the odd dress of the ambassador, and the customs he'd told Teiryn about. When he got to the part about the ambassador's marriage, she couldn't help looking up. "His father had nothing to say about it?"

Teiryn's black eyes were amused and he kissed her forehead. "Apparently not. You know, I don't believe we've had an ambassador in Morovol for some years now. Perhaps I should send one. I don't know why I didn't think of it before." He looked out the window. "Actually, there are a lot of things I can't understand that I've done since becoming king. And especially since Brenicia died. Now that I have you, I feel so much stronger, more able to face the ministers. Even my cousins." He hugged her tightly and she laid her head on his shoulder. "With you by my side, so much seems possible that wasn't before."

He was quiet for some time, but he had tensed up again. "What's wrong?" she asked. "Won't you tell me? Did the ambassador upset you somehow?"

"No, no," he said. "It was Novardan. He had another girl waiting for me."

Lythera's heart froze. She had been replaced already? "A new consort?"

"No," he said with some anger. "I told him no more. And I sent her away. I'm done with that. Even if you did not want me, I would be done with it. I don't know why the law was implemented that said a king can't take a second wife, but a new law needs to be made." He sighed. "There's no reason I need to be bound by that law any more."

Lythera thought about Gomeril and the way he'd spoken about Teiryn being too easily led. He'd be pleased to see a more active king in Teiryn. "I think you would have Gomeril on your side," she said. "I know he can be trying, but he's loyal. Surely you can count on some of the others, too."

He chuckled. "I don't think you know Gomeril as well as you might think, but perhaps you're right. In any case, even the ones who might oppose me at first could be softened with the right inducements. Property or positions for their sons at court. Something. I'll figure it out. Now, tell me about your day with Jarris."

Lythera recounted her time at the school, the meeting with Jarris' inner circle, the room she'd be sharing with Aiza. Happiness over her good fortune bubbled out of her. But Teiryn was still. She stopped and looked up at him. Strangely, his face was troubled and stormy.

"What's wrong?" she asked. "Everything is perfect."

She could see him struggling for something to say and held her breath. He had always been so understanding, so supportive. He had spent days at her side after the miscarriage. Now that everything was coming together, how could he look so unhappy? They could both have everything they desired.

"It seems like so much of your life will be lived away from me," he said. "I had thought to move you back into the palace as soon as my ministers agree. Some of them have already left for Harvest, so it will have to wait until after that, but I need you with me. Not here, not at the school."

She was confused. "But then why ask Jarris to find me a job?"

He shook his head. "It wasn't to be permanent. I knew you would find it enjoyable, since you'd liked being in the records-room with Jarris. But after you become my new queen, you'll be too busy to teach or be part of Jarris' team of scholars."

Her heart sank and she felt she could very well be sick right there, in front of him. She felt dizzy.

"But...you told me once you thought Brenicia's days were full of gossip and embroidery. Even if I'm queen, why can't my days have scholarship and students? Maybe I couldn't travel to the school all the time, but the students could come to the palace. Jarris' group could even meet there sometimes."

Teiryn shook his head. "But that's not the life of a queen."

"Why can't it be?"

Teiryn removed his arm from her shoulders and stood up. "It just isn't. My mother was a strong woman, too, and learned. But once she married my father, her life revolved around the palace—planning the celebrations, mixing with the ministers, helping my father by listening to the gossip he never heard. That's the life of a queen."

She was taken aback. "I have no interest in gossip," she said at last. "And I'm sure I can, with the help of the staff, plan any celebrations you might want. I love you and will support you and your plans for the kingdom, but that doesn't mean I have to give up everything else."

Her heart ached with disappointment and fear. How could having plans to teach or study truly interfere with being Teiryn's wife and queen? "I don't have to behave exactly like your mother, or any other queen," she said softly. "Can't I be myself? Don't you love me as I am?"

"Of course I love you. That's why I want you with me! I'll make you my wife, give you a throne and a crown!" His eyes were sad, his voice pleading with her.

Lythera stood and held her arms out. "I only want you. If that means being queen and having a crown and a throne, then very well. But if I want that, it's only because it means sitting beside *you*. You are what I want."

"Then why change things? Be my queen, as my mother was to my father."

She dropped her arms. "Why must that be my only choice? Why not be your queen, *and* have at least some of the things that are of value to me? If Brenicia could have much of her time free for gossip and sewing, then there's no reason I couldn't fill my time with other things."

He shook his head. "I have to think."

Panic tinged her thoughts. Lythera thought of telling him she'd give up everything for him. Jarris, the school, Aiza—she couldn't bear to think of her life without Teiryn. Or a life beside him where she made him unhappy.

But she couldn't get the words out. He might not like this idea now, but she had to give him time. He was only now realizing how much his ministers had bullied him; he would need time to realize how much more she could be to him than someone who planned parties and gossiped.

"Could we not talk about this some other time?" she asked. "Can I ask the staff to get you food or wine? There's no reason for any decisions to be made right now. We can just be together."

For a moment, she saw a glimmer of love in his eyes, before confusion clouded his face once more. He opened his mouth, then closed it, then turned away from her, his shoulders bowed in defeat. Her own heart turned to ash in her chest.

"I don't understand," he said. "But if I say anything more now, I'll say something I'll regret forever."

He strode out the door.

"Teiryn, wait!" she called after him, but he did not return. She went to the window and watched him get into the carriage. She waved, but he did not look up.

The carriage moved away and Lythera sank onto the floor, unsure if she would be sick or merely die right there of misery. How could he turn away from her? After they had been through so much together. After he had stood by her side even when his ministers did not wish him to. He had cherished her and protected her, and loved her. Tears ran down her cheeks but she paid them no mind.

She was unaware of time passing; the night moved on while she alternately dozed and wept. All over again, she was plunged into a pit of grief that seemed to have no bottom. It was worse than when she'd lost the baby; at least then she'd had Teiryn at her side, grieving with her. Now she was alone.

Someone shook her awake. "Lythera, what are you doing on the floor?" It was Aiza.

Lythera lifted her face and it registered dully to her that it was morning. She felt like staying where she was until she died, but Aiza had other ideas.

"I'm so glad that sour-faced house mistress let me in here to see you," said Aiza as she helped Lythera to her feet. Aiza's broad form had significant strength in it. "She said you'd had no breakfast yet, and wanted me to leave, but I marched right up here saying I'd have breakfast with you, and, look here, I was right." Aiza guided Lythera to the bed and allowed her to sit on it. "What an unpleasant woman! Now, what in the world is the matter with you?"

But Lythera could not talk around the great pain in her heart and just shook her head.

"Well, whatever it is, I'm sure some tea will set you right—at least righter than you are now," said Aiza. "So be good and sit right here. I'll tell your house mistress to send up tea and breakfast and we'll eat right here. After that, well, we'll just see how things go."

Lythera closed her eyes, too weary to reply. She was vaguely aware of Aiza bustling about, ordering the servants imperiously as befitted an ist-Lord's daughter, and managing Lythera's affairs to suit herself. In short order, Lythera found herself in a chair, in front of a small marble-topped table brought in from another room, with steaming tea in a cup held in her hands and bacon, eggs, and biscuits on a plate in front of her.

Aiza sipped some tea of her own. "I'll get them to pack up some of your things after breakfast so you'll have a few dresses and underthings in our room."

Lythera's heart lurched. Pack. Yesterday she'd been so willing to leave here, but now she wasn't so sure. Teiryn had been angry with her; she hadn't expected that. She shook her head.

"Oh, don't worry. I'll take care of everything," said Aiza. "I've been ordering servants to do what I want since the cradle." Her beatific smile belied the mischief in her voice.

The smile relieved Lythera more than anything had in the past twelve hours. She drank her tea and managed to eat a few bites of her tasteless breakfast.

Aiza kept up a monologue during breakfast. "My father said you came by yesterday while I was out—I was afraid I'd miss you but Gadriena

Standren insisted we go since she's leaving today for Standren Hall for Harvest. Her brother Galladon's supposed to marry Holliwen Segrithr, did you know that?"

Lythera let Aiza's gentle patter soothe her fears; she was sure she'd heard the names before, but didn't care enough to try to sort them out. It wasn't important right now, anyway. Teiryn would get over his anger, she was sure. If he didn't return to the house, she could go to the palace, or wait in the park. He rode his horse there so often, she was sure to see him soon.

"I'm sure my father simply blurted out all his prize theories about the prophecy and the Rulikarien Progression and never let you get a word in edgewise. My father can talk a lot when he wants to, you know. My mother was a quiet soul so you know I had to get it from somewhere. My sisters are more like her, very staid and reserved. Anyway, don't let my father upset you too much. He's just so excited to be able to witness the fulfillment of the prophecy."

Lythera put down her fork. She could hardly bear the thought of remaining awake, let alone eating another bite.

"Oh, finished?" asked Aiza. "All right, let's get your things together."

"But," began Lythera. She couldn't finish. How could she even talk about what had happened. She took a deep breath. "But Teiryn didn't like it that I would be staying somewhere else sometimes," she said at least, measuring out each word like it was poison.

"He'll get over it," said Aiza confidently. "Good fortune, Lythera, make a man pursue you once in a while! It's not right for you to just be here for his whims. Even wives have more freedom than that. I'll leave the address of the room with the doorman, so if Teiryn wants to see you on a day you're not here, he can find out exactly where you are. How about that?"

Lythera hesitated, and Aiza took that for assent. In a matter of minutes, Lythera and her trunk had been collected onto a carriage and Aiza was directing the driver where to go. Lythera allowed the other woman to bring her to the boarding house and install her belongings in the cramped room. Aiza excused herself after a few minutes, saying she had an appointment, and that she would return in the evening.

By noon, Lythera realized she needed to get herself moving, to get her mind working, again. She had a class to teach at four. She was truly on her own now and couldn't ignore her responsibilities to the school, no matter how much she wanted to sleep and forget the outside world.

She moved so slowly, though, that it was after three before she made her way to the school and climbed the steps to the classroom. She laid out the work for the students and waited. It seemed only moments before they arrived, just as much a tangle of adolescent energy and rebellion as they had been before.

She smiled wearily at them. "Please, take your seats and look at the papers I've prepared. I'd like you to translate some sentences for me, and we'll go over them together."

There was a small spattering of grumbling, but nothing serious. She could see the boys remained determined to learn from her, if only to prove to themselves that they couldn't be bested by a female instructor. At least, not for long. They studiously translated the sentences she had for them in relatively neat hands—they at least had paid attention in penmanship—and gave Lythera their work with more than half the class time remaining.

By the time class was over, and Lythera and the boys had discussed the intricacies of declining masculine and feminine nouns in the dative case, Lythera felt much better than she had since seeing Teiryn the night before. She couldn't believe that his anger would last. Not Teiryn. Not with her.

So it was with much-improved spirit that she walked into the late afternoon sun and saw Aiza waving at her. She waved back and even managed a smile. She had a place to stay when she needed it, and a beautiful house to stay in otherwise. She had friends. And, sooner or later, she would have Teiryn again.

"Lythera!" called Aiza. Her hair, which had always been pulled back before, now flowed down her shoulders freely. Lythera liked the look on her; she thought it was much more flattering on the large-boned woman than having her hair bound. "How are you feeling now? I see you're smiling, at least."

Lythera nodded. "I'm better. I'm sure I can work this out with Teiryn. He has to realize how important this is to me. I'm sure he will."

Aiza laughed. "I'm sure. Meanwhile, come with me to my father's house. Threndayl's already there. We want to talk to you about Harvest."

Lythera's good mood disappeared. Even if Lord Gomeril had pledged to be loyal, she wasn't sure how far she could trust him. What did loyalty really mean to him, anyway? She hated to say no to Aiza, who had been so friendly, but she didn't want to go back to the Gomeril house.

Aiza saw her hesitation and linked her elbow with Lythera's. "Don't worry, my father's just very excitable about his studies. Besides, what do you have to fear? He thinks you're the next ruler of Evandia, so even if he's crazy, you know he won't hurt you."

Lythera shuddered. "But I won't do anything against Teiryn. Your father should know that. And if I won't, then whatever he believes, nothing is going to happen. Teiryn will continue to sit on the throne, and I'll teach at the school, and your father will be duly disappointed that nothing's changed."

"Threndayl's somewhat of that mind, too," said Aiza. "Otherwise, he and my father get along excellently well and agree on everything."

Lythera still found it odd that Lord Gomeril could favor a poor boy so much, even when it came to his daughter's company, but she said nothing. She allowed herself to be led to a coach that Aiza had waiting, and was silent during the drive to the Gomeril residence.

Of course, what did she know of ist-Lords? The first one she had ever met was Lord Novardan, and he fit her preconceived mold perfectly. Arrogant, dismissive of those below him in station, complete with haughty demeanor and a cold sneer. The others had seemed so quarrelsome and unpleasant when they'd interviewed her that first day, she'd assumed they were rude, condescending boors.

Even then, Lord Gomeril had seemed different. He had not joined in the laughter at her expense during that meeting. He had seemed thoughtful, and he'd been very quiet. After that, if she saw him in passing, he nodded to her. He hadn't sought out her company or spoken to her, but she remembered now that Teiryn had said that Lord Gomeril had been the first of his ministers to send condolences after they'd lost their baby.

So maybe he wasn't like the others after all. Lythera still wasn't sure she wanted to meet with him again, but Aiza was right, she wasn't in any danger. Lord Gomeril was just an unsettling man with strange ideas. She glanced at Aiza, who was watching the people along the street out the carriage's window. What would it have been like to grow up with a scholar-father who liked odd ideas and entertained strange fantasies borne of old prophecies and dusty texts? Certainly it would have been nothing like being Marlun Halevern's daughter. For one thing, it had probably been much more pleasant.

The carriage pulled up outside of the Gomeril residence. Aiza hopped out and Lythera followed more slowly, only now realizing she was wearing one of the dull travel gowns and not something more fitting a visit to this residence. But Aiza hadn't seemed to notice. Perhaps her father would be gracious and overlook Lythera's dress.

Lythera glanced down the street toward the Segrithr house. She just caught a glimpse of the stag banner flying in the autumn wind before being ushered into the Gomeril dwelling.

Once more, Lythera was struck by the hominess of the great house. Even though the architecture could not have been more formal, nor the furniture more stately, the rugs and tapestries and small personal items scattered about, like a tiny wooden box engraved with the letter G, made Lythera feel welcome all over again.

Aiza ushered Lythera into the conservatory behind the house. Her father and Threndayl sat behind the table, nearly obscured by a haphazard pile of books and loose parchments. They did not seem to notice the women's entrance.

Finally, Aiza picked up a book and slammed it shut. Threndayl jumped in his chair. Lord Gomeril merely looked at his daughter. "Come, come, sit down," he said. "We think we've found something useful."

Aiza plopped herself down in a chair, decidedly unladylike, and Lythera followed suit. The casualness and familial closeness of the setting made her suddenly lonely for a childhood with a man like this. Someone to talk to, study with, or simply lounge in a chair next to and be at ease with. Lord Halevern, or her mother, would have scolded Lythera for such behavior, even in the privacy of the family rooms even when doing backbreaking chores that servants should have been doing. The noble bearing her parents wanted to see in their daughters could not be relaxed anywhere in Halevern Hall.

"So?" asked Aiza. "Are you going to tell us? Perhaps today, before we expire of boredom?"

Threndayl glanced up, a fierce fire blazing in his eyes. Lord Gomeril's eyes reflected no less excitement. "Yes, yes," said the Lord. "Recall that I was disappointed I could find no omens that Lythera was indeed the true Bandryn ruler we have been waiting for. Now we think we know why. We think we have discovered how to make the signs concerning Lythera reveal themselves."

24

"What?" asked Lythera. "What do you plan to do to me?" She got up and backed away from the table. Aiza glanced at her, worry on her broad face.

"Nothing, nothing," said Lord Gomeril. "Would I do anything to you, child? It's just that there is an incantation here which is designed to make the Bandryn heir reveal himself—or herself, as the case may be. The wording is deliberately murky on the point. I'm assuming that if the author of this tract had baldly stated that a female Bandryn would take the throne, his work would never have been copied and he'd have been laughed out of scholarship entirely."

"Let's try it," said Aiza. "Let's see if it works!"

"Wait," said Lythera. "What is this text, and how did you get it? Does Master Jarris know about this?"

Lord Gomeril smiled easily. "No, he doesn't. He doesn't have the resources I do. I've been able to put out discreet enquiries for old texts that mention magic, Fortuna, and Bandryns. Sometimes, impoverished families discover they have moldy tomes that can sell to me for a good price, whereas Jarris can only offer them his thanks. I have especially been interested in contacting those families who intermarried with the Bandryns over the years, because they have been more likely to have family papers. The effort has been worthwhile."

Lythera felt silly standing when everyone else was sitting, and no one had made a move toward her or offered her any insult. She sat down cautiously. "What is it you want of me?" she asked.

"Nothing," said Lord Gomeril. "No, really," he said when he saw her expression. "I want to read this incantation and perform the accompanying ritual. If I'm wrong and you're not the next ruler of Evandia, or if this is all a fool's errand, then nothing will happen. If I'm right, then we should see or hear something that indicates I'm on the right track. But nothing happens to you, dear. Nothing at all."

Lythera hesitated, but there seemed to be no danger. "All right."

"Very good," said Lord Gomeril. Threndayl, who had been silent beside him this entire time, merely nodded.

"What do we need for this ritual?" asked Aiza.

Threndayl picked up a list he had in front of him. "A feather. Some flower petals. A sword. Smoke. Water. And something precious to the person doing the ritual."

To herself, Lythera wondered about the symbolism of the items. They had to do with blessings, power, transformation, and communication with another world. She shivered, recalling once more the feather that had appeared on her windowsill prior to her father sending her away with Novardan. The more she thought about it, the more she could not dismiss it as mere coincidence. Some force had been telling her something. It had been a message.

"Any particular kind of petals?" asked Aiza. She gestured arbitrarily at a flowering bush. "This conservatory is full of them."

Lord Gomeril glanced around. "I think Lythera should choose."

Gomeril looked at her, and Lythera nodded. "All right." She got up and walked around the conservatory, carefully noting all the flowers she knew. Most of them, however, she did not. Gomeril was quite a gardener; so many of the plants in this room were exotic and colorful. Bright oranges and yellows, brilliant whites, and even spotted red-and-yellow flowers. They were all beautiful. But which one should donate the petals Gomeril needed for this incantation?

She found a bush that looked familiar. This was the same sort of bush that Jarris was trying to save in the palace gardens. And yet here was a perfectly healthy one. She wondered if Jarris knew about Gomeril's garden and what it contained. Jarris had told her the name once, after she'd agreed to help him save it. A nystrion.

The purple flowers of the nystrion were almost lily-like in their tapered, thick petals and long stamens covered in yellow pollen. Lythera was attracted to the delicate scent that surrounded the bush. It was sweet like honeysuckle, but something about it seemed darker and more mysterious. She didn't want to disturb the bush, but something prompted her to take three of the flowers anyway. She couldn't help herself. This was the proper flower for this ritual.

She returned to the others to find they had cleared off the table. On the table was a marble bowl full of water. A feather. A candle, the sort that smoked to keep away insects in the summer. An ancient sword black with age. Lythera laid down the flowers.

"Excellent," said Lord Gomeril. "Now all we need is something precious. That is coming."

In moments, the steward arrived with a bottle covered in dust. He handed it to Gomeril, who thanked him and placed it on the table. "Sixty-year-old cognac from Selandia," he said. "I've had it for thirty years with the thought that I'd save it for New Years in 1298. So it's about as precious an item as I own, at least to me personally."

Threndayl handed Gomeril a thin unbound book whose pages were sewn together. "First, we have to ask for a blessing for our, um, propitiation," said Gomeril. He squinted at the handwriting. "I'd prefer first to curse the scribe, but that can wait."

Gomeril's voice rang out loud and clear.

Fortuna, bless us, each one
Look upon us with kindness
Grant us success in our endeavors
And support us in all we do.

"Hmm," he said. "Rhymes in Old Vedatic. Oh well, now I ask you all to close your eyes, clasp your hands together, and I'll finish the incantation in the original."

Lythera did as he requested. In her mind, she translated the text as Gomeril read it out loud.

The winds of time have brought us to this place
The end of an age, a time for your grace
The Progression is finished; the new age is at hand
Reveal to us the one who will take hold of the land
Return to smile upon us and let us hear your voice
And put forward the one who bears the choice.

A loud crack filled the room. Lythera jumped and opened her eyes. The cognac bottle had shattered, sending its contents all over the table. It had soaked the feather, doused the candle, and even, somehow, tipped over the marble bowl so that the water also flowed onto the table and on the floor.

But what caught Lythera's eye was the sword. It was bright and shiny as if newly-forged. And it had swung around so that its wet hilt was directly in front of her. Without thinking, Lythera dropped Aiza's hand and grabbed it. The moment she touched the sword, every bush in the conservatory blossomed with even more flowers and their combined scents weighted the air, which already smelled heavily of cognac.

The petals which Lythera had brought to the table were now in her lap. For a moment, the tableau held. Lythera couldn't breathe, couldn't think. Her head felt as if her senses had been swathed in cloth for her entire life and now that had been removed for the first time. She heard every bird in the yard, even through the glass of the conservatory. She felt the slow ebb and flow of the sap in the bushes around her and in the trees nearby and her own blood seemed to move in concert with it.

Lythera leaped up from the chair and threw down the sword. It clattered to the floor; Threndayl jumped out of its path.

"What did you do to me?" she screamed around uncontrollable shaking. Her voice was too high, too frightened; she didn't recognize it. The world around her was altered, or she was; everything was alien. Nothing was familiar.

"What happened?" asked Aiza.

Gomeril leaned forward, concern on his face. "I'm sorry, child, I had no idea the results would be so dramatic. Are you all right?"

Lythera wanted to reach out and strike him, hit something, do something which would distract her from the growing maelstrom in her mind. She was being sucked down into a dark place and couldn't resist. Dimly, she was aware that others were talking around her, carrying her, placing her on a bed. They were unimportant.

The darkness swallowed her. It seemed to her that she was spinning out of control with no way to know which way was up. And yet she was falling. She screamed but didn't know if she could reach the others any more with her voice. She was cut off. Alone.

Not alone, said a deep, feminine voice.

Who are you?

Who do you think? The voice contained an element of humor that Lythera clung to. It helped her banish the topsy-turvy spinning in her head. Soon she felt as if she were floating on the surface of a dark, bottomless sea. She did not want to sink.

I don't know who or what you are. Something named Fortuna? Something like the Selandi sacrifice to? The one who changes the seasons, and causes the moon to rise and set? I don't have a word for that.

Some have called me a goddess. Your people have long forgotten both me and the word.

Lythera struggled to grasp what she was being told, but she couldn't really make sense of it. She fell back on what she did understand.

Lord Gomeril thinks I will rule Evandia. But I won't do anything to Teiryn!

That is your choice. The prophecy will be fulfilled, but not necessarily in any manner which can be predicted. The choices of the people involved can never be foretold.

If I don't take the throne, then there will be no Bandryn ruler. Teiryn will continue to be king. The prophecy won't be fulfilled, said Lythera.

Do you really suppose you are the last scion of the Bandryn line? You have four sisters. Your mother had other relatives. There are others you do not know. The prophecy will work itself out one way or another. With you or without you.

So you don't care who is the next ruler of Evandia? You don't care about Teiryn? Lythera felt herself growing afraid of the voice. It was so calm, so detached. It did not seem like the voice of any entity she wished to know or be involved with.

Of course I care. But to force the choices of others is wrong, even for me. The choice is yours. Teiryn's life is within your hands, not mine.

I want him to live.

You cannot both choose his life and deny the throne.

Why not? yelled Lythera. There was no answer.

Lythera floated on the odd dark waters while overhead, a full moon rose. The full moon, she recalled, meant completion. Fulfillment.

At Harvest, the choice will be made.

Lythera wanted to argue with the voice, make it tell her more, assure her that Teiryn would live. She opened her mouth, but the oily waters rushed down her throat and she began to sink. She struggled and tried to scream, but she couldn't swim, couldn't float, couldn't do anything to help herself. Her body spasmed and changed, bones and sinews melting, taking new forms they had never had before. She was being crushed under the water, under the weight of her own bones. With a last desperate burst of energy, she flung her arms out with all her might and willed herself to rise.

The water parted and she flew upward, light and free. She had wings. She looked down and saw the old white-maned lion with the body of a goat, the feet of an eagle and tail of a serpent on an island in the midst of this peculiar sea. The lion creature smiled and said, "I knew you would come. But be careful. The outcome of the striving is the one thing that is not foretold."

Lythera turned away from the animal and flew into the icy sky toward the full moon. But then her wings failed her and she fell toward the earth far below, shrieking her rage and sorrow and defiance.

25

Teiryn slept fitfully and got up early. The confusion and anger he had felt during his visit with Lythera had surprised him. It was true she was educated and he'd asked Jarris to find her a position at a school, so he should have known when she accepted that she would be pleased by it. He simply couldn't fathom why she would want to continue on that path once he had found a way for her to sit beside him as queen.

Teiryn ignored Velrudin's attempts to get him to look over some papers after breakfast, and he waved off Yawneil when it was time for the morning cases. Not this morning. Not only was he in no mood, but he had no idea what he might decide, or put into motion, today. Now that the lassitude of the past few years was dissipating, he needed to find a new way forward that would mark this reign as his own. Stamp it with his name and his image. But how that reign would take shape, he couldn't imagine. Not yet.

Teiryn strode to the stables, his mood so obvious that not one person approached him when normally he was besieged by petitioners. He looked at no one and noticed nothing until he stood in front of Trailblazer's stall. The horse lifted its head over the stall door and brushed its nose against his chest.

The familiarity of the horse, and the soft feel of his velvety black muzzle under his hand, calmed him somewhat. Teiryn grabbed a brush and entered Trailblazer's large box stall and began to brush the already impeccable coat. The repetitive motion helped ease his mind even more.

Lythera. He loved her; she was as dear to him as Brenicia had been. He knew she loved him. But he wasn't the only love in her life; she had scholarship, and students, and a new friend in Aiza Gomeril. Her life had opened up in front of her in ways it never would have at Halevern Hall. She could have everything Teiryn could provide, and yet...and yet, she wanted more.

Brenicia had always smiled and cooed over every present he had given her. And Lythera had treasured his morning gift and the hair ribbon—it had been in her hair last night. He had noticed it as soon as he walked in. In fact, he could not remember seeing her without it since he had given it to her. It was either in her hair, or on the table next to the bed. So some gifts she was more than willing to accept.

"Hey, Blazer!" called someone from outside the stall. His young cousin Evinard Nivain appeared and stopped as he saw Teiryn already in the stall. "Majesty," he said, obviously surprised by the king's presence. "I, uh, hope you don't mind. Sometimes I bring Trailblazer here a bit of something from the kitchens."

Teiryn smiled and hoped the turmoil and pain in his heart were not so evident now that he had had a chance to begin thinking about what happened. "No, not at all. I'm glad he has more visitors than just me and Dendryl."

Evinard smiled easily; he looked so much like his father rather than Teiryn's cousin Morvania. He had the Segrithr coloring, but his features were softer, more rounded, more pleasant. He was an affable young man and Teiryn liked him. He was glad Lythera and Evinard had become friends.

"I'm always in the stables in the morning," said Evinard happily. "And this morning is special—I thought I'd ride out to the park, maybe stop by to see Lythera. Velrudin told me where she's staying. I'd like to see her again. Maybe she'll come back to the palace for more riding lessons. Or I could take a horse over to the house and we could ride in the park. I think she'll be a good horsewoman in time." He shook his head. "Strange to think of a noblewoman who'd never been on a horse before."

Teiryn tried to look pleasant through this monologue, wondering if everyone and everything would be reminding him of Lythera today. He didn't want to say anything, but Evinard deserved to know that Lythera was gone.

"She might not be there," said Teiryn. "At the house, I mean. She's might be at the school. Or somewhere else." Somehow, he couldn't force himself to add that she might be in a rented room with Aiza Gomeril.

Evinard looked troubled for only a moment. "Then I'll ask the doorman, and if she's not there, I'll head toward the school. And if she's not there, someone will know where to find her."

"Just like that? Don't you think she should remain at the house?" Teiryn put the brush down and walked to the stall door to face the young man.

Doubt flickered across Evinard's face. He did not seem to want to have this conversation with his king. But Teiryn stared at him and did not relent.

"No, not really," said Evinard slowly. "She always had courage, but you know that, Sire, better than anyone, I would think. I never really thought Lythera seemed the type to sit in a house and do nothing, anyway, and I guess I was right. With a position at the school, and with your support, she can finally pursue any interest she might have."

Teiryn didn't respond, but he turned over Evinard's words in his mind.

"When she was here, she was always busy doing something," said Evinard, now sounding a bit more confident. "Riding, or studying, mostly. Or walking in the garden, discussing the plants with the gardeners. Helping the servants with the palace cats—feeding the runts of the litters, and such. I don't picture her sitting around a solar stitching with the ladies all day, Sire, she's got far too much she wants to do and to learn. Now she'll be teaching, and who knows what else she'll find to occupy herself with. I bet she'll have interesting stories to tell. I can't wait to see her again."

Teiryn still had nothing to say. After a few moments, Evinard bowed slightly, stepped away, and said, "Please excuse me, Sire."

"Wait," said Teiryn. A question popped into his head. "Are you saying she would feel trapped in the Water Street house?"

Evinard looked doubtful all over again. "I don't know, Sire. But, well, I think I would. I've been, um, seeing a girl lately, from a wealthy merchant family based in Ensdrun. They travel all the time, and they've seen more of the country, and even some other countries, than my parents would dream of visiting. They have so many interesting stories, and seem to know everyone. I think I might like a life like that."

Teiryn recalled some slip Morvania had made recently about Evinard's new "friend." Morvania seemed resigned to the possibility her youngest would marry beneath him, but with five elder children already provided with titles or inheritances, perhaps she was content to let Evinard find his own way. It appeared he was happy with that, and had no need or desire for his mother to arrange a marriage or provide for him for life.

That seemed to be what Lythera wanted, too. It was just that he didn't understand that. For Evinard to do such was one thing—he was a young man. Younger sons had always had to rely on their parents and eldest brother or else strike out on their own. But daughters were always cared for within the family. Always.

Lythera didn't have a family now, but she did have him. He would provide for her. That should be exactly what she wanted. Security. All the privileges of wealth without the duties. Everything.

But it seemed he was wrong.

"Sire, are you all right?"

He managed another smile for Evinard's sake. "Yes, thank you, Evinard."

The young man bowed and left, no doubt glad to get away from such a strange and difficult conversation with his king.

Teiryn was glad to be alone with his thoughts again. He recalled Lororo's story about how Morovolo women handled their own affairs, and men competed for their attention. It had seemed a chaotic system, full of uncertainty. Why not let the fathers arrange everything? It worked out for the best most of the time.

Even Lythera's father, though motivated by greed, could not have arranged a better situation for Lythera than to send her to Teiryn. Unless, he thought grimly, he had been a cruel man, or a heartless one. And what of all those other girls who had been sent to him and whom he had sent away? What of Eithnira Nevelein, brought to the palace because she resembled Brenicia, and because her father was titled and poor? At least Teiryn had been able to make sure Velrudin sent money to her family, but he had to be honest. Fathers did not always have their daughters' well-being at heart. Sometimes they only had their own.

Teiryn was sick of thinking and his heart still felt wounded. He wanted to see her again, to talk this out some more, but he did not have time now. He was supposed to leave shortly to enjoy Harvest with the rest of the Segrithrs at Novardan Manor. Teiryn's heart fell even lower. He had put aside his tasks this morning, but he couldn't do so for much longer. There were many errands and duties ahead of him if he were to leave the capital on time in two days. It would take a further four days to reach Novardan Manor, leaving just days to spare before Harvest. Metricia had already written him saying that she and the lady of the manor had many diversions and entertainments planned and looked forward to his arrival. He couldn't disappoint them.

Teiryn returned to the palace. He wanted to avoid his apartment, though, since the servants were busily packing away what he would need for the visit to Novardan Manor. And here was his cousin Lord Novardan himself coming toward him, his traveling cloak and hat already donned.

"Good fortune," said his cousin.

"And to you."

"I am just leaving," said Novardan.

Teiryn nodded. He was glad that Julinand and his lady were the true caretakers of Novardan Manor. If it were up to this man, nothing would have been done in time. Harvest was rapidly approaching and he was still in the palace. By now, the food should have been delivered and stored, and the wines carefully chosen, and some of the beasts already slaughtered. If only their uncle had not willed the title to Ilvinard. Julinand would have been a much better choice. At least this man had never married. The title might yet pass to another, preferably one of Julinand's sons.

Teiryn flushed a little. That sounded a bit like he was wishing ill-fortune on his cousin.

Novardan had been waiting for a response, something more than a nod, Teiryn was sure. But he said nothing. Novardan looked slightly uncertain.

"Sire, I know you have been in a deep despair of late. But do not worry; the girl I have for you at the manor is a bright, happy thing."

"Send her back to her family."

"Sire!"

"Send her back. I told you before I will accept no more consorts. I am finished with that. Are you deaf, man?"

Novardan leaned forward, rage flashing in his eyes. Teiryn wondered just how far his cousin would go, and if he cared.

"Sire, I am doing this for the kingdom and you are not helping. I'm sorry your last consort miscarried. And it's too bad you sent the Nevelein girl away after I searched so hard for someone like her. You never gave her a chance to win your heart or conceive your child. Another girl might appeal to you..."

Teiryn cut him off. "No."

"No?" Novardan's voice was strangled, as if he could not believe what he was hearing. "For our family, for the throne! What is so objectionable? There are hundreds of maids in Evandia and all the same..."

Novardan fell to the ground. It took Teiryn a moment to realize it had been his own fist which had knocked the other man down. Novardan stared up at him, one hand on his jaw where Teiryn had struck him. In his eyes, there was no longer rage, but hate. "That was ill done, Sire."

Teiryn knew he should apologize, but he couldn't do it, not at this moment. Novardan had pushed girls on him for the last time, and, after Harvest, if he protested too much about Lythera's return or hinted that she should be sent away again, Teiryn would send him back to his estate and ensconce him there. The old Teiryn who could be bullied by Novardan was gone.

"No more consorts," he said. "You are my minister, but remember this—I am your king. If any woman comes to my bed ever again, it will be at my invitation, not yours. I do not need you to agree, only to obey. Send word to the girl you've chosen to go home. Give her a gift for her time and her obedience to the throne, but I will not bed her, nor any other woman of your choosing, ever again. Is that clear?"

Novardan climbed to his feet slowly. "Very clear, Sire."

"Good." Teiryn stalked down the corridor and those who had witnessed the altercation flung themselves out of his path. Except one rotund figure who stood squarely in his way. Gomeril, of course. He was clapping.

"I would say that was well done, Sire. Too bad I haven't the courage to smack the young snot myself."

"What do you want? Shouldn't you be at Gomeril Hall by now?"

"I want nothing," said Gomeril. "You mistake me. I am simply working on some last-minute arrangements. I will be away home shortly. May you have a good Harvest."

Teiryn almost strode by the man without responding, but he had been rude far too much recently, especially in the last few minutes. "Good Harvest to you, too."

Gomeril smiled and bowed slightly, as much as his large belly would allow. Teiryn walked around him and passed on into the hall to the throne room. It was rarely used except for coronations and state functions, and almost always deserted. The guards allowed him in and closed the door behind him.

Teiryn walked down the long narrow room which was draped in red banners, the floor covered in red carpet. At the end of the room stood the seat carved from the granite of the Segrithr mountains and covered in red felt and red cushions. Behind the throne, on the wall, was a tapestry depicting Keival Segrithr's victory over the last Gomeril king. Always before, the room had made Teiryn feel a bit awed. To think his forefathers had such strength, such conviction. Now he wondered where all that courage had gone. If Keival Segrithr had wanted a woman, surely he would have found a way, something more forward and heroic. He wouldn't have allowed her to reject him, to turn away from his generosity and his desire to protect and care for her.

Teiryn sat down on the steps which led to his throne. He wasn't the king his father had been, or his grandfather. Songs were still sung about Warin Segrithr, about how strong he had been in battle with Evandia's enemies. And about how his wife Queen Palia, had rallied the people at home, astride her great white horse Starshine. Little children still sung nursery rhymes about that steed. And their son, Majelon, Teiryn's father. He had not been required to go to war, as his ancestors had. But he had faced a ten-year drought. Riots had broken out in the hardest-hit regions. Teiryn's father had personally inspected the areas and spoken to those in need. He had organized the relief efforts, and made sure those areas which had more provided to those with nothing at a reasonable cost.

Teiryn had thought about those deeds when he'd married Brenicia. But all during their years together, they had faced no such hardship. Their personal tragedies had been many, but when it came to true leadership, none had been required. Teiryn had allowed the ministers to bend him to their will. He would have to find the strength, after Harvest, to take back the authority of the king.

He might not be Majelon, or Warin, or Keival. He was only Teiryn, but he had a lot to live up to. He had never felt up to the task, and since Brenicia had died, he felt even less competent than ever. Allowing the ministers to convince him to accept consorts was one of the mistakes he had made, though at least that had brought Lythera to him. Still, he would have to learn not to make similar mistakes in the future. He was too old to be so foolish.

Last night he had been foolish again, allowing rage to overcome him. To turn away from Lythera without even trying to understand why she wanted to be on her own, why she felt she needed more than he could give.

He got up, tired of self-pity. He had one more stop to make before he could leave. Underneath the throne room was another, more silent room. The crypt which held the remains of the kings and queens of Evandia. All the Uldreths, Gomerils, and Segrithrs who had sat on the throne. Their families had crypts elsewhere, but the rulers themselves remained safe in the crystal palace, surrounded by its blue and violet-shaded walls, where the very air seemed to drip with color and riotous light.

Teiryn took one of the oil lamps from a side table and went to the staircase behind the throne. He descended it slowly. The stairs weren't terribly steep but they were worn with age and uneven.

He pushed the doors at the bottom of the steps open and strode into the violet-hued room. He walked to the right wall, where Brenicia's sarcophagus lay. Most of the Uldreths and Gomerils were in niches in the wall which had long ago been sealed. The Segrithrs had chosen not to fill the remaining niches, though, but to have their dead in sarcophagi. Teiryn didn't know why.

"It's been another year," he said. "Three years now since you left me." She didn't speak to him here. She never had. He placed his hands on the marble lid and leaned forward, rested his forehead against the cool stone. He thought about her bubbling laughter and the way she'd smile after they made love. But the details were fuzzy now. It was getting harder to see the particulars of her face any more, as if she were fading from his inner sight. He was losing her all over again as she became part of the dim fabric of his past, along with his childhood and his parents. Even Lythera was gone for the moment, absorbed in a new life she was building for herself. A life Teiryn wasn't sure he would have a place in. He felt so alone.

"I have to find a way to live up to my name. My mother said once I should do something to ensure songs were sung of me until the end of the age. But I have no idea what that would be, and even if I did know, I couldn't do it alone. If I find a way to give Lythera what she needs to be happy, will that make things the way they were when you were with me? Will that help me be the king I need to be?"

There was no answer, of course. Wearily, he turned and went back up the steps.

26

When Lythera awoke, it was full dark. A single lamp glowed on a table by the bed, illuminating a dozing Lord Gomeril in a large chair near the far wall. Lythera wondered if the world would start spinning again if she got up, but she wanted to try. The voice that had spoken with her had told her she had a choice to make, and that Teiryn's life was in her hands. She was impatient to go to him, to do whatever it took to save his life. Nothing was more important than helping Teiryn.

Lythera eased herself up gradually and then swung her legs over the side of the bed. Everything in the room stayed where it was supposed to. No darkness threatened, no vertigo, no strange sensations. Certainly no wings! She was herself again, small and unimportant.

She felt strangely weary and very hungry now that she was sitting up. Her stomach protested and grumbled. Lythera glanced to her wrist, but her purse was not there. She looked at the bedside table and found it in a drawer. So she had money. She glanced at Lord Gomeril. Should she try to slip out of the house? She was sure the ritual he had performed had surprised him and that he had not been aware of what would happen to her.

Lord Gomeril blinked and jerked. "My child, you're awake!" He heaved himself out of the chair and padded across the room to her. He held out his hands and Lythera took them and allowed him to pull her up.

"I need to go," she said, realizing belatedly how rude she sounded.

"It'll be dawn in a couple of hours," the lord said. "Aiza will be here then; that's when we decided she would take over the watch."

"The watch?" asked Lythera dumbly. "Why were you watching me?" Her mind seemed to be taking in information too slowly. She felt groggy.

"My dear, you frightened us terribly. You passed out and have been yelling and struggling in your sleep—or whatever it was. Sometimes I thought I recognized a word in Old Evandic but mostly I've had no idea what you've been saying. Something about drowning, or flying, or falling. Or maybe all three."

"How long was I unconscious?"

"Two days," said Gomeril. "Nearly everyone who's leaving the capital for Harvest has left Rayn Avinon already. We need to go today if we're to arrive at Novardan Manor in time."

"Novardan Manor?" Lythera couldn't understand what Gomeril meant. Surely he was going to celebrate Harvest in his own residence.

"This is the Harvest season where everything changes," said Gomeril. "Something is going to happen, to Teiryn, to you, maybe to others. We need to be there. Or, you need to be there. I want to be there. Besides, the Segrithrs are used to my tricks. They'll grumble but they'll have the manners to take in an ist-Lord and his train for Harvest. And Julinand's wife is a cousin to my late wife, and was much beloved by her, so her welcome, at least, will be genuine."

Lythera couldn't think past the growling in her stomach. She'd been asleep for two days? She could hardly believe it. It had seemed like minutes. But that would explain the hunger. And the confusion in her mind. She needed to eat; maybe then she would be able to think straight and understand what Gomeril was trying to tell her.

Gomeril noted the rumblings. "Here I go rambling about plans and you must be starving. Wait here and I'll bring something to you. I instructed the cooks to keep some of their mutton stew on the fire, and there's always bread and fruit at hand."

"No, Istan, you shouldn't," said Lythera, suddenly embarrassed by the attention from an ist-Lord. Her knees shook and she wondered if she'd have the strength to find the kitchen. She felt as though she'd been running for two days, not sleeping. "I'll go get something for myself."

"No, you won't," said Gomeril firmly. "You're trembling already and I'm sure it's hunger or exhaustion—the way you were struggling the past two days, I'm sure the sleep wasn't restful. You come here," he led her to the chair he had been sitting in, "and let old Ulindein fetch you some food. After all, it's my house and you're my guest, so it's my honor to serve you.

Besides, remember what Jarris always says—there's no rank between scholars."

Lythera slumped into the chair, grateful to him, but unnerved that he would serve her himself rather than waking a servant as her father or Teiryn would have done. But she was too tired to make an issue of it and sat in the chair, letting her mind drift to thoughts of Teiryn. If he had left for Harvest, could his life be in danger already? Before her, she pictured his kind smile, his tanned, careworn face, and his black, black eyes, pools so dark she felt she could sink into them forever. The man she loved. A man who was in danger. Lythera had to get to him.

Wearily, she put her face in her hands. Tears of frustration rolled down her cheeks. How could she fail Teiryn? She could not imagine the rest of her life without him.

Memories of Teiryn plagued her; as soon as she had considered one, another took its place. Teiryn giving her the hair ribbon. Teiryn beside her in the bed when Wenvia discovered them together. Teiryn sitting with her on the bench under the Hellfren Willow. Teiryn feeding the fish in the fountain.

"Fortune's Blood, child, you are a wonder."

Lythera glanced up. The oil lamp burned more brightly than before, but even more impressive was the vine that had crept in the window, crawled along the wall, and blossomed into small white, fragrant flowers.

Lythera blinked, afraid of what this meant. Had the ritual changed her somehow, changed her into someone Teiryn wouldn't like, or love? What was happening to her?

Gomeril came to her and placed a tray on the table next to the chair. "Very interesting, dear, very interesting. Much like your demonstration in the conservatory the other day. You are definitely the Bandryn we've been waiting for all these years. The signs prove it."

Lythera picked up a piece of bread, which had already been buttered, and nibbled on it. She was desperately hungry but didn't want to choke. She simply ate with a fierce focus until the bread was gone. Then she picked up a second piece.

Gomeril, meanwhile, had sat down on the end of the bed and waited for her to finish. Lythera ignored him until the rumblings in her stomach ceased. Then she looked back at the vine.

"The vine has been coming in every so often since we placed you in the room," said Gomeril. "As an experiment, I brought one of my saita flowers to your room. Its pot broke last year and it hasn't done well since the repotting. But two hours in your company has greatly improved its health. I have a feeling you're going to be difficult to hide."

"Hide?" Lythera picked up a pear and bit into it. The pear was sweet and perfectly ripe.

"I don't think we should just drive up to the gate of Novardan Manor and announce that we've brought you to see the king. A little more subtlety is called for. You'll be Aiza's chaperone—she's a bit old for one, but since she's unmarried, it'll do as an excuse. Besides, everyone expects me to do odd things as it is. Once we get you inside, then we all need to keep our ears open. We must know from what quarter danger will come."

"Why should there be danger if I'm to be the next ruler of Evandia?" asked Lythera. "Aren't you the one bringing danger to Teiryn?" All over again she heard the voice, *Do you suppose you are the last scion of the Bandryns?* Well, she knew her sisters would have no reason to be at Novardan Manor, and her mother's cousin, her tutor, was too old to be king. She didn't know any others among her mother's family. But there could be many scions of the Bandryn line after thirteen hundred years. The one who would threaten Teiryn could be anywhere.

"No, no, I'm sure of where your loyalties lie," said Gomeril. "Whatever or whomever is going to instigate the change must already have put events in motion. We must be alert and ready for anything."

Lythera put down the remainder of the pear. "Tell me something, Lord. Why is it so important to you for there to be change? Is it just so you can leave land to your daughters?"

Gomeril frowned. "Why shouldn't it be? I love my daughters. If I'd had a son, perhaps I'd think differently, but with four girls, I've been plagued by doubt for years. How do I care for them after I'm dead? How do I ensure, not only their survival, but their happiness? Marrying them off to hand-picked sons of other ist-Lords or nao-Lords is the usual custom, but I haven't met one I cared to spend an hour with myself, much less saddle a daughter with for life. So, what else can I do? Legally, nothing. The law says I should marry them off and let their new husbands care for them, and leave my land to a cousin, or the eldest daughter's husband. I don't consider that acceptable."

He paused. Lythera waited, content to sit while she rested. Already she could feel some benefit from the food, and her mind felt clearer.

"You love Teiryn, I know, so perhaps you can understand that Mailin and I loved each other very much. She was the daughter of sei-Lord Kelldon, and he was grateful to be able to wed his daughter into an ist-Lord's family. My father thought her an odd choice. Still, he didn't particularly care one way or another as long as the woman I married was noble. But the reason I married her was that I loved her, and she me. I'd seen how miserable my parents were, had seen plenty of unhappy couples at court, and I had vowed never to be wed to someone just for a bloodline. I want the same for my daughters. I don't want to send them to a stranger's bed, to be treated well or badly at some spoiled brat's whim."

"What will you do?"

He smiled. "I'm going to wait to see what happens after Harvest, and if things change enough, I'll be able to leave wealth to my daughters directly. Then it won't matter whom they marry."

"Even if it's a poor boy from the north?" Lythera gulped, surprised the thought had made it to her tongue and had been said out loud. She blushed with shame. Was it so long ago that she had been tutored in manners by her mother? But everything was topsy-turvy around Gomeril. He spoke to her as an equal; he treated her with a fond affection as he might the daughter of a friend. He owed her no respect—she was the king's whore to the court, after all—but he insisted upon it. He seemed contrary to everything Lythera expected in a lord of his rank. She remembered her first sight of Lord Novardan, with his sneer and his dismissiveness. Gomeril was nothing like him. In Gomeril's presence, she was reminded that this man was the son of kings.

"Even if. No rank among scholars, remember? And Threndayl's a good man. Hard-working, smart, honest. And he loves her. Even if he worked in a stable for the rest of his life, he'd give everything he ever had to her, and pledge to give her everything else he ever gained. Aiza is his world. He would take her even if I cast her out, even if she had nothing but the dress on her back. Nothing would stop him from protecting her, claiming her, loving her. How could I ask for a better man than that? If things change enough, then by this time next year I expect to see Aiza and Threndayl wed. And my eldest, Lianellen, has a man in mind, too. But it all depends on this Harvest."

Lythera closed her eyes. Everything seemed to depend on this Harvest. But as long as she could find a way to choose Teiryn's life, then nothing else mattered. Teiryn would live. She would go to Novardan Manor as Aiza's chaperone, and watch, and wait for her opportunity to stand by Teiryn's side and fight for him. Everything she had, and everything she was, she would devote to his survival.

She hoped it would be enough.

27

Lythera watched with trepidation as Novardan Manor grew closer. She wasn't too worried about being recognized; no one would look at a chaperone closely to begin with, and Aiza had worked several cosmetic miracles en route. Lythera's hair was now black as Teiryn's and fell only to her shoulders. Her hair had never been this short and she missed the weight of it, but most servants, even highly prized ones like chaperones, would keep their hair in this style. She consoled herself with the thought that her hair would grow back.

Her hair was not the only change. Aiza had carefully plucked her eyebrows and applied traces of cosmetics to draw attention away from her hooked nose and strong chin. A light dusting of powder on her face was designed to make her appear more rosy than usual. The effect was subtle; the hair and costume alone would probably have done the trick. But Aiza was determined to do her best for Lythera, so Lythera calmly submitted to the application of cosmetics every morning. Nothing could be done about her height, of course, but Aiza was nearly as tall as she. Her height would be less noticeable since she did not tower over her "charge."

Novardan Manor was an imposing edifice worthy of the royal family. The approach wound down into a valley and across a river, then up the far side of the valley. The manor itself was nestled in the roots of the western mountains, which loomed high above. Lythera had never seen mountains before, and they made her uneasy. It was as if the earth had thrust giant spikes into the sky. The mountains seemed to be about violence and anger, unlike the gently rolling hills of home. She shuddered. The mountains dwarfed the manor, which was impressive enough on its own without the dramatic backdrop.

The manor was built of the same gray stones as the mountains, and looked as solid and eternal as them. Unlike the palace, which rose gracefully from the ground, this structure appeared to loom in a threatening manner. Crenellations on the walls reminded Lythera of teeth. And the dark windows seemed to stare at her accusingly. *You are here under false pretenses and bearing a false name. Enemy!*

Just her imagination. She sighed and sat back in the carriage. She was frightened of what might happen, but also terribly eager to see Teiryn again. Gomeril had warned her not to approach him, but she knew she had to find some way to get to him, to let him know she still loved him. She had to feel his hands in hers, his lips on hers, to assure herself that he loved her. To tell him over and over again how much she loved him.

Aiza clasped her hand. "Softly, my friend. Look."

Lythera glanced out the carriage window again and saw flowers blooming in their path. She bit her lip. "Sorry." She hadn't found a way to keep things from blossoming around her every time she thought about how much she loved Teiryn. Yet how could she keep him from her mind now that she was so close? He was in the manor up ahead. He might overlook her, seeing her in his mind's eye as she had been before Aiza's attentions. But she would not be able to overlook him. If she saw him, what would happen? Would wilted flowers suddenly stand up straight and renew their beauty? Would birds land at her feet? Or his?

She had to stay hidden to do whatever would be necessary to help Teiryn. She didn't care what Fortuna had said about her, only that she had hinted that Teiryn might die. Lythera could not let that happen.

"I hope you visit Gomeril Hall someday," said Aiza. "It's much more attractive than this hulking thing. The builders must have wanted to scare everyone away! It looks like it's staring at us."

Lythera relaxed and smiled. "I thought that was just me."

"Hmph," said Aiza. "I think it's a deliberate choice on the part of whichever Segrithr had this place constructed. I don't think that would have been a man I'd have wanted to meet. I wonder if the inside is as cold and imposing as the outside?"

"Probably."

"Well, it's only for a few days. But when you visit our home, you'll see how pleasant a manor can be. The local stone is a rosy color, flecked with gray and very pretty. All the windows are meticulously cared for and the grounds are maintained by a well-trained staff who are proud of their work. This place looks like no one cares about it. I've always loved Gomeril Hall. The city house has a different feel, much more one of power and elegance. The manor is more relaxed, more welcoming. It's my favorite place in all of Evandia."

"I thought the city house was quite welcoming. But then, you've never seen the hulk that is Halevern Hall," said Lythera. "It's crumbling and has—or had—broken windows. For generations, my father's family has been unable to afford adequate repairs or servants."

The carriage was allowed through the outer gate. The manor loomed even more awkwardly and threateningly over them. Lythera shuddered. When the carriages stopped just outside a wide open doorway, Lord Gomeril alighted from his. Aiza watched him from the window, but Lythera hung back. Now they would see if the Segrithrs would accept them as hospitality demanded, or would attempt to turn them away. Gomeril had not been stingy with his personal retinue: besides his daughter and Lythera, he had arrived with a coterie of servants, perhaps thirty people in all, Threndayl among them. Novardan had no doubt stocked a complete larder for the company he was expecting, but thirty additional people would be a strain.

It was just the sort of thing that amused Lord Gomeril, Lythera was learning. He could have arrived with fewer staff, but that wouldn't have been as much of a goad to the Segrithrs.

Lythera glimpsed Lord Novardan himself coming out of the doorway. He walked up to Gomeril. The two of them spoke briefly before Novardan turned away, his face expressionless. But Gomeril walked to the women's' carriage, his face a less-well-concealed mask of delight. He leaned toward the window.

"Fortunately, he didn't make an issue of our arrival," he said. "There will be porters here shortly to show us where we will be staying. I doubt our accommodations will be the best, but then, we are the last to arrive."

Aiza nodded. "And it's only for a few days."

As promised, the porters arrived quickly. Lythera got out of the carriage behind Aiza and kept her eyes downcast, but as Gomeril had suspected, the Segrithrs who came to observe their arrival kept their eyes on Lord Gomeril. Lythera recognized Vandencia, but to her relief did not see Evinard. Surely he would know her.

A few of the men let their eyes linger on Aiza, but no one had any attention to spare for a chaperone in Gomeril livery. Lythera felt a surge of triumph. She was as invisible as Gomeril had hoped she would be.

The only bad moment came when Lythera followed Aiza to her room and the porter attempted to stop her. "Servants' quarters are on the fourth floor," he said. Lythera froze. Their plan called for her to be near Gomeril and his daughter at all times.

Aiza solved the problem. She waved her hand airily at the porter. "Riadyn will stay with me. See to it." The careless arrogance in her voice and attitude almost made Lythera smile, but she resisted the urge and kept her eyes on the floor. The porter hesitated a moment, but then moved Lythera's trunk into Aiza's room. She stared at the trunk a moment. She had brought the nauvynnor and hardly knew why. She hoped her feeling that she needed it was merely foolishness, but if not, it was here.

Aiza stepped into the room first and Lythera followed. The room was small, fitting merely a bed, a wardrobe, a chair and a fireplace. It smelled musty as if it had been unaired in a long time. Aiza sneezed.

"Please inform Lord Novardan of our gratitude for his hospitality," Aiza said to the porter as he left.

Lythera went to the room's one small window, only to find that the catch was broken. She wriggled it, but the window did not budge. "I can see why the room hasn't been aired in a while."

"Well, at least it's not summer," said Aiza. She stared gloomily at the small, lumpy bed. "We can try sharing the bed, but honestly, considering the state of the room, I'd almost rather take my chances on the floor. It'll be hard, but no telling what might have taken up residence in the mattress in the past hundred years since it was placed here." She scanned the floor. "Mice for sure, anyway. I see droppings and some mattress fluff in the corner. Ugh."

Someone knocked on the door. "Come in," said Aiza. Lythera slipped to the side of the room to be as unobtrusive as possible.

A chambermaid entered with a basin of water and a towel. "Here's something to refresh you after your journey," she said to Aiza. "Will you be needing anything else?"

"No, that will be sufficient, thank you. Oh, tell me, when will the next meal be served?"

"Noon, Lady."

"And my chaperone?"

"She can eat in the kitchen with the others," said the chambermaid.

"Very well. That's all."

Aiza looked down at the single bowl and towel. "I guess we'll be sharing more than the floor," she said. "At least in Gomeril Hall we would have offered water to the staff as well. I suppose Novardan will want to get as many small insults in as he can to get back at my father for the inconvenience. I don't expect we shall find many hospitalities extended with grace." Aiza splashed water on her face and dried it with a towel.

Lythera shrugged and performed her own ablutions. "Not that it really matters for what's going to happen, I suppose, but the level of hospitality offered to guests does show the quality of the lord. At least that's what my mother always used to say."

"She was right. My father wouldn't dare insult his worst enemy while the man was a guest in his house. I haven't met the king often, but he struck me as the same sort of man. But apparently Novardan thinks differently. Now, let's get you fixed back up."

Aiza reapplied the cosmetics to Lythera, and then Lythera carefully combed and braided Aiza's hair. She made seven braids and then pinned them on Aiza's head. It was a style her mother had favored. On Aiza, the effect was striking.

"I saw several Segrithr cousins watching you," said Lythera, trying to find a way to lighten the mood. She was unused to this new, nervous Aiza. "If you're not careful, one of them will come looking for your hand."

Aiza snorted. "Gomerils have married Segrithrs before, but those who are still available aren't worth marrying."

Lythera thought of Teiryn, and Evinard. "Not all male Segrithrs are worthless."

"No, not all," agreed Aiza. "But it's not just them, you know. You haven't spent your life around the capital—most noble families don't train their sons in anything besides duty and politics. Things like husbandly virtues are something they discover for themselves—if they're intelligent enough or if gentle behavior is part of their nature—or they don't. Did you—no, you wouldn't have."

"What?"

"The Lady Trenstarl, you never met her husband, Borganden Trenstarl. I don't see how she could stand to be married to him and not turn into a complete shrew herself. He was boorish man who liked crude jokes. He'd pinch chambermaids' breasts and invite them into his bed. He openly leered at younger women with his wife sitting by his side. The man was a goat, complete with the stench. Yet she always treated him with honor. But she's not the only one. When you're a daughter of an ist-Lord, you know your choices are likely to be limited, and you just pray your father can find the man who's been raised not just to be a good politician, but also a decent man. When my father looks on arrogant boors like Lord Yawniel's grandson, and compares him to someone like Threndayl, it's the nobleman who comes up short. Well, enough of that. Come along; let's find our way around and see what we can see."

Lythera followed Aiza into the hall and down the steps, which led to a back hallway in the manor. The way to the main area of the house was tortuous and not easily discovered by someone without a guide. But after a few false turns, Aiza and Lythera ended up in a wide open space full of trees and flowering plants. Aiza strolled into the space as if she owned it. Lythera followed and tried not to look around. She didn't want to see anyone she had met at the palace.

"Good morning," Aiza said to someone. "It's been years."

"Yes, of course," said a young man. Lythera lifted her eyes just briefly. The man wore a light yellow surcoat with a tree and vine symbol embroidered on it. Lythera was not familiar with that livery. He bowed to Aiza.

She simpered prettily. "I'm so sorry that my father has brought a horde of people upon you at the last moment. It was all his idea, you know."

The young man nodded. "Lord Gomeril is well known for his, ah, habits. But House Gomeril is always welcome at Novardan Manor."

Aiza and the young man kept up a boring, polite dialogue in which neither said anything of importance. Lythera did not listen to all the social niceties.

She froze. Teiryn strode into the room. He looked older than she remembered, and more weighed down with care. She longed to run to him, to comfort him, and to assure him of her love. But she clenched her teeth and held her place. The flowering bushes near her began pushing forth buds and Lythera closed her eyes. She needed to think of anything else besides her love.

"Riadyn?"

Lythera opened her eyes. The young man was gone. As was Teiryn.

"You look unwell," said Aiza, though Lythera had no doubt the other woman knew exactly what had happened. Aiza, too, must have seen Teiryn enter the room. "I'll have lunch sent up to you. Why don't you wait in our room?"

"Very well, Lady," said Lythera in her mildest voice. "Thank you, Lady."

Lythera turned and slid back into the dark corridor. As quickly as she could, she retraced their steps and returned to the room she shared with Aiza.

Once in the room, she flung herself onto the rug in front of the fireplace and wept bitterly. To see Teiryn, but not be able to touch him, or let him know she was here! It was too much to bear. She resolved she would seek him out, no matter what Lord Gomeril said. She had to see Teiryn. Tonight.

28

Ultimately, it took Lythera two days to figure out where Teiryn was staying while in Novardan Manor. It was difficult getting the information she wanted when she was supposed to escort Aiza and otherwise stay in their room. But she managed to get lost a few times and establish from the various porters and chambermaids who challenged her presence just where she was and how it related to where she needed to return. After two days, she thought she had most of the main levels mapped out in her head.

She didn't see Teiryn again, which was both a searing pain and a relief to her. She wanted to be with him desperately, but she was afraid that something would give her away if she saw him in public. But she also felt she couldn't wait until tomorrow night to see him again. Whatever was going to happen, Gomeril believed it would happen with the Harvest's full moon. After that, if things went wrong, she might not see Teiryn again. He could be dead. She could be dead. Anything could happen. She had to see Teiryn now. The anxiety and anticipation in her gut made the air almost crackle around her.

She waited until Aiza was asleep and slipped out of the room. She made her way carefully down the corridor and the steps, taking a route she had memorized so well she could have walked it in the dark. But sneaking around in the dark without a light would be too suspicious. Instead, she had a small oil lamp with her, hoping she would appear as a servant sent on an errand.

A man came around the corner. She recognized him instantly; it was Valeron Trenstarl, the young man she'd met in the palace who had the same eyes as she.

"What are you doing here?" he asked imperiously.

"An errand for my lady, Aiza Gomeril." Lythera kept her eyes on the floor and hoped he would let her by.

But the man came closer until he stood in front of her. He was so close she thought she might swoon from the fetid feeling that hung heavily in the air around him. He had not felt like that to her before. Something had changed. "Oh, yes, I remember you were with her earlier. You know, seeing you gives me the strangest feeling I should know you."

"There is no reason a lord like yourself would know anyone like me," said Lythera. She trembled but tried to keep it from showing. To be so close to Teiryn and not to be able to get to him!

"Still." He hesitated.

Lythera waited a few moments before asking, "May I continue on my way, Lord?"

He stepped even closer to her and she resisted the urge to run away from him. The reek of his presence seemed to flow from him like a dank wind. Before her mind's eye floated a vision. The goat-footed lion, staring at her, then at him. Her heart froze. Was this the Bandryn scion she was to fight? Was this man the one who posed a danger to Teiryn?

"No," he said at last. "I think you should come with me."

"But..."

He grabbed her arm. Lythera nearly collapsed from the shock that overwhelmed her. Her senses shifted somehow; she couldn't hear the man speaking to her, but she heard the owls in the courtyard. Her vision faded to gray but a bright verdant field opened up before her. She opened her mouth to scream, but only a gasp came out. She sagged against the wall.

The man obviously felt something as well. He let her go and she fell to the floor. "Who are you?" he demanded. "Who are you? Are you the one the old man talked about? The other Bandryn?" The man paused, then laughter escaped his lips. "You must be, but why was I worried? You're just a servant girl. The descendant of some old lord's by-blow. You can't do anything to me."

"I'll never let you kill Teiryn," said Lythera through the choking miasma of the man's presence. The man stepped back and considered her again.

"Now that's an interesting thing for a servant to say," hissed the man. "What are you?" He patted her body as if searching for something. It didn't take him long to find her pouch hidden under the dress. Lythera tried to pull away, but her legs wouldn't obey her. She waited helplessly while the man reached for the pouch.

His touch on her bare skin was a hundred times more horrible than his presence alone. Lythera blacked out for a moment. When she awoke, she lay on the floor and the man stood above her with her pouch. He opened it and poured out the contents. Out rolled the remains of Lythera's money. Her hair ribbon.

The man appeared enraged but he kept his voice down. "Nothing important. Nothing that tells me who you are. So, who are you? Tell me!"

"Lythera," she said, unable to dissemble anymore. One word was all she was able to get out; her throat felt as though it was closing up. She would suffocate!

She pushed herself up and almost made it to a sitting position, but the man kicked her in the shoulder. She hit the floor hard and the shock sent a spike of pain through her. She bit her lip and tried to get air into her lungs, but her body wouldn't obey her.

"You? You're the king's wilted flower? The one I met in the records-room?" The man knelt down and grabbed her arm again. He was breathing heavily as if he were having trouble getting enough air himself. For a moment, his gaze seemed to soften, but whatever kind thought he may have had toward her, he pushed aside. "Well, it doesn't matter. You are nothing but a whore."

Valeron, still gasping, dragged her up onto her feet. Lythera's stomach rebelled at the renewed nearness to him and she nearly vomited. The urge passed but it left her shaky and weak. She shivered, feverishly hot and cold at once. She managed one shaky gulp of air but her throat was too rebellious for her to make a sound.

Valeron dragged her down the corridor, away from Teiryn's room. Her heart called on her to recall her strength, to wrestle herself out of this man's hands, and to run to Teiryn. To at least scream. But she could do nothing while this man touched her.

She managed one last despairing glance down the corridor. In the dimness, she could barely make out the sight of her hair ribbon, crumpled on the stone floor.

29

Valeron dragged Lythera to the cellar of the manor. At the top of the steps, he was joined by Lord Novardan, who merely raised an eyebrow at Lythera's presence and ushered Valeron and his captive down the staircase and into the dank, dark basement. In a back corner stood an iron cage. Valeron tossed Lythera inside. Her injured shoulder connected to the wall and she cried out at the sudden and renewed pain. She slid to the floor.

But, blessed Fortuna, as soon as he released her, she could breathe again. She gulped air greedily, pushing aside her other hurts for a moment.

"After tomorrow night, when I'm king," he said, "I'll take care of you. Teiryn will already be dead, and Lord Gomeril...well, he has won a special place at the Harvest celebration tomorrow night. I wasn't going to, but Lord Novardan thought it wise I show the lengths to which I will go to achieve my destiny."

"I'll never let you hurt Teiryn!" she screamed. "Never!"

"Enough," said Novardan. "Even speaking to her is unseemly. Let her rot here."

The two of them went back up the stairs and shut the door. The room was plunged into complete darkness. Lythera leaned against the wall and didn't try to keep the tears from coming. The memory of Valeron's hands on her kept her shivering for many minutes and she furiously tried to wipe off his lingering presence with the filthy straw from the floor. Even damp and moldy as it was, it was still more wholesome than the miasma that surrounded Valeron.

After a while, her tears subsided. She was ashamed. Crying and sitting in the dark was no way to help Teiryn. Tenderly, she got up on her knees and crawled around the cage. It seemed solidly built, with the bars set into the cold stone floor. She could find no way out. She sat against the wall in despair—she had to find a way to get to Teiryn! She had to tell him about Valeron and Novardan.

A scream split the air. She couldn't tell where it came from; it echoed through the cellar as if the person were next to her. A second scream followed. Angry voices yelled words that were unintelligible and overshadowed by more screams.

The angry voices became more frustrated; whatever they wanted, they were not getting it from their victim. The next scream was silenced with a horrid finality. Lythera waited, but heard nothing but the drip of dank water in the far corner of the room. In a terrible way, the silence was even worse than what had come before.

Suddenly, Lythera stood on the lakeshore she had visited in her dreams. The old lion was there, its skin loose and ragged. It lay on the shore, tongue hanging out of its toothless mouth. Flies covered its eyes and its hide was alive with sores.

Lythera rushed to it and brushed the flies off. What could she do? She couldn't help Teiryn, hadn't been able to help whomever was being hurt in the dungeon, had no idea how to help this lion.

I am old and it is time to go. Let me go.

As clearly as she had ever heard anything, the lion's words rang in her mind, weary and full of grief and pain.

"No," she said. "Not everything that is old need die. Or at least not today." Lythera ripped the underskirts of her dress into strips, dipped them in the waters of the lake, and bathed the lion's hurts. She cast about for more she could do, but no one had taught her how to be a healer, and who would—or even could—have told her how to heal a lion?

Instead, she lay beside it, and put her arm under its neck, wrapped her free arm over its shoulders. "I'll stay here with you," she said.

You are the sum of the choices you make. How will you choose?

"I choose Teiryn. I choose you. I choose life," she said.

Maybe you can not choose all those. How will you decide?

She didn't know what to say to that. She hugged the lion and pressed her face into its mane.

A strange sound caught her ear. She looked up; a shadowy figure holding a shining lance stood over the lion. "Die," it said. "It is time for the old to pass away. The new is coming."

It is time. I thank you for your kindness. You will have kindness in return.

"No!" shouted Lythera. Awkwardly, she got her arm out from under the lion and threw herself on top of it as the lance flashed down...

...and she was back in her cell in the dark. Despair battered her heart; was there no one and nothing she could help without failing?

Tears threatened, but she would not give in to them again. The lion's last words to her echoed in her mind and felt sure she could expect something to happen.

Within moments, without knowing why, she began whispering in Old Evandic.

Hider, stealer, thumper, squealer,
Biter, squeaker, runner, leaper,
Aid me, guide me, hear my call.

She repeated the words over and over. Soon she heard a strange rustle, as of dry leaves being blown in the wind. An odd whispering sound.

Something stepped on her. She shrieked and pulled back but the first was only the beginning. Now dozens of little paws swarmed over her hands and feet. Some began to crawl up onto her calves. For an instant, Lythera wanted to scream and fling all the things away. They must be rats; rats always lived in manor cellars. She was covered in rats.

But the instant of panic passed, swept up in a sense of hope. The lion had promised help and the words had come to her unbidden. Now the rats were here, all around her, waiting. Waiting for her. "I must have a way out of here," she said to the rats. "I must escape."

The teeming rodents milled about for a few seconds, but then at once, they left her. She thought for a moment they had gone, but soon she heard gnawing. The gnashing and grinding of rodent teeth.

Lythera didn't know what they were doing, but they were obeying.

Thin rays of light came in from cracks in the foundations and from under the doorway to the main house. Lythera's spirits lifted. She tried to see what the rats were doing, but it took some time for the light to grow strong enough for her to make out any details.

The rats were gathered around several of the metal poles. At first she thought they were trying to gnaw the iron, but then she noticed that they were concentrating on the flagstone floor. The stone was cracked from age and much use and the rats had nibbled at the cracks, making them wider and deeper. Flake by flake, they had worn away the stone.

Lythera crawled forward to examine their work. The floor appeared slick and red with blood. After a few moments, Lythera realized the sharp edges of the stone flakes were cutting the rats' noses, lips, and tongues. They were mutilating themselves for her.

"Stop," she said. She couldn't bear it, not the thought of more pain, even rodent pain. It was too much.

The rats stopped gnawing. Several slumped down, apparently from sheer exhaustion. Lythera picked up a rat and looked it in the face. It wriggled its blood-soaked nose at her. She could sense its weariness.

"Back up," she said. "I'm going to see if I can remove any of these bars now."

Most of the rats obeyed. A few could barely lift their heads. Lythera picked those rats up carefully and carried them to the back of the cell. Their fur was softer than she had thought it would be and their limp bodies seemed very frail.

Lythera went back to the iron bars. This time when she shook them, they were loose at the bottom. She threw her shoulder against them several times and two of them came out of the floor. She pushed them as hard as she could and the bars bent outward a short ways.

She thought she'd be able to slip under the bars if she tried. Lythera laid down on the floor and worked her way under the bars. The sharp edges tore at her dress and scratched her, but it only took her a few minutes to get out. She turned to the rats, who were waiting for her. "Many thanks," she said.

The rats trotted past her and were gone to holes within moments.

Lythera went to the top of the steps but the door was locked. Perhaps there was another way out. She went back down the steps. Far past the cell and behind some discarded, broken furniture, she found another staircase, this one choked with cobwebs. Dead leaves coated the stairs. Lythera put one hand in front of her face and waved her other arm in the air to try to keep most of the webs out of her face and hair. But they were everywhere.

Small dark forms in the webs fled at her approach and she tried not to think too hard about spiders crawling on her.

The stairs were slippery and she nearly fell twice, but she caught herself on the slimy, mold-covered walls. At the top of the steps, she had a choice. To enter a dark passage where the dim light from the cellar no longer could aid her, or to go down an identical set of steps. She chose to go down. The cobwebs were just as thick here and by now she was covered in white silk. She didn't care anymore.

Lythera put her foot down where a step should have been, but the step was broken and she fell. Her shoulders and head banged against the wall of the narrow staircase as she rolled the rest of the way down. Sudden pain brought a shriek from her and she lay still at the bottom for a few moments, waiting for the pain to fade. After a minute or two, she twitched her feet and hands and took a deep breath, but all she felt was battered.

Cautiously, she got up. She ached all over, but the pain did not get any worse. A short distance away was an old scarred door. She stumbled to it and pushed it. It wouldn't budge. She pulled and the door slowly came toward her. The hinges were so rusted, they protested loudly and she had to pull with all her strength to get the door open enough for her to slip through.

Once on the other side, she immediately wished she hadn't come. Perhaps she could have found another way out. Some way. Any way. But not through this.

A body hung by its wrists from a rafter in the center of the room. The body itself was a hundred and one times worse than she could have imagined.

It was red. Blood was everywhere—flagstones, walls, rafter. Lengths of purplish intestines had fallen out of the abdomen onto the floor. But the face had remained whole, and the hair. Blood had coagulated under the body. It was Lord Gomeril and he was clearly dead and had been for some hours. Lythera's breath caught in her throat and she felt faint. It took her several minutes to stop shaking, to brave the sight again, to figure out how to get around him to the door on the opposite side of the room. She had to get out; she had to reach Teiryn. If Valeron and Novardan had something similar planned for Teiryn, she had to find a way to stop it.

She opened the door and found a stairwell on the other side. She stumbled to the stairs and climbed them warily. At the top, she listened, but heard only a strange scrabbling sound. Then whining. A dog. Automatically, she remembered dogs were a sign of faithfulness. She took it as a good omen.

She worked the latch and opened the door carefully. A small white powderpuff of a lapdog stood there, waiting for her. She knelt. If she could suddenly talk to rats, why not dogs? The ridiculousness of it almost made her laugh out loud, a crazy laugh with no sanity in it. But she stifled that dark impulse. She had to keep hold of herself a while longer. She wasn't safe yet. "I don't want to be seen. Lead me to the third floor of the south wing and stay away from people."

The dog let out a small "whuff" and trotted off. Lythera walked after it, sore and covered in blood and sticky white silk. Her dress was shredded down the front by the iron bars and her head was pounding. She felt half-dead.

The vision of Gomeril's body stayed before her. He had believed in her, and now he was dead. He had thought she would be such a hero.

But what a hero she had turned out to be! Unable to help anyone, barely able to help herself. She needed rats to rescue her and a dog to guide her. It was as if she herself were nothing without constant assistance from others. And she hated herself for it. For her weakness. For her helplessness.

The dog led her faithfully to the room she shared with Aiza. She went inside, where Aiza was standing in front of the dirty window, scanning the courtyard below.

"Riadyn?" she asked, apparently assuming Lythera might not be alone. She turned, saw Lythera, and clapped her hands over her mouth to stifle a scream. Lythera stumbled forward, tears springing from her eyes. She barely got out a strangled "Aiza!" before Aiza's long arms wrapped around her shoulders and held her as if she would hold her until the end of the age.

30

Teiryn lay awake in the darkness. Earlier, he had considered taking a walk, but he'd thought he'd heard Valeron talking to someone in the corridor, and he didn't want to be seen. He just wanted to wander, alone. In the palace, he was constantly watched, constantly approached. He was needed everywhere by everyone. Or at least it seemed so most days. Things weren't so bad here, but all of his cousins—and there were dozens— wanted some of his time. His days passed in one unsought conversation after another.

So he had not gone out upon hearing Valeron. But the itch to get out of bed and wander continued to press on him, and he finally gave in. Surely by now, after midnight, he would have the corridors of Novardan Manor to himself. Though he might not—nearly everyone kept odd hours at Harvest, some staying up until morning and sleeping most of the day, others rising early to watch the Harvest sunrises. No one's schedule would be normal, so his solitude would not be guaranteed. Still, he needed to get out.

He took an oil lamp and opened the door. He looked both ways but he had the hallway to himself as he hoped. Teiryn smiled a little at his foolishness; here he was, a king, and he felt like he were a small boy trying to sneak a snack from the kitchen behind his parents' backs. But when you were a king, your time was rarely your own. Finding some time for yourself was sometimes a chore, but always a treasure to be savored.

He looked forward to getting out to the courtyard. The weather had turned chilly, but not yet truly cold. It was his favorite time of year; invigorating and beautiful, full of the smell of burning leaves and mulled wine. Even the low gray skies of late autumn could not shake his love of the season.

Something caught his eye in the small circle of his oil lamp's light. Something red on the floor. He leaned over and lowered the lamp to knee level.

His heart froze. It was a hair ribbon. Lythera's hair ribbon.

For a moment, Teiryn couldn't move, could only stare at the proof that the woman he loved was somewhere nearby. In Novardan Manor. How could that be?

He reached down and grabbed the ribbon, stood up and brought it to his nose. It still smelled like her. She must be nearby.

He suffered only one moment of shock and indecision. But that passed quickly. Lythera was here!

Was Lythera the person to whom Valeron had been talking earlier? On the face of it, that seemed ridiculous. Valeron would have no reason to keep Lythera from seeing Teiryn. Novardan, even, had no reason to keep her away from him at the moment. After all, he had installed her in the Water Street property. Everyone knew she was his and that he wouldn't give her up.

Why was she here, and why she had not come to see him? Or had she tried to come and been prevented? That was the only explanation he could think of that would explain her abandonment of the cherished ribbon. Teiryn's heart beat harder at the thought that she was here, somewhere. Possibly being kept from him against her will.

Teiryn made his way down the main staircase of the manor house and walked to the door warden, who opened the door to the courtyard for him.

"Thank you," said Teiryn. "Tell me, have you seen Lord Trenstarl lately?" He had noted that Valeron always seemed to be about this Harvest, no matter the time.

The man nodded. "Not very long ago, Sire. He was headed toward the family's dining room."

Teiryn nodded and turned around. The family's informal dining room was near the kitchen. It was used for individual meals, or small, intimate family dinners when the banquet hall was not appropriate. Teiryn had eaten there many times as a child.

It did not take him long to walk through the maze of familiar corridors. He opened the door of the dining room and found it occupied, but not by Valeron. The person sitting at the heavy walnut table was Reyva Segrithr.

Teiryn had only spoken with Reyva a few times and had always found her to be a sullen, unpleasant conversationalist. He would have left immediately but Reyva spotted him and grinned. He realized she was drunk. "Teiryn, cousin," she said, her voice slurred and indistinct. "So nice to see you today." Reyva accented the word "today" in such a way that Teiryn was baffled. She said it as if she did not expect to see him today, or indeed, ever. Which of course she would, since the Harvest dinner was tomorrow night, and everyone would be there.

"You should get back to your room and rest," he said. "Sleep it off."

She laughed. Teiryn didn't understand what was so funny, but then, he had little experience dealing with those who were too far into their wine.

"Yes, give me orders, put me in line with everyone else," said Reyva. "But I won't take your orders much longer. I'm going to be queen of Evandia, you know that? I'll sit on a throne and everyone will do what I want."

"You're not only drunk, you're dreaming," said Teiryn gently. "I'll send for someone to help you to bed."

"I'm pregnant."

He froze. Reyva wasn't married. If what she said were true, she had shamed herself and the entire Segrithr clan. Why would she reveal such shameful secret to him? Or was it just the drink?

"He's gonna be king someday, right after my husband," said Reyva.

Now he knew how badly the wine had affected her. Reyva's father had made no announcement about an engagement, let alone a marriage. Nor was there any way for Reyva to become queen. She was imagining things, or dreaming while awake. Teiryn had heard rumors of people who did that.

"You're talking nonsense," he said. He turned to go. She laughed again, a horrid shrieking laugh that bounced off the rafters and rattled Teiryn's ears.

"Poor Teiryn, always trying to be so kind, so helpful. Always failing," said his cousin. "You can't help me; I don't need your help. But those who do won't get it. You can't help Gomeril, or your little whore, either. Pretty soon you won't even be able to help yourself."

That stopped him. What could Reyva possibly know about Lythera, or why would she even care? He went over to her and touched her on the shoulder.

"Reyva, I don't know what you're raving about, but let me help you back to your room." At this point, Teiryn was worried he couldn't leave his cousin alone long enough to fetch a servant.

"Raving?" She smiled up at him, a ghastly smile that he'd never seen before. He shuddered at the sight of it. The beauty of her face was terribly offset by the ugliness of her expression. "I'm not raving," she said slowly. "I just can't bear to keep all the secrets any more, the weight of them. But you shouldn't worry about me. Worry about yourself. The storm comes. Tomorrow at Harvest." She cackled and the sound was so inhuman, Teiryn's blood froze.

Teiryn fled, unnerved at her expression and the hatred in her voice. He had no idea why Reyva had said what she did, but it frightened him.

Teiryn stopped in the kitchen, relieved to find no one about yet. It would be several hours before the bustle of breakfast-making truly began. He passed through to a small room that was normally used to store dishes before they were taken to the main banquet hall. Teiryn could use the door on the other side to get to the hall, but that was hardly likely to be someplace he would find Lythera.

A voice came from beyond the door. Teiryn leaned forward on the rickety chair. It sounded like Novardan.

"Valeron? Where were you? I..." the rest of Novardan's sentence trailed off.

"Just checking on things," came the reply, almost too dim to be heard. "Now that the king's whore..."

Lythera! Teiryn would have stood, but the chair creaked slightly. He froze.

"Did you hear that?" asked Novardan.

"A mouse or a rat," said Valeron. "Don't worry; nothing can go wrong now."

A pause.

"That fool Gomeril," said Novardan at last. "She was with him. He...in here to...king, anyway."

King? Teiryn's heart nearly stopped.

All those pokes and prods over the years—late taxes, short levies—he had been wrong to take them so lightly. Gomeril wasn't just an annoyance. He would betray his king! It all made sense. For generations, the Gomerils must have watched and waited for their chance to regain the throne. Now the time had come, or so Gomeril thought.

But what part did Lythera have to play in this? He couldn't believe Lythera would turn against him of her own will. She loved him! His heart was sure of it. But she would have had to come with Gomeril's train to get here, so she was cooperating with him for some reason. It couldn't be to put Gomeril on his throne, could it?

No, Lythera would not betray him. Never. It was unthinkable. She might do strange things or hold unconventional thoughts, but her love was true.

Teiryn knew he wasn't the king his father or grandfather had been, but of this, at least, he was sure. He couldn't let Gomeril steal the throne, not for any reason. And he certainly would never permit Lythera to be forced into anything against her will ever again. Even if she were sick of court intrigue and chose a life as a teacher over a life at Teiryn's side, still, she would have whatever life she chose. No one would gainsay her. Not while Teiryn lived. Not while he was king.

Teiryn set his face in a stark grimace; his heart was a stone within his chest. He was king of Evandia. He would remain king of Evandia, whatever Gomeril did.

3 1

Aiza finally let go and stood back, looking at Lythera with a mixture of astonishment and concern. "What happened to you? And what have you been crawling in?"

Lythera tried to speak, but her voice broke and all she managed was a squeak. She closed her eyes, took a deep breath, and tried again. "Spider silk, mold, blood. I don't know what else. There were rats and it was dark and Fortuna spoke to me and..."

"And what? What happened? You're not making any sense."

Lythera nodded, not wanting to say what she had to. "I know. Is there any way for me to get clean? This is awful."

Aiza narrowed her eyes and did not seem satisfied with the answer. "Yes, there is. A bath is being drawn for me as we speak, but you obviously need it more than I do. We'll sneak you into the bathing room. Now, what happened? Where were you all night?"

Lythera raised her eyes to meet Aiza's, still unwilling to come out and speak the truth. "Have you any news of your father?"

"Not since last night. But he often keeps odd hours, especially at Harvest. Do you know where he is?"

Lythera bit her lip and hesitated. How could she just blurt out what happened?

"What do you know?" Aiza grabbed Lythera's shoulders and shook her. "Where is he? What's happened to him?"

It took three tries for Lythera to get the words out of her mouth. "He's dead."

"Dead?" Aiza wailed. She dropped her hold on Lythera and hugged herself with crossed arms. "How did you even know this? Who killed him? How? Why?"

Lythera shook her head. "Valeron Trenstarl and Lord Novardan. They're the ones plotting to kill Teiryn. I'm not sure why. Maybe they wanted to make an example of him." She didn't want to go on, but Aiza should know before she came across any evidence of her father's remains. She should be prepared.

"An example?"

"I think so. They hurt him. Made him scream. I was in a cage in another room and heard him scream, and scream again. I heard them yelling at him, as if they wanted something. But I don't know what."

Aiza fell to her knees and whimpered. Her face was colorless and her jaw worked back and forth as if she were trying to speak, or scream. Her eyes were wide with horror.

Lythera's tears escaped her control and the two women clung to each other and sobbed for several minutes. The strength of her own grief surprised Lythera; she hadn't known Lord Gomeril very well, but somehow, his affable manner and charm had wormed their way into her heart. She missed him, almost as if he had been a father she had never known. How much worse must it be for Aiza! Lythera kept her arms around the other woman until Aiza's sobs quieted and she dropped her own arms from around Lythera.

"Valeron says he'll be king, that he's a Bandryn. How is that possible? He's a Trenstarl."

Aiza shook her head.

Someone knocked on the door. "Your bath, Lady."

To her credit, though her face was covered in tears and she was still pale with shock, Aiza managed to say "thank you" and sound calm and collected. Lythera doubted she could have done the same.

Aiza roused herself and sniffed. She wavered on her feet a moment, but took a deep breath and immediately looked steadier. "My father would expect me to be calm and efficient and put off grief until later. Tonight is too important to give in to tears again now. Tomorrow is time enough. Now. Let's get you in the bath. Getting all that silk out of your hair will be a mess." She got up and went out the door a moment. When she came back in, she said, "No one's out here right now. So come, quickly."

Lythera hurried after Aiza down the hall to the bathing room. A large brass tub stood inside, half-full of steaming water. Mounds of soft towels and a multitude of soaps were piled on several tables near the tub.

Lythera hurriedly pulled off the ripped, soiled dress and left it to lie on the floor. She stepped into the warm water and gratefully let it slide over her bruised, aching flesh.

Aiza handed her some sweet-smelling soap and Lythera began scrubbing. Her hair was a complete mess of tangles, and Aiza was eventually convinced to fetch some shears to cut it very short.

Eventually, she was as clean as one bath could make her. She climbed out of the water and toweled herself dry, glad to see most of the grime left in the tub and little left on herself. She would have liked to bathe again with fresh water, but that would have to wait.

"That's a beautiful jewel," said Aiza, her face still grief-stricken. Lythera assumed she was trying to distract herself from her pain. "You've never worn it where I could see it before."

Lythera fingered the necklace. "It's from Teiryn. A morning gift."

Aiza raised her eyebrows. "I've never seen its equal. I'm surprised he was willing to give it up. The Segrithrs don't often let their own rubies fall into the hands of others. You usually have to inherit them."

Lythera looked at her jewel briefly. The jewel was special. Proof of Teiryn's love, a promise he would love her again, she thought. She had to believe it. He had to want her back. But first, she had to get through the Harvest dinner and whatever Novardan and Valeron Trenstarl had planned.

"Come on," said Lythera. "We need to get ready."

Aiza nodded. She went to the door and looked down the hallway. "No one's here."

The two women snuck back to their room. Lythera went to her trunk and pulled out the red dress she had first worn in the palace. If Gomeril and Avaidan and Valeron Trenstarl were all correct, then this was the night that decided the future of Evandia. Whether it went well for her, or not, she would look her best and face her foes, and the consequences.

Aiza helped her into the dress. It displayed the Segrithr jewel that rested between her breasts in spectacular fashion, just as she remembered. Aiza ran a comb through Lythera's hair—though there wasn't much to be done about that now. It would just have to be short and choppy.

"You're a vision," said Aiza.

"You're kind," said Lythera. "But I know I'm not pretty and my hair's a mess. It's the dress."

"No, there's something more to you than just a dress, my friend. And whoever said you weren't pretty didn't know what they were talking about. Just because there's only one sort of beauty fashionable at court doesn't mean there's only one form of beauty in the world."

Lythera let that thought sink in. She didn't think Aiza was simply flattering her. She sounded sincere.

Someone knocked. "Lady? Food has been laid out for Harvest, and Lord Novardan wishes everyone to know there will be games this afternoon."

Aiza's face was wretched with dismay, but she managed a polite, "Thank you. Please inform Lord Novardan that I am feeling a little unwell and will see him at dinner."

"Very well, Lady."

When the servant's footsteps had retreated, Aiza sank onto the bed. "I might be able to be calm during dinner, but I can't manage it all day. Why don't we go over these books again and look for any clues about what's supposed to happen tonight." She pulled out the tomes Gomeril had acquired from Bandryn sources and immediately flipped one open. Lythera doubted Aiza was actually reading, but she supposed they had to find some way to fill the hours. She sat down beside Aiza and put an arm around the other woman's shoulders.

"We'll read them together," she said. Aiza nodded. Lythera felt tears stinging her own eyes, but Aiza's eyes were clear. She stared ahead, unseeing. Lythera began reading the tome out loud, knowing she would find nothing knew, but hoping the sound of her voice could bring some level of comfort to her friend.

Her voice was tired long before evening, but by then, Aiza had recovered enough to read for herself. Without something to do, Lythera felt trapped and restless. She was exhausted but knew she had no way to sleep before whatever happened tonight under the moon had been settled. The day passed with agonizing slowness, but at long last, a servant came by to announce dinner.

The women stood. Aiza curtseyed. "Before I go down to dinner, let me say this. As far as I'm concerned, my loyalty to you in no way impinges on my loyalty to Teiryn, because I know you love him." Her voice grew hard. "But I have no love or loyalty for Novardan or Valeron Trenstarl. Or Valeron Bandryn, or whatever he wants to style himself. If you need aid tonight, remember, I am yours."

Lythera reached out to hug her friend, who was shaking. "And I say, that no matter what happens tonight, I will always be your friend. If it all goes wrong, we will at least have each other."

She released Aiza and the other woman nodded. "It's time to go down to dinner." She faltered and her eyes filled with tears again. "My father?"

"I'm sorry," said Lythera. "I think you will be forced to see what they did. It will underscore the lengths to which they're prepared to go. Who would oppose them with your father's remains facing them?"

Aiza sniffed again, then nodded resolutely. "I can bear it. He would want me to, for your sake." Without another word, she turned and left the room.

Lythera waited. She wanted to make sure everyone was well into dinner before she crept down to observe as well as she could. Her own stomach grumbled at her; she hadn't eaten since last night. Despite that, she had no appetite. She felt slightly woozy, but at the same time, she felt stronger than she ever had. Or perhaps more determined. She was tired of not knowing what would happen and eager for this to be over.

Eventually, she left the room, crept down the hall, and went to the staircase. Everyone was at dinner, so she found her way unimpeded to the courtyard. And then across the courtyard to the dining room. Lythera stood in the shadows and looked inside.

The room was decorated for Harvest—vines and branches had been woven together into green ropes and were mounted on the walls. Broken crockery decorated tables around the room in a Harvest celebration of newness and excess. Sheaves of grain had been set up in the corners and fall flowers were on every table. The guests at the feasts had plates heaped high with venison, beef, chicken, and pork. Fish and mussels. Vegetables and breads of light brown and dark. Large bowls of jellies and butter were generously distributed on the tables. The smells wafted around her and made her ravenous.

Everyone seemed to be having a grand time. Servants passed among the tables with bottle after bottle of wine.

To the side, just within her range of vision, was a table piled high with cakes and pies. The Segrithrs and their guests were definitely eating well this Harvest.

On the far side of the room, at the head table, which was raised on a platform, sat Valeron with his mother, Metricia. Metricia looked strangely sullen for a woman whose son was about to make himself king. Lythera dismissed that; Metricia was not her problem, Valeron was. To the other side of Metricia was her brother Novardan. To Valeron's left was Teiryn, Vandencia, and a man Lythera assumed was Vandencia's husband. There were also several other people Lythera didn't know. They must be the other siblings of Metricia and Novardan. The eldest was surely Evinard's mother, Morvania, Lady Nivain, who looked more regal and proud than any woman Lythera had ever seen. Her hair was nearly white but some of it still showed the deep black that marked many of the Segrithr kin. The elderly man on Morvania's right must be Lord Nivain, Evinard's father. The other two men must be Julinand and Malagert. Both of them had ladies beside them. Lythera did not know how to tell which was which. Neither had the black Segrithr eyes or hair, apparently taking after the distaff side of their family.

Once she had scanned the occupants of the table, Lythera had eyes only for Teiryn. He stared furtively around the room and Lythera noticed guards in Segrithr livery moving slowly throughout the hall. Teiryn seemed anxious, but also focused. He must know something was coming. He made no effort to engage his tablemates in conversation. He was like a dark hole of silence in the middle of the festive gathering.

Lythera watched while servants began to spread the pies, cakes and candied fruits around the tables. While Teiryn sat silent like an immovable block, Valeron stared around him in utter contempt. What would he do, and how would he begin? He was her true foe. She had thought, when she came here, that Gomeril meant for her to seize the crown from Teiryn, and she had never believed she could do that. But now she realized that Valeron had already planned to do so. It was Valeron she had to stop.

After the Segrithrs and their kin began eating their desserts, Lord Novardan stood. He rapped on the table to attract attention. Soon, conversation died as all eyes turned to him.

"I welcome all of you here for the Harvest in the year 1297," he said. "For the past thirteen centuries our forebears have made Evandia a strong nation and a prosperous land. Tonight is a night to celebrate that. And to make a special announcement."

Guardsmen dressed in purple poured into the room from either side, swords drawn. Teiryn's guards looked stunned for a moment, then to a man, they rushed to put themselves between the new arrivals and the king. They encircled the head table and drew their swords. Gasps went throughout the Segrithr kin in the room. Teiryn himself looked relieved, as if he finally realized what he faced, but also puzzled, as if the direction of the threat was not what he had expected.

"Tonight is the night when the line of Gelain Bandryn finally asserts its right to the throne," said Novardan. "The reign of the Segrithrs is over."

A renewed shock of screeches and gasps came from the assembled family. Teiryn's face hardened into an expression Lythera had never seen on him before; stony, determined, almost cruel. He must be steeling himself for the coming battle. She wished she could reassure him she was here, that she would give her life for him.

Novardan held up his hand for silence.

"Many years ago, a prophecy foretold that on this night, in this year, a Bandryn lord would rise to power," said Novardan. "Master Jarris did try to warn you."

People turned to look at a table Lythera couldn't quite see. Jarris was here?

"I know nothing of this!" protested her friend.

"True enough," said Novardan. "Jarris only predicted that the time was near. But tonight is the night, and so he was invited here to witness the birth of the new age. He will be able to write the account, and tell the world about the new Evandia, under the rule of a new king."

"New king?" shouted someone else. Lythera thought it was Aiza. "That's treason!"

"In the face of prophecy, there is nothing to be done but to cooperate with it," said Novardan. "It is not treason to bow to the inevitable. Anyone who opposes us shall die. And now, I introduce you for the first time to the man who will be our new king, the chosen one of the prophecy, and the fulfillment of the Rulikarien Progression—Valeron Lord Bandryn."

Teiryn swung to confront Metricia and Valeron. "You're mad!"

Valeron stood and took off his outer tunic. Underneath he was clothed in purple. "No, cousin," he said. "I am king."

Outraged shouts echoed across the hall. Lythera saw Teiryn reach for his side, but he was not wearing a sword—well, who would need a weapon at a family Harvest dinner, after all?

The purple-clad guards rushed Teiryn's guards. Lythera wanted to jump forward, to prevent the bloodshed, but she stood frozen on the spot. Something inside her would not let her move. This was not the moment. She had to wait. Silently, she fought the stiffness of her limbs, tried to bend the force that held her in place. But she couldn't. *Patience*, said the voice to her again.

She hated the voice now. It didn't care about Teiryn. *Let me go to him!*

Teiryn's guards were overcome quickly; there were just too many of the guards in purple. Lythera was glad to see that not all had been killed. Some of the faces were familiar from her time in the palace, and she did not know how she could live with herself knowing people she knew had died while she had stood unmoving.

Teiryn stood by his chair at the table; around him his family sat dumbfounded in their seats. And something else. Lythera could detect a certain unfocused look in their eyes. She scanned the room; the same look was worn by most in the room. Had Valeron and Novardan poisoned their entire family? If so, why did they need guards? No one besides her seemed to have noticed yet.

Teiryn spoke slowly, but his eyes did not leave the bodies of his guards. "You can call yourself king, Valeron. You can even kill me. But that doesn't mean you will ever rule Evandia. You are a Trenstarl, and they have no right to the throne."

Valeron crossed his arms and smirked. He glanced toward another side table, this one covered in many thick layers of cloth. "Perhaps you'd like to see the remains of the last traitor I dealt with—for it is you who are the traitor now, if you defy the prophecy."

Guardsmen went to the table and threw off the covers. In the center of the table on a silver platter was Lord Gomeril's head.

"Father!" shrieked Aiza. "No! Father! What did you do to him? Why did you kill my father?"

Lythera felt a surge of sympathy for Aiza. Indeed, the Segrithrs at her table encircled her with their arms and the others looked not merely shocked but personally offended and outraged.

"House Gomeril will see you pay, Valeron Trenstarl!" said Aiza.

"House Segrithr should as well," shouted someone else. Lythera recognized Evinard's voice. Her heart was cheered by the thought of his presence.

One of the Segrithrs at the head table stood. Rage had turned his face nearly the purple of Valeron's surcoat. "Traitor! You would commit treason in my home!"

Novardan glanced at the man in disdain. "It's my home. You're only the caretaker, Julinand. Now sit down. When this is all over, if you decide to cooperate with my demands, you can keep the books for me again."

"Demands?" Julinand appeared ready to die of outrage. The pregnant blond at his side rose ungracefully and grabbed his arm. She seemed equally outraged, but also sickly pale.

Novardan glanced at the woman. "There will be concessions, Julinand."

The woman grew even paler, if that were possible, but managed to get Julinand back in his seat. The shock and outrage on their faces were mirrored in the faces of everyone else in the room.

Teiryn shook his head. "Julinand is right. This is treason. And a violation of all we hold sacred. You did this to your guest? How could you do something like this—to anyone, but especially to someone welcomed into your home?" He took a deep breath and looked away from the gory display. "Congratulations, Metricia. I hope you are proud of your son."

Lythera looked over at Valeron's mother. The woman couldn't stop staring at the remains.

"She trained me to be king," said Valeron. "I will make sure she is rewarded as is her due under my reign."

Metricia slumped in her chair. She seemed twenty years older. Lythera felt a surge of triumph. Metricia had fooled them all, had been so loving and kind, but all the while she had plotted to put her son on the throne. Now she knew the true cost of what she had done.

"You get to die more quickly," said Valeron to Teiryn. "But I have others to make familiar with my little knife. The other ministers on your council." His gaze swept the room. "And anyone in my own family who opposes me. Listen well, everyone. From tonight, I am king. Oppose me, and I will resurrect the old methods of execution. You will find your skin flayed from your bones and your head on a pole. I couldn't arrange a pole this evening for Lord Gomeril, but for any of you, I'll be sure to plant your head on a spike outside my window, where I can spit on it whenever I choose. But before I can officially become king, Teiryn, you have to die. So die, cousin. Die now, and be grateful your passage will be easier than Gomeril's." Valeron reached behind him and a guardsman handed him a jeweled sword. The jewels flashed purple.

Lythera wrenched free from the binding that held her in place. The pain of it made her gasp, but she ignored it and ran forward into the room with no concern for herself. Teiryn couldn't die! "You will not harm him," she shouted over the hubbub of raised voices in the room.

All eyes turned to her.

32

Lythera stood in the center of the room while every Segrithr family member stared at her. Teiryn did not seem as surprised as everyone else, and he was frowning at her. Why would he do that?

Valeron glanced once toward Novardan, who shrugged. Apparently they had not realized until now that she had escaped.

"The king's whore. Lythera Halevern. How sweet of you to join us to watch Teiryn die."

"He's not going to die," said Lythera with more conviction than she felt.

"That's what you think." He lifted the sword. Teiryn stood and tried to back up, but several guardsmen grabbed him and held him still.

"Foul creature!" shouted Master Jarris. Beside him stood Evinard. Neither of them wore the glassy look of the others in the room. Jarris continued, "Lord Novardan is correct about a prophecy. But where are the omens, Valeron? Where is the moon-bird? Torturing ist-Lords is hardly an act which qualifies you to be king in Teiryn's place."

"Whatever's going on here," said Evinard, "it has nothing to do with flaying people and killing the king. You've got to be stopped." He pulled out a long knife from under his tunic.

Novardan laughed. "Omens? Moon-birds? You're the one who's insane, old man. And he is a Bandryn, descended from the last lord and Islara Segrithr. Aylward Trenstarl never fathered any child. Guards—kill them."

The purple-clad guards leapt toward Jarris and Evinard. Those coming from the left fell as Aiza Gomeril suddenly lurched out of her chair and flung herself in their way. Valeron brought his sword down on Teiryn.

"Teiryn!" Lythera rushed forward, though there was no way she could cross the room in time to save her love.

Teiryn twisted against the men holding him and the sword bit into one of his captor's shoulders. The man screamed and let Teiryn go. The other man stumbled and Teiryn pulled loose. Before Valeron could swing again, Teiryn had danced away from him.

"Abomination!" shouted Aiza. "That's what you are, Valeron Trenstarl! A child of deception and rape can't inherit the throne!"

"You defy the prophecy rather than fulfill it!" said Master Jarris as he backed away from the approaching men in purple. Evinard stood in front of the old man and lifted his knife against the swords of the guards. "The prophecy speaks of a legitimate Bandryn. If you are indeed the descendant of Valeron and Islara, then you are not legitimate. The prophecy is not about you."

"I am the prophecy! I must be!" Valeron screamed. He leaped onto the table and down to the floor in a fluid motion, as if he were a serpent. He flung his own guardsmen from his path, which gave Evinard and Jarris an opportunity to back farther away from those who opposed them. In fact, the purple-clad men seemed confused now that Valeron had rushed into them and knocked them down in his effort to get to Lythera. Perhaps this battle was not progressing as Valeron had promised them.

Lythera did not try to avoid Valeron. As he bellowed in rage and ran at her, she stepped to the side. Valeron went rushing by her and out of the room into the courtyard. The moment the moonlight touched him, he froze.

Valeron began shaking, then crying. He whirled around and yanked on his hair as if trying to remove something. Lythera walked toward him, unsure what she should do. She couldn't overcome a man physically, especially when he was trained to fight and she knew nothing of the art.

As she reached the doorway, she was flung aside. The nauvynnor she had carried here spun from her hands and rolled into the courtyard. At first, she didn't realize what had happened, but within moments she had regained her balance and saw Teiryn in the courtyard.

"Traitor!" Teiryn shrieked. His voice was nearly unrecognizable. He held a wickedly pointed but short dinner knife and lunged at Valeron, who grabbed Teiryn's wrist. The two of them fell onto the flagstones and rolled around. Lythera's heart was in her throat and she ran forward.

Valeron kicked Teiryn off of him and the king spun backward toward Lythera. He slammed into her and they both fell inside, onto the dining room floor. Teiryn grunted.

"Are you hurt?" she asked. She sat up quickly and knelt over him. Teiryn appeared dazed, his head having smacked smartly into a table leg. Beyond, she saw Valeron shaking in the moonlight.

Teiryn rolled onto his side and flinched when she touched him.

Evinard and Aiza rushed to her. Evinard flashed Lythera a friendly but strained smile.

"Is he all right?" asked Evinard.

"I think so," said Lythera. "But I'm not sure. Why aren't the rest helping?"

"Drugged, or so Master Jarris surmised. He made sure we didn't eat anything," said Evinard. He looked at deathly pale Aiza, who shrugged.

"I wasn't hungry," she said, her voice heavy with grief and anger. "I knew Valeron would have my father here somewhere."

"You'll ruin everything!" shouted Novardan. He grabbed a candlestick and ran toward the group huddled on the floor around the dazed king. "Fortune's curse on you, bitch! I wish I'd left you with that scheming father of yours in Halevern Hall."

Evinard stood and rushed his uncle. The two of them squared off, Novardan bringing the candlestick down toward Evinard's head, Evinard deflecting it with his knife. Their fight took them around a table and they were lost to Lythera's view. But she could hear the ringing of the candlestick and knife making repeated contact.

Master Jarris tottered over to them and sank down at Teiryn's side. "Lady," he said to Lythera in Old Evandic. "I don't know how you came to be here, but you must be the one, just as the sundial said. If you are truly the fulfillment of the prophecy, now is the time to show your powers. Your true foe is in the courtyard. We will protect the king." He bowed to her slightly.

"Very well," she said in the same language, as a strange calm settled over her for a moment. This was the time she had been told of. The time to make a choice. It was time for the future of the kingdom, as well as her future, to be decided. But there was no choice, not really, because she would not give up Teiryn to Valeron's attentions.

Lythera stood quickly and lurched outside. The moment she stepped into the moonlight, she could go no farther. She tried to keep walking, but she was frozen as if the moonlight were ice and she a mere leaf caught up in it.

In front of Lythera, Valeron also stood as if frozen in the moonlight. Lythera felt as if the world were waiting for something. Even the breeze had quieted and from behind, the only sound from the dining hall was that of Teiryn moaning.

Lythera struggled against her entrapment; she had to escape for Teiryn's sake. He was what mattered most, though she fought also for her friends. Evinard, Master Jarris, and Aiza had helped her. She couldn't let them down.

But she couldn't move. Her bitter disappointment of this morning came back to her. She was nothing by herself. She couldn't help Teiryn, or escape, without the aid of dogs, or rats. Without Gomeril she couldn't have come here. In her whole life, and especially in the past few months, she hadn't managed to accomplish anything on her own.

Everything is connected, daughter, said the voice of Fortuna in her head. *You are nothing alone. But then, that is true of everyone. It's for you to choose which connections shall bind you close, and which you will loose.*

Lythera wanted to scream that the only connection she wanted was with Teiryn.

He has his own choice to make.

Slowly, the moonlight around her became more fluid. It no longer kept her from moving; rather, it was like water. She almost felt she could swim in it. She took a step, then another. Valeron was in front of her, crazed rage blazing from his eyes. He fought to move, but he was as trapped as Lythera had been.

Slowly, Lythera bent down and picked up the nauvynnor. Now she realized what it was; more than a calendar, it was the arbiter, the watcher. It would have been found in time for this night no matter what. It would have made its way here somehow.

Its runes read *elenvi vaurrikas bandrynoi.* Ever faithful. That was the destiny of the Bandryns. To serve and wait, and finally, to realize the promise of previous ages. To rule. Gelain Bandryn may have cursed Fortuna, but his line had never abandoned her as everyone else had done, not until the last lord had turned away from his wife to take Islara in secret. Since then, Fortuna had been waiting, both for Valeron and for Lythera. For two Bandryns, legitimate and not, to come to this full moon, to be witnessed by the nauvynnor, to struggle for the fate of the kingdom.

Lythera threw the nauvynnor above her head, where it sailed to a point some twenty feet up, began spinning, and spread forth a bright shining silver light tinged with purple, like moonlight through an astar. The light bathed Lythera and Valeron.

This was the time for them to decide. Lythera was tired of waiting. She reached out and grabbed Valeron's outstretched fist.

Lythera was blinded by a tremendous flash of purplish light and flung backward toward the doorway. Around her swirled ribbons of sparkling colors, as if the very air had come alive.

The ribbons touched her, stroked her skin, touched something inside her and blossomed and spread throughout her body. It was raw power. It emanated from her skin like heat, rising from her and filling the courtyard with a purple glow. The radiance of it filled her brain and filtered into every corner of her being. She felt as if she had been living only half a life until now and only at this moment was she whole. She was finally the person she was destined to be.

She opened her eyes. Valeron had also been freed from the moonlight by the flash of light. In his eyes, she saw triumph. He had also discovered power. But his power was different from hers; she could sense it. Hers was the power of nurturing and compassion, but his was a great, sucking neediness that would consume the world if it could. A deep hunger that could never be satisfied. She was creation, he destruction. They were equal in power, but reflected different faces of Fortuna. Each face had a function, each had times to be pre-eminent. But which one would win tonight was not decided.

The light still surrounded them. Lythera could not see beyond it. It kept the two of them separated from the rest.

The lion creature of her dreams walked into the circle of light, just as ragged and laden with sores as it had appeared to her last night. The lance that had come down upon it had not struck it dead, though it showed a new wound in its side. It had not escaped completely unscathed. It looked at Lythera, then Valeron.

"Who will it be?" it asked. "Who will free me?"

"What are you?" shrieked Valeron. "This shouldn't be happening! You're a dream. I am king now!"

"You are hardly master even of yourself," said the lion. "I am the face of Fortuna as she was last seen in this land, back in the days of the astars. The world was a different place then, full of wonder and light. But then the ages changed, the tides came and went, and darkness fell over the land. The people departed. The tides changed again, people returned, and the Uldreths swore to build a kingdom and worship Fortuna. But they were small-hearted and they lied. They wanted to keep the throne and not give it up as the Rulikariad instructed. They are gone now. All others fell away except the Bandryns, but even they could not keep their faith through the centuries."

"But that is the past," said Lythera. "What about the future? Will we have wonders again? Will the astars shine with an inner light like they do in my dreams? Will you walk among us, and teach us?"

"That is up to you," said the creature. "One of you is the moon-bird, and will usher in the new era of splendor. And the other is not. The coming age will be full of wonders, or an abyss of darkness and death."

"This is nonsense," said Valeron. "Utter nonsense. I reject it entirely. I can kill one little whore and take my place on the throne of Evandia."

"That remains to be seen," said the creature. "I am waiting to see."

Lythera looked over at Valeron, at the young man with her coloring, who looked almost like her. They could be siblings. But in his eyes there was nothing but anger and hate. He would kill her. Kill Teiryn. And others—Evinard, Jarris, and how many others. How many would Valeron slaughter to be king? Not just tonight, but next year, and the year after.

Valeron would tear the hearts from the people just as he would cut the skin from his enemies' bodies. He would spread terror throughout the land and do it for the glory of Evandia.

And yet he is my son, just as you are my daughter. All things change in time. If he wins, Evandia will cease to be, at least for an age. If you win, it will flourish and be renewed. It is time for Evandia to wither, or blossom once more. Like the moon, everything waxes and wanes. The two of you will decide which it is to be for the land at this turning.

Valeron took one step toward her. Lythera spread her hands and let the words come to her.

"*Elenvi vaurrikas bandrynoi!*" She was faithful. She was herself, and at the same time, she was part of Teiryn. His *verrika*. She did not have to be alone, nor did she have to let others choose her path for her. There was a middle way, full of love and devotion, and also compromise. Giving and taking.

With the words, she felt a change in her body. Within moments, her hair had grown back out to be waist-length. It twisted around her in the moonbeams and whipped against her face. The light of the moon stroked her skin and made her feel light as air.

Valeron spat at her. "Luckless whore." He pulled the metal lance head out of his surcoat and pointed at her. "Die, bitch."

His power slammed into her and she fell to her knees. The dreadful hunger of his power tore at her mind, draining her will, spreading pain through every joint in her body. She gritted her teeth and pushed herself to her feet. She would not give in. If she did, Teiryn would die. She would suffer anything to prevent that.

Lythera climbed to her feet, and walked toward her rival. His power battered at her and she felt as if she were walking against a terrible wind. Her dress whipped around her feet, nearly tripping her. The pain grew bad enough to steal her breath. But she would not relent. Twice she was driven to her knees, the pain in her body searing her joints, threatening to pin her to the flagstone pavement. The second time, she could barely breathe. It was agony to move her feet back under her, to stand and face her foe. His power ripped at her. It threatened to shred her mind. As she grew closer to him, it became more difficult to focus her thoughts. Numbly, she let her thoughts go and let instinct take over.

She reached out and grabbed his hand again. Her hand slipped and she grasped the lance instead. Fire flared up around their hands as their opposing powers slammed into each other. Lythera gritted her teeth and did not let go.

Valeron screamed and lurched away. "I'll kill you," he said.

The power of the moonlight that they shared twisted between them. His darkness, her light. Black and violet ribbons of power twisted around each other, ripped through the courtyard, tore limbs from trees and tossed leaves everywhere. The wind spun around them so tightly Lythera had no air to breathe. Black spots danced before her eyes and her ears rang. She was drowning. Drowning in ebony moonlight.

Valeron pushed his will onto her, and his darkness was so strong, she bowed before it. But she would not surrender. She thought of Teiryn and held her ground. He was her life, and her happiness. She would keep him safe, whatever the cost.

The power rose within her as she raised her eyes to meet Valeron's. Eyes the same color of her own. Bandryn eyes. Yet she could not recognize the person looking out from those eyes, the person whose soul held such dreams for destruction and a terrible hunger for pain that could never be assuaged. Yet Lythera would only accept the pain, she would not submit. She would never submit.

The rage in his eyes changed to surprise as she continued to stare at him. Now she extended her will to him, but she was not stronger than Valeron. Tears of frustration welled up in her eyes. Why had Fortuna brought her here just to withhold the power from her she needed to defeat Valeron.

But then, why did she need to defeat him? When Keival Segrithr had wrested the throne from the last Gomeril king, he had not killed his rival. As much as she hated the idea of allowing Valeron to walk away from here, she could do so. She could even offer him her assistance and support, if not her love. Death did not have to be the only choice.

Lythera let go of Valeron's hands and he stumbled backward.

"I won't kill you," said Lythera. "Join your power with mine and let us learn to rule together. Darkness and light, allied. Two rulers, side by side. A new age of peace and balance."

The world seemed to stop; the wind suddenly halted, the ribbons of power coming from the two of them fell apart into glittering sparks that rose into the sky and dissipated into the night. Lythera smiled and held her hands out to Valeron. The lion blinked in astonishment, but said nothing. The world waited for Valeron's answer.

For a long moment, Lythera was sure Valeron would accept. He stepped forward, confusion on his face, as if he could see the way through the darkness he had chosen for himself, a way toward health and light that he had never considered.

Between them, she sensed the possibility. Though she could not see it clearly, the vision floated before her of a land united under both light and darkness, the promise of a mythical, beautiful age that might never end. A dawning of a new world that might encompass more than mere human minds could even dare contemplate. It was possible. It had always been possible, if those striving at the turn of the age would only reach out and take it. Together.

"I...I killed two people," he said, his voice that of a young boy. "I plotted treason. You can't mean to trust me to be a co-ruler with you."

"I would. We could forge a new age such as the world has never seen. It could be brought into being if we only choose to do so. We just have to choose."

For a moment more, just a moment, his violet gaze softened and Lythera's heart swelled with compassion and forgiveness. Then the darkness settled on his features once more and her hope turned to ash.

"Never, bitch. I know my duty to my ancestor Valeron Bandryn, and to the throne. And to myself! Rule with *you*? Share a throne? My destiny doesn't include sharing anything with anyone—not my mother, not my cousins, no one!—much less a wretched whore like you."

Valeron raised the lance head and thrust it straight at her heart. Lythera quailed but refused to move. This was her choice: she would not kill him, or even try to kill him. He was a son of Fortuna just as she was a daughter of Fortuna. They were kin. Family. She would not bow to him, but neither would she raise her hand against him. She let the lance come and did not defend herself.

The lance impacted her body and a purple flash of light flared around her. She grunted and fell backward in shock as the light raced up and down her limbs, stung her fingers and toes, and stole her breath.

It took precious moments before she could breathe again, get her feet underneath her. She hauled herself up and stood unsteadily on the flagstones, trying desperately to see. Where was Valeron? She had to stay between him and Teiryn.

The flash faded. In front of her stood Valeron, the lance buried in his own chest. He looked down on it in shock and despair. Slowly, he collapsed. Lythera rushed forward and he sagged against her shoulder. "Kill...you..." he whispered.

"No," she said. "There will be no killing, not anymore. That is my choice."

A grotesque parody of a grin crossed Valeron's face. "The old man said, we make our choices, and then we..."

His body slackened and he stopped breathing. Slowly, his body became dead weight in her arms. Lythera kissed him on the forehead and laid his body down on the flagstones. With shaking hands and sorrowing heart, she removed the Bandryn signet ring from his finger and placed it on her own.

You are king. The throne is yours. I shall return to Evandia and you will rule with my blessing.

She sighed to herself and dashed away tears. King. How could she be king? But the power within her would not be denied. She would rule. Nothing less would be acceptable to Fortuna.

Lythera turned to the assembled onlookers. Many of them still looked glazed; she sensed that whatever Valeron had put in the food would do no permanent harm.

Evinard stood to one side, a large welt on the side of his face. His knife dripped with blood. She grieved to see it, but was glad her friend was all right.

Lythera finally realized someone was screaming. It was Metricia. She stood and beckoned to the woman, who had no choice but to walk toward her. "No!" Metricia pleaded. "No, I was kind to you when you first came to the palace. Have pity!"

Teiryn walked up to stand beside Lythera. She reached out to offer him her hand, but he did not take it.

"Pity?" snarled Teiryn at Metricia. "First you will tell the truth. What have you done, besides groom your son to take the throne? Speak."

Metricia began babbling in fear. "With the nestriana's help, I poisoned the queen so that you would have to rule without her. We needed you weakened. And the nestriana and I caused all the queen's miscarriages."

"And Lythera's as well?"

"Yes."

"And you raised your son to take the throne."

"Yes."

"What else?"

Metricia stared at Teiryn in hate. "The nestriana dosed your food, too. To make you more amenable. To make you timid. We've been directing you for years."

A gasp went through those assembled in the hall. Despite their hapless, drugged state, it seemed they were shocked by Metricia's admissions. Lythera was beyond shocked. Her baby had died at the hands of this woman, and at the hands of the healer sworn to aid her. Every one of Teiryn's children had been denied life by Metricia. How good she had been, how supportive, how compassionate. It had all been an act.

"How could you do that?" she screamed at the woman she'd thought was her friend. "And the nestriana—how could she bear to break her vows?"

"Break them?" For the first time, Lythera heard the voice of the nestriana. It was filled with anger. She ripped the strings of black pearls from her veil and threw them down at her feet. "You have no idea what my life has been like, what I've dreamed of, what I've wanted. No matter how tonight ended, the nestriana are finished, and I couldn't be happier about it." That drew a shocked gaze from Metricia. Apparently, the nestriana had had her own motives about which Metricia knew nothing.

But there wasn't time to sort all that out now. All around the room lay the injured and nearly everyone in the room was too drugged to be of assistance. If there were no nestriana to help them, Lythera, Aiza, Jarris, Evinard, and Teiryn would need to be their healers until other help could be arranged.

Teiryn had already stepped forward. "Guards, take these traitors away, and remove the dead with honor. For now, I am king once more," here he sent an indecipherable look at Lythera, who nodded and smiled at him. "And this matter is finished."

33

Lythera had no knowledge of healing, but she did what she could, bandaging the wounds of those merely injured and holding the hands of the dying. But within an hour of the battle, it was clear that the majority of the wounded would survive and the deaths would be few. Most of the dead came from Teiryn's personal guard, and he was shaken by each one who had fallen in his defense.

Slowly, the rest of the gathering recovered from whatever had been in the food, though they were exhausted. One by one, they were led to their beds by the servants, who had a tendency to jump at every sound. Lythera was sure everyone in the kingdom would be like that for a while. She felt the presence of Fortuna all around her and realized that the return of such a powerful entity to the realm would put everyone on edge at first. No one would know what to expect. Not even she.

As the last of the injured were taken away to recover in their beds, Lythera made her way to Teiryn. She held out her hand to him, but he did not take it. Confusion reigned on his face.

"My love?" She couldn't keep her sorrow out of her voice. How could he doubt her anymore?

Evinard led a sobbing Metricia up to Teiryn. "She says she needs to speak with you, Sire, but I doubt she has anything worthwhile to say." He pushed the woman forward with disgust.

"I can tell you everything we planned. I can reveal it all. Just don't kill me!" She turned to Lythera. "I was your friend; don't forget that."

"A friend who caused my miscarriage?" Lythera was dumbstruck that Metricia thought such a declaration of friendship might work to her benefit. "Who poisoned my predecessor? Who drugged the king for years?

Who, with your brother, arranged for every consort to the king, including me? In what way were you my friend?"

"I'm not going to kill you," said Teiryn. "But you will be stripped of all your holdings, your jewelry, your fine clothes. You will have nothing, not even your freedom. Take her away." Two of his guards who had only been lightly injured dragged a hysterical Metricia from the room.

At last, Teiryn turned to her. Lythera smiled shyly at him, hoping that they could find a small space of calm in which to speak. But Jarris and Aiza approached and bowed to both of them.

"I suspect things will be confusing here for a while," said Master Jarris. "But the prophecy has been fulfilled. A Bandryn will sit on the throne of Evandia."

"I'm not a Bandryn," said Teiryn.

Master Jarris nodded at Lythera. "But she is, Sire, through her mother's line. She will be the first king of the new age."

"I don't understand. A woman can't be king."

Aiza shrugged. "Perhaps sovereign is a better word? In any case, it's clear that Lythera is the one."

Master Jarris patted Teiryn on the arm. "Remember the prophecy? The one that mentioned that this year Segrithr rule would become Bandryn rule? I tried to tell your father that years ago, and you, too, when you came to me for lessons. But your father dismissed it as nonsense, and once he knew I was telling you the same, he forbid me to speak of it again."

Teiryn shook his head and narrowed his eyes at Jarris. "I don't recall that."

Master Jarris nodded. "I think it will take some time for all of us to sort this out. But at least you have your lady back, and the traitors are dead or imprisoned. Though we have seen betrayal and death, we seem we have come to the beginning of a new age without the level of upheaval and violence I feared. I am glad that is so, and that I am alive to see it. I am only sorry Ulindein is not."

Aiza flinched and Lythera embraced her friend. Aiza hugged her back and kissed her. "He would be happy to know he was right about you."

Aiza let her go and stepped back. Threndayl, whose nose was bloody, approached and took Aiza's hand. The two of them bowed to Lythera, and then to Teiryn. "My king...kings," Aiza said. "Let me be the first to swear my allegiance to you both as we transition to this new age of Bandryn rule."

Teiryn's expression hardened. "I don't even know what that means," he said. "I am still king and I am a Segrithr."

"Of course you are," said Lythera. "But Fortuna is insistent that I am not merely queen, but a ruler as well, and I am a Bandryn." Again, she held out her hand to Teiryn, praying he would take it. She could face this new uncertain future if only Teiryn were beside her.

Slowly, Teiryn backed away and walked out of the room. Lythera ached to run after him.

Patience, daughter. He must make his own choice freely.

She closed her eyes a moment, trying to gather her courage. Finally, she took a deep breath and looked back at the sea of faces.

"There are decisions to be made," said Aiza. "Who will be Lord Novardan? Who will rule in Trenstarl Hall?"

Master Jarris nodded. "Important considerations, my dear, but that can wait for the dawn. Or even the dawn after that. Tonight, we should be grateful merely to have survived, and take the time to mourn those we have lost."

Tears rolled down Aiza's face. Threndayl hugged her and she buried her face in his shoulder.

Master Jarris' own eyes teared up, but he dashed the tears aside. "I don't understand one thing. The circle of the prophecy must mean the signet ring. And the struggle that is, or rather was, to take place is obvious. But what is the moon-bird?"

Lythera smiled at him but did not answer. She stepped out of the room, back into the soft purple moonlight. It called her. It caressed her. It wrapped around her like a lover's embrace. She reached her arms for the sky, and was changed before them all.

Her powerful wings flapped once, twice, and she was airborne. Under the full moon, she flew into the sky and let the starlight fall upon her like rain.

Teiryn sat in his room and realized he had been a terrible king. He was sure his parents would be ashamed if they could see him. He had to have shamed his name, his father, his family, his crown, or he would have known

Metricia had betrayed him. That she and Novardan had killed all his children. His queen. That they had drugged him, even. In a way, that was the worst of all. Did that mean he was a different person without the drugs? What would he be like when their influence was gone? Would he even recognize himself? Would Lythera recognize him?

Would she still love him?

Teiryn ached to see Lythera again, but he was afraid. Something had happened to her, had changed her into someone else. Lythera Bandryn. Someone he wasn't sure he recognized. If he stayed with her, he realized she would never bear his name. Nor would their children. Bandryn rule for Evandia, after thirteen hundred years. Master Jarris seemed to think it so easy, but how could Teiryn let that happen? Let his family name go, let his children be raised as Bandryns? It was beyond his understanding how Lororo could take his mother's name, and he wasn't even from Evandia! How could Teiryn let his children do the same?

At least now he knew Lythera had come to his aid. Gomeril had not brought her here to betray him, but to help him against Valeron and Novardan. That was the only answer that made sense, and it made him mourn old Ulindein more than he ever thought possible.

Other questions tormented him. Was Lythera still the same woman who said she'd belong to him forever? How could she be? She had a different name, even a different form. He had glimpsed her transformation from the balcony and it had shocked him to his core. Lythera had become a large, purple bird and had flown away.

How can you doubt her?

He startled. He hadn't heard Brenicia's voice in his head for some time; he'd almost believed she'd abandoned him, too.

"How can I not?" he said with tears in his voice. "I love her with my whole heart. But I don't understand how she could do what she did."

My love, you are a fool. You were so sure it was Lythera that needed rescuing by you that you never realized you also needed her.

"That doesn't make sense," he said, his sense of propriety shocked even more than during his conversation with Lororo. "It's..." He couldn't think of anything to say. What kind of man needed a woman's help? Women didn't act while men sat by and did nothing.

Lythera is strong, but even the strong need the love of others. And you do love her. Would you deny that, and reject her for the sake of your pride?

"Reject her? She flew away from me! She became a bird. I don't know her anymore." His heart ached with the knowledge that his sweet Lythera had changed so.

She loves you. Now you have a choice to make. Remain faithful to her and your love, or turn away.

He would have argued further, but his heart wouldn't let him. Brenicia was right. Lythera loved him. He had seen her last despairing look, her eyes begging him to stay with her, to be with her.

The changes in the wind this night only underscored the strange times that were coming, that Lythera was a part of. From his window, Teiryn could see the blossoming bushes in the courtyard. Strange birdcalls he'd never heard before came from the sky. Once, an odd, brightly colored bird landed briefly on his windowsill. It looked like a wren, but it seemed comfortable with only moonlight to see by. Its feathers had been iridescent and beautiful. It sang to him briefly and then flew away.

Over everything seemed to lie a strange sheen that was part moonlight, part something else. It was as if the land had been holding its breath, waiting for these very things to happen. It was as if Evandia had been asleep for thirteen hundred years and was only now awakening. Teiryn felt in his soul that the land was fully alive now in a way it had not been for ages.

Grudgingly, he realized that Gomeril had been right to bring Lythera here. She was meant to rule. She was meant to bring Evandia into a new age. Master Jarris, too, had been right. The prophecy had been real after all, and Lythera was the one foretold. He still didn't know how a woman could be king. Understandable or not, however, it was simply so. And Lythera was the agent who had brought the change.

What is really keeping you from her? Would you prefer the changes Valeron promised?

He didn't answer right away, instead leaning over to sniff the fragile fragrance of a new vine's flowers. "Everything seems to belong to her now. Would I be an equal with her or just a consort? How can I live like that? Men aren't consorts."

How can you live without Lythera, without someone by your side? Do you wish to be alone all over again?

No, he definitely didn't wish that, not for himself, and certainly not for Lythera. After all, how often had he wished he hadn't been king? How often had he envied the fish their boring, responsibility-free lives? He'd never worn the crown with the grace or power of his ancestors. Now he had the chance to change his life, to be part of the court without having to be the one making all the decisions. Being king was hard, so hard. Especially when there was no one in your life to share the burden with.

Oh, yes, especially then.

Lythera needed him, as much as he needed her. That, ultimately, was the only thing that mattered. He loved her, and she needed him. She wanted him to be at her side.

He didn't relish their return to the palace, but he'd have to find the strength to endure it. There'd be unkind ditties sung about him behind his back, and no doubt there would be disrespectful nicknames and ugly rumors. He'd undoubtedly be stared at, whispered about, and shunned by many. But wasn't that what Lythera had faced when she had first come to the palace? She had stood up to it with her dignity intact. If she could do that for him, could he do any less for her?

Shame or not, fear or not, he belonged with her and nowhere else. The rest of the court could think what they liked about their arrangement but he would not live without Lythera. As he realized that, Brenicia spoke one last time to him.

Goodbye, my love. I wish you every happiness.

Lythera flew tirelessly around Novardan lands, amazed at the effortlessness with which she skimmed through the air. Below her, the towns, roads, and rivers glimmered eerily as the moonlight bathed them in its rippling glow. She could feel the land changing as she flew over it. By morning, Fortuna's presence would have spread farther, perhaps even to the capital, and soon the entire land would once more be full of wonderful creatures, and brilliant magic. Lythera had no idea what it would be like— she couldn't even conceive of what the land had been like before Fortuna left—but she knew it would be beautiful. The light bathing the land below was nothing like the darkness which would have covered it if Valeron had won.

But also it was not as beautiful as it would have been if his darkness and her light had been forged into a common cause. That, truly, would have made Evandia an incomparable place of magic and wonder. She was grieved that would never happen now.

But she had chosen, and Valeron and chosen. As much as she might regret the thought that Evandia could have been so much more, she was pleased to know that its future was to be wondrous indeed.

The threads of her life seemed clear to her now. Her mother, anxiously waiting for the day Lythera would demonstrate some omen or sign. How disappointing it must have been for her mother when Lythera displayed none of the signs her mother had been searching for. But the time hadn't been right.

Her mother. Her tutor. Her father selling her away. So many people had played a part in making sure she was prepared and present on the right day at the right time. Lord Gomeril was simply the last piece of the puzzle.

She could see the connections now, the connections that Fortuna admitted everyone had. Lythera had wanted to free herself from them, but what she really needed to do was to choose the ones she wanted and dispense with those she didn't. Teiryn was one she would not let go of unless he chose to leave her. And even then, she knew she would never turn from her love for him, or her hope that he would return to her. She would simply not attempt to keep him against his will.

She had no idea what would happen when the sun rose—besides the fact that she should be back at Novardan Manor before moonset. Her new form, the moon-bird, would only come to her under moonlight, she knew instinctively. But the consequences of last night had yet to be faced. She trembled to think of facing them alone if Teiryn turned away from her.

For now, she could sweep through the skies and ponder her fate at leisure for a few hours. She would have to return to the capital and she hoped Teiryn would be with her. By the time she—or they—returned, everyone would know the world had changed. Fortuna's lion, young again and strong, would arrive there tonight, and take up residence in the beautiful garden and make its home under the Hellfren Willow; how she knew that she didn't understand. She simply knew. She even knew its name now, a secret name she could not speak aloud. A bond existed between her and the creature; she would always be aware of it at some level.

Even if the ministers grumbled about Lythera's return to the palace, even if they did not wish to see her with a title, they would not be able to deny Fortuna. For thirteen hundred years the ministers and kings had ruled together. Now there was a deity involved as well. Everyone would have to get used to that.

Suddenly, Lythera remembered her classes at the school. Lythera would be sad to see her time at the school be so short, but surely she could find a way to fit scholarship into her new duties somehow. Perhaps Jarris would be willing to let his study group meet at the palace. Perhaps she would find a way to attract scholars in the far provinces, poor boys like Threndayl—and girls, too—and bring them to good schools, provide them ways to make a living doing something other than begging or forced marriages. There was so much that could be done; her mind was awhirl with it all.

One thing that was vitally important would be to continue Jarris' work. More scholars would need to be trained to dig for the past, so that they could learn from it, and understand where they had come from. Know the darkness they had crossed without a guide, how far they had come with no light to show the way.

As the moon drew close to the horizon, she swept back down toward the manor house. Without even thinking about it, she knew which room was Teiryn's. It was the sole window surrounded by vines. She banked down toward it, flew in the window, landed lightly, and was herself again.

Teiryn sat in a chair, and was staring at her with wide eyes. He looked tired, as if he had not slept, but he did not look angry. The look in his eyes was awkward but kind, a little unsure. Except for the uncertainty, he seemed as she remembered from her first encounter with him. She could not stop staring, tracing with her eyes every wrinkle, every line of his face. Every touch of gray in his hair. She drank in the sight of him and felt as if she had forever, it still would not be long enough to fill the emptiness in her heart.

"I thought," he began. Then he stopped. Lythera's heart nearly stopped along with him. Wordlessly, she reached out to Fortuna, but the entity would not speak to her now. This was Teiryn's choice. Not Lythera's. Not Fortuna's. Everyone, man and woman alike, had the right to make the choices presented to them.

He got up and walked toward her, hesitantly, like a boy caught doing something wrong. The words tumbled out of him, confused and rambling; his eyes begged her to understand. "I was afraid I didn't know you, that you'd changed so much your heart would forget me." He held out something to her. It was her red ribbon and her heart nearly seized up with hope. "Now I'm hoping I was being an idiot. I'll be your consort if you'll have me, and share the throne with you, and be co-ruler of Evandia and raise our children as Bandryns. Is there still a place for me beside you?"

Tears ran down her face and she threw her arms around him. She took the ribbon and crushed it in her hand. "Always," she said as she covered his face with kisses. "I will never have any man but you. Never. I'll swear it again if you like. I'll swear it anew every morning. I am yours."

He kissed her back, then held her close. "And I swear I am yours, my *verrika*, whatever you become, whatever you do, whatever it costs me." His hands ran through her hair. "My mother said I should do something that would ensure songs would be written about me. Do you suppose this might be it? I doubt this was what she was thinking."

"Of course songs will be written about you, and about our love," said Lythera. "Everyone wants to hear songs about love."

He stopped fiddling with her hair and wrapped both arms around her. He murmured, "Will you give me a morning gift?"

She laughed through her tears. "I'll give you the world."

He carried her to the bed and they took their time undressing and relearning each other. Lythera's worries melted away. She embraced her friend, her lover, her consort. Inside the circle of his arms was her true home. With his support, she could do anything. A life that seemed gray and meaningless when she was apart from him would become full of laughter and love. He would not merely ease her burdens or she his; they would support each other. She would wake up every morning knowing his was the face she would see, her whole life long.

Well done, daughter. Many blessings on you both.

Lythera sent a silent thanks to Fortuna and then forgot everything but Teiryn. She welcomed him in every way she knew how. Wordlessly, they remembered how to bring each other joy.

The red ribbon she kept in her hand. She would not let it go, ever again.

About the Author

 Marella Sands is a native St. Louisan who has published various fiction and non-fiction works. Her historical novels, *Sky Knife* and *Serpent and Storm*, were set in 5th century Central America. Sky Knife has also appeared in a German edition as *Der Mayapriester*. In addition, she co-wrote two King's Quest novels with fellow St. Louisan Mark Sumner under the name Kenyon Morr. Her book *Pandora's Mirror* was released by Word Posse in 2014.

Marella earned degrees in anthropology from the University of Tulsa and Kent State University. The author's household includes the author, her husband, and a multitude of pets. She and her husband travel whenever they can.

Word Posse Fun Fact

Some of the writers that inspired me were Walter Farley, Richard Adams, and J.R.R. Tolkien. Books like *The Black Stallion, Watership Down*, and *The Lord of the Rings* kept me spellbound; I read my copies so many times they became quite ragged. I desperately wanted to go to the places I read about and meet the characters I loved so much. Of course, I didn't dream of entering the rarefied world of writing myself, authors being mystical beings that I could never understand. It was only when I was in college that I realized that writers were people like anyone else, and I could be one, too.

www.ingramcontent.com/pod-product-compliance
Lightning Source LLC
Chambersburg PA
CBHW071252170626
46809CB00001B/187